"To sin as little as possible is the law for men;
to sin not at all is a dream for angels.
All earthly things are subject to sin;
it is like the force of gravity."

- Victor Hugo in,
Les Miserables

"If you want a happy ending, try Hollywood.
Life's the wrong racket for you.
It will only make you cry."

-Kinky Friedman in,
Meanwhile Back at the Ranch

FORWARD

It is amazing how much goes on in small towns right under the noses of people who are too busy with their own lives to notice or care what's going on around them. As unbelievable as it all may sound, this story is wild and involves real people. The events are tied together with truth and fiction because I had to embellish the facts somewhat in order to tie the events together in a colorful manner. This book is partly based on what the author was accused of, rather than what actually transpired. I have also taken liberties with the timelines of the major events. In other words, I have condensed events that spanned over several years in order to alleviate any boring intervals. I have used many of the peoples real first names, while avoiding real last names, for obvious reasons. In the drug world it is a general practice not to ask for last names. Many people use nicknames or we associate them with their looks or what they drove. We kept it simple. The old saying that truth is stranger than fiction fits this book well. I would like to have included a number of other events, but the book would have been far too long. Many people will be thankful that I only used their first names and nicknames, because their conduct was often shameful and heartless. I'm sure they would not want their grandchildren to know how they urinated on people's dreams. Mixed with all the craziness, some of us managed to have some fun, even though we experienced a lot of sorrow. I feel lucky to have lived through it all. Many of my old friends have passed away. Too many to name. I miss them all and I hope they are in a better place. One thing that I want you to remember when you finish this book is, evil has a face and sometimes it looks like your next door neighbor.

                      Jeffrey Dan Williams

CHAPTER ONE:

Nightmare

It was a picture perfect night. Like you would see in a fairy tale. The kind of beautiful sight that many have grown to love and enjoy on the country roads of rural Oklahoma. There was a huge full moon shining bright just above the old dirt road, right in front of the car. The barbed wire fences on each side of the road, glistening with fresh raindrops, almost looked like tiny runway lights lighting the way for takeoff. To the man sitting in the driver's seat it must have looked like the old forest green Plymouth Fury III was going to drive right up the hill and into the moon. Fairy tales are like that just before something evil reaches out its hand and crushes all your fragile little dreams into one big nightmare from hell.

The musty smell of the warm rain was hanging heavy in the spring air.

All you could hear was the low rumble of the car's big engine and the tires sucking up mud as the car rolled slowly along. When the car approached an old weathered mailbox at the end of a driveway leading to a small farm house, the brake lights flared and the passenger door popped open, just as the car came to a halt. Then a dark form that could only be a human body is roughly pushed out, down onto the muddy road. The car door quietly closes as the car quickly pulls away and vanishes over the hill.

As the crickets resumed their cadence, the body issued a low moan, as it lifted its mud covered face from the road and began to cry. When the dog on the front porch of the old farmhouse heard the broken voice crying one word, over and over, "grandpa -- grandpa," it jumped to its feet barking and running to inspect the problem, because it knew that voice and could tell it was in pain. By the time the dog (Buster), whining and barking, reached the person a light came on in the house. An old man stepped out on the front porch in his t-shirt and boxers, letting the screen door slam shut behind him as he surveyed the yard. It was past 2:00 a.m. and he knew something was wrong. He was headed down the steps and in the direction of the barking dog when he noticed the dog standing over the body and heard the tiny voice crying for her grandpa.

Grandpa, panic stricken, ran to his granddaughter and dropped to his knees beside her and said, "Oh, Ali, God no." He always called her Ali, short for Alice. She looked like her mother. Ali and grandpa were all each other had. Grandma had succumbed to cancer before Ali was born and grandpa loved her so much that he couldn't even think about remarrying. They didn't know who Ali's father was and Ali's mother had moved away to Las Vegas, two years before, in search of her "dream." Her mother never called or sent letters. It was just Ali and her grandpa. Ali is what made grandpa's life worth living and brought joy to his heart. She was sixteen now and had been doing very well in school. But for the last year Ali had been partying with her friends and staying gone for days at a time. Grandpa talked with her about it, but he didn't have the heart to scold her. He knew she was depressed because she missed her mother. So, he tried not to pressure Ali. He didn't want to lose her and he hoped she would get it out of her system. He was worried that if he was too strict Ali might leave. Then he would be alone. Life sure wasn't fair, sometimes.

As grandpa scooped Ali up in his arms he grimaced at the sight of her face. Her once beautiful smile was gone. Replaced by a swollen face, busted lips and a cut cheek. The blood was mixing with the mud and tears.

Even though her eyes were mostly swollen closed, he could see the vacant expression in her eyes. He gently carried Ali to his truck and placed her on the seat. Then he ran into the house for his pants and keys. This kind of thing just didn't happen in Beggs, Oklahoma. All grandpa could think about was getting Ali to the hospital and making somebody pay for what they had done to his baby.

The closest real hospital was about 12 miles away in Okmulgee, Oklahoma. Grandpa drove as fast as he dared to the emergency room where he carried Ali through the door. He didn't have to ask for help. The need was obvious. All at once the entire emergency room came to life. Emergency room doctors and nurses seemed to appear out of nowhere. One came running with a gurney. Some were barking orders and others were rushing to gather equipment. It looked like a well orchestrated dance as grandpa laid Ali down carefully on the gurney. The nurse was already asking grandpa questions ("Is she allergic to anything") as two doctors wheeled Ali away. He said "No, she's not allergic to anything." He knew that he had to let them take care. of her so he went with the nurse to answer all the questions that he never thought he would have to answer again after his wife passed away. The questions were cold and he was thankful he had his insurance information in his wallet. A nurse came by and asked if Ali had been in a car accident. He told her he didn't know, that he had found her in his driveway and came straight to the hospital. When the questions were over and the forms signed grandpa was relieved that he would now have time to think. Who could have done this? How could it have happened to his sweet little Ali? Was it his fault for not taking a firmer hand with her?

On one hand he was furious at who had done this. On the other hand, he was thankful that she was dropped at the end of their driveway, rather than dumped in a river or the woods to die. As he stood looking out the doors of the emergency room, watching the sky slowly lighten with the morning sun, grandpa thought back to his life in California when his wife was alive and Ali's mother was a child. Things were so simple then. He was a substance analyst for the State of California for over thirty years. He spent his days analyzing chemicals and drugs that were seized by law enforcement officials, then preparing lengthy reports that could later be used in prosecutions.

It was a job. It paid well and he was able to leave his work at work and go home every day to a normal life. The many stories about the atrocities that people inflicted upon one another just didn't seem real. Those things may happen to other people, but not his family. Now he was living a real nightmare.

Grandpa was a little cold. He realized that although he had had enough sense to put on his pants and boots, he was only wearing an old, thin t-shirt that he used to sleep in. He went to the nurses station and asked about Ali and was informed that the doctors were still working on her and that they should know more soon.

It had been almost four hours, but it seemed like days. The thought of the nurse's words, "Working on her," brought on a whole new round of grief.

Grandpa decided to find a phone and call his friend Jonas, who was a prominent attorney there in Okmulgee, Oklahoma. As grandpa was walking down the hall, in search of the phones, he noticed a nurse crying in the hallway, with another nurse consoling her. As they saw him coming they stepped further down the hall and through a door marked the break room. To grandpa it looked like everyone must be having tragedies that morning. He had no way of knowing that the nurse was crying about what she had seen of Ali's condition in the emergency room. All of the presiding staff were very shaken-up about it. It wouldn't be long before just about everyone in the whole area would be crying over what happened to Ali.

Grandpa found the phones where the real waiting room was. He thought that it was only right that there were phones in the waiting room. People needed to call someone in an emergency to share their grief. Grandpa called Jonas and his wonderful wife Sallie answered the phone. She knew right away that there was something wrong so she said, "let me get Jonas for you." When Jonas came on the line it was all grandpa could do to maintain his composure. His voice cracked repeatedly as he told Jonas what was going on and where he was.

Jonas assured him that he would bring him a shirt and be right there. After hanging up, grandpa told the nurse that he would be in the waiting area. A short time later Jonas and Sallie came walking down the hall. Jonas carrying a shirt, with Sallie carrying a McDonald's bag in one hand and three large coffees in the other in one of those little cardboard cup trays. They were trying to smile.

Grandpa stood up from his seat in the otherwise empty waiting room as Jonas and Sallie approached. Sallie said, "John, what in God's name is going on? I called one of my friends here at the hospital and she said Alice has been tortured."

"You know more than I know," John said, "They haven't told me anything yet. The dog woke me up last night and I found her lying in the driveway." Just as Jonas announced that he was going to find a nurse and find out what he could, they all three saw the doctor come out of the emergency room headed their way.

He looked too tired for his young age. As the doctor walked up, John was putting on the shirt. It's normal for people to want to look good for important people and right then the doctor was very important to John because he held Ali's life in his hands.

The doctor said, "Mr. Connor, is it okay if I call you John? Your granddaughter is stable and in intensive care. Judging from the needle marks on her arms, her accelerated heart rate and her non-responsive state, I would say she has been injected with a combination of stimulants and barbiturates. I'll know more about that when the toxicology report comes back. I was concerned about giving her pain medication so I used mostly locals. Her facial cuts and bruising are fresh, so they will heal nicely. However, the other damage is more extensive and some of the wounds are several days old."

Grandpa said, "What wounds? I didn't see any other wounds."

The doctor continued. "The other wounds were hidden by her clothing. They were inflicted and then her clothing put on over them. She has lacerations on her back. Some of them are several days old. Some were beginning to heal then were broken open by more lacerations. It must have gone on for several days, because some of the older cuts were getting infected and some are new, probably as recent as yesterday. There will be some scarring, but they should heal okay. The worst part is the burns on her inner thighs and vaginal area.

Sallie said, "Oh, God. Somebody whipped her and burned her?"

"Yes, Ma'am," the doctor said. "And I'm sorry to tell you that she has been repeatedly raped and sodomized. There is old and fresh tearing, but that will heal. My concern is the burns on her thighs and vaginal area. She was burned with something about four inches long and one inch wide. Some of the burns are infected and will scar. They are third degree. She has lost a lot of blood and is very weak.

She's dehydrated and I am sure she hasn't eaten in several days. I have two IV's in that are administering antibiotics and fluids. All we can do now is wait. I will feel better once her heart rate gets back to normal and she is out of intensive care. I would like to add that I am outraged about this and when they catch the person that did this be sure to call me to testify."

During the doctor's rendition of the facts Sallie had sat down and began to cry. The doctor looked at Sallie, then at Jonas and Grandpa and walked back down the hall towards the emergency room. The doctor knew that not only would his patient's life be changed forever, these people would be changed too. Now they knew what evil was. They just hadn't put a face to it. Nothing more could be said. They were all too stunned to speak.

While Sallie cried and Jonas consoled her, grandpa Connor walked down the hall to intensive care where he looked at Ali through the window. She looked so small in the hospital bed with all the wires and tubes running into her. He wanted to hold her little hand, but knew he had to wait until she was out of intensive care.

A moment later Jonas and Sallie walked up and Sallie started another round of crying. Jonas put his arm around her and then they all three walked back to the waiting area where they ate cold McDonald's breakfast burritos and drank stale tepid coffee.

A short time later a reporter from the local newspaper showed up. In small towns news travels fast. Often a reporter will show up before the police. Newspaper people are pretty smart, it seems. They had this gorgeous lady reporter and just looking at her made you want to talk to her. But grandpa didn't feel like talking. Jonas escorted the reporter to the side of the room and had an animated discussion with her. Anyone looking could tell that the reporter was visibly distraught by what she was hearing. Jonas had abandoned his usual "No, comment," and went for shock treatment. She kept looking back and forth between them all with her tear streaked face. The reporter left with her head hanging.

True to form, the cavalry showed up after the press left. It was no comfort. Deputy Sheriff Tim Newsome came in with his usual two gun toting sidekicks. He didn't like doing paperwork so he brought other officers to take notes. Newsome always wore a big silver cowboy hat. Behind his back, people would say, "I'd like to have two of them hats. One to shit in and one to cover it up with." He also drove a big silver Cadillac. Everyone knew that Newsome couldn't find his boots without an informant to show him where they were. Without a rat, Newsome couldn't find a stolen car if he was riding in it. People made comments like, "He's no Dick Tracy," or "He's no Sherlock Holmes." He was a big man with a badge who liked to push little people around and to him everyone was considered little.

Once again, Jonas, knowing that grandpa Connor didn't have any patience for incompetence, came to the rescue. Jonas intercepted Newsome and told him everything they knew and told him if he had any questions to call his office.

Jonas gave Mr. Newsome his card, indicating that the conversation was over and that was the final word. Newsome knew better than to try and argue with Jonas. He had faced Jonas from the witness stand too many times. Newsome didn't want a repeat in the hallway next to the emergency room waiting area.

Jonas had taken charge and grandpa was grateful for it. Jonas came back to Grandpa and Sallie and said, "Okay, we need a plan. The doctor says that Alice will be in intensive care until tonight. Then they will likely move her to a recovery room if all is well. We know she won't be waking up for several hours, at least. So, I propose that Sallie stay here. I'll go to the office and John, you go feed your livestock and get cleaned up. We'll meet back here at 5:00 and get a status report. Then we can grab some dinner and figure out what we are going to do from there. Any arguments?"

Grandpa Connor couldn't help but smile and say, "No, arguments." Jonas was forever the attorney and a good friend. Sallie agreed, hugged them both and they were on their way.

Alice was on her first day of what would be a two week hospital stay and many years of recovery and nightmares.

CHAPTER TWO:
The Plan

Everyone needs a plan and I was about to have one. My name is Jeff.

I did not know Alice at the time she was so badly hurt. The sad talk and rumors were starting to circulate that first week she was in the hospital. I felt sorry for her and didn't even know her.

I lived in Henryetta, Oklahoma. Thirteen miles from Okmulgee, where Alice was in the hospital. We didn't see much violence in those days. Henryetta was a great place to live. I had it a little rough when our family first moved there. It was me, my mother Mary Ann (who looked like a movie star), my big sister Susan with her long red hair and my baby sister Jody who brought us all so much joy. My mom was cool. She drove a 1966 Ford Galaxy 500 convertible, yellow with a black top. I didn't count my new step dad, who was not a nice person.

Being small and the new kid in town, I was picked on a lot by the local boys. I just didn't fit in too well. I was an aspiring hippie, sort of. I believed in being nonviolent. We had moved from Lawton, Oklahoma the summer of my sixth grade year. Lawton is the home of Fort Sill Army base and the local schools where my sister and I attended had a lot of diversity. We learned a lot from one another and everyone seemed to get along. The Lawton schools were a memorable place for me. I started seventh grade in

Henryetta as an outcast with few friends. It did not help that my mother had divorced from my step dad, Bob. He was the only dad I knew and I missed him. My mother did the best she could, but I had a new step dad who was a drunk. That took a lot of the fun out of my home life.

When we first moved to Henryetta, a town where dancing was illegal, the town had a dancing man. I never knew his name. He would stand on the corner of 3rd and Main next to the movie theater. When anyone would drive by and honk their horn he would dance a little jig. I remember him wearing a suit with a tie and a brown hat. We loved that old man. One of the biggest tragedies in Henryetta was when some drunks beat the dancing man to death trying to rob him. The whole town mourned for him. He didn't deserve to die like that. He always had a smile and brought joy to our hearts, the dancing man. I don't know why he danced. It may have been because of the happiness he knew he brought to others, or because he was old and wanted to feel young again and be remembered for something good. Maybe he just wanted to see our smiles. A wonderful dancing man, murdered in a town where dancing was against the law.

It was contradictory to what we believed and just didn't make sense.

He was killed right on the corner where he danced. The blood stain stayed on the sidewalk for a long time. Every time I pass by the movie theater I look to where he used to dance and remember. A few years later, my mother and a local pawn shop owner (Ross), put together a great big dance in the old JCPenney building on main street in order to protest and challenge the City's dancing ordinance. Some people were actually arrested for dancing. This was in the days when disco ruled and John Travolta was the king. It was a great time to be a kid. People came from miles around to see the spectacle and it received national coverage. Police, news people and cameras were all over. It was great.

That's what I call the good old days. Back when the police were your friends and neighbors. If the police pulled your car over and found that you were drinking or smoking a little pot, they would just take it away from you and dump it out then either send you home or take you home if you weren't in any shape to drive. They had hearts and they let kids grow up without putting them in jail. Things were a lot different then.

Rather than go to High School and put up with more abuse, I quit school in the ninth grade and went to work full time for a preacher at Street's Auto Repair on West Main. I could fix and/or repair almost anything. Mr. Street was a good man and he taught me a lot about the car repair business, God, life and integrity. It all worked hand-in-hand.

I wish I could have frozen time right then when life was simple and innocent. I had grown up working around my grandfather, watching and helping him rebuild and restore old antique airplanes and cars. Every day I would drive to work in my 1970 Dodge Challenger, 440, Sixpack, 4 speed.

It was a competition orange with a white strip and it was fast. It was a hot rod set up to drag race. I used to race it on weekends against all comers. I was only outrun one time and that was because I hadn't learned to drive it yet.

Mr. Street closed his repair shop and moved away. I started supplementing my income by selling marijuana to help support my hot rod habit. Back then I could buy a pound of Columbian gold or redbud for $300.00 and sell ounces for $50.00. That made me a hefty profit of $500.00 a pound. I was selling about a pound a week, which bought a lot of hot rod parts. The pot business was going so well that I worked it full time. I was saving up my money to open my own mechanic shop. That was my plan.

Soon, an opportunity opened for me. A local auto repair shop owner was selling his home and business and moving back East because his wife had cancer. He wanted $50,000.00 for the building, inventory and some of the equipment. I made a deal with him where I paid $30,000.00 in cash and would make monthly payments for the balance. It was my first real business venture and it went sour on me. The man was holding the deed and the only copy of our contract. I had no reason not to trust him. But when his wife passed away a few days later he sold the business to another man and moved away. All in one weekend. With my money. It made me look like a fool and it toughened up my business sense. On Friday I was telling the pretty little girl who worked at the gas station next door that I bought the shop and on Monday I was watching somebody else move in and take over the place.

It wasn't the new owner's fault. I had no idea where the previous owner moved to or how to find him. It was a total loss.

It didn't take me long to put some money together to try again. I leased the old Street's Auto Repair building and changed the name to "The

Garage." I did most of the work myself because I had a reputation to maintain and I wanted it done right. I had my friend Jimmy working with me who took care of a lot of the minor routine repair work. Between the marijuana and the repair business I was very busy. I was also buying broken down cars and trucks, fixing them up and reselling them. I usually had 10 or 12 used cars and trucks lined up out front for sale. I had the prettiest little secretary and parts chaser working for me that you ever did see. Her name was Phoebe. We all looked out for her real well because she was so young and sweet. I just had to give her the job. She walked right into the shop one day and told me she went to school half the day and wanted a job for the other half of the day. I had to admire her. She had more nerve than most of the men I knew. She wasn't intimidated by anything. Things were great. I had my plan in action. But that plan was about to take a hard turn.

It was a sunny day in the last week of April when grandpa Connor pulled into the driveway of my shop. I had recently celebrated my birthday.

I didn't feel any older. Maybe a little hung over. I had two friends, Smokey and Big Jim who also had birthdays in April so we partied pretty much the whole month of April. Smokey did the right thing. He got a real job. Got married to a nice girl and settled down. Big Jim got Lou Gehrig's disease and died some years later.

Mr. Connor got out of his truck and started looking over one of the trucks I had for sale. I walked out to greet him. "Are you looking for a truck?" I asked.

"Not really," he said, "I'm looking for Jeff."

"That would be me," I said. As I extended my hand. He had a firm work hardened hand shake.

He said, "I'm John Connor. I would like to talk to you if you have the time."

I recognized the name but I didn't know where from. I said, "Nice to meet you. Would you like to come in where it's cool and have a Coke?"

"That would be nice," said Mr. Connor.

I liked Mr. Connor from the moment I shook his hand. He reminded me of my own grandfather. As we walked into the large center bay door of my shop I was telling Mr. Connor that I tried to keep a few inexpensive cars and trucks for the people around town who couldn't afford to buy a new one. When our eyes adjusted to the darker interior of the building I pointed out an area where I was in the process of building shelves to stock new and used parts and accessories. I was already stocking the most common batteries, starters, alternators and a variety of other things.

Mr. Connor followed me through the door that led to the reception area, two offices and a restroom. We went to the reception area where I had one of the old antique Coca-Cola pop boxes. The nickel machine with the arched top that held the small glass bottles of Coca-Cola. I kept it turned down as cold as I could without the Cokes turning to ice. After getting our drinks I asked Mr. Connor to come back to my office. I kept my back office as my sitting room, so to speak. It had a couch, bed, stereo, two chairs, coffee table and a gun safe. It was fixed up nice with some pictures and a Snap-On clock on the walls. My private space where I went to relax. My own personal break room.

I had given Mr. Connor a play by play on where we were going and explained the significance of each area as we went. It was the grand tour.

I was proud of my meager accomplishments. I worked hard and it was beginning to show.

When Mr. Connor sat down he exhaled in the way a tired man does when he has a lot on his mind. He said, "I'll get right to the point. I have a problem and I think you can help me with it.

I've heard some good things about you and I have talked to some people that think you have the nerve for the job. I know you have been selling pot for a few years and have a reputation of treating people right."

He looked at me like he expected me to say something but I wasn't going to touch that pot comment, so he proceeded.

"I figure you know most of the people in the surrounding area that use and deal drugs. I will show you how to make more money than you can imagine if you will put three drug dealers out of business. I want you to ruin them."

I'm sure he could tell by the way I went "Humph," and sat up that I thought this was a set up or that he was crazy as hell. The man pulled up out of nowhere in a ten year old truck dressed like a farmer telling me that he was going to show me how to make more money than I could imagine. I was pretty sure he wasn't a cop, he was too old. I didn't think he was crazy because he knew too much and looked serious. I wasn't going to admit to anything or agree to anything until I knew what was going on. All of the sudden I didn't feel comfortable talking to him in my back room. I wanted outside to see what was going on out there so I could try and get a better picture of what was happening.

I said, "Sir, please excuse my skepticism. I don't know you. You come here out of the blue talking about making me a lot of money."

He held up his hand to stop me and without further ado he told me the name of the person who referred him to me. I was momentarily shocked into silence. He handed me a slip of paper with a telephone number on it and suggested I call the number. It was a number I knew well. I recovered quick. The fact that he had that number meant he wasn't whistling Dixie.

In a way I felt better. Like that feeling you get when someone you know gets hurt bad in a car wreck and is in the hospital with two broken legs and everyone is saying, "Thank God he's alive." It is pretty bad when you are looking at being alive as your consolation prize. I was hoping that I wasn't the one about to be in the wreck. But I have always been a people pleaser. I wanted to make people happy. I said, "As long as it doesn't involve killing anyone I'm your man. Let's go to the In-And-Out drive-in and get some lunch and you can fill me in. I like the idea of being wealthy.

In fact, I couldn't think of anything nicer at the moment.

As we walked out of the shop the air was so hot and still it felt like the Devil was holding his breath in anticipation of what Mr. Connor had to say. I had just finished putting on a water pump, flushing the cooling system and replacing the air conditioner compressor on a black-on-black 2-door

Lincoln I had for sale. This was a good time to test drive it. We climbed in and took off for the other end of town. I hadn't gone two blocks when I pulled in at Kern's Corner to use the pay phone.

The tiny voice that answered the phone said, "Who is it?" She was so little and got so excited that she often forgot to say, "Hello," when she answered. "It's the Big Bad Wolf," I said.

She laughed and said, "No, it's not. You're kidding me. Where you at?"

"Oklahoma," I told her.

She said, "Are you coming to see me?"

"Pretty soon," I said.

She told me, "My daddy says I can get married when I'm 35."

"That's about right," I said. "But there are no boys good enough for you in Louisiana."

She laughed and said, "I'll get daddy." She must have seen a cat walk by, or something, because she lost interest in the phone.

Every time I went to see them I brought her some kind of little toy.

The last time I brought this windup, spring loaded top, spaceship and little round propeller thing. It came with a handle to wind up the toys on. Then you pushed a button and the top would take off spinning on the floor with a "whrrrring" sound, or the propeller would fly across the room with a "whrrrr."

She got a lot of mileage out of it. All day long I heard "whrrrr" over here and "whrrrr" over there. She was fun to watch with her tiny hands and little smile. Children are wonderful. All they require is a little attention and love.

When her daddy came on the line he said, "Hey, Pete. I've been expecting your call. You must have gotten a visitor."

He always calls me Pete, for the same reason I always used a payphone when I called. Anonymity and deniability. "Yes, Sir," I replied.

"Has he told you what's going on?"

"He's about to," I said. "But I wanted to speak with you first."

He said, "It's a terrible thing Pete. I wanted to take care of it for him, but he wants to handle it his way. I understand where he's coming from. I know it is a lot to ask of you. However, he wants to handle it, take care of it for him. If things get too rough I'll send someone up there to give you a hand. This will be a good payday for you. And remember, there are some people down here watching how you manage this. It could be very good for your future."

"I don't know whether to be excited or nervous," I said, as I laughed.

In my usual manner I said, "Whatever it takes. You can count on me."

He said, "Be careful, Pete," and hung up.

At that point I had committed myself and I didn't even know for what. I had a feeling my life was about to change. I got back in the Lincoln that was still running and cool and headed for the drive in. On the way Mr. Connor asked me if I knew a local methamphetamine dealer who people called Bopper and his two friends Harold and Richard. Bopper and Harold were meth monsters and Richard was a cocaine carnivore. I knew them.

They were part of the older crowd I didn't hang out with. To call them simple drug dealers would be to clothe them in more nobility than they deserved. Tagging them as mere reprobates would be sorely insufficient. Bopper was known for stealing horses that were about to foal. The horse would just disappear after the colt was born.

Bopper would keep the colt hidden and bottle feed it and later claim it came from his own horse. Sorrier people never lived. They would break into houses and steal guns. People in town were pretty sure it was them. But they couldn't catch them at it. Bopper was a pile of shit with boots and a cowboy hat and his two running buddies were no better. They were festering sores on the ass of humanity. There really isn't a euphemism sufficiently degrading enough to describe them. That is why I stayed away from them.

Mr. Connor said, "I always liked this little town. The people here keep to themselves and wash their own dirty laundry." I didn't say anything. It didn't call for a response.

We got to the In-And-Out drive-in and ordered Rex boneless chicken, which I dearly loved. The drive in was owned and operated by a very sweet lady who I've always thought the world of. As we sat in that Lincoln eating our meals, Mr. Connor started the grisly story by telling me all about Alice.

He painted a picture of a perfect little granddaughter who had brought joy to his life and who did well in school. A picture of a little girl whose mother had moved away leaving her sad and feeling unwanted. A child without a father.

Mr. Connor had tried to fill that awful void in her life by being a loving grandfather, but he knew it just wasn't the same. Then he explained the recent event that brought him to my door. Alice had been released from the hospital after a two week stay. She hadn't spoken and she cried any time her grandpa was out of her sight. Sallie, Jonas's wife, was the only one that could calm her when Mr. Connor was away. By the time he finished the story of how Alice (Ali)was raped, beaten, burned, whipped and dumped, I was almost ill. It didn't even sound real. It sounded like a script for a horror movie. I was mad and amazed at the man's restraint.

My first question was, "Are you sure it was Bopper and his gang?" He said, "As sure as I can be. You know the one they call Knife?" "Yes, Sir," I said.

Knife hadn't been around long. He did some of Bopper's dirty work.

They called him knife for two reasons. He liked knives and he wasn't the sharpest knife in the drawer. He was a dim-witted transient that followed Bopper around like a puppy, because Bopper would give him drugs and feed him.

"Knife is the person who dumped Ali in my driveway. Him and Bopper had a falling out because Bopper told him to take her out and dump her some place. Thank God knife was so stupid he didn't know what that meant. He took her home and dumped her in the driveway. Knife told some people that Bopper was mad at him for being so ignorant. He also said that

Ali wouldn't stop crying on the way home so he kept slapping and hitting her to make her shut-up."

I wasn't sure I wanted the answer to my next question but I asked anyway. "Where's knife?" I had some questions for him too.

When Mr. Connor said, "Louisiana," I knew what that meant. Knife was more than likely alligator food. I didn't want to know and I wasn't going to ask.

I said, "I'm surprised that you haven't killed Bopper already."

"That was an option, obviously," he said. "But dead people don't suffer. I don't want Bopper or his two sorry friends dead. I want them to suffer. I want to take everything from them. I want them so broke that they can't pull in here and buy a hamburger.

I want them so desperate that they start taking bigger risks. They will eventually get caught at something and end up in prison. Maybe they will rot in prison spending every day thinking about their sorry lives.
There are far worse things than death or prison. Going from having money to having nothing is one of those things. I want them to suffer, Jeff. And I need your help to make it happen. I want you to put them out of business.

Every place they are selling their shitty meth I want you to go sell them pure methamphetamine at a cheaper price." "Before long Bopper and his friends will be stuck with a cut-rate product that they can't sell any place in the country. I want you to flood the meth market and drive them right out of business and over the edge. Can you do that for me? Can you do it for Alice?"

"Oh, I'll do it," I said. "I'll be like the little boy poking the big bad dog through the fence with a stick. I'll have to make damn sure that dog can't get to me. That, and where am I going to get all this pure meth you're talking about?"

"I have that part taken care of," Mr. Connor informed me.

We rode around some in that old Lincoln and worked out all the details and the emergency plans. By the time we arrived back at the shop I knew that this was one intelligent man. I had learned more in that short drive than I thought possible. With almost every idea Mr. Connor shared with me a new idea popped into my mind.

He made it clear that I wasn't a little boy poking a bad dog through a fence. I was an avenging Angel pissing in the Devil's face. I knew I had a new friend in Mr. Connor, but at the same time I knew I was about to make some hellacious enemies. It was for a good cause and the money was great.

When we got back to the shop I followed Mr. Connor to his truck where he calmly extracted an old brown leather suitcase from the cab and handed it to me. t was heavy. It turned out to be a heavier load than I could have imagined. Mr. Connor drove away without looking back. He was confident I would accomplish my task. The most important thing I learned that day was to never judge a man by the clothes he wears.

I walked into the shop and looked around thinking life sure takes some odd turns. My mechanics, Dean and Jimmy, who were also my good friends, walked over to me. I'm sure they could tell that something was on my mind by the way I just stood there with a smile on my face.

I said, "Boys, change of plans. We're going into the meth business."

CHAPTER THREE:

Action

My first day as a methamphetamine mogul didn't start out like you might think. I had a business to run. The night before I had put my new plan into action by assigning new jobs to Dean and Jimmy. I also called in a friend of mine, Terry, who Dean and Jimmy both liked, as well.

These three guys trusted my judgment. I couldn't tell them everything. Only that we were about to put Bopper, Harold and Richard out of business and that there was a good reason for it. I informed them that it could be dangerous and gave them an opportunity to pull out.

I told them to take turns following our three targets and to report back to me every afternoon at 3:00 to give me a list of all the addresses these guys went to. What time it was. What they were driving and the names of the people they went to see, if they knew them. This was straight spy stuff and they were liking it.

I also gave each guy an ounce of meth weighed up in 8-balls, told them to sell each one for $250.00 a piece and to keep $50.00 from each one they sold. That made them very happy. I also told them to make sure that everyone they sold to understood that the supply was unlimited if they made sure Bopper, Harold and Richard didn't know about it, didn't get any of it and if they stopped dealing with the Three Stooges. That's what we were calling Bopper, Harold and Richard. It fit. My own personal Mission Impossible team left on their new missions happy and excited.

When the phone rang at 6:30 in the morning it wasn't a drug deal.

It was an older gentleman with a tractor problem. I loved making service calls. The idea of helping someone in need put a big smile on my face. When people have a problem they really appreciate it when you come right out and take care of it.

I told the man, "Yes, Sir. I'll be right there."

I slept at the shop so I was ready to go. I brushed my teeth and was out the door. I had a 4-wheel drive Chevy truck for a service truck. It was equipped with most anything I needed and could go just about any place I wanted to go.

When I got there, it was an easy fix. The choke cable on the old John Deer tractor had broken. I got the tractor started and noticed that it was only running on three out of its four cylinders. It needed a distributor cap, plug wires and spark plugs. I gave the man the news and headed to town for parts. It was only about five miles back to town and the part store was just opening up when I got there. Small towns wake-up early. I bought the parts I needed and was soon back on the job. When I finished the tractor was once again running smooth. I had greased every fitting on the tractor. Those old tractors will just drink up grease and they need it. I had also made a list of the things I saw that would need further repair soon. The people that I did work for knew that they had to pay attention to that repair list because I was usually right. I wouldn't just tell them what was wrong, I would show them. I always gave them the parts receipt so they knew I wasn't jacking up the price of the parts and so they would have it for their farm taxes. Along with my labor receipt. I had a good reputation for being quick, fair and reasonable.

I liked working on equipment out in the county where the wind was blowing and you couldn't hear much but the cows and birds. I did some welding projects for some of my customers. Fixing cattle guards, fences or farm equipment. Most of it was done in nice weather, but I did have some winter weather calls that were pretty nippy.

Often the people would insist that I stay and eat breakfast or lunch and when I left they would give me homemade jelly or pickles or green beans canned fresh from their gardens. That was great.

I didn't know that this was going to be my last service call, for a long time. On my way back to the shop I swung by the house to give my mother the jars of jelly and green beans the lady had given me when I left the tractor job. And to take a shower. I gave my mom a kiss and headed for the In-And-Out drive-in for lunch, which was my usual routine. My mom was great. She supported me in most everything I did. But I had a feeling she was going to have a hard time with my new methamphetamine enterprise. When mom hugged me extra long and looked me in the eyes and told me to please be careful, I had no way of knowing that my mom knew Sallie and that Sallie had already called mom about Alice. Sallie had also explained my future role as avenging Angel to my mother.

When I got back to the shop Jimmy was waiting for me. He always opened up at 8:00 a.m. if I wasn't there. He was dependable and trustworthy. The most loyal friend I had. It wasn't long before Dean and Terry showed up to report and pick up some more meth. All three of them had sold everything they left with the night before and still managed to keep loose tails on their subjects. It seemed that the Three Stooges were pretty lazy. They were letting their customers come to them. So, all my boys had to do was find a place to watch from and take notes.

The people they didn't know, they followed and found out where they lived. It was an easy way to get your customers. Once the new customers got a sample of the high quality meth they weren't going back to Bopper and his cohorts for anything. The one thing that I didn't want was people coming by my shop to get meth. I didn't want anyone but my three guys pulling out of my shop with meth and I was about to change that, as well.

However, as the next few days progressed more and more people were pulling into my driveway looking for Dean, Terry or Jimmy. We had initially come to an agreement that they would only take one ounce at a time in 8 balls. That way if the police got after them they could throw it away and it wouldn't be too big a loss. Or if they got caught it would be such a small amount they would get probation. But the money was good and the demand was growing fast. People wanted ounces. I had discovered that the Three Stooges were selling their ounces of poor quality meth for $1,600.00, so I started selling my ounces of pure meth for $1,400.00.

I took care of all the ounce deals myself.

I was trying to minimize my guys' exposure. I had one rule, never come by my shop. Just call me and ask me to come by when I have time. They knew why. They didn't need to say anything on the phone. So I treated it like a service call.

I got a call one day from a man that hadn't lived in Henryetta long.

I knew he was shady. The story was that he had robbed a drug dealer some place and had moved to our quiet little town to get away from the heat that his robbery had created. He had money and he didn't work, so I figured the story was likely true. When he called and said he wanted an OZ I automatically knew that someone had told him my routine. I told him I would be there in a little bit. Lucky for me I smelled a rat. I drove in from the back side of his place rather than just pulling up out front. Bopper's red and white Ford Bronco was parked behind the man's house. It was a set-up.

I went to a pay phone and called Mr. Connor with the news. It hadn't taken long for Bopper to get wind of my new business venture. Now we knew that Bopper and his partners were on to me. Mr. Connor advised me to start packing a gun. I knew it was necessary but I hated the idea of carrying a gun. I was soon glad I decided to carry one.

My next call was to the man waiting on that ounce. When he answered I said, "How did you know to call me?"

He said, "A friend of mine told me."

"His name wouldn't happen to be Bopper, would it?"

The man said, "No. I don't know anyone called Bopper."

My next question was, "Then why is his truck parked behind your house?"

I hung up before he could answer. Then I drove back to my shop and told Dean and Jimmy the news about Bopper's Bronco being parked behind the man's house and how I figured it was a set-up to rip me off.

Dean Said, "I saw Bopper's Bronco parked across the road in the trees in front of the shop yesterday."

I couldn't believe he hadn't told me this sooner. I asked him, "Why didn't you tell me yesterday?" He looked dejected at my scorn and said he had just remembered it. I went into the back office (my private sanctuary) and opened my gun safe. Mostly I kept my important records in it. But I also had an M-1 carbine with four thirty round banana clips, a pistol grip 12 gauge riot gun and my trusty Colt Python six inch vented rib .357 magnum. I took the pistol out and loaded it. I love guns. I have had guns most of my life. I was raised in a family where everyone had guns and went hunting regularly. I respected guns and I knew I was not supposed to use them in the manner I was about to use them. I looked at the gun and wondered if I'd made the right choice about getting involved in this mess. Then I thought about what these low life people had done to Alice and I dismissed all reservations. I was already obligated to some important people and there was no turning back. In for a penny, in for a pound. I took the pistol into the shop with me and started putting the head back on an old six cylinder Ford Econoline van I was working on. The van was parked half in and half out of my center bay shop door. All three bay doors were open and Jimmy was sweeping the floor on the empty bay next to the passenger side of the van I was working on.

Jimmy yelled, "Here he comes." Just as I heard the roar of an engine and tires spinning on gravel. Then Bopper's Bronco shot into the empty stall with all four tires sliding to a halt.

Bopper jumped out of his truck, faster than you would think a fat man could, he strutted up to the front of his Bronco and yelled, "All you big'ns line up on the left and all you little'ns huddle together on the right, because the Bopper's here. Ain't nobody sells dope in my town unless it's my dope. Where's Jeff?"

I had a two-foot three eighth drive extension in my left hand and my .357 magnum in my right. When I hit the left front fender of Bopper's Bronco with the extension it not only made a dent, it banged so loud is sounded like a gun going off.

As Bopper spun around, I yelled, "I'm right behind you Bopper. Don't you ever pull into my shop like that again. Now get your fat ass back in your truck and get out of my shop. Now."

I was watching him and the man that had called me, who was still in the truck, as I waved Bopper towards his truck door with my gun. I had no doubt that Bopper could see how mad I was. His face first registered shock, fear, then pure rage.

As Bopper slid into his truck, he said, "You made a big mistake. I run this town. I'm not done with you yet." He was trying to get his courage back, but it was a failed attempt.

"That's good," I said, "Because I'm just getting started with you. You are the one that made the mistake. You might want to think about moving to McAlester and getting a job as a rodeo clown."

I could tell he understood what I meant because a new wave of rage went over his face as he backed out of my shop and pulled away. I had found out that he was getting part of his meth supply from a rodeo clown who lived in McAlester, Oklahoma. I had already driven to McAlester and had a talk with the clown, who was a great guy. Bopper was out of that loop and the clown was now buying quarter pounds of the best meth he had ever seen, from me, for $4,000.00 each and I was delivering. I wasn't just going to stop Bopper from selling, he was about to be stopped from buying too.

I had also heard that Bopper and Harold were making trips to Dallas, Texas to buy meth. I knew the mail man who ran the mail route that included Bopper's house. So I went to him and gave him an ounce of the best Columbian Redbud there ever was and asked him to make me a copy of Bopper's telephone bill. He was reluctant at first, but he knew Bopper was an absolute jerk. He agreed to make a copy for me.

I already had a copy of Bopper's phone bill in my pocket as Bopper left my shop. I was about to turn the heat up another notch.

I was so mad when Bopper left I couldn't sit still. I got in my service truck and went to Walmart. I bought some cases of oil, antifreeze and cleaning supplies. On the way out I picked up a sale flier. Back in the truck I read the flier and noticed that Remington 12 gauge pump shotguns were on sale for $159.00. It was a great deal. I went back in and bought four of them and four boxes of No. 6 birdshot.

By the time I got back to the shop Terry was there too and my guys were talking about the Bopper incident. They helped me unload the supplies from the truck, paying special interest to all the shotguns. Even though it was really May I told them Merry Christmas and handed them each a new shotgun and a box of bird shot. Then I informed them that we would be duck hunting and Bopper was the duck. I told them that the next time they saw Bopper parked in the trees across the street to calmly empty the gun where he's at in the trees. Then come get me. At over 50 yards the bird shot would harmlessly pepper the trees, but Bopper wouldn't know that it was only bird shot.

I got on the phone and called my new friend the rodeo clown in McAlester and told him that Bopper was on the warpath and to get ready for a shit storm. He made some comment about Bopper not having big enough balls to mess with him. I could only hope he was right. I was starting to like the rodeo clown. He was a down to earth guy with a pleasant way about him.

After my call to the clown in McAlester I pulled out Bopper's phone bill and called what turned out to be the nut from Dallas, Texas.

When I first started this misbegotten adventure I had Dean, Jimmy and Terry buy samples of the meth Bopper and his people were selling. It had a brown/tan tint to it. I showed it to Mr. Connor, and being a substance analyst, he was able to tell me why it was such poor quality and he explained how to fix the problem.

Mr. Conner had been teaching me about the chemicals used to produce meth, their reactions and the manufacturing process. I was a fast learner.

When the man answered the phone in Dallas he simply said "Snake." There was loud music in the background and I thought it must be a bar.

I said, "Snake, you know Bopper from Oklahoma, he is about to become a problem. We should talk. I can help you with some other problems you're having, as well."

"I don't have problems," Snake said.

"Sometimes people have problems and don't even know it." I said.

"I'm the guy that knows how to fix problems. Meet me in Ardmore, Oklahoma at Budroux's Pig Shop at noon tomorrow. I'll buy you lunch.

If you don't like what I have to say you can tell me to piss up a rope."

Snake said, "Why should I trust you?"

"Nothing to trust," I said. "I'm not asking for anything. I'm just going to tell you some things about Bopper that you need to know and share some other information with you that you might find helpful. I'm not going to be asking any questions. Just doing some talking. You'll be glad you listened."

"Pretty sure of yourself," Snake said. It came out like a statement, not a question.

I said, "That's why people like me."

"I gott'a eat. I'll be there. But you need to know that if I'm not happy with what I hear, you won't be happy with this meeting." And he hung up.

I left early the next morning for Ardmore. I wanted to visit with Budroux a while before my visitor arrived. Budroux had the best barbecue around. I tried to go there as often as possible. I was trying to get my name on a bar stool. Budroux has over 100 foreign and domestic beers. To get your name on a bar stool you have to drink 100 different beers. Not in the same sitting, of course. The only problem was, I'm just not much of a drinker. I prefer ice tea with my meals. By noon the place was busy, as usual, and I had a table by the front window. I saw two Harleys pull in and I figured it was Snake and a friend. Snake was big. But the guy with him was huge. He was the biggest man I had ever seen. He had to duck coming in the door. I held my hand up when they looked my way. The guy was so big he wouldn't fit in the booth. He had to pull a chair up to the end of the booth. I thought the chair would break.

I said, "Damn, what do they feed you in Texas? You're the biggest person I have ever seen in my life.I hope I never piss you off." He laughed and growled, "Me, too."

Snake was nervous. He was looking around like he was expecting a SWAT team to jump out at any second. You could tell he didn't like being there.

I introduced myself and we ordered. We got a pitcher of beer to break the ice. Everyone knows that cops can't drink on duty, so drinking beer kind of softened the atmosphere. I told them why Bopper and his buddies were a problem, which included an accounting of what they did to Alice. The big guy, who was ironically called muscle, obviously didn't like what he was hearing. He kept looking at Snake for a reaction.

Snake said, "Why's that my problem? He pays his bill."

"People like Bopper carry a lot of heat with them," I said. "He is hanging out with a guy who recently ripped off a drug dealer in Dallas. And some friends of Alice's grandpa from Dixieland are not pleased, to say the least.

They want Bopper shut down."

"What's the guy's name that ripped off the drug dealer?" said Snake.

I pulled a piece of paper out of my pocket with a name and address on it and slid it across the table. It included the fake name the guy was using, as well. Snake pushed the paper over to Muscle who picked it up and read it, smiled and put it in his pocket. I had hit the jackpot.

Snake said, "Why don't you just kill Bopper and be done with it?"

I had been waiting for the opportunity to say, "Dead people don't suffer. The people down South want him destitute. They want him so broke that he can't buy a hamburger.

They figure Bopper will work himself into prison from there. It would probably be best if you're not in the picture when that happens. It will happen a lot sooner if you cut him off. I just gave you a token of my good faith. If you agree to cut him off, I'll turn that tan powder you have crystal white for you." I smiled that yes I can do it smile.

"You're already one up with that name and address," Snake said.

"If you can turn tan powder crystal white maybe you should be working for me."

I said, "Look at me as an independent contractor. I'll tell you how to correct your problem. If it works, not only will things be crystal white, your yield will increase. If you have other problems you can call me and I'll come show you how to fix them. If you lose a batch, you can save what you have and I'll come in and recover it with little loss. Of course, I'll want a percentage every time I fix a problem or recover something. I'm flexible on the amount. Whatever you feel is fair. Call me your damage control specialist."

"Bopper is a bum anyway," Snake said. "Consider it done. Now how would a person go about making things crystal white?"

I pulled another piece of paper out of my pocket with detailed instructions on it. We all smiled. I paid the bill and we walked out.

I said, "I like your bikes."

Snake said, "These are Hogs. Bikes have pedals on them. What are you driving?"

I pointed to my Challenger. He raised his eyebrows and we walked over to it. I liked to show it off so I popped the hood. It had three two barrel Holley's, a "Six-Pack," sitting on top of a chromed out 440 engine. I had just changed the camshaft and put in roller rockers. I got in and fired it up.

It had a great lope to it. I handed Snake an 8-ball of the meth I had and closed the hood. I think my car made Snake and Muscle look at me in a different way. I told him to call me if he had any problems with my instructions and off we went.

I went by grandma's house in Elmore City, Oklahoma on my way back home. My grandmother is the most wonderful person ever. I love her homemade hot rolls and blackberry cobbler. I think she hung the moon and the stars. It was my grandfather that I inherited my mechanical abilities from. He taught me so much. I had been helping grandpa restore antique airplanes and cars since I was a little kid.

I hadn't been back to the shop ten minutes when the rodeo clown from McAlester showed up with a black eye and a story about a guy with a mask coming in his house and robbing him that morning. He was sure Bopper was behind it, but was sure it wasn't Bopper. He was positive that it was a guy called Schlimp from Beggs, Oklahoma that hung out with Bopper.

Schlimp was hard to miss. He was well over six feet tall and had a bushy head of black hair. The rodeo clown was on his way to Beggs to find Schlimp and he wanted to know where Bopper was. I had just gotten back and didn't know but I assured him I would get right on it and find out.

I went in the shop to get Dean, Jimmy and Terry outfitted and supplied for the night. They said they didn't know where Bopper was at that moment but they had each seen him drive by the shop that day.

Jimmy said he was pretty sure Schlimp was in a motel in Okmulgee and he gave me the room number. I pulled my Challenger into the shop and asked Jimmy to change out the rear tires with the slicks. I had a race at 10:00 that night with a guy coming in from Broken Arrow, Oklahoma. It was time to get ready. After the race we were having a party.

I got in my service truck and headed for the motel room in Okmulgee.

I figured I could reason with Schlimp and get him to give the dope and money back. Everyone knew it was him that took it. The girl with Schlimp in the motel room even told Jimmy that Schlimp had robbed a guy. I drove the 13 miles to Okmulgee hoping I was right. I pulled into the motel parking lot and drove around back to the room I was looking for. It faced the parking lot in the back. I no sooner knocked on the door when I heard a gun shot from inside the room. It was loud and a man was yelling. I had just stepped back and was about to turn and leave when the room door popped open and a good looking girl came out, while the man was yelling, and shut the door. She was visibly shaken. You could see the fear in her pretty face when she turned around. She had her purse in one hand and a leather bag I recognized in the other.

She looked at me and said, "Damn." Then she handed me the bag.

She knew who I was and who the bag belonged to.

I said, "let's go before the cops get here. I guess you know I have a reward out for this bag."

She smiled and we got in my truck and left by a side road. I could already hear sirens on the way.

"What happened?" I asked.

She said, "He was so paranoid. When you knocked on the door he grabbed his gun from under the pillow and shot himself in the leg." She laughed that kind of I don't know if I should be laughing laugh. We later discovered that one shot went through both of Schlimp's legs. He was lucky it didn't hit an artery. He was released from the hospital directly to the county jail where he later pled guilty to being a felon in possession of a firearm. He received five-years in prison.

As we were driving back towards Henryetta I said, "This calls for a party. I have a race tonight so why don't you come with me. I'll introduce you to some of my friends. I've seen you before but I don't know your name."

She said, "Elizabeth, but my friends call me Crystal. I know who you are. But you don't look crazy."

"How about I call you Elizabeth," I said. "Why in the world would you think I'm crazy?"

"Schlimp said only a crazy man would take on Bopper," she said.

I said, "Surely you've heard why I am at odds with Bopper, haven't you?"

"It's about what happened to Alice," she said. Elizabeth and Schlimp were from Beggs, the same town Alice was from.

"Yes, it is about Alice," I agreed. "However, I would like to keep that quiet for a while. After what happened to her I can't believe you would be in a motel room with an idiot like Schlimp."

"He's my uncle," she said. Looking a little sad and embarrassed. "He would never let anything happen to me."

I said, "You may be right, if he doesn't accidently shoot you. Or get you hurt because he robbed someone. We have to get you some new friends.

First, we're going to get you some new clothes and I'll give you the reward I mentioned.

How about $100.00 and an 8-ball?"

She smiled, a beautiful smile, and said, "How about $200.00 and two 8-balls?"

"You drive a hard bargain," I said. "But it's a deal. And I'll buy your new clothes too and get my friend to give you a reward also."

That made her very happy. I was already enjoying her smile. We did some shopping and had something to eat. I called Jimmy and told him the news and asked him to find the rodeo clown. When we got back to the shop I introduced Elizabeth as the hero of the day. I sent my secretary Phoebe and my new friend Elizabeth to get their hair done for the party. A friend of mine's wife had a beauty salon at her house and she didn't mind taking late customers. By the time they made it back we had the beer on ice and the stereo going. They both looked hot all decked out. Elizabeth was the center of attention telling her story about Schlimp shooting himself in the leg. She and Phoebe made quick friends. Elizabeth wandered over and I introduced her to my girlfriend, Deena. Elizabeth told me thank you and kissed me on the cheek. She had already taken a liking to the rodeo clown and he had given her another reward.

Deena said, "You do this knight in shining armor thing pretty good, big boy." I smiled and kissed her big. She was a very special person. I should have married her and moved away right then. A little bit later the guy I was about to race showed up with his friends. I heard one of the newcomers ask Deena out and she said, "Why would I want one of you little fishes when I have Moby Dick over there?" Pointing at me and smiling her wonderfully seductive smile.

The place we used as a drag strip was a mile West of town on the old highway by the Sundowner Ballroom. We mostly raced at night when it was a little cooler and the sun wouldn't be in our eyes. We raced straight into the West. The man from Broken Arrow brought his own pit crew with him. They put his slicks on at the shop and we went to our makeshift drag strip. I was about to race a 1969 Camaro with a 427, 4-speed.

There must have been a hundred people there. We were all friends, just having good clean fun. We lined up heading West into the dark. We had cars and judges parked at the far end of the quarter mile with their headlights shining across the road marking the quarter mile line. A big block Chevy matched with a big block Dodge. It was going to be a good race.

My girlfriend, the sexy Deena, got between our cars to start the race. When the flag dropped we both shot out fender to fender. When I hit second gear I was pulling ahead. The Camaro's engine started popping. His valves were floating. The valve springs were too weak to shut the valves fast enough to keep up with the RPMs the engine was trying to crank out.

I slammed into third gear and beat him by four car lengths. It cost him $500.00 to lose that race. We went back to the shop to continue the party. Me and the man from Broken Arrow had a discussion on the importance of stronger valve springs. He assured me that he was headed home to replace his valve springs, promising to return one day soon to try his luck again. It had been a great day. The kind of day memories are made of. My real reward came later after everyone left. Deena took me by the hand and led me to my back office bedroom where we made wild love until we fell asleep in each other's arms.

I don't know what I dreamed that night. I'm sure it was something nice, because I still hadn't got a full dose of how crazy the meth world was. That was about to change.

CHAPTER FOUR:
Making Progress

The next few days were fairly uneventful. The marijuana and methamphetamine business was booming. I spent my days working at the shop and making a few pot and meth deliveries. I was keeping up with the growing popular demand.

At night I was spending a considerable amount of time with Mr. Connor getting an education in chemical engineering. Mr. Connor had used a backhoe to dig the floor out of his large pole barn, where he built an underground laboratory. The lab included a variable control ventilation system with water activated charcoal filters that vented through a four inch pipe that ran all the way out the top of the barn. The system was so efficient we could restrict the incoming air flow and increase the ventilation fan speed, thereby lowering the barometric pressure in the lab.

The lab had a hidden entrance and a large storage area. It wasn't long before I built my own lab and- underground storage facilities.

To get me started Mr. Connor had obtained the first ten pounds of meth from our friend in Louisiana. From here on we would be manufacturing our own. To accomplish that task, we had to have a secure place to manufacture the meth, which we now had. Then we had to obtain the equipment, glassware and chemicals that are necessary for production.

Some of the equipment, glassware and chemicals were common and could be easily obtained without raising a red flag and alerting the Drug Enforcement Agency (DEA). However, some of the glassware and chemicals are heavily watched and regulated. A person can't just walk into a chemical warehouse or distributor and ask for 500 gallons of acetic anhydride, which is a chemical bonding agent used in organic synthesis, or phenylacetic acid, or methylamine without running the risk of being arrested and going to prison.

We set up a deal where we could get most of what we needed in Louisiana and Texas, out the back doors of some chemical companies.

Some chemicals like sodium acetate, although used chiefly in organic synthesis, photography and Dr. Pepper, it's also used in bakery products and was easy to get. However, the key ingredient, Phenylacetic acid, which was heavily watched and monitored by the DEA, was going to be a problem. As we worked on our plan to obtain the more difficult chemical, I took a trip down South to Louisiana to pick-up glassware and some chemicals. Things went smooth. I had to stay two days while the chemical man gathered up the things I needed. Then I had to rent a U-Haul trailer to bring everything back. We were making progress.

Getting the other things, we needed turned out to be more of a challenge. I had to get creative. First, I went to Oklahoma City and bought a few things at a chemical warehouse that would not set off any alarms or be suspicious. While I was there I picked up some business cards from the man running the place. I also picked up some advertisement brochures and an order catalog. Then I went to a pay phone and called directory assistance for the number of a large wholesale chemical distributor.

I then called the distributor and asked who manufactured phenylacetic acid. Once I determined who one of the main wholesale distributors where I bought a nice suit, new shoes and expensive sunglasses. Then I got a new haircut and rented a furniture delivery truck (with no name on the side) from a guy I knew and headed for Kansas.

I spent the night in a fancy motel and had dinner in a posh restaurant. I thought it might be my last meal as a free man. The next morning, I started real early. When the chemical company opened I was already backing the truck up to the loading dock. I went in and asked for the boss by name. I had asked for his name when I called. When he came out I introduced myself as the man on the business card I handed him.

I told him my company was participating in a DEA sting operation and that I was there to buy phenylacetic acid. He asked me how much I wanted and I asked him how much he had.

I bought it all. As he had the truck loaded I paid the bill with cash and signed my fake name to the ticket. When I left the place, I had twenty three 110 pound barrels of phenylacetic acid in the back of the truck and a nervous smile on my face. He also gave me a hat that sported the company logo.

I drove back to Oklahoma and put all of it in a storage unit I had rented a month prior for a temporary holdover. I didn't want to take anything directly to the lab in case I was being followed. After I returned the truck and picked up my car I met Mr. Connor at the Sirloin Stockade in Okmulgee for dinner. By buying the large bulk quantities of chemicals, we were eliminating return visits to the chemical places and minimizing our exposure. Once a person has the required chemicals and equipment the likelihood of getting caught manufacturing was slim, as long as a person has a hidden secure place that nobody knows about.

I soon realized that the lab is the one place that everyone is trying to find. That included the cops, drug dealers, thieves, tweakers, nuts and rats.

That was why we were getting all of our supplies stocked piled and hidden before the shit hit the fan.

When I got back to the shop Dean and Jimmy were worried. I had been gone a lot and doing "secret" things that I wouldn't discuss with them. They were partly out of the loop and they didn't like it. Deena showed up mad because I was neglecting her, as well. I couldn't tell them everything.

They had no way of knowing how much pressure I was under, or how many things I had going. I wanted to tell them that all their little problems were nothing compared to mine. It would have been nice to actually be able to talk to them about my week. They didn't know that I was effectively taking night classes from Mr. Connor in chemical engineering, that I had just helped build an underground laboratory, that I had been to Louisiana and Kansas buying truckloads of chemicals, or that I had met with the rodeo clown and Snake to try and undermine Bopper and his bunch. I had a full plate. I also had a shop to run, bills to pay, money to manage and I was in the process of learning how to hide money and assets.

My guys were used to me being there more and they didn't understand the change. Deena was mad and hurt because she thought I had another girl on the side. I didn't. I was just really busy working my rear off. I later discovered that someone was lying to Deena trying to get in her pants and I wasn't around to defend myself. She went with the person who was paying her the most attention. It ended up being one of Bopper's friends who was just using her trying to get information about me. I learned another valuable lesson.

When I was younger, my first experience with love was with my junior high sweetheart Darleen. That short lived relationship had left me brokenhearted. My ability to trust had been substantially diminished.

It has affected me all my life.

With Deena walking out the door and my life in turmoil, I was once again brokenhearted. It was easy to fix the problem with Dean, Jimmy and Terry. All they wanted was more meth to sell. They understood that the meth was coming from some place and that I had to take care of that end.

Deena was gone and I had just gotten matters settled with my guys when I received a phone call from Stillwater, Oklahoma, home of the Oklahoma State University (OSU). It was my marijuana man informing me that a new shipment had arrived. That put a smile on my face. I told him I would be there the next afternoon to pick-up my issue.

I spent the next morning taking care of shop related business, then I drove my service truck out to an old man's house in the country that sold firewood. I bought a rick of fresh cut firewood and piled it in the back of my truck. The drive to Stillwater only took two hours. I was there in time for dinner. My friend, the pot man, talked me into staying the night and going dancing at Eskimo Joe's. I had to buy some new clothes, but soon I was outfitted and ready for a night on the town. At Eskimo Joe's that night I let all of my worries slip away. For a little while I was just Jeff, an ordinary man who was laughing and dancing with a bunch of really wonderful people. We danced until closing time. Then we took two college girls back to my friend's place and had wild sex. That morning we went to a pancake place for breakfast then took the girls back to Eskimo Joe's to get their cars.

We said our goodbyes with hugs and kisses then parted company. It had been a great night.

When we got back to my friend's house, I packed 100 pounds of Columbian in green Army duffle bags. It was pressed in bricks. I placed the bags in the bed of my truck then I piled all the firewood back in on top of it. The freshly cut wood would mask the pot smell to all but trained dogs.

If I got pulled over the police were too lazy to unload the truck to see if something was under the firewood. The only way I would get caught was if someone told on me and the police were waiting on me when I returned to Henryetta. I was not concerned about the ride home, only my return to the shop. To solve that problem, I was stashing the pot and other things in the woods outside of town in a little spot I'd fixed up. It meant I had to unload and load that firewood several times, but I didn't mind. After I dropped off the pot, I drove all the way around town so I would be coming in from the other direction. I stopped at the In-And-Out drive in, with my load of firewood and had a cheeseburger. While I was there, my cute secretary, Phoebe, drove in to pick-up food for the guys at the shop. She was happy to see me. It was Saturday. Payday. Everyone loves payday.

Not much had happened in my absence. Phoebe had sorted the mail and gotten checks made out for bills and pay. I signed the checks and Phoebe mailed the ones that needed mailing. Dean and Jimmy were anxious to sample the new weed shipment. Life was good. The only new development was disturbing. The reason we hadn't heard much from Bopper and his boys was they were trying to follow me to find out where I was getting the meth. That wasn't going to happen because I'd had it all along. I didn't have to go get it. I had expected them to start trying to follow me. I was taking precautions. Unbeknownst to me, Bopper had tried to follow me when I went to Ardmore to meet Snake. He had tried to follow me when I went to Louisiana. He was following me the day I rented the furniture truck and went to Kansas. He watched my car sit in the parking lot of the furniture place for two days and he had attempted to follow me towards Okmulgee on several occasions. Jimmy had found all this out while I'd been gone to Stillwater. We had a lot of friends and someone Jimmy knew told him to warn me. We certainly had more friends than enemies. Bopper had recruited some help. Their plan was to follow me until I led them to the source and then initiate a robbery.

To help foil my enemies plot I moved three of the cars I had on the lot for sale to different locations. I kept one in the parking lot of a friend's shop in Okmulgee. I parked one on campus at the vocational training school in Okmulgee, where I could park my truck in one parking area, walk across campus and get the car without being spotted. I parked the other one in a friend's old barn behind his house in Pauls Valley, Oklahoma so I could change vehicles on the way to meet with Snake in Ardmore. I also put my motorcycle at a friend's house two blocks from my mother's house. I had things fixed up where it would take some doing to find out where I was going.

One morning when Jimmy and Dean got to the shop at 8:00 in the morning they woke me up and told me Bopper was parked in the trees across the road from the shop.

He was obviously waiting on me to leave so he could try and follow me. I was pissed. I grabbed one of the new 12 gauge shotguns with No. 6 birdshot and headed for the door. The first shot sent Bopper running for his truck and I let go of the other four shots right on his tail. I had no doubt that Bopper could hear the birdshot hitting the tree leaves. Bopper never watched from the trees across the road again. I found out later just how crazy and mad Bopper was about me shooting in his direction. It must have hurt his pride a little.

That evening I was driving out of town on the back roads and Bopper showed up in his red and white Bronco with two of his friends. He came up behind me real fast. As he was passing he weaved in my direction. I did not give an inch. The person in the passenger side of Bopper's Bronco shot my truck twice trying to get me to pull over. It worked.

I slammed on my brakes and jumped out, gun in hand.   He had gone past me and was backing up. I could see his friend Carl's face looking out the back window.

I was using my gun to wave him back, yelling, "Come on, come on."

I don't know what he was expecting, but I sure wasn't just going to give up. They saw my gun and panicked. Bopper and his passengers ducked down below window level and took off forward, driving on nothing but fear and instinct. Weaving like a drunk. I went from mad to laughing.

My mother received a phone call the next day, from someone's mother, letting her know that Bopper and his friends were overheard at a bar planning a way to capture me and torture me until I told them where I was hiding the drugs and the money. That got my attention.

I was a little shaken after getting shot at and I was amazed at how much of a coward Bopper was. I realized that I didn't have to shoot him. He just needed to know that I was ready and willing to shoot. When I got to Mr. Connor's and told him what happened he was livid. I finally got him laughing with the story of how Bopper freaked out and drove off weaving when he saw my gun. We had come too far to stop and now we had proof that our plan was working. It was time for some psychological warfare.

Mr. Connor gave me an H & R 10 gauge single-shot shotgun. We sawed the barrel off to 19 inches. Just over legal length. The next day I bought two boxes of 10 gauge 3-inch super magnum extra long-range geese loads. Then all I had to do was make sure Bopper got the news. I put my 10 gauge in the gun rack of my truck and went to visit a guy who lived in the country that I knew would call Bopper as soon as I left his house. I told the man the story about Bopper and his buddies shooting at me, then I showed him my new sawed-off shotgun and announced that I was ready for Bopper to try again. I even threw an old five-gallon bucket into the man's yard and demonstrated how mean my new gun was. When I fired it, it sounded like dynamite going off. Unless you have fired a 10-gauge shotgun with that type of ammunition, then you can't even imagine the deafening sound and the kick. I just smiled. I never let on that it kicked so hard it bruised me and I didn't want to shoot it anymore. It hurt. I had a cannon that would stop a truck.

I didn't call Louisiana and let him know what Bopper had done. I could handle it on my own and I figured he would find out anyway, in due time.

Later that week one of Snake's representatives showed up. Perfect timing. Snake had sent a scout to scope things out and to bring me a bonus.

A quarter pound of pure crystal white meth. My instructions had worked and Snake was very happy. The guy was also on a reconnaissance mission. He wanted me to show him where the guy lived who ripped off the drug dealer in Dallas. We climbed in my truck and I took him by the guy's house to show him. I also showed him several ways to come and go from the area and told him about Bopper and the same guy shooting at me and trying to rob me earlier that week. When he left town, he had a pretty good picture of what was happening and the lay of the town. I sent a message back to Snake that I was in the market for large quantities of two of the chemicals I needed to get started. I thought he just might have an idea where I could obtain them. The thing about asking for a certain chemical is, people are pretty smart. The fact that I didn't ask for the more difficult to obtain chemical was an indication that I probably already had it. Often the person wants to trade chemicals, which can be a dangerous business.

Two days later Jimmy told me that the guy who ripped off the drug dealer in Dallas, the guy that was with Bopper and shot my truck, had apparently packed up in the middle of the night and left. Nobody had actually seen him pack up and leave, but he was gone. He hadn't told anyone he was leaving and didn't leave a forwarding address.

Imagine that. I figured, maybe he got Snake bit, but I knew better than to say it out loud. Some things are just better left unsaid.

When the telephone rang at 2:30 in the morning I figured it was something crazy and it was.

I grabbed the phone and said, "Jeff's Road Service."

Snake said, "What, you fix roads too? He laughed and said, "I got a problem needs fix'n, fast."

"Where am I heading," I asked.

"You know where Ringling is?" Said Snake.

I assured him I did and that I could be there in three hours. He told me to meet him at Denny's in Ardmore at 6:00a.m. It concerned a large spill in a house. The fumes were so bad that Snake's people couldn't go in. I knew what I needed. I quickly removed the tool boxes from my service truck and put two air tanks in the back that had full face masks like firemen use.

I threw in some empty boxes and headed out.

This was my first recovery job and I intended to look good doing it.

I kept lightweight coveralls and work boots in the truck along with a change of clothes and an overnight bag. I was ready.

I was eating sausage with biscuits and gravy when Snake got there.

The guy who was cooking meth in the house had left it cooking and went to town, where he was arrested on back warrants and found in possession of meth and a gun. When Snake's boys went to the house to move the lab they couldn't go inside because the fumes were overwhelming. Obviously, something had broken. We had to hurry and get it cleaned up before someone drove by and smelled it, or the police figured out where the guy lived and went to search the house. No problem. I went to Walmart and picked up the additional supplies I would need.

When I got to the house it was a nice house with an attached garage. My truck was too tall to fit in the garage, so I backed up to the garage door to help hide my license plate and unloaded everything I would need into the garage. The fumes were bad in the garage. But with the door open I was able to unload everything real fast into the garage then close the door and put on my air tank.

When I went through the inside garage door into the house the fumes were so bad it was smokey in the house. My eyes were burning even with the oxygen mask. I carried a fan in with me and went right to the back door, opened the door, plugged in the fan and turned it on high blowing out the door. Then I walked through the house opening every window.

The spill was in the master bathroom. In the bathtub. The man had set up a 22 thousand milliliter triple neck boiling flask in the bathtub. He had put a stopper in the tub in case he had a spill so the tub was a foot deep with a heavy dark yellow oil, P2p. The flask was huge. It had fallen off of a hot plate and broken. The hot oil had drenched the hot plate causing the circuit breaker to pop, luckily. But the instant the large flask broke the hot burner vaporized part of the chemical filling the house with smoky fumes.

The hot oil had cooled making my job easier.

I scooped up the oil and poured it into two new five-gallon gas cans. I even sprayed a little water in the tub to rinse off the ruined hot plate and broken glass in order to get every drop of P2p. By then I was out of air and had to change tanks. The smoke had cleared but the fumes were still too bad to go at it without the air tank and full face mask. I was working back and forth between the bathroom and the garage. I had all the trash bagged up and all the glassware and chemical containers cleaned, packed in boxes and sitting in a neat stack by the garage door. I scrubbed the bathtub and had hot soapy bleach water in it, soaking towels so I could use them to clean the bathroom.

By the time I ran out of air in my second tank, (each tank had forty-five minutes of air) I had the place looking good and was able to do the final cleanup work without the air tank. Lucky me. The man had lined the bathroom walls with heavy plastic so the walls were in good shape. I had a load of laundry going, coffee brewing and was washing a few dishes, all by noon. I had packed up everything in the house that might have been called manufacturing paraphernalia. Including the guns and drugs I found too. As I went I straightened and cleaned the whole house with Pinesol and lemon fresh Pledge. By the time I was done anyone's mom would have been proud. I was ready to go. It looked and smelled like nothing happened.

When I opened the garage door to load my truck there was a Buick Regal parked next to my truck with a very cute little blonde sitting on the hood smoking a cigarette. She didn't look old enough to smoke, or drive.

She said, "Hi. I'm Little Bit. It smells okay out here."

Playing innocent, I said, "It certainly does." I smiled.

It was about 2:00 p.m. and I was hungry. I ask the pretty little gal, "Have you had lunch yet? I am about to get a bite to eat. Would you like to join me?" I was talking and loading my truck as fast as I could and still look like I was supposed to be there and that everything was cool. I had already changed clothes and had my dirty clothes in a bag.

She calmly said, "We thought you might be dead, so I came out here to check on you. Then I heard you in there and thought I better wait for you out here. Did everything turn out okay."

"That was thoughtful of you," I said. "Yes, everything turned out fine." Not committing myself or admitting anything as I closed the tailgate of my truck. I had no idea who this girl was, but apparently, someone had sent her out here to check on me. I later found out that she had volunteered for the task.

I said, "I just made coffee, or there's a coke in the fridge if you want one. But I think it would be best if we didn't stay here long."

She slid off the car and headed in through the garage entrance like she had been there before. She went right to the ice box and got a coke then headed down the hall. I had the central air on high and all the windows were still open.

She said, "Damn, it smells nice in here. You cleaned the whole house. Snake's going to like this. He didn't think you could do it. They were going to burn the house down tonight."

I was starting to like this girl. She was obviously older than she looked. I said, "Well, let's get out of here. I'm hungry and I need to make a call." Little Bit followed me to town where I called Snake from a pay phone and informed him things were taken care of. I told him Little Bit had shown up to check on me. He asked to talk to her and she told him it was "Amazing," the whole house was clean and smelled great.

I told Snake I would be in touch in a few days, then followed Little Bit to a Mexican restaurant called Polo's where we ate and she told me about the dumbass that made the mess in the house. It was his mother's house and she was gone to Florida for two weeks. Fortunately, she would still have a home when she came back.

It was getting late and I didn't want to be driving at night with all that stuff in my truck so I told Little Bit I was going to get a motel room and asked her if she wanted to stay with me. She said, "Sure," and off we went.

When we got to the motel room I made the mistake of saying, "You sure are cute."

She said, "Puppies are cute. I'm not a puppy." No, she wasn't.

But that didn't stop us from doing it doggy style several times that night. She was hot and sexy and I couldn't get enough of her. When I got ready to leave the next morning she said, "My name is Loretta.

You're Jeff, right? Are you going to come back and see me?"

I had made it a point in life not to ask people their names or to make many promises. I told her that I had to come back in a few days to meet someone and "Yes," I definitely wanted to see her when I came back.

If I made a promise I intended to keep it. We parted with a kiss.

I had a place in mind to store everything but the two five-gallon gas cans of P2p. It was only an hour from Ardmore, not too far from my grandmother's house. I was taking the P2p back to Mr. Connor's to process it into powder. That was when I learned that you should never bury anything on a creek bank just because the dirt is soft and easy to dig. Four days later, on my way back to Ardmore, I went to dig everything up and move it to a better place. It had rained. When the water came up it floated everything up out of the ground. It was all triple trash bagged. Lucky for me the water only floated the stuff partly out of the ground and the weight of the bags kept it from floating down the creek.

Back at Mr. Connor's he showed me that the color, texture and smell, combined with the fact that the cool liquid did not reform any crystals, indicated that the P2p process was complete. We separated the P2p oil with lye water then distilled it. The next stage was the speed cook, then we turned it into five-pounds of crystal white powder.

I took Snake three-pounds and kept two for my trouble along with the lab equipment, chemicals and other things I had recovered. Everyone was happy. Especially me.

I was back to see Loretta to work on what became a long, fun relationship. I made many trips to Ardmore after that ordeal. I wasn't living a double life. I was living a triple life and boy was it fun. At first.

My motto was, "You can't have too many irons in the fire, all you had to do was build another fire." I was establishing my reputation as a methamphetamine guru.

One time a wonderful girl I knew, Suzanne, asked me how I kept from getting in trouble. I put on my best John Wayne and said, "I cover my tracks before I make them."

CHAPTER FIVE:

Vengeance

While I was thriving on the excitement, Bopper was getting bold. I went to a guy's house in Okmulgee to deliver an ounce of meth and some pot.

I usually did not stay long when I delivered something. I would show up, go in an unoccupied room with the person I was there to meet, make the deal in private and go. I never carried extra dope in my truck and I only left the place with cash. That way if I got pulled over leaving I was clean, except for the money and two very large guns. That day I decided to stay for a while. The person I came to see had some friends over and they were ordering pizza. There was a girl there, Glenda, who had the stunning beauty of a Greek goddess. I couldn't keep my eyes off her. When our eyes met I was sure the other people in the room could see sparks fly between us. We were talking and eating pizza when the front door banged open and in walked Bopper, Harold and Richard. Everyone got quiet.

Bopper said, "Nobody sells dope in my town, unless it's my dope."

Not very original. It was the same thing Bopper said when he came to my shop. I always sit with my back to the wall facing the entrance, no matter where I'm at. As Bopper and his two friends came through the door I stood up and pulled out my gun, holding it beside my leg. The gun was partly hidden by the table in front of me that had pizza and beer covering it. As soon as he blurted his little speech, I raised my gun, pointed it at Bopper's chest, from across the room, and pulled the hammer back with a loud double click.

Then I announced, "That's a nice revelation Bopper. But as you can see, we're having a pizza party here and you're not invited."

I was slowly easing around the table, still pointing my pistol at Bopper's chest. Harold was right behind Bopper and Richard was behind Harold, half in and half out the front door. I was thinking that, if the bullet makes it through Bopper's fat ass, it would probably take out Harold and maybe even Richard.

It was clear that Richard and Harold must have thought the same thing.

Richard backed out the door and Harold stepped to the side, just enough to get out of my line of fire. This all took place in an instant. Less than thirty seconds had passed.

"Didn't your mother teach you to knock and get permission before you entered?" I continued.

Bopper said, "You're not always going to have that gun." There was nothing between us and he was looking right down the barrel.

I replied, "Yeah, I am. And you're always going to make an ass of yourself. If you keep showing up where I'm at, one of these days you are liable to catch me in a bad mood."

He knew what I meant. He turned and headed out the door with Harold on his heels. I holstered my gun that nobody knew I had under my leather bomber jacket and apologized for the rude interruption.

Everyone in the room was smiling and excited like they had just witnessed Doc Holiday in a gunfight. I was feeling out of place.

I didn't mean to bring Bopper and his crap to a peaceful pizza party. I looked at Glenda and said, "I guess that blew any chance I had of getting you to go to a movie with me."

Some people laughed and Glenda jumped up, hugged me and said, "No, I would love to go to a movie with you and if we hurry we can get there before it starts."

My smile must have been ear to ear. We said our goodbyes and headed out the door. I also warned the person I came to see to keep his doors locked. I don't remember what movie we went to see. What I do remember was looking at Glenda's smile and thinking how lucky I was.

After the movie Glenda suggested we go to the lake.

We drove to Okmulgee lake. I had never been there. It was a little cool. We spread a blanket out on the grass and soon things warmed up just fine. Before we knew it, it was so hot that we had to take our clothes off. Glenda was very energetic. She could move her hips in a way that drove me over the top and kept me coming back for more. For a little while she made me forget about Bopper and his craziness. When I dropped Glenda off at home, the sun was just peeking through the trees.
Glenda and I saw a lot of each other that summer.

Even though I hadn't let it show at the time, I was thoroughly peeved at Bopper's bold outburst. I wasn't the only one mad. Bopper and his partners, Richard and Harold, were mad and getting desperate. I had cut deep into their supply and sales. After I ran Bopper off with a gun, he went back to Henryetta to get even. When I got back to the shop the next morning, after spending a wonderful night with Glenda, it was 6:00 am and Jimmy was already there. I knew something was wrong.

Jimmy had been in the shop that night and heard something out back. Jimmy opened the back door to a raging fire.

He then grabbed the water hose and was putting the fire out when he saw Bopper's Bronco tail lights driving away on the road behind the shop.

He could just see the tail lights through the trees, but he knew it was Bopper. Not only because he saw Bopper's tail lights, but because Bopper had used yellow spray paint to paint a big B on the back of the shop where the fire was started. Bopper had sprayed the B on the building then poured gas in my scrap iron pile that was against the back of the building, then lit it and ran. Fortunately, the scrap iron was metal and so was the building. Jimmy was able to put the fire out quickly with only minor damage.

I'm not the kind of guy to get crazy mad and go off halfcocked. I'm more calculated and cool about my vengeance. I was really starting to understand the reason why Mr. Connor chose to handle Bopper and his two buddies in the manner we were handling them. As crazy as it was, I was having fun. Besides, I was tired. Glenda had given me a workout. I woke up in time for lunch, with a new idea.

When I came out into the shop Phoebe was there. I had fun playing with my secretary. I sent her to the In-And-Out to buy a sack of cheeseburgers. She came back a little later and asked, "How many are in a sack?" I laughed. I sent her back to get ten cheeseburgers, five orders of cheese tater tots and five large chocolate malts. Cheese and chocolate are two of my major food groups.

While Phoebe was gone for sustenance I ran my new idea by Jimmy.

He agreed it was pretty daring and that it might send Bopper over the edge. I didn't want Dean or Terry to know. Dean was doing too much meth and Terry was acting strange. When Phoebe got back with the food we all five gathered around a big work table and ate like a family. We'd been missing that.

My mother was making Phoebe's prom dress. It was beautiful, purple and black. Phoebe was excited about it and she certainly had a right to be. She looked so cute in that dress. It made me wish I was ten years younger and had better sense.

Phoebe said, "We need to go by your mother's so you can get cleaned up and I can try on my new prom dress."

I agreed and off we went. Mom liked Phoebe. When I came out of the bathroom all clean Phoebe was standing on a little stool and mom was pinning the hem of her prom dress. Phoebe looked like a doll smiling and clapping her hands. Her smile and joy were infectious. Mom and I stood together looking at an angel. Phoebe was happy and we were happy for her. She had worked hard and was about to graduate with her whole life ahead of her. It made me wish I could start over.

My first idea for getting back at Bopper was simple. All it was going to take was a little planning and big balls. I was just the guy for the job.

Until then, all I had been doing was trying to undermine Bopper's dope business. Bopper was getting nasty and it was time for me to hit back.

I needed a truck that couldn't be traced back to me. But first, I had a chemical deal to finesse.

I set up a deal to buy acetic anhydride from two crazy brothers that were cooking meth down on the Red River. Snake was the go-between.

I wanted a lot, but I was only going to get fifty gallons on this trip.

We were meeting at an old oil field location and Snake was supervising the exchange.

Snake and I had been doing some other business together and he was starting to like me. He didn't trust these two brothers. We picked a nice night for the exchange. It was hot and sultry with a mild breeze blowing.

Snake and his friend were a little tense and it was making me somewhat uncomfortable. The oil field location was secluded. A great place for a covert transaction. Snake and his friend and I were smoking a joint when the two brothers arrived. They both got out of their truck and were walking towards us. One was over weight and had shifty nervous eyes. The other one was skinny, with a bounce in his step and a big grin.

Both had pistols tucked into their belts.

As they approached, I asked, "Are we good?"

The skinny hyper one said, "Yeah, but on the way out here we decided to rob you," as he went for his gun. Snake must have had his gun in his hand. He jerked the gun up and from five feet away shot the guy in the neck. Then he fired at the brother who was ducking and running. The guy shot in the neck flipped backwards and landed on his back, just for an instant, then he rolled over and was scrambling away on all fours.

Snake was shooting back and forth between the two brothers, left, right, left right, boom-boom-boom. The other guy with us was alternating shots between them too, boom-boom-boom. Dirt and dust were flying and gun smoke was slowly drifting away.

Snake slammed a new clip in, but both of the brothers were nowhere to be seen. They had run into the trees and even though my ears were ringing I could hear them crashing through the brush running away from us.

The smell of cordite was heavy. The cloud of gun smoke was slowly floating away with the wind.

I hadn't moved. I'd just pulled my own gun and stood there watching things unfold, or collapse. I laughed and said, "That didn't go very well." Then I yelled at the trees, "Now who's robbing who? Or should I say whom?"

I gave Snake the money I had in my pocket to pay for the acetic anhydride, said thanks and informed him that I was taking the brothers truck and chemicals and going home. Snake just chuckled and told me to be careful. I told him I would come get my truck later and handed him the keys. Then I scooted into the brothers truck, where the keys were hanging in the ignition, and drove away. I didn't know, or care, what would become of the two stupid brothers. I was hoping the one shot in the neck wouldn't die. I figured since he was in good enough shape to run he would probably make it. It was a hell of a night. Not only did I get part of the acetic anhydride I needed, I had gotten the truck I needed for my new Bopper idea.

After I stored everything I drove by Bopper's house then went looking for my friend Jimmy, who was the only one that knew what I was about to do. Bopper's lights were off and his Bronco was gone. He had been spending a lot of time at Harold's house in Okmulgee, playing around in Harold's work shop. They had been getting some meth from somewhere.

I just hadn't figured out from where, yet.

Jimmy was at my house on Fourth and Merick playing foosball with Doug and Delbert. I had a very nice burner foosball table with a dragon under the glass sitting in my living room. It was already 4:00 in the morning, but people on meth didn't care about time. My house and shop were open to my close friends, mainly Jimmy, who had keys. I asked Jimmy to drive the thirteen miles to Okmulgee and call me if Bopper's Bronco was parked at Harold's house. Thirty minutes later Jimmy called and informed me that the Bronco was there and Bopper was in the garage with the door open working on something. I told Doug and Delbert to hold the fort down and ran out the door to my stolen truck. I knew I had at least thirty minutes. It was ten minutes to Bopper's house and it was getting light outside. I drove to Bopper's as fast as I could. When I got there, I pulled in the driveway, drove over the little fence and into the back yard. Then I backed the truck up to the back door of the house. The house sat low to the ground with an added room on the back. I left the truck running, jumped out and ran to the back door and kicked it open. Just inside the back door was a chest type deep freeze. I pulled one end away from the wall and raised the other end up until it stood on end. I worked it to the door then let the tail gate of the truck down and backed the truck to within a foot of the door. Then I simply pushed the deep freeze over halfway into the truck and slid it all the way in, closed the tail gate and drove off.

Henryetta is an old coal mining town. There are strip pits on the East side of town that are full of deep blue water. I had told Jimmy where to pick me up when he called from Okmulgee. Bopper had put two pad-locks on the deep freeze.

By the time Jimmy got back from Okmulgee and to the strip pit, I had used a large pry bar to break the locks and hasps off. Jimmy and I took everything out of the freezer and opened it. Bopper was known for keeping his drugs and money in his deep freeze. We hit the jackpot. Four thousand in cash and almost an ounce of meth. Then I found a pistol, a .38 caliber revolver. It was an old collectors piece. I was sure I knew who it belonged to. But I wasn't sure how I was going to get it back to that person and still keep my deep freeze secret. I tied the steering wheel with a rope. Pushed down the accelerator pedal with a stick and braced it against the seat.

Then I reached in the window, started the truck and popped it into gear. The engine roared, the tires spun and the truck shot forward over the edge of the bank of the strip pit for a thirty foot nose dive into the water. The truck slowly went under but the deep freeze didn't want to go down. It was slowly inching under.

I knew there would be a shit storm. I went back to the house, got cleaned up and called reinforcements. Then I went to the shop to act like it was a normal day.

About noon, Carl and Wade showed up at the shop. Two of Bopper's running buddies. They told me that Bopper thought I had something to do with his stolen deep freeze. I played dumb and asked them, "Why in the world would I want Bopper's deep freeze?" They asked me if I had a truck with Texas tags. I said, "No." Then I played it cool and invited them into the back room to do a little meth. After they left, a city cop showed up and asked if I had a truck with Texas plates and if I knew anything about a break-in at Bopper's house. I said I didn't, on both accounts.

This was a new development. Bopper had called the law on me. I was wondering what else he told them. As soon as the officer left I gathered up everything in the shop that could ever remotely be considered illegal and sent Jimmy out the back door with it to hide it in the field behind the shop.

I drove home and cleaned out my house too. Then I took a risk and called the man the pistol belonged to and asked him if I could come by his place for a little talk. The man was older, wealthy and very upset about his guns being stolen. He had already accused Bopper and Carl of stealing them. The man's house was on lake road. We were talking outside under a nice shade tree. I asked him if he knew about what was going on between me and Bopper. He said he knew. Then I told him about Alice and what brought me to his doorstep. He was getting madder by the second. I went to my car and retrieved his gun and brought it to him. It had been his father's gun and he was grateful to get it back. He asked about the other guns that were stolen from him, but I didn't know anything about them. I figured Bopper had them too. As the man and I were talking, Bopper's Bronco came racing around the curve in front of the man's house. Bopper saw my car and slammed on his brakes, screeching to a stop.

I pulled out my gun and looked at him. I expected him to start shooting. He looked at me, with his big black cowboy hat on and slowly shook his head up and down. Then he drove off. I knew my chance of making Bopper think someone else stole his deep freeze just went right out the window.

I saw Bopper connecting the dots with that look. He knew that the only reason I was there was to return the man's gun. I asked the man to keep it quiet about my returning his gun and assured him that if I came across any of the other nine guns that were stolen I would return them to him. I later recovered three more from people who bought them from Bopper.

I went back to the shop and told the guys to be vigilant. Then I went to the McDonald's that is by the turnpike tollgate on highway 75 on the way from Henryetta to McAlester. I met the rodeo clown and Elizabeth to deliver another quarter pound of meth. Then I headed to Okmulgee to meet Glenda at the same guy's house where I first met her. I delivered an ounce of meth and some pot. Glenda and I went to dinner, then to her girlfriend's house where we used the bedroom for an hour. By the time I got to Mr. Connor's the ten o'clock news was on. I parked behind the barn then went in the house to bring Mr. Connor up-to-date on the recent events. He was pleased.

Alice poked her head around the hall corner, then eased into the room to cuddle up next to her grandpa. She was so pretty. Even with the two little scars on her face. She was starting to get more comfortable around me. She still wasn't talking, but she tried to smile. She had sad, scared eyes. When grandpa Connor sent her to bed she left without a sound. My hatred for Bopper grew. It was a long time before Alice said anything or trusted me enough to give me a hug.

I showed Mr. Cannor the meth I had taken from Bopper's deep freeze.

It was in the same ounce bags I was purchasing from Oz head shop in Tulsa, Oklahoma. Bopper was getting my meth from someone. It had to be one of four people, I just had to narrow it down.

Mr. Connor told me that Louisiana was looking at putting a 100 pound deal together. A biker group called the Sons of Satan, from Indiana was putting the cash together and putting out feelers. If we could put the quantity together we could probably get the deal. It would be great to make all the craziness pay off. At that point we were spending money as fast as we could make it on chemicals.

Everything was quiet when I got back to Henryetta. It was late. I went by my house, ate two hot dogs, took a shower and went to the shop to get some sleep. I'd had a long week. I liked sleeping in the back room of the shop. It was totally dark - no windows – quiet and secure. If anyone tried to break in I would hear them long before they could get to me.

My mom was going to grandma's that weekend so I had her drop me off at Biscuit Hill truck stop in Wynnewood, Oklahoma. Loretta would pick me up and take me to my truck. We had to drive to Fort Worth, Texas to get my truck. We met Snake at his bar and grill. It was a nice cozy place with good food. A little loud for my taste. Then we followed Snake to his place to pick up my truck. His shop was a hodgepodge mixture of little addons. It was fully equipped. He had a nice little salvage yard going behind the shop. While I was there I made a deal on a 1970 Chevy truck. A black, short, wide bed with a 350 engine. I borrowed a trailer and his guys hooked up the tail lights while I loaded the truck. I was having fun. I followed Loretta back to Ardmore where we ate at Budroux's and got a motel room. We had sex for a little while to help knock the edge of missing each other.

Loretta wanted to go to a party at her friend's house. I usually didn't go to parties around people I didn't know. It was somewhat awkward with people knowing that I'm the big drug dealer packing a huge pistol. It's an invitation for trouble. Hell, I was starting to like trouble. I should have changed my last name to Gerous, so I would be Jeffrey Dan-Gerous. Trouble was my new middle name.

There were a lot of people at the party. I didn't really care about meeting anyone. That really didn't matter, most of them had already heard of me. Loretta was having fun showing me off and pointing out people, telling me who they were. It was a money crowd. She pointed to a young woman with breasts so large you can't believe they are real, and said, "That's Sandy. She's the local cocaine connection." I was impressed. When

Loretta went to the restroom, Sandy walked over to me and gave me a slip of paper with her number on it and said, "Call me. Soon." In a very seductive voice that made me hard.

"I will," I replied. Life was getting better by the day.

Loretta and I were going from room to room saying our hellos. We passed a guy coming out of a room saying something was absolutely crazy.

I had to see what it was. Loretta and I went into the room where all the commotion was. I walked around the room to see what it was. To my surprise, it was the guy Snake shot in the neck. He looked bad. His neck was swollen much larger than his head.

It was bright red and stretched so tight it looked like the skin was going to split. On closer inspection, I could see a straw poked through the bullet hole. The guys there had perforated the straw and were pouring peroxide through the straw to try and kill the infection. The guy was about to die and the people working on him were laughing. The man clearly had staph infection and a fever so high he was delirious. I told the guys to take him to the hospital right then. They said they were planning to take him to the hospital if he wasn't any better tomorrow.

I said, "He'll be dead by tomorrow." I didn't leave them any options.

I told one of the guys to drop him off at the emergency room. I walked with them while they helped him to a car. All the way to the car, which was a painful trip for him, the shot brother with the straw through his neck kept saying, "Thank you, man. Thank you." He lived, but it was a miracle.

Loretta and I went back to the motel and played ride'm cowboy until we fell asleep covered in baby oil.

The next morning was Saturday. I took a shower, kissed Loretta bye and left her to go back to sleep. I drove to a gas station, filled up my truck and called Sandy to see what was on her mind. She answered with the sexy deep voice of a woman who partied half the night then was awakened by the phone, way too early. I said, "Damn, you sound sexy."

She informed me that she had two tickets to the ZZ Top concert in Oklahoma City that night and asked if I would like to go with her. My mind thought, "Hell, yes."

But my mouth said, "I can manage that." We agreed on a place to meet.

I was excited. I drove back to Henryetta in time for lunch. It sure seemed like I was driving and eating a lot. I had called Jimmy on the way and asked him to find Dean and Terry and meet me at the shop. They were waiting on me when I got there. Glenda, Loretta, Deena and Denise (a girl I met in Tulsa at the drag races) had called. I told the guys I was going to be tied up until Sunday night or Monday morning and got them supplied for the duration. I went to my house and restocked my overnight bag and got an extra change of clothes. I had bought a 1976 Vette. A bicentennial edition, black with the silver spacy interior, 454, 4-speedy. The engine was blown when I bought it. I rebuilt it and fixed the air conditioner and put in a new stereo system. I kept it parked behind my mom's house. I drove up ninth street to mom's house, told her where I was going, switched cars, and hit the highway. I got to Oklahoma City early.

I was being presumptuous. I picked up a bottle of champagne and rented a room on the top floor of the historical Skirvin hotel, not too far from the Civic Center where the concert would be. I put the champagne on ice, placed a bottle of coconut oil on the table between two champagne glasses and laid a single red rose next to the coconut oil. I think my intentions were expressed fairly well. When I met Sandy, she looked amazing. Like one of those sexy girls you see in the fancy clubs on Miami Vice. I was impressed. I felt a little naked myself. I wasn't wearing my customary gun and bomber jacket. When we got to the Civic Center I had the prettiest, sexiest girl in the place on my arm. The memorabilia stand was selling red satin collector ZZ Top jackets. I bought us both one. The first person I saw was Glenda. She was there with another guy. We waved at each other and there was that unspoken, "Oh, hell," between us.

Jeff Healy opened up for ZZ Top. He was great, but he looked a little lonely down there on the big stage by himself.

When ZZ Top came out it was a whole different story. The set was huge. It was their recycler tour. There was an overhead crane, crushed cars with large TV's in them. Dusty and Rusty were picked up by a crane and dropped into the recycler. Then they came out on a conveyer belt and popped out of crushed cars with their fuzzy guitars. It was all too cool. Then, Sandy had backstage passes. We went back stage where everyone was laughing and drinking. A-Jax couldn't have wiped the smile off my face.

It was a new world for me. I wanted to change the words of Elenore Rigby to, "Ahhhh, look at all the lovely people." It was fun. Sandy jumped, clapped and squealed when three very pretty girls (all dressed the same), who were also jumping, clapping and squealing, came up and kissed and hugged her. Sandy introduced me. They were a local three girl lesbian band. They invited us to come hear them play at some club I had never heard of and off they went.

Sandy looked at me with those sexy eyes and said, "They love to play."

I had no doubt. I showed Sandy the room key and told her I had champagne on ice. As soon as we got in my car, Sandy undid my pants, pulled out little Elvis and went to work with her mouth. I don't even remember the short drive to the Skirvin hotel. When we got to the room I popped the cork on the Champagne, toasted to "Us," took a sip and then didn't drink any of it. We were preoccupied. Hell, I don't like champagne anyway. She was a seductress who loved to lick and be licked. She liked it rough. I learned I did too. The next morning my jaw muscles and little Elvis were tender. I had to help Sandy brush the knots out of her hair. We looked a mess and I loved it. We did it in the shower. Got out of the shower and did it again, then took another shower. A wonderful night and morning. It was like that all day.

We decided to go to the horse races at Blue Ribbon Downs in Sallisaw, Oklahoma.

It was a straight shot East of Oklahoma City on I-40, an hour on the other side of Henryetta, almost to the Arkansas line. We did some cocaine and meth and on the drive to Sallisaw, she put her mouth to work on me and played with herself. I got so worked up I had to stop at a rest area and do her real hard from behind with the passenger door open and her leaning inside the car holding on to the gear shifter as cars roared by on the highway. We got to Sallisaw and had lunch, then we did it again in the restaurant restroom.

I lost some at the track and Sandy won some. Story of my life. We did it again in the race track parking lot, like we did it at the rest area. We then drove to my shop in Henryetta and did it again. By the time I drove her back to Oklahoma City to pick-up her car I was give out. But we did it again in the parking lot before she left. When she drove away I thought, "This girl will be the death of me." What a way to go.

CHAPTER SIX:

Busted

When I got back to the shop I was give out. I fell into bed and didn't move until Jimmy woke me up the next morning. That day I assembled an engine for a hot rod Jeep I was overhauling. A lot of engine work is waiting on parts and machine work. There is the tear down and cleaning stage. The wait on parts and machine work stage. Then the assembly stage. I was also rebuilding the engine for an old black convertible Dodge Dart. It was a restored collectors' item I was working on for an out-of-town friend. I had Dean and Jimmy doing odds and ends and taking my 1970 Chevy truck apart cleaning and painting each piece as they went. In the evenings we were doing pot and meth deliveries. At night I would go to Mr. Connor's and start a P2p cook. It had to boil for twenty-four hours. I had four twelve-thousand milliliter triple-neck boiling flask to work with. Each with two reflux condensers. That way I could keep two running at all times. The heating elements were on timers. I timed everything so I would arrive thirty minutes before the first two turned off. I would pour the chemicals in the other two, add boiling stones, and start them by the time the first two cut off. My condenser cooling system was working great. I made it from an old refrigerator. It was keeping the cooling water at thirty-eight degrees. I built racks on the walls to hold the condensers when not in use and kept the water continually running through eight condensers. It was a regular production line.

I would separate the P2p with lye water, which is a hot, violent chemical reaction. The lye water bonds with the acetic anhydride and as it cools the P2p floats to the top. Using a large separation funnel I would drain off the sludge and save it in a plastic drum so I could distill it later and recover about sixty percent of the acetic anhydride.

Then I would pour the raw heavy dark red P2p in another plastic drum to store until I could distill it later. It was easier to work with large quantities of raw P2p when distilling and resulted in better quality and higher yield. I was reducing the volume of our large stock pile of chemicals by turning it into P2p as fast as I could. The nights I couldn't make it Mr. Connor would take over for me.

That week I finished the Jeep and the Dodge Dart. The hopped up Jeep was too much for my friend. He rolled it a few days later trying to show off.

He said, "It got away from me."

Jimmy and Dean were making progress on my 1970 Chevy truck.

I had parts ordered from all over. My only problem was that I was running out of meth. Some of the P2p I was making was about to get processed into speed. All I needed was anhydrous ether.

I'd already bought twenty lecture bottles of hydrogen chloride gas (which is used in the manufacture of plastics), but I was experiencing some difficulty obtaining large quantities of ether. Ether is hard to store, hard to use and highly flammable. You can smell it for miles and it is one of those chemicals you can't walk in a buy without question. I was buying most of my chemicals from far away so I didn't draw any local heat from law enforcement.

or attention to us. I knew a guy that worked at an oil field chemical supply. He wanted double the price and a quarter ounce of meth for the ether. When he went to Tulsa on his regular chemical run for the company he picked up six five gallon cans of anhydrous ether for me. That was a start.

I couldn't drop the ether off at my storage place because it smelled bad even in the sealed cans. I took it to my friend Russell's in Preston, Oklahoma and stored it behind his house way back in the trees. I gave him a little bag of meth and told him I would be back in a few days to pick up the stuff.

When I got back to the shop, Jimmy informed me that Bopper had been arrested over two stolen Honda four-wheelers. Then Bopper's friend Richard had also been arrested in a motel in Okmulgee with two ounces of cocaine, some meth and a gun. And Bopper's friend Harold had been arrested in Beggs on a meth deal. All three were out on bond. I was seeing a pattern. On top of that, my friend Terry was unaccounted for, ever since Bopper and his boys got out of jail. Terry's Plymouth Roadrunner was parked at his dad's house, but no one had seen Terry.

I told Jimmy and Dean not to carry or sell anything. Then I sent them on a mission to look for Terry. Jimmy was pulled over and searched before he got to the other end of town. Dean was pulled over and searched an hour later when he left his mother's house. Shortly thereafter, two guys that I didn't know, who were surely cops, came to my shop and asked to buy some meth. I told them I didn't sell drugs and strongly recommended that they did not come back. Then I cleaned my shop out, again.

The next morning a guy I knew, Mark, showed up in his van and asked me if I wanted to buy a riding lawn mower and a remote control airplane.

"Sure," I said. I bought them and helped him unload them. A short time later a police car turned into my driveway with an old school buddy of mine, Shane, riding shotgun.

The officer said, "We know you bought a riding lawn mower and a remote control airplane from Mark today."

I said, "Yes, sir." The mower was sitting right in front of his police car.

Shane said, "They are mine. They were stolen from my house last night."

I apologized and told Shane that I had no idea they were stolen and offered him the use of my truck and helped him load the mower. I was just as upset as Shane. I felt bad. I didn't want anything that was stolen. I told Shane that I would take the loss and apologized again. Shane left to take his mower and airplane home.

Then the officer informed me that he had to search my shop, on the pretext of looking for additional stolen property. I said, "No," and started closing and locking the doors. I was locking the last door but the officer would not leave my shop. By this time, my parking area was full of City and County cop cars and a few Highway Patrol cars, all with their lights flashing.

They decided to search the place anyway and came in in force. I could only stand there and watch.

I didn't think anything was in my shop. In the end, they found a pound of pot and less than two grams of meth that I really didn't know was in there. I was arrested and made bond before I could be put in a cell. My friend Shane felt terrible. I told Shane not to worry. It certainly wasn't his fault. It was my fault for having anything to do with the type of sorry people that were hanging around me. The police tried to question me but I wouldn't answer any questions.

I hired an attorney out of Tulsa who got the charges dismissed on search warrant grounds. The cops had the building secured and could have taken an hour to get a warrant but they chose to go in and search without one.   Case dismissed.

At that point, I knew I couldn't keep my shop open, as bad as I wanted to.

I was depressed, hurt and mad. Bopper and his buddies had urinated on my dreams. I didn't know if it was Mark (who sold me the lawn mower and airplane) or Bopper that set me up, but I was sure it was one of the two. Bopper was the first one arrested.

I made bond and went to a pay phone to call Mr. Connor with the news. We had to put everything on hold for a few days while I cleaned out my shop. I assured him I would be back on the job in a couple of days.

I had so much shop equipment, parts and supplies that it filled up my little work space at my house. The back yard was full of cars. When we were getting our last load from the shop Terry came stumbling down the driveway, beat-up and ill. Two of Bopper's friends, Carl and Wade, had picked Terry up at his dad's house and took him to a house in the country where they were doing drugs, drinking and having a party. Terry thought he was doing a shot of meth, but they tricked him. It was a mixture of demerol and meth. It incapacitated Terry to the point where he was awake but couldn't move. The same thing Bopper had done to Alice. Then they roughed him up some and asked him questions about me and where I was getting the meth. He really didn't know. Thank God. To scare Terry, Bopper staged a fake shooting. Bopper shot Carl with blanks, with Terry tied to a chair watching. Then Bopper and his friends rolled Carl up in a rug and hauled him out the door. Terry was freaked out. He thought he witnessed a killing. Bopper kept Terry there for two days threatening to kill him if he didn't tell where I hid my dope and money. Then Bopper dropped Terry off close to the shop and Terry walked the rest of the way to tell me what happened. It affected my friend Terry so bad that, when I took him home, he got in his car and drove to another State to live with his mother.

To say I was mad was a grave understatement. I called Mr. Connor and told him the news. He said, "Don't go kill him. Come talk to me." I went to meet Mr. Connor and he told me that "Bopper and his friends were broke and on their way to jail." That was a little comfort. At the time we figured that the most I would get was probation. We didn't know the charges would later be dismissed. Our plan was to keep undermining Bopper and to get busy putting the 100 pound deal together with the Sons of Satan.

That was a million dollar split. We had enough of the primary chemicals to make a lot more than that, but after we made the 100 pound deal we were going to scale things back some and coast.

After what happened to Terry, I had to talk my friend Tink out of killing Bopper. Bopper had also slapped around Tink's nephew over twenty dollars and had taken Tink's nephew's new washer and dryer to settle the debt. We were all mad about that too.

I told Tink about Bopper's deep freeze and got him laughing.

Bopper was a very lucky man that night and he didn't even know it. Tink was a hell of a great guy and most of the time pretty easy going.

He was the kind of man that would do anything for you. It was wise not to make the mistake of getting Tink mad. He got very serious, real quick. Reluctantly, Tink saw it my way. We sat in my living room, had a few beers and talked about old times. It seems that the old times were always the best times.

I assured Tink that I had it taken care of. Tink was also upset because Bopper had caused me to lose my shop. But in the end Tink gave me one of his big Tink bear hugs and went home.

The next day I was sitting on my motorcycle at the In-And-Out having a deluxe cheeseburger. Mark pulls up in his van and parks next to me so he can talk to me out his driver side window. I told him what the police said and that I had assured them that he must not have known the mower and airplane were stolen. He hadn't been arrested so I was thinking the whole thing was a setup. But I liked Mark and didn't want to believe he would do something like that. My good friend Mr. Roundsville was standing on my left talking to me. We were expressing our opinions that Bopper was the likely person behind the bust, when Bopper drives past in his Bronco with the top off. Bopper hit his brakes and turned the corner a half a block away. He was circling around to come in from the back.

I said, "That's my cue to leave. See you guys later."

Roundsville said, "No, you stay right there. I'll handle this."

It is always best to try and avoid trouble when you can, but you can never allow people to think you are running from it. I decided to sit there and see what happened. Mark was looking nervous. Bopper drove around the drive-in and pulled up in front of us sideways, blocking our forward egress. Bopper got out of his Bronco and walked up next to me and shakes Mark's hand like some cheesy politician. Then he walked around the front of my motorcycle and shook Roundsville's hand. When Bopper let go of Roundsville's hand he tried to backhand me in the face. I saw it coming and pulled back so he would miss. Roundsville hit Bopper in the face about five times before you could say Jack Sprat. It was fast. Bopper went down, hard.

What most people didn't know was that Roundsville was a championship boxer for five years in a row when he was in the Army.

Roundsville said, "You son-of-a-bitch. Don't you ever use my handshake to try and sucker punch one of my friends."

I was trying not to laugh. Bopper's friend Carl jumped up and was coming out of the Bronco. I opened my jacket and showed him I was reaching for my gun, as I shook my head "No." Carl sat back down with a mean look on his face. It was kind of funny watching Bopper scramble up and get in his truck with a bloody nose and busted lip. Then Bopper stood up in his Bronco (he had taken the removable top off) with a gun in one hand and a knife in the other, holding them up high for all to see and yelled, "You bunch of goddamned cowards. Follow me outside of town and we'll settle this once and for all." Then he flopped his big ass down in the seat, backed out and took off with his tires spinning. He was mad.

Naturally, the other customers and the people working in the drive-in saw him waving the gun and the knife, yelling. He was right in front of the order window. They called the police. My friend Roundsville wanted to go after him and finish things.

I said, "No."

A lot of good that did. He climbed in Mark's van and they headed after Bopper. I was right on their tail hoping I could divert a gun battle.

Bopper went to the strip pit, the same one where his freezer was floating in the pretty blue water. Mark pulled in behind Bopper and Roundsville jumped out of the van and him and Bopper started going at it with fists. Roundsville was putting it on Bopper. Bopper went down twice and couldn't even hit Roundsville. Then Carl threw Bopper a knife. Bopper bent down to pick it up and Roundsville hit him in the face and knocked Bopper down, again. Bopper grabbed the knife and came back up, dazed and furious. I pulled my pistol and fired a shot between Bopper and Carl. I had my eye on Carl, he had the gun. I yelled, "Carl, put the gun in the truck or I'll shoot you deader than shit. Bopper, get your ass in your truck and get the hell out of here. Now."

I don't know where I came up with such creative language, "Deader than shit."

It didn't matter, they knew I meant it. Carl laid the gun on the seat and Bopper stomped over to his Bronco and they spun his tires all the way out of there.

I said, "Roundsville, you're amazing. And a little crazy. Thanks for sticking up for me. Come on. I'm buying you guys something to eat."

Then I pointed to the deep freeze floating in the water and said, "Hey, doesn't that look like Bopper's freezer?"

We had a good laugh and headed for the truck stop to eat.

I already had a cheeseburger, but I was ready to eat another one.

On the way back to town we passed Bopper. The police had him pulled over with him and Carl handcuffed, laying on the ground. As I passed I saw the gun, knife and bags of drugs laying on the hood of the police car.

Bopper and Carl were arrested for the incident at the drive-in, which resulted in additional firearm and drug charges. Bopper was still on bond from his other arrest. He made bond again and was back out the next day.

A short time later I heard that Bopper had a preliminary hearing scheduled. I got dressed up nice and went to the courthouse to watch.

We were in the Courtroom and Bopper's attorney was telling the judge that his client would be there any second. At that point, Bopper flung the Court room door open and strutted in like a Tom Turkey on crack.

The judge asked the attorney, "Is this your client?" The attorney sadly replied, "Yes, You Honor."

"How dare you come into my Court room dressed like that," the judge yelled. Bopper was wearing his big black cowboy hat and overalls, with a sweaty red bandanna tied around his neck and no shirt. We were all stunned that Bopper was that stupid. I was just there as an observer and I had on a suit. The Courtroom deputy walked over to Bopper and pulled a syringe out of big Bopper's bib overall pocket that clearly contained some type of drug. Bopper's mouth fell open and the deputy handcuffed him and took him away. Old Bopper wasn't looking too good on the home stretch.

When I got back to my house my mom was there. I was a grown man and my mom was still cleaning up after me. I kept up with most of the cleaning myself, but mom liked to come by and make sure I was keeping on top of things. Mom told me that Sandy called. She thought Sandy sounded like a wonderful girl and I agreed. I liked the fact that my mother was always trying to find me the perfect woman. I needed help from someone, because I sure wasn't doing a very good job myself.

I called Sandy. She wanted me to meet her at a club in Oklahoma City where her three lesbian friends were opening for a bigger band. She suggested that we show up early and leave by midnight and go to the three girls' apartment for a party. That sounded great. I just happened to have plenty of party material. I could handle a little R & R.

I got to the club early so I could watch Sandy walk through the front door. I was getting a little annoyed because this gay guy kept trying to flirt with me. He knew it was embarrassing me and he thought it was rather funny. I was thankful when Sandy walked in and made me forget everything and focus on her. Yes, she had it like that. Every man and woman in the room stopped and looked at her, even the gay guy. I stood up so she could see me. When she spotted me, she smiled and headed across the room toward me, swinging her cute ass like there was no tomorrow. She reached up for two hands full of my jacket and pulled herself into me and kissed me hard. I heard a collective sigh throughout the club. Everyone in the club was wishing they were me.

Sandy said, "God, I missed you", in her sexy deep voice. I replied, "I like it when you call me God."

She laughed and the party was on. She kept brushing her hand across little Elvis as we danced. I was hard all evening.

We left the club at midnight as Sandy had promised. The three girls lived in a nice upstairs, spacy two bedroom apartment on the Southeast side of Oklahoma City. The party started small and grew to about twenty people. The girls placed a large mirror on the kitchen table and I plopped down two very large spoons full of meth in the middle of it. Sandy dished out two matching spoons full of cocaine. One of the girls started mixing it all together and making little lines for everyone.

Sandy and I kept easing into the back room for quickies. Sandy and one of the girls started kissing each other with deep sexy French kisses. Then they would snuggle up to me and tell me what they were going to do to me later. I was certainly looking forward to getting them alone.

The night was moving along well. A guy from out of town showed up with a cheap white styrofoam ice chest. In the ice chest, he had two pounds of freeze dried hallucinogenic mushrooms, some high quality cocaine, and some top of the line connoisseur marijuana. I bought a little of everything. Sandy and the three girls· and I each ate a good size mushroom. Being freeze dried, they were shriveled, crunchy and tasted like peanut hulls. In about thirty minutes I was starting to trip a little.

Colors were getting brighter. I could hear each note and word of the music and each kiss was electrifying. I was buying more of the mushrooms so anyone who hadn't tried one could join in the fun. And it was fun.

Everyone was smiling and having a great time.

Until we heard a scream from the living room. It was one of the three girls that lived in the apartment. She was shouting, "Help, help!" It all happened in slow motion. I ran from the back bedroom, down the hall to the front door where the girl was yelling. She was in the process of pointing at the far end of the small living room where the guy who brought the mushrooms had both hands wrapped around a girl's neck, choking and shaking her like a madman. I didn't even pause. I ran across the room and hit him from the side with a full body blow that sent him flying into the wall. Only there wasn't a wall there.

He went between two pretty potted plants and was enveloped by the blue curtains as he crashed through a picture window and cascaded to the ground below. I remember a cool breeze blowing in my face as I looked out the window at the guy laying on the ground, two stories down. I looked just for a second and I was sure he was dead.

I turned around and the girl that was being choked grabbed me and hugged me, as I yelled, "Time to go. Everybody out and don't come back."

Sandy was looking out the window at the guy on the ground and people were leaving, fast. I snatched up a dish towel and wiped all the meth and cocaine into the floor and rubbed it in with my boot, as I calmly told the people to go and not come back. Then I poured beer on the table and mirror and wiped it off again. Everyone was out but Sandy, the girl who was choked and me. I told them to head for my car. As I turned the light out I noticed the white ice chest. I picked up the ice chest and closed the door behind me. The three of us went down the stairs, past the guy on the ground and walked to my car. I smashed the ice chest into the little storage compartment behind the seat of the Vette. The girl sat in Sandy's lap and we drove away. The girl was crying, Sandy was consoling her, telling her it would be alright. I was thinking, "Bullshit!" And wondering what I might have left my prints on and hoping that nobody knew my name.

The bars were closing and cops were all over. It seemed like red lights were flashing in every direction I looked. I just kept driving. We took the girl to a friend's house and dropped her off, as she requested.

Sandy said, "Oh, God. What are we going to do?"

I said, "There you go, calling me God again. You know how that makes me hot." I was trying to lighten a situation that couldn't be lightened.

She repeated, "What are we going to do?"

I said, "It won't be 'we' Sandy. It will be me. I'm the one who killed the guy, even though I didn't mean to. We'll figure everything out tomorrow when we have clear heads. Right now, we're going to a motel."

We had no way of knowing that the guy wasn't dead. In fact, he wasn't even cut and didn't have a broken bone. He was knocked out for a bit.

We were told the next day that when the police cars and ambulance came blazing into the parking lot of the apartment complex, with sirens blaring, the guy woke up and took off running.

That night, on meth, cocaine and mushrooms, there wasn't any sleeping. All the excitement and danger made the sex more intense. We did manage to sleep, or at least close our eyes for about two hours, then got cleaned up and left by the noon checkout deadline. I took Sandy back to the club to get her car. She was sad and nervous when she left.

She asked me, "How can you stay so calm?'

I said, "What's done is done. I can't take it back, so I just have to deal with it." It wasn't like me to ever freak out over something, but killing a man was a pretty big something and it was weighing on me heavy.

I didn't go back to Henryetta that day. I drove a different route and went to Tulsa. I sold my Corvette to a friend of mine who had been trying to buy it from me. When I was unloading my things from the Vette, I pulled out the ice chest. It was loaded with mushrooms, cocaine, pot and money. It certainly wasn't worth the man's life, but of course, I kept it.

I called my mother and asked how things were going. She told me that Sandy called and told her that "everything was alright, the guy wasn't dead." Mom wanted to know what the "hell" was going on. I told her not to worry and that it was too much to go into on the phone. Mom called Sandy back and Sandy made me out to be a hero.

That was one of those turning points in my life where I had a revelation and was seeing things from a different perspective. I went from a person who thought he killed a man, to a person who had almost killed a man.

Having not killed him was a tremendous relief, but not much of a consolation. I was still depressed and ready to get out of the crazy lifestyle I was living. Now I knew what it felt like to kill someone, or think I did and I didn't like it.

I had my friend from Tulsa drop me off at Okmulgee Votech, where I kept one of my cars parked. I then called Glenda and she was happy to hear from me. Seeing me at the ZZ Top concert with another woman had the opposite effect than I thought it would. Glenda was impressed and excited at seeing me with the classy, sexy, mystery woman. She asked me who the pretty girl was and I said, "I can't tell you."

Glenda said, "She looked rich and famous."

I changed the subject. I thought it best to avoid the topic. I told her that I would like to spend more time with her and she agreed. We decided to meet the next day for lunch. Then I went to Mr. Connor's house and worked in the lab for a while. I slept that night in the barn in a little area I had fixed up with a hammock. The next morning, I told Mr. Connor what happened. He was feeling bad about me losing my shop. We were planning a little business adventure. He and I agreed that it was best for me to stay out of Oklahoma City for a while.

At noon, I picked Glenda up for lunch. We drove to Tulsa, went to a nice restaurant, then took an "actual" walk in a park. It was the closest thing I'd had to a normal day in a long time. Glenda wasn't a druggy, as I often referred to some girls that liked to indulge in chemically induced euphoria. She was a down to earth good girl and I blew it. She deserved better than me anyway. I wish I would have had enough sense to clean up my act and give her the kind of attention she deserved.

When I dropped her off at home we kissed and discussed going out again, soon. But we never did, to my regret.

I wasn't in a hurry to go back home. My meth supply was fairly depleted and I had used the majority of the profits to purchase a vast amount of chemicals. I called Jimmy, then met him on a back road between Henryetta and Okmulgee at Cry Baby Bridge. Terry had moved away and Dean had all he could take, he dropped out of the picture and went to work in the oil field. Jimmy and I had taken on a heavy load. We were delivering meth and pot as fast as we could make the rounds and we were both making a lot of money. I fixed up a small hiding spot next to Cry Baby Bridge out in the woods so I could leave things for Jimmy without the need to go into town. When I met Jimmy, I gave him a pound of the freeze dried mushrooms, two ounces of the high quality cocaine and a quarter pound of meth to sell. Then I gave him two ounces of the really good pot to keep for himself. That would hold him over for a few days and he was happy.

I went back to Mr. Connor's and got busy distilling the raw P2p.

When I was done I had twenty-six gallons of finished P2p. I also distilled the waste from the cooks, which was a smelly process and recovered a significant amount of the acetic anhydride.

I mixed it half and half with unused acetic anhydride and put it on the shelves for future use. Even though I was very meticulous about not making a mess it still took me a considerable amount of time to clean things up, dispose of the trash and get ready for a large speed cook.

When I recovered the P2p in Ringling on the emergency mission for Snake, Mr. Connor and I used the old recipe called "Hitler's Revenge," using methlyamine to make methamphetamine. It was a messy procedure that had to be carefully watched and attended to throughout the cook. It was not practical on a large scale basis and methlylamine was getting hard to come by.

We decided to make amphetamine with a 60 over 40 under ratio mixture of formamide and formic acid. It was a clean, easy cook that resulted in a high quality product.

Turning the speedy oil to powder is very dangerous. Ether is highly volatile.

A person runs the risk of an explosion and fiery death or asphyxiation.

The only incoming air came in through the entrance of the lab. The vent pipe ran out the roof of the barn. To help slow the evaporation rate of the ether, I needed everything cold. I placed two five-gallon cans of ether in a chest type freezer. Then I built an enclosure around the lab entrance, using two-by-fours and heavy black plastic. Then I rigged an air conditioner to cool the enclosed area and stacked bales of hay, four high, around the enclosure for insulation. When I was done, I had a little plastic room built over the lab entrance inside the barn. I wanted to cool the air before it was sucked into the lab which would also help with the humidity. The vent for the industrial vacuum pump was tied directly into the outgoing vent pipe which would help reduce the ether fumes in the lab, as well.

By midnight it had cooled off outside enough for me to get started.

The lab was cold from the air coming in from my little air-conditioned enclosure and the ether was ice cold after being in the freezer all day. The work area I was using to powder was under the ventilation system so it would pull the fumes right off the top of the five-thousand milliliter open mouth flask I placed on top of a magnetic stirring table.

In order to manage things easily and not make a mess or waste anything I was only powdering about two pounds at a time. The vacuum pump and vacuum flask worked great. I powdered half the oil into white powder with a perfect pH of seven. Then I powdered the other half of the oil with a lower PH, turning it slightly pink.

I wanted people to think it was coming from two different places. When I was done, I had eight-pounds of crystal white powder and eight-pounds of pretty pink powder and I was so cold my teeth were chattering and my hands were blue. By morning I had everything cleaned, sealed and put away. I let the lab air out while I tore down my makeshift enclosure. When I was finished nobody could tell I'd been there. After handling that much meth it took me two days to wind down enough to sleep.

CHAPTER SEVEN:

Drama

After I finally got rested from my manufacturing adventure I was pleased with myself. My noble cause, that started as a way to put Bopper out of business for what he did to Alice, was expanding across the State.

The pink meth was a hit. As I planned, people were assuming that the white and pink meth was coming from two different places.

Someone started a rumor that the pink meth was "fed dope," put out by the federal government. That was an interesting development. I helped fuel the rumor by never denying it. Before long, the meth-heads thought I was getting the pink meth from a top secret connection in the federal government. It was an odd turn of events, but I didn't see the harm in letting the tweaked out druggies believe whatever they wanted.

Bopper was still managing to buy some of my meth, but his customer base had to be small. During the day I was watching Bopper and driving around making a few deliveries and trying to figure out who Bopper was getting meth from. At night I was diligently working to process as much of the chemicals as I could into P2p.

It was a lot bigger project than I'd anticipated. I hadn't made a good dent in my large quantity of stockpiled chemicals.

In the long run, it was Jimmy who accidently figured out how Bopper was getting my meth. It was through Floyd, who was selling cocaine for Bopper's friend Richard. Floyd was also the person who had lied to Deena, turning her against me. Bopper was having Floyd buy ounces of meth from one of the guys that was buying them from me. There were several ways I could have handled the situation. I could have confronted the guy, telling him I knew what was going on, or I could play with him. I chose the latter. It meant that I would end up with Bopper's money.

Jimmy told me that Floyd was at the guy's house. Therefore, when the guy called me and said, "come see me," I was reasonably certain he was buying an ounce for Bopper, by proxy. I still had the ounce of meth I recovered from big Bopper's freezer. Bopper had cut it for resale. It was only right that Bopper get his cut ounce back. I put Bopper's cut ounce in my left pocket and a pure ounce in my right pocket. Then I went to see the guy.

When I arrived, I said, "I just sold you an ounce yesterday."

He promptly informed me that he was buying another one for a friend from out of town. That was my cue to give him the bag of Bopper's cut dope from my left pocket. In my opinion that is why God gave us two hands and two pockets. For those necessary sleight of hand tricks.

Two hours later, as I expected, the guy came by my house and said, "That ounce you sold me was heavily cut."

I said, "Have I ever sold you cut dope before?" "No," he replied.

"Then whoever you got it for is trying to play you for a sucker," I said.

He paused and I saw his expression change as the other possibility dawned on him.

He said, "That damn Bopper."

I acted stunned and said, "I warned you about doing business with Bopper. You know he is a no good sorry individual. He's probably laughing at you right now."

Oh, what a tangled web we weave. Bopper and I were the only two that knew what actually happened. I had no doubt that Bopper was pissed. Lord knows that Bopper's anger wasn't justified, because it was the same dope that Bopper had cut to sell to his friends. I didn't feel bad about putting the guy on the spot. He was told not to deal with Bopper.

As it often goes in the dope business, new and unexpected drama pops up that I couldn't have foreseen. My friend Lee had been buying a little meth and pot from me. He and his wife Teresa were splitting up and Lee was moving away to accommodate his job on the railroad. Teresa became fixated on me. I didn't see it at first. Teresa was living with her mother a few blocks from my house. She and I had been seeing each other, doing drugs and engaging in wild, hot and wet sex. The kind of thing two young healthy, horny people enjoy. We were doing fine. Until she started carrying a gun and wanting me to front her meth so she could go into the retail drug business. That flipped me out a little. It was completely against my unwritten policy and moral code. My policy and code include things like, always being kind to women, children and animals. Never killing people, and not selling drugs to women. Women are mothers who are supposed to take care of our children, not sell drugs. Okay, that may sound chauvinistic, but it is a code I have always lived by. Doing a little meth, or smoking a little pot with a wild woman and having sex was one thing.

I wasn't crossing the line and having a woman sell drugs for me and her possibly end up in prison. I didn't want that on my conscience.

Teresa was spending a lot of time with my mother. Mom liked her, until Teresa started carrying a pistol and talking like a character from a 1940's gangster movie about prohibition. Mom and I informed Teresa that it was not wise to pursue the kind of lifestyle she was seeking. It didn't help.

One night I came into town from the back way, avoiding the popular well traveled roads. I pulled quietly into my driveway and killed the engine in my truck.

Then I sat there for ten minutes, looking around, waiting to see if anything was happening. It was 3:00a.m. and all was well. I got out of my truck, closed the door softly, then rolled under my truck to cut loose a pound of meth I brought back with me. When I rolled out from under my truck Teresa was standing there with her gun in her belt.

Smiling like everything was fine, Teresa said, "I thought you might need a lookout."

I just about crapped my pants. I thought, maybe I do need a lookout if this girl can sneak up on me that easy. I would have been in serious trouble if it would have been Bopper or one of his cohorts.

I invited Teresa in for a heart-to-heart talk. When I was finished she had missed the point completely. She said, "I knew you liked me. You're just too busy. You need some help."

That night, what was left of it, we canoodled a while, had breakfast, canoodled some more, had lunch and canoodled some more. Then I took her home and didn't come back to my house for a month. By then she had moved on to a new boyfriend named Donny. That was another lesson well learned. I later discovered that she was selling dope for Donny, who was a friend of Bopper's.

One day I showed up unannounced at my friend Russell's house in Preston, Oklahoma. I had already moved the ether I stashed there.

Russell was selling some meth and even though he was a great guy he just wasn't real bright. His Old Dodge truck was parked in his driveway so I got out of my truck and knocked on his front door. It was so quiet all I could hear was the little bees buzzing around in the grass. When I knocked on the door it was so loud it felt like I was disturbing the peace. I looked over at the dog that was asleep on the porch. Fine watchdog it was, it hadn't even moved its head. I nudged the dog in the rear with my boot.

It jumped up with a "yip," spun around and bared its teeth with a low growl. I think it was offended.

I announced to the dog, "See there, all you needed was a little motivation." The dog must have been embarrassed by its lack of protection efforts; it trotted off the old rickety porch and headed around the house.

I thought that the dog might know something I didn't so I followed.

There was a small shed behind the house. As I came around the house a person in a white environmental suit, that was belted at the waist with a gun belt, was backing out of the shed. I knew it had to be Russell.

"There you are," I said.

Russell jumped and started turning around in the bulky suit as he drew his six-shooter and shot a hole in the ground. As the blast from the .44 echoed I could hear Russell's muffled yells of, "shit, shit, shit."

I held my hands out in that universally known "Easy does it," position. At the same time, I was slowly attempting to keep out of his line of fire.

"Russell, is that you in there?" I said.

He replied, "You scared the shit out of me."

It was a little hard to hear him through the face mask of the hood.

I knew by his gestures that he was freaked out and had been awake for a few days. Lack of sleep, drugs and guns are not a good combination. He was wearing a hazardous waste containment suit that required an air supply. I could see the air hose connection and noted that it was not attached to an air source.

I said, "Where's your air line?"

Russell said, "I don't have one. Man, it's hot in this thing." He didn't know that he was slowly suffocating.

"You might need some air." I stated. "Let's get you out of that thing."

As I helped him take off the hood and suit, normal color started coming back to his face. I asked him what he was doing. He'd heard about a new way of making meth, so he gathered up the required chemicals and was trying it out. That was about the time I heard a low rumbling and dark red smoke started pouring out of every crack of the shed. The smell was horrendous. There was a muffled whoosh and fire started coming out of all the cracks, as well. I grabbed his water hose, but it was like trying to piss on a bonfire. I couldn't get close to the shed for the heat and there wasn't enough water to do any good. I helped Russell hide the environmental suit, dope, guns and other illegal things he didn't want found out in the trees. Just in case the neighbors saw the smoke and called the fire department.

He got lucky. The shed burned extremely hot, real fast, right to the ground and nobody noticed. By then I had forgotten the reason I stopped by to see him. I helped him think up a good lie to tell his wife and left.

I didn't know it at the time, but Carl and Wade had seen me parked at Russell's on several occasions. Of course, they told Bopper and he was planning on running in on Russell and robbing him. Bopper thought that I was getting my meth from the guy at that house, Russell. Russell knew about the problems I was having with Bopper and he was already on high alert.

That night I was at Mom's having dinner when the phone rang.
Mom said, "There is a Snake on the phone for you." She got a good laugh out of that.

Snake was also feeling bad about me closing my shop. He was mad at Bopper for causing the problem. But at that moment, Snake had another emergency. It was in Ardmore and had to be taken care of fast. He figured I had twenty-four hours to do the job before someone had reason to go in the house. Snake was pretty sure it wasn't a spill. It was just a bunch of chemicals that needed to be moved. The man that lived there had freaked out and left, leaving everything in the house. Snake assured me that the man wasn't coming back. In fact, the man was hiding in Texas. That sounded to me like the law was after him, but I didn't ask.

I drove straight to Ardmore and met a friend of Snake's at Denny's.

I was becoming a regular. The guy showed me the house and told me not to be seen and not to leave any prints. The house was on a corner in the country. There was a home across the road on the corner in front of the house I came to plunder.

I parked my truck in the trees at the back of a field, about two-hundred yards Southeast of the house. I walked in from behind the house carrying five flattened boxes and a small backpack that contained duct tape, trash bags, rope and a few other necessities. It was a nice brick home. I slipped the lock and went in the back door. It was still daylight. My plan was to get everything ready to move by dark. That way nobody would see lights on in the house, or see me move the stuff across the backyard.

The first thing I noticed when I went in was that somebody had cut a large square section of carpet out of the living room floor. My thoughts were that some dumbass must have spilled chemicals on the carpet.

I started looking in the garage, the washroom, kitchen, bathroom and then the bedrooms. The house was clean except for the back southeast corner bedroom. The bed and other bedroom furniture had been removed.

The walls and floor had been covered in plastic. Two twelve

thousand milliliter triple-neck boiling flasks were set-up, with condensers and were full of what looked to be chemicals for a P2p cook. It was partially done, but someone had turned off the heat and left. There was a large amount of boxes stacked against two walls that were full of all kinds of chemicals and lab supplies. I used duct tape to plug the holes of the triple-neck flasks then wrapped them in several towels and packed them in their original boxes. I packed all the small items in the sturdy boxes I brought.

Then bagged-up all the trash. I took all the boxes into the kitchen and stacked them in a nice line by the back door. I then tore down all the plastic lining the bedroom walls and rolled it up with the plastic covering the floor. The room looked nice.

I wasn't about to carry thirty two boxes, four trash bags, a large roll of plastic and my backpack a quarter mile to my truck. Something was telling me that I needed to get out, and fast. I found a two-wheel furniture dolly in the garage. It was dusk, so I started moving three boxes at a time across the back yard into the trees where I placed them next to the fence, out of sight from the house. It was at least a seventy five yard trip. By my last load I was soaked in sweat. I locked the back door and was glad to be going.

Walking back to my truck, I took notice of my surroundings and plotted my return route. In the dark it would be a little tricky without lights. I could only get to within thirty yards of where I had everything stacked.

By the time I got my truck in place it was fully dark. Rather than lift everything over the old rusty barb wire fence, I just cut it so I could walk through. The dolly had worked well bringing everything across the open yard, but in the trees the ground was too rough to use the dolly.

I had to make thirty five trips to my truck carrying heavy boxes in the dark. I used bailing wire to tie the fence back together. Even with two boxes inside the cab of my truck the other boxes were stacked so high in the truck bed I had to tie them on with rope. It was a big load, almost as tall as my truck cab.

As I was easing across the field I started hearing police sirens. By the time I made it across the field and was ready to turn into the road going away from the house I could see flashing lights coming from the direction I needed to go. I backed up, using my emergency brake so no one could see my lights. Then two police cars sped by and stopped in front of the house I had just left. More police cars were arriving from other directions. I was less than a quarter mile from the house, but even with the commotion, it was time to leave.

I drove out of the field and into the road with no lights heading away from the house. I made it around a small jog in the road and over a little bridge before I saw more flashing lights coming towards me. The moon was up and I could see fairly well. When I spotted a dirt driveway going into a pasture I turned in, running over the little barb wire gate as I went. I went down the dirt path a ways and stopped with my emergency brake, again.

I was only a mile from the highway. If not for the wailing sirens I could have heard the trucks passing on the highway. I was that close to freedom. After two more police cars passed, with flashing lights, I headed for the highway. I wanted out of the area and right then wasn't soon enough. I figured that I would be fine once I passed the Ardmore exists.

Before I traveled the short distance to Ardmore I passed two more cop cars, with emergency lights ablaze, heading in the direction I came from. It was not a good sign.

I had a friend who lived in Gene Autry, Oklahoma, slightly North of Ardmore. I went to his house and parked in his driveway until daylight.

That morning I had a talk with my friend and ate breakfast with his mother and father. They were all glad to see me and it was nice to see them.

I was back on the highway by 7:00a.m., headed to the underground storage place I had been working on for months. It was a big project. I had precut my lumber for the ten foot deep hole I dug, that was twelve feet long and ten feet wide. I had to haul out three pickup loads of dirt. Then I built a box in the ground and buried the whole thing. It was a lot of work, but I needed a secret hiding place. It took me two hours to unload, inventory and safely lower and organize the boxes in my storage spot.

When I was done I went to Pauls Valley for lunch. I was sore all over from the hard work and tension. I called Snake and told him that I got everything, just before the cops stormed the place. He wanted me to come to Texas, but I was too tired to drive two miles, care less a hundred.

I was calling from a motel room where I was about to take a shower and sleep the day away. Snake was corming my way. I woke to the sound of the phone ringing. I'm a very light sleeper. I had the phone before the second ring. It was Snake calling from the truck stop across the road from the motel. I asked him to order me a double cheeseburger and fries. I dressed, brushed my teeth and headed out the door with my hair slicked back and wet. I walked in as my food hit the table. Perfect timing.

Snake brought company. The guy I knew and the girl was Lisa. Snake brought her to meet me. She was Snake's gorgeous younger cousin, sitting there smiling, looking all of eighteen, I hoped.

Snake told me that the man who owned the home I'd sanitized had started a P2p cook when a friend of his showed up, pounding on the front door. The man was telling his friend that he needed to leave, when another guy showed up. The second guy was demanding that the first guy pay him some money for a past debt. The debate became physical. The first guy shot the second guy. Killing him in the living room, hence the missing carpet in the living room. The first guy cut the carpet and rolled the second, dead guy, in the carpet and hauled him away. The owner of the house drove the dead guy's car away, to get rid of and never came back. The owner of the house was obviously scared. He called some people, in a hysterical outburst, asking them what to do. Snake got the man to shut-up and sit in one place until I got the lab equipment out of the house.

Evidently, one of the people the man called had called the police.

I was lucky to get in and out before the police arrived. My help meant that the man who owned the house would only be looking at accessory to murder, not an additional manufacturing case. Gosh, the man was only looking at ten years, rather than thirty. Once again, I was the hero.

The dead man's body was recovered several months later when a politician's plane crashed near McAlester, Oklahoma. The search team looking for the downed airplane came across a shallow grave. The remains of the body might have been difficult to identify, but the person who killed and buried him left the man's wallet in his pocket. Criminals aren't very smart.

When Snake was ready to leave, Lisa said, "I'm going to stay with Jeff for a couple of days. He can bring me home when I get ready." Lisa had spoken.

I shook my head "Yes," and Snake slapped me on the back. He said, "Take care of her, big guy." Snake thought I was an enigma, because I looked like a college student.

I had slept all day so I was ready for a night of play. Lisa and I stayed in my motel room across from the truck stop that night. Her body was a perfect little dream come true.

The next day I had some deliveries to catch up on. Lisa rode with me to meet the rodeo clown and Elizabeth in McAlester. I was happy to see that the clown and Elizabeth were still together. She brought out his wild side and he kept her from going completely wild. It was a great combination. Then we drove to Okmulgee and on to Tulsa.

Lisa asked, "Is this what you do all day?"

I replied, "Yes, but at night I'm a superhero, bounding around, trying to save the world from imminent destruction. And I do make a pretty good Teddy Bear, if I may say so myself."

We went to Red Lobster for dinner. Spent some time at the Tulsa Drag Strip, where I introduced her to a few old friends. Then we stayed in the executive suite on the top floor of the Camelot hotel on Peoria, in Tulsa.

It was classy, right down to the champagne that I don't care for.

The next day I took Lisa by my mother's house to meet mom. We went to my house where we stayed part of the day having a sex-fest.

We played Foosball and she met Jimmy. Then we drove to Ada, Oklahoma and had dinner at Polo's, which is a nice Mexican restaurant. Lisa indicated that she needed to go back home the next day. Her parents were getting a divorce and things weren't real great at home.

We drove to Ardmore after dinner and got a room where I did my best to show her that I was not a drug crazed idiot. Lisa did not do drugs and I really liked her for that reason. She was also very intelligent, sweet and lovable.

I was sad when morning came. I wanted to keep her. We went clothes shopping, then headed for Texas. When we arrived at Snake's I told him, "We need to do something for Lisa. She is incredible. She wants to start college next semester. Let's get her an apartment close to campus."

Lisa's parents had bought her a new Mustang. All she needed was an apartment. I stayed two days in Texas, playing with Lisa and apartment hunting. Snake and I split a years' rent on an apartment close to the college Lisa wanted to attend. Then we let Lisa pick the furniture she wanted and we split that, as well. It was a good start for her. Even though Snake would never admit it, he had as much fun as I did. I saw Lisa a few times after that.

I didn't get too close because she was a nice girl that didn't need to be mixed up in my messes.

When I got back to Oklahoma, I drove straight to Budroux's and called Loretta. While we had lunch, Loretta told me that she'd heard about me saving the girl in Oklahoma City by knocking the guy out the window. It was Loretta's subtle way of informing me that she knew I had been with Sandy.

That didn't stop her from spending the night with me.

Russell was waiting on me when I got home. Bopper had been driving by his house a lot. Russell figured that Bopper was waiting on me to show up before he came in and tried to rob the place. Russell had been awake awhile and was a little bit overly excited. I followed Russell home. Sure enough, a short time later Bopper drove by with three other guys in his Bronco. Bopper looked like he was going to stop then he drove away.

Russell's wife was gone visiting family. Thank goodness. I had Russell call her and tell her to spend a couple of days. It was obvious that Bopper was working his nerve up to do something.

After dark Bopper pulled into the driveway and got out of his Bronco and Richard, Carl and Wade got out on the other side. I yelled across the yard for Bopper to get back in his truck and leave and to never come back. Bopper yelled back that he didn't want to talk to me, he wanted to talk to "The other guy."

I walked a little closer and said, "Well, if that's the case, you should have come alone, not with an army. Because this looks like you're planning a robbery."

Russell yelled, "Leave," from the porch.

Bopper said, "You're just a lot of talk with that gun."

I pulled my pistol and fired two shots next to Bopper's and Richard's feet. Little rock chips blasted up from the gravel drive and hit Bopper in the hand.

I said, "The only reason I haven't killed you already is, it would be too big a burden to bury your fat ass and these witnesses."

As they were leaving I told Carl and Wade that they were keeping bad company and following bad advice. I figured Bopper would either go to the police, or come back when he thought I wasn't there. I moved my motorcycle back into the trees and told Russell to keep watch while I got some sleep. About 2:00a.m., Russell woke me and told me that Bopper and his friends had parked down the road. I was getting very tired of Bopper's ignorance. Someone was bound to get hurt, or killed.

I started to walk down the road to meet them, then I decided to let them come to me. I got four small pieces of firewood, good throwing size and settled down to wait. I had Russell get his deer hunting spot light and told him to wait until he heard me talking before he turned the light on them. The first thing we heard was the squeak of the barb wire fence as Bopper and his team climbed over.

We could hear them trying to walk softly in the crunchy leaves and whispering to each other. As they approached I could identify which one was Bopper by the moon light. I threw a chunk of firewood as hard as I could, hitting Bopper in the chest, knocking him down.

I said, "Bopper, you're a slow learner."

Russell hit them with the spot light. I ordered them all to drop their guns and they obliged. Bopper was starting to recover, cuss and get up at the same time. I stepped into the edge of the light, with a pistol in each hand.

"Bopper," I said, "You are becoming too much trouble. I ought to just shoot you and be done with it. Nobody would know. But truth be told, I'm having fun watching you act a fool. And you guys, you should pick your friends better. The way I see it, you're leaving me no choice but to kill the lot of ya. Surely to goodness you can see where this is headed. If you keep it up some of us are going to die and I'm going to do my best to make sure it isn't me. Now, leave your guns where you dropped them and get the hell out of here."

My lecture was over. Bopper was hurt and grumbling, as his friends helped him to his feet and they walked away. Russell kept the lights on them as they walked away.

I picked up their guns and Russell and I went back to his house. We talked and decided that they weren't coming back. Russell was going to stay out in the trees and watch his place, just in case and I was going home.

It was still dark, but dawn was close at hand. I climbed on my motorcycle and headed South back toward Henryetta. I hadn't gone a mile when I saw a muzzle flash and felt my motorcycle jerk as the bullet ripped through the gas tank. Gas splashed all over me and into my eyes. I hit the brakes and my motorcycle slid out from under me. I landed on my back and hit my head on the pavement.

I may have died that morning. I'm not sure. I didn't see a bright light or a tunnel. I felt like I was painlessly floating in a misty cloud and people I couldn't quite see were looking at me. One came a little closer and said, "Get up. He's coming."

I jumped up with a sense of clarity and calm that certainly didn't fit the situation. I had no intention of shooting anyone, unless I had no choice. My gun was already in my hand. Bopper was crawling over a fence, twenty feet from me, when he looked up into the barrel on my gun and saw me smiling. He was coming to finish the job.

I simply said, "You missed."

Bopper panicked, pissed his pants and got hung in the fence. He wasn't going anywhere.

Bopper pleaded, "Please, don't kill me."

I said, "Bopper, if I wanted to kill you, you'd be dead right now. I want to see your cowardly bushwhacking ass broke and squirming. Drop that rifle, get off that fence and get out of here."

I was only five feet from him, with my gun pointed in his face. He obeyed and took off running across the field. I was starting to accumulate quite a gun collection. I retrieved Bopper's rifle, picked up my motorcycle and rode it back to Russell's house. It wasn't far. I took it slow so the last bit of gas wouldn't slosh out. I was able to make it to Russell's.

Russell heard the shot. He was getting his nerve up to come check on me, when he heard me coming back. The gas was chapping my skin. I undressed and took a shower while Russell put my clothes in the washer. I picked gravel from the back of my head. It bled like crazy. I looked in the mirror and one of my pupils was huge.

I had a concussion. I was too tired to care. I figured, since the wreck didn't kill me, I wasn't meant to die.

I put on a pair of Russell's shorts, took four aspirin, chased them with a beer and grabbed a towel. I folded the towel in a square and laid down on the floor, using the towel as a pillow to catch the blood.

I then asked Russell to wake me if Bopper showed up again. I was exhausted, in many ways.

CHAPTER EIGHT:

Big Deal

When I woke up I had Russell take me to pick up the car I had stashed at my friend's mechanic shop in Okmulgee. I then drove to a little medical clinic where the doctor picked and cleaned more gravel out of my head.

He gave me a tetanus shot in one cheek and a penicillin shot in the other. I paid my bill and was on my way, with an admonishment about driving. The doctor wanted to x-ray. The swelling was so severe he thought my skull was fractured.

I told him, "Thank you," and said, "If I have any problems I'll come back." The doctor said, "Playing tough is not smart. You could die."

"I'm figuring that one out," I said.

I didn't feel well, to say the least. My head hurt and I was nauseous.

I couldn't let that stop me from "Taking care of business in a flash," as Elvis would say. However, my ego would not allow me to let anyone see me hurt. I took Jimmy a hefty supply of meth to our stash spot at Cry Baby Bridge, then called him and told him I'd dropped it off. He knew to leave the money for the last load in the stash spot. I also told him to be extra cautious, because Bopper had shot at me and I was about to turn the heat up, again.

I was tired of Bopper and his boys following me and showing up unexpected. I decided to take proactive measures. I'm the kind of guy who takes care of his own dirty work. I didn't want anything from Bopper or his partners, but I had taken on the job of making sure they didn't have anything. It was time to get to work. The next phase of my plan required the services of a friend of mine from Tulsa who owned a salvage and crushing yard. I gave him a call and he agreed to meet me in a secluded place we both knew. I then loaded all the tools I would need into my service truck.

I met my friend and told him my plan. He thought it was rather fitting and funny. I probably wouldn't have done so many outlandish things if my friends would have encouraged me not to). He drove me back to Henryetta and dropped me off down the road from Bopper's house. I stayed in the trees and walked to within watching distance of Bopper's place.

Bopper had four vehicles. His red and white Bronco, a green Chevy truck, a blue Dodge Charger and a gold Buick. My target was the Charger.

Bopper had been working on it for a year. It had a new motor, new tires and a fancy stereo system.

I waited until Bopper left in his Bronco then I walked into his yard and got in the Charger with my little tool bag. I took the steering wheel off and removed the key switch. Then I put the wheel back on, started the car and drove away. I was later told that Bopper didn't notice the car missing until he realized his boat was missing, two days later.

I drove the Charger to where my truck was parked. The motor and transmission hadn't even cooled completely down before I had them both removed from the car, using a big tree to hold my hoist. I loaded the motor and transmission in my truck, along with the car's tires and wheels, the fancy stereo system and some other parts and accessories and delivered them to my friend Russell. Russell subsequently used the parts to fix up his old Dodge truck.

I went back to the Charger and used the owner of the property's backhoe to crush the top, trunk, hood and fenders of the car. It looked like it had been hit by a train. Using the backhoe, I loaded the stripped, smashed Charger on a car trailer and hauled it to my friend's crushing yard.

After crushing Bopper's car, I borrowed one of my friend's trucks and put Bopper's Charger tag on it. I made sure the truck had both size trailer balls, drove it back to Henryetta where I got lucky and Bopper wasn't home. I backed into Bopper's yard, hooked on to his boat trailer and drove away. I didn't take it far. I towed the boat to the handy strip pits, removed the outboard motor, gas tank, battery and fishing gear and pushed the boat and trailer over the edge of the steep bank. The drop to the water was so far that the boat and trailer bounced and flipped upside down into the water. I had anticipated a problem with sinking the boat. After all, boats are made to float. I brought my 10 gauge shotgun. The boat was bottom up, with the trailer sticking up in the air slowly floating away from the shore. I slid down the bank to the water's edge and shot four huge holes in the boat. The boat sank, with the trailer, before I could shoot it a fifth time.

I changed the tag on the truck and threw Bopper's Charger tag in with the boat. I gave the boat motor and fishing gear to Russell.

Before I could get another one of Bopper's vehicles an interesting development occurred. Bopper was pulled over leaving a club and the police found a pistol under the seat of his Bronco. As it turned out, the pistol was stolen. It was the same pistol I found in Bopper's freezer and returned to the owner. The old man had someone plant the gun in Bopper's truck, then call the police and report the infraction.

When the police got a warrant and searched Bopper's house they found two more of the man's guns and some other stolen property.

Obviously, it was not a good night for Bopper. After being arrested, he made bond again and was back in business the next day. Bopper had to sell his Bronco to make bond.

I decided to let things cool off for a while. But as luck would have it, cooling off was not in the cards. A person I knew, who had developed a reason to be mad at Bopper, told me that Bopper and Richard had a small camping trailer. It was parked at the back of a friend of Bopper's property.

The person told me that he was sure that Bopper was hiding something in the camper. The man who owned the property never left his house, so I couldn't drive past his house without being noticed. I had to walk in from the back side of the property. The person I was with dropped me off and I asked him to come back and pick me up after dark. That gave me about five hours to walk in, find out what was going on and walk out.

I found the camper without too much trouble. Careful not to leave prints, I broke the lock off the camper door. I was amazed at the vast amount of property hidden inside the trailer that was undoubtedly stolen.

I spotted three expensive hunting rifles and I knew to whom they belonged. I took the three rifles and left. After I was picked up and taken to my truck I called the owner of the rifles. It was late, but he invited me over. I told him the story and gave him the guns. He was pleased. I made it clear that it was my position that the old man that owned the property didn't know the camper was full of stolen property.

The next day the man I'd returned the guns to and his friend, who was a deputy sheriff, went to the old man and advised him of the problem.

They told him that no charges would be filed against him if he would allow them to go in and get the trailer. A lot of hard working people got their stolen property returned that week. Saddles, TVs, guns, tools, chainsaws and more. It was kind of like Christmas and I was Santa Claus.

Nobody had seen me come or go, just like Santa.

I woke the next morning with someone poking me, saying, "Are you going to sleep all day?"

I knew that voice. It was my little sister, Jody. I opened my eyes and low and behold, Phoebe was standing next to her. They were both smiling and laughing at me. My hair always sticks up in the mornings. Mom wanted me to get up and go eat with them.

Great idea, I loved to eat. I had missed Phoebe's graduation, on purpose. She invited me and I declined. Graduation is for teenagers who are in the beginning of starting their lives. I was an adult who had already messed up his life. I knew Phoebe had a crush on me. Truth be known, I had one on her also. But I was smart enough to know that it was best for Phoebe to find someone, other than me.

My life was too crazy. She knew why I backed away from her. At first, she was hurt and mad, but she was starting to understand and liked me again. She came to bring me graduation pictures. We all went to eat together and talked about normal things. While we were eating the deputy, sheriff drove by pulling Bopper's camper full of stolen merchandise. My role as avenging angel was coming together pretty well.

Making P2p almost every night was getting monotonous and tiresome.

I had two, thirty five gallon plastic drums full of un-distilled P2p and over twenty gallons of distilled P2p. With the large glass I had, I got eleven P2p cooks from each 110 pound drum of phenylacetic acid. I had cooked twelve of the 110 pound drums and had eleven more to finish.
Passing the halfway mark was a relief. I was in the process of pouring raw P2p into a third drum when Mr. Connor came in and told me that Louisiana had called. The order was in for the one hundred pounds. I had more than enough distilled P2p ready to handle the order.

I started four twenty-two thousand milliliter speed cooks. I felt like a mad scientist. The lab looked like something from a science fiction movie.

I had twelve hours to get things set up and ready to powder. I put three five gallon cans of ether in the chest type freezer, that was all that would fit at one time. I also placed three more cans next to the freezer to put in as I removed one from the freezer. It took some time to build my plastic room around the lab entrance and set up the air conditioner.

I then made breakfast. Biscuits, sausage and gravy for myself, Mr. Connor and Alice. I didn't talk about things in front of Alice. We were trying to keep things as normal as possible around her. I had become almost a household fixture. The three of us were eating and looking out the back sliding glass door as the sun started peeking through the trees, shining on the heavy dew blanketed over the field behind the house. During the night one of Mr. Connor's cows had a calf. The new born calf was stumbling and wobbling around trying to get acquainted with its legs. It was a cute sight, watching the calf learning to run and turn. It was the first time I'd heard Alice laugh. And it was music to my ears. Mr. Connor and I laughed, as well. Only our laughs were laughs of relief, accompanied with tears of joy at hearing Alice laugh. Hearing Alice laugh was one of the happiest moments of my life. She didn't say anything and we didn't try to get her to, we just enjoyed the moment. Alice was coming back.

I silently vowed, once again, to make Bopper suffer.

When I climbed into my hammock in the barn I was thinking about the best way to powder one hundred pounds of meth. The steady drone of the air conditioner put my exhausted body to sleep, but my mind kept working. I woke up later with an easy solution to my problem. I went to Walmart and bought four large plastic containers. The big rectangular kind that people put clothes or quilts in and slide under the bed, or stack in closets.

I was going to alternate dumping the meth in each of the four containers so it would have time to dry before I poured more on top.

Each of the containers would hold well over twenty five pounds of meth and still give me plenty of room to stir it all together, turning it over and over, to help it air out and dry.

I also bought six, five gallon plastic cans that had lids that snapped on and off. My plan was to pour my used ether into these new clean cans so I could re-gas it after I was done with the bulk of the powdering project.

I figured I would work about five hours then take a break. That didn't workout. I was on a roll, I didn't stop until I had all the oil powdered, ten hours later. It took all six of the five gallon cans of ether. I was higher than a kite.

At that point I took a break. Sleep was completely out of the question. I was wired. I forced myself to eat, used the restroom and went back to work.

I had powdered everything with a PH of seven, so I re-gased all the used ether lowing the PH to five and a half. That caused any remaining oil that was suspended in the ether to form pretty pink meth. After I strained all the used ether through filters, using the vacuum pump, I put it back in its original containers. To dispose of the used ether, I later poured it into an oil tank, where it mixed with crude oil being pumped out of the ground, then it went to a refinery to be recycled.

When I was done I had one hundred and twenty six pounds of white crystal meth. Four pounds of pink meth and two pounds of pink sticky, moist meth that I scraped from the sides of the four flasks I used to powder and the six, five gallon cans I used to re-gas the ether. My nights work had run through most of the day.

By the time I moved all the hay, tore down my plastic enclosure and drove down the road to dump all the used ether in the oil field tank, I was tired. I flattened all the ether cans with a backhoe so I could dispose of them easier. I then grilled myself a big cheeseburger on the outside grill, while I drank a margarita and smoked some really good pot. After eating I went to sleep for ten hours.

It took me most of the next day to get all the meth weighed and packaged into pounds. I knew I had powdered over one hundred pounds, but I was amazed at how much over. Then I took another trip to my favorite place to shop (Walmart) and bought five matching canvas tote bags. Each bag held twenty pounds. I was ready to make the deal.

I called Louisiana with the news. He suggested that I deliver the load to Indiana. I told him that I already had a spot for the exchange and if they wanted the meth, they had to come get it. Louisiana assured me that everything was okay and would go smooth. I gave Louisiana a pay phone number and told him I would be there for an hour waiting on a call from the person I would be meeting.

When the call came, the man identified himself as "Jay." I said, "I'll be damn, that's my name too."

Jay wanted to meet me halfway. I told him I didn't mind meeting him any place he liked. I just wouldn't be hauling anything with me. I suggested that we meet at a bar and grill in Tulsa, just to look each other over, because it was close to where I was comfortable doing the exchange. If things looked alright to both of us, I would show him where we would make the switch. I told him that, if he liked the situation once he'd seen it then we would do our thing. He agreed. With Louisiana vouching for the guy I figured the deal would go fine, but I wasn't taking any chances.

Two days later I had everything ready and was waiting at the appointed place and time. It was after the lunch crowd so the place wasn't busy.

First, four bikers walked in and took a table. Then Jay walked in looking like an attorney. He fit his description and I fit mine. I was certain he wasn't a cop. He was too small and nervous. And cops don't bring four big wild looking bikers with them. I waved him over and we shook hands. Before we ordered, I asked Jay if he wanted two of his guys to check out the product. I gave Jay a key, told him the motel room number and that there was an ounce of meth under the pillow. I also told him to be sure and have the guys take the dope, because I wasn't going back to the room.

He took the key and walked over to the bikers' table.

Then two of them got up and left. The motel was on the other side of the parking lot. Jay came back and I recommended the chicken fried steak. He said he was too nervous to eat. I told him if he couldn't trust Louisiana then maybe he should call off the deal and walk. He relented and I ordered chicken fried steak for both of us and the four bikers. There isn't much better than a chicken fried steak with brown gravy. If someone told me I could have my choice between a chicken fried steak or sex with a beautiful woman, I would probably pick the chicken fry (unless I had already eaten) and then talk the beautiful woman out of her pants later.

We were just starting to eat when the other two bikers came back.

One of them shook his head "Yes" and gave us the thumbs up.

I told Jay my plan was for him and I to drive out alone to see the dope and the exchange spot. We would drive back and if he thought the situation clear, his boys could follow us to the location for the deal. After finishing our meals, he told the guys the plan. They agreed and went to my motel room to wait on our return.

Jay climbed in my truck and we drove a short distance to a dirt road leading into a pasture. The road, which was not much more than a path, went a half mile into the trees and around a small hill to an oil well that had three tank batteries sitting on location. On the way out, I informed Jay that I had two watchdogs. I really only had one, Jimmy. Jimmy was waiting in the trees until he heard my truck coming. He would then climb the steps of the tanks and lay down on top of one of the tanks with his high powered deer rifle. He would supervise the exchange through his scope. Jimmy was up there waiting when we arrived. I showed Jay the five bags with the hundred pounds of meth and we headed back to town for me to see the money.

Back at the motel I told Jay I wasn't going to put myself in a position where I had to shoot my way out of a motel room. I figured the money was in one of their vehicles anyway so why not just look at the money in the parking lot. All four of the big bikers came out and one of them opened the truck and unzipped a bag showing me the money. I knew it wasn't a million dollars.

"That's not a million," I said.

The biker closed the trunk and said, "We got six hundred thousand. We'll bring the other four hundred back in two weeks."

I said, "When you bring the other four hundred you can pick up the other forty pounds. Six hundred gets you sixty pounds."

As I talked, I stepped away from the car closer to Jay.

"Jay here wasn't honest with me," I said. "He left that part out. Louisiana told me that there wouldn't be any problems. I don't like problems."

Two of the bikers were fanning out in what looked like an attempt to get behind me. I put my hand in my jacket and laughingly told them not to even try and get behind me or I would shoot everyone in the parking lot.

They stopped moving.

Jay said, "Calm down. We came for one hundred pounds."

"Then you should have brought the correct amount of money," I said.

" I'm not fronting forty pounds to no man. I've a good mind to walk all together, but if you want to get sixty, let's get it over with. But y'all need to know, if we get out there and one of you guys pulls something stupid, nobody will be leaving. You are getting pure dope for your money and if things go well there is plenty more where this came from. I'll still throw in the extra pound of special pink meth I have ready for you, but things better go smooth from here on. When I go home and count that money it better all be there or I sure as hell won't be doing any more business with you."

They said the money was there and that they would take the sixty pounds. I could tell by their expressions that if they saw an opportunity I was a dead man. For that kind of money, they would kill me and take whatever they could get and make their next deal with someone else. I advised them to stay close to their car when we got there and Jay and I would get the meth. Jay rode with me as the guys followed us to the location. Jay knew I was pissed. We didn't say much on the way. When we got there Jimmy was back on top of the oil tank. Jimmy didn't know how big the deal was. All he knew was that I needed backup and he was ready to help. I was sure that once Jimmy saw these guys he would be on high alert.

When I got out of my truck the four bikers were looking at Jimmy on top of the tank with the hot sun causing heat waves to rise off the tank and Jimmy's hair blowing in the wind. I was certainly thankful he was up there.

I had Jay follow me to the bags. Jay carried two and I carried the one I knew had the extra pound of pink meth in it in my left hand. I pulled my pistol out of its shoulder holster and held it in my right hand. My six inch vented rib Colt Python .357 magnum made an impressive sight. I wasn't taking any chances.

Jay and I walked to the back of the bikers car and placed the three bags on the ground.

I told them, "The extra pound of pink meth is in this one."

The lead biker opened his trunk, took out the bag with the money in it and dropped it on the ground, as he stooped to look in the three bags.

He looked happy with what he found. As he put the three bags of meth in his trunk, I put the bag of money in my truck. I kept waiting for the hammer to fall, but nothing happened. I told him to call Louisiana when they were ready for more. He said he would and they got in their car and drove away. It was a close call and I was thankful I handled the deal on my own terms.

Jimmy came down from his hot lofty roost and I gave him a pound of meth and my motorcycle, that he was riding with a new gas tank, for his trouble. I loaded the other meth and we left by another dirt path that took us out a different direction.

Mr. Connor was not a happy man. He was upset with Louisiana for putting me in that precarious position and he didn't think we could trust Louisiana's judgment any longer. He was also mad because the deal was supposed to be both our paydays.

Mr. Connor had already proceeded with his plan to build a country convenience store. I told him to go ahead and keep five hundred thousand and I would take one hundred thousand and the meth. That helped a little, but the thing with Bopper had gotten out of hand and I'd almost been killed, on more than one occasion. Mr. Connor was ready to shut everything down.

We had pushed our luck as far as Mr. Connor thought we could. He didn't think it was a wise idea to continue down the same path we were traveling. I understood that, because I was feeling apprehensive myself.

Even though it was Mr. Connor who got the old proverbial ball rolling, he wanted out and I sure couldn't blame him.

He was worried that too many people knew what was going on and he no longer wanted the risk. He had Alice to think about. He felt that he had accomplished his goal. With my help he put Bopper in the poor house and he made the money he wanted. He figured Bopper would eventually go to prison and Alice was getting better. He was old and scared of losing everything he had.

Mr. Connor decided that I should have all the meth, chemicals and lab equipment and that I should move it all that day. I didn't have a problem with that. Getting everything out of his hair was a good move for him and Alice and I respected that. One hundred thousand in cash, plus what I already had and enough of the necessary base chemicals to make about five million more was one hell of a start for me.

I borrowed Mr. Connor's large horse trailer. (It held four horses). It took me the rest of the day and half the night to get everything loaded and the horse trailer was full. Everything, including my hammock, went into the trailer. That morning I drove half-way across the State to Pauls Valley and put all the heavy items, the huge vacuum pump and drums of P2p in storage. The lighter items, the ones easy to manage, I put in my underground storage, which was then as full as I could make it and still move around. I knew where I was going to build my lab, but I had so much meth I didn't need to worry about that for a while. At that moment, I needed additional hidden storage space. Hiding things is not easy. If one other person knows about it then it's not hidden.

The other problem I had was, I wanted to buy some land. I had the money, but I needed someone to owner finance some property so I could make monthly payments. A person can't just pay cash for a bunch of land without the long arm of the law reaching out with questions of where the money came from. I went to my friend Kevin and told him that I was in the market to buy some property. (He knew most everyone in the area).

He said he had sixty acres he would sell me. I could just pay him cash, wait about five years, like I paid it all in payments, then transfer the property into my name when I got ready. We drove out to look it over and it was perfect. The land was mostly grown over with black jack trees and had a few bigger elm and pecan trees. Exactly what I was looking for.

He was my best friend, like a big brother to me, I had no reason not to trust him. I paid him cash for the property. I wasn't in a hurry to transfer the property into my name. My main concern was storage.

It was several years later that I found out that the land actually belonged to Kevin's father and Kevin was planning to sign it over to me after he inherited the land, someday.

Digging another storage hole by hand was out of the question. I brought in a backhoe and dug my storage like a large cellar, because I planned on using it for a cellar when I built a home there. The only difference was, I made the entrance a ramp instead of stairs. It only took one afternoon to dig my hole. It then took four days to build the box in the ground, frame the door for the entrance, then bury everything. I felt much better once I had all the chemicals and equipment buried. With the precautions I had taken, it would be almost impossible for someone to find the place.

With everything buried all I had to concern myself with was my meth and pot business and making Bopper, Richard and Harold miserable. I hadn't forgotten about what happened to Alice. I sure hadn't forgiven Bopper for shooting me off my motorcycle.

Fall was rapidly approaching. Some of the trees were already turning colors. Halloween was coming and Thanksgiving was on the way. Fall is a pretty time of year in Oklahoma. I went back to Henryetta to take care of business. I pulled Mr. Connor's horse trailer back to his house. He invited me to have Thanksgiving dinner with him and Alice and I assured him I wouldn't miss it for the world.

Even though I was selling meth to the rodeo clown and a few other out-of-town friends, I was concentrating on the local areas where Bopper was hanging out. I hadn't given up on my goal to break Bopper and Richard.

However, Harold had dropped out of the picture and was working for his family's business. I had come to believe, over the months, that Harold didn't have anything to do with what had happened to Alice. I was sure that he knew about it, but ever since Bopper had tortured and raped Alice, Harold had been limiting his exposure to, and keeping his distance from, Bopper. It was Richard who was sticking with Bopper, so it was Richard who would be suffering along with Bopper. I was also going to make sure that if Carl, Floyd and Wade kept helping Bopper they weren't going to fare very well either.

For obvious reasons, when I heard a car pull into my driveway I glanced out the window. When I saw Richard's primer brown Chevy Blazer pull into my driveway, I was somewhat surprised. Especially when there were two police cars behind him with their lights flashing. I was smart enough not to keep too much in my house and it didn't take me long to flush what I had. Luckily, the police weren't after me. The police searched Richard and the Blazer, finding cocaine, guns and drug paraphernalia. Richard was arrested and the police hauled him away. But they didn't tow the Blazer and they never even knocked on my door. It was like they were in a big hurry to get away from my house. My guess was that Richard drove into town from the back roads. When he noticed the police following him he was close to my house and thought he could pull in my driveway and the police would go on by and leave him alone. It didn't work out and I was pissed that he brought that kind of heat to my door.

Two days later when Richard's friend Floyd came by to ask about the Blazer, it was too late. Richard had cost me a thousand dollars by pulling into my driveway with the police behind him, just in what I had to flush.

I took the Blazer to a friend of mine's shop in Meeker, Oklahoma and stripped it down to nothing. The Blazer had a new engine and transmission and new oversize tires and wheels.

It took me less than a week to put all the Blazer running gear under a 1977 burgundy Chevrolet Laguna that had a white stripe and swivel bucket seats. I was the only guy around, at that time, that had a jacked up four wheel drive car. I drove it around a lot that winter so Bopper and Richard could see the new tires and wheels and know that I built the car out of Richard's missing Blazer. Oh, what fun it was to ride in Jeff's new Chevrolet.

CHAPTER NINE:

The Wizard

My mother liked the fact that I was spending a lot more time at home.

I kept my four wheel drive Chevrolet Laguna parked in my front yard, so it would drive Bopper and Richard crazier. From the stories I was hearing it was working. Big Bopper was telling people that he was sure I was behind the disappearance of his Charger and boat. I told the same people that, if I could make things disappear, then I must be a Wizard.

Some of them agreed that I must be a Wizard because I turned Richard's Chevy Blazer into a Chevy Laguna. Welcome the birth of my new nickname, "The Wizard."

The holiday season was quickly approaching. It was time to renew my marijuana supply. I didn't sell large quantities of pot. Most of my customers for that commodity bought ounces or half ounces. One hundred pounds lasted me awhile. I called my pot connection in Stillwater and told him that I had so much fun the last time I was there I was ready to go dancing again. He informed me that it would be a great time to visit, meaning he had what I was looking for. Everyone I knew liked to get high for the holidays. Generally, the people who smoke pot are a lot better crowd than the ones who use meth.

After I picked up a rick of firewood I headed for Stillwater. Upon arrival, we got the business end of things out of the way and I loaded one hundred pounds of pot in my truck, covering it with the firewood.

At Eskimo Joe's that night a friend of ours showed up unexpectedly.

We called him Shitty Leg because of the way he kept breaking his girlfriend's heart. She put up with it, but we wouldn't let him live it down. Him showing up at Eskimo Joe's without her was yet another example of him being shitty.

We were having a great time dancing and flirting with half the girls in the place. I remembered something I'd seen in a movie, so I explained it to Shitty Leg and asked him to try it out. He thought it was a grand idea. I had to go over it and explain it twice, but then he was ready. Following my detailed instructions, Shitty Leg turned to the table next to ours where three gorgeous young women were sitting. He pulled his chair around between two of the girls and asked the prettiest girl if she would like to dance.

She said, "No."

Shitty Leg said, "No, what?"

She said, "No, I would not like to dance."

He said, "I didn't ask you if you would like to dance. I said, you look a little fat in those pants."

We all cracked up laughing. She threw her drink at him. He moved and part of her drink hit her girlfriend. It was a hoot. Before things progressed to blows I jumped up and made an apology. I took responsibility for putting him up to the stunt.

I said, "it's my fault. Y'all looked bored and I thought it would liven up things a bit. I must add that, you are not fat. In fact, you have a fine ass. How about when this place closes I take you and your friends to breakfast?"

The pretty girl boldly announced that, "My boyfriend has a ten inch dick." Hearing that comment come out of her mouth stunned me some, but I recovered quick. I said, "Well then having sex with me shouldn't be too much of a burden for you."

That got a laugh and a smile out of her so I said, "I named my penis little Elvis."

She said, "Why, it is little?"

"He's smaller than my truck." I said. "But that's not why I named him Elvis. Sometimes, at night, when I'm all alone, by myself, I hear him singing 'love me tender, love me true, never let me go.'" I sang it in my best Elvis voice, which got everyone laughing.

"And besides that, I'm a mechanic!" I said.

Pretty girl said, "what's that have to do with anything?"

"I'm glad you asked," I said. "Didn't you hear the story about the girl who was married four times?"

She shook her head "No."

I continued, "The first time she married a doctor and all he wanted to do was examine it. The second time she married a police man and all he wanted to do was lock it up. The third time she married an attorney and all he wanted to do was talk about it. The fourth time she married a mechanic and he tore it apart the first night and has been working on it ever since."

We all enjoyed another laugh, but the wet girl who ended up wearing part of the thrown drink, she was still unhappy. I told her I was sorry she got wet, then told my friend Shitty Leg to use his mouth and suck all the alcohol out of her shirt so it would dry faster. Combined with Shitty Leg begging her to please let him suck her shirt dry, the joke got her laughing.

I was on a roll so I asked the pretty girl to dance.

The pretty girl said, "Yes," and added, "My name is Patricia and don't ever call me Pat."

We danced together and I danced with her friends. At closing time, we all met at an all night diner where I bought everyone breakfast. I always loved to pick up the tab and I was a big tipper.

I leaned over to Patricia, as we ate at the big table and quietly said, "I don't know if I can measure up to your big boyfriend, but you ought to try me on for size."

Patricia said, "You're pretty wild."

"You ain't seen nothing yet," I said. I was thinking, "Just wait until I do a line of meth and do you every which way for about four hours."

While we were eating we got on the subject of my friend Shitty Leg's nickname. The girls thought it was rather funny and fitting. One of the girls said she had a nickname and told us all how she got it. When I saw the direction the conversation was heading I got an idea. When Patricia asked me if I had a nickname, I avoided answering the question. Good ol' Shitty Leg jumped right in there and said, "They call him The Wizard." The girls got excited and wanted to know why. Shitty chimed in and said, "Because he can make things disappear."

They all wanted to see me make something disappear and they were having a big time teasing me.

I put a French fry in my mouth and said "There you go. It disappeared."

I calmly added, "Wouldn't you rather see me make something appear?"

They said, "Yes." I told Patricia to hold out her hand over the table palm up.

She did and I made a show of rubbing my right fist with my left hand, then I held the closed fist over Patricia's open hand.

I told her, "Say any magic word that you ever heard."

Patricia said, "Abracadabra."

I opened my hand and dropped a diamond tennis bracelet in her hand. There was a collective gasp at the table. Even the waitress who had stopped to watch said, "Wow."

Shitty Leg, true to form, said, "Son-of-a-bitch."

I guess they were expecting something cheesy, like a nickel, or something I had palmed off the table. None of them knew I had it in my pocket all night. I brought it in hopes of seeing the girl I was with the first time I went to Eskimo Joe's.

She wasn't there, so this was perfect, a real show stopper.

Patricia said, "Oh, my God. Is it mine?"

"Of course," I said. "I had it stored in my mind with hopes of someday giving it to a beautiful woman."

I never told anyone how I did it and Harry Houdini couldn't have pulled it off any better. The rest of the morning went in a blur of sweaty orgasms. When the girls left I was fairly confident that Patricia would remember The Wizard.

Shitty Leg said, "I don't know how you pulled that off, but thanks."

Traveling back to Henryetta the next morning I had a smile of satisfaction on my face. I had a lot of fun. Most of the time, for me, it was work and no play. I treasured the moments I got to enjoy myself.

Even though I had spent a significant portion of my money on the land I bought from Kevin, I was looking for ways to legitimize my money. I met with a friend of mine who had inherited two hundred and fifty acres from his grandfather. His name was Mike, but people called him Mikey. The land had two ponds just sitting there, not in use.

Mikey lived there in a little house that came with the land. I went to see him and Mikey and I came to an agreement that, after winter was over, we would go into the cattle business together. I would go around buying calves from some of the local cattle men we knew, paying cash and he would watch after them. As they grew we would breed some and sell some, splitting the money. I went ahead and bought four yearlings to put in the pasture to make it look like we were doing something. I paid to build a long low roofed barn to store hay and feed. Mikey and I built a corral with a squeeze shoot and loading gate. I looked at it as a sound investment and a great idea. I didn't see how anything could go wrong. We ever decided on a name, we called it TSCC. We weren't going to tell anyone that it meant "Tough Shit Cattle Company."

Halloween morning, I went to Walmart and got two plastic pumpkins and enough Halloween candy to fill them up. When I pulled into Mr. Connor's driveway Alice was sitting on the front porch. She got up and went in to get her grandpa. They both came back out as I walked up the steps. I handed each of them a pumpkin full of candy and said, "Happy Halloween."

Alice smiled as a big tear rolled down her cheek. Then she hugged me and went in the house as she wiped her eyes.

Mr. Connor said, "She's missed you. She sits out here like she is expecting you to drive up any moment. It's good that you came. Stay for lunch. We'll grill cheeseburgers. Your favorite."

I had lunch with them and it was a good time for all three of us. It was as close as anyone could get to being family. I was driving my four wheel drive Chevy Laguna. When I was leaving, Mr. Connor said, "A car like that probably draws a lot of attention."

I said, "I hope so, I built it out of Richard's Blazer."

Hr. Connor laughed. I didn't have to say more. He knew I was still causing Bopper grief. I told Alice I would be back for Thanksgiving. She smiled and hugged me goodbye. Alice was making progress, but it broke my heart every time I saw her.

Halloween night I went to the Freakers Ball in Tulsa with a girl named Summer.

I went as Count Dracula and Summer went as a six foot tall blond version of Elvira. Our costumes were top of the line. I was decked out in a long tail Dracula tux, top hat and cane. We danced until midnight then went to see The Rocky Horror Picture Show. We stayed at a classy motel and bit on each other half the night. Summer

was getting into the whole dress up for Halloween trick or treat thing. She was wearing a sexy push up old fashion meets modern day vampire corset. She was hot. Sitting on top of me with little Elvis deep inside her, she said, "I'm going to cut your neck and suck your blood." I smiled, thinking she was playing.

She then pulled a small knife from her corset, opened it and reached down and made a small cut on the left side of my neck. She did it without breaking rhythm. Then bent down to suck blood out of my neck, working her hips, until she climaxed. She fell over on the bed next to me and said, "Come on, it's your turn," with my blood on her lips.

She spread her legs to let me in, took the tip of the knife between her fingers and cut the left side of her own neck. It was one of the most erotic sexual experiences I ever had. When I let go inside her, with the taste of her blood in my mouth, I erupted with every inch of my body. The taste of sweaty sex and blood was intoxicating.

I was learning that it would be impossible to write an instruction manual for women. (Women for Dummies). No two women are alike. You can't tell what type they are just by looking at them. Women don't come with emblems, identifying them as mild, hot or kinky. It is not until you get in the bedroom and they say, "Be easy with me," or "Harder," that you can identify their personalities and adjust yourself accordingly. This was very confusing to me and I think women do it on purpose to keep men thrown off track.

Things were moving along quietly after Halloween. As I expected, I was selling a lot of pot. I had slowed down on my efforts to sell meth, but my regular customers were keeping me busy. I found out that Bopper and Richard were selling cocaine and meth out of a tire shop in Okmulgee.

That made sense, because all their vehicles had new tires and wheels. Even the Charger and Blazer I'd liberated had new tires and wheels.

I decided to investigate. I just happened to have a car that needed new tires. The first couple of times I drove past the tire shop, Bopper was there. When Bopper left I pulled in and told the man I needed new tires.

I could tell the guy was nervous. I said, "Do you know who I am?"

He said, "Yes and if Bopper and Richard catch you here they will kill both of us."

I said, "I doubt that. I'll tell you what I'll do. If you want out of this mess, I'll buy you out right now. You can close the doors and walk away. I'll buy all of your inventory and tools and equipment and you can just drive off. I know you owe Bopper and Richard a bunch of money. If you sell out to me, I want you to take the money and run. If you are interested it's now or never. All you have to do is lock the door and put out your closed sign and I will make sure you get away clean."

I knew he leased the building and I could see his inventory was small. He said, "let me pull my truck in and lock the door."

After he pulled his truck inside I got out a legal pad and we walked around his shop writing down each piece of equipment and all the inventory, putting a price beside each thing. I then called his landlord and asked if there would be any problem breaking the lease. I did that for show, because I'd already talked to the owner of the building.

He was a friend of Mr. Connor's. The man was glad to get this bum out of his building.

After we added everything up I was surprised at how low the figure was. I started making out a detailed receipt and called Jonas, Mr. Connor's attorney friend and asked him to come by and witness the contract.

While we were talking Bopper and Richard came back and banged on the door. The man was visibly shaken.

I said, "Calm down. I told you I would help you get out of here. I keep my word. I'm not like Bopper and Richard. I won't mess you around. I'm giving you a way out."

By the time Jonas arrived Bopper and Richard had left. Jonas witnessed the signing of the contract and the cash payment and I paid him for his services. When Jonas left the man left also. I had bought out a tire shop in less than two hours.

That night I had Jimmy come in with my truck. We picked out some tires and wheels I intended to use and mounted and balanced them.

We then loaded them in the back of my truck with what little other equipment I planned to keep. We were actually just killing time waiting on a moving company to show up the next day. I had hired a moving company to come with a semi and load the whole place up and take it all to Snake's shop in Texas.

While Jimmy and I sat inside laughing, Bopper and Richard were outside waiting for the tire guy to come back. I called four of my friends and asked them to pick up some food and cokes and come by the tire store.

It was my idea of a going out of business party. I told them that Bopper was outside and that there would most likely be trouble when they arrived. They didn't care. When my guys got there I raised the big shop door so they could all walk in together.

Bopper and Richard got out of Bopper's green Chevy truck and asked, "What the hells going on here?"

I stepped into view and said, "I bought the tire shop, so we're having a party." When Bopper and Richard heard my voice and saw me they were pissed.

Bopper said, "Where's Chris?"

Chris had been the previous owner.

I said, "After my attorney witnessed the sales contract Chris left. I think he went back to Kansas. He said something about Dorthy and getting lost."

Bopper started walking towards me and said, "I own half this tire shop."

I pulled out my trusty pistol and said, "No, you don't. I own it all. But if you think you have a claim, have your lawyer get with my lawyer. Be sure to bring your contract."

As Bopper turned to leave, he said, "I'm going to kill you." Then he drove away.

Jimmy and I stayed in the tire shop that night talking about all the crazy shit we were into. We helped the movers load everything the next morning. When the movers left I called Snake and told him what was coming his way. Then I called the owner of the building and asked him to come by and inspect the place before I left. I wanted to make sure he was happy in case I needed something from him later. Plus, he was a friend of Mr. Connor's and I wanted him to know it was me that was leaving his building in good condition.

I was spending money as fast as I made it. I didn't mind. You can't take it with you when you die and at the rate I was going, I could bite the bullet at any time. To prove my point, I was sitting in my living room talking to Snake on the phone, we were discussing the necessity of building another addition to his shop to hold all the stuff I sent him, when someone drove by the front of my house and shot two of my front windows out.

Snake said, "What the hell was that."

I could see the car still moving up the road.

I laughed and said, Bopper's friend Carl just shot at my house. I better go so I can call the glass place and have these windows replaced before they close."

Snake said, "You don't sound too excited. You just got shot at and you sound as cool as a cucumber."

"Carl's not a very good shot," I said. "I'm surprised he hit the house. But, if I don't call back tomorrow, remember the guy's name is Carl."

Snake told me to be careful and hung up. I called the glass place and they were there by the time I had the broken glass cleaned up.
What bothered me most was I couldn't go by Carl's and shoot his windows out, because he lived with his mother.

Since I knew who it was I decided to get him back when it was convenient for me and when he wasn't expecting me. I figured the whole crew was at Bopper's house with their guns ready, looking out the window, waiting for me. The joke was on them. I let them wait.

When I called Snake the next day he was glad I wasn't dead. Snake was a great guy. All the bikers I knew personally were good people. They would do anything for you. And even though they were truly tough guys, they had hearts of gold. I can honestly say that my biker friends have more integrity than any attorney I have ever met.

No matter where I'm at or what I'm doing, if I see a biker in need I'm going to help him because I know in my heart he would not hesitate to help me.

Snake said, "Why don't you come down here for a couple of days. I've got a little problem you can help me workout and there is someone here who wants to see you. Hold on."

Lisa got on the phone and said, "May I speak to a Mr. Wizard, please?"

I could hear Snake in the background just busting a gut.

I said, "Why certainly, but wouldn't you rather talk to him in person?"

She agreed that she would and I hung up the phone, packed a bag and headed for Texas. On my way down, I stopped by my hidden storage and picked up a couple of things.

When I walked in the door of Snake's club Lisa ran over and jumped into my arms, wrapping her legs around my waist. I held her there as we kissed. People in the bar were clapping their hands for us. The scent of her peach shampoo floated in the air as she hugged me, then led me by the hand across the room to where Snake was sitting.

Just seeing her smile and smelling her peach shampoo brought joy to my heart and made me happier than words can express. From that day forward the smell of peaches always triggered my wonderful memories of Lisa. I used to call her my Mona Lisa, my beautiful work of art.

After we ordered I asked Lisa to hold out her hand over the table, palm up. I made a show of rubbing my left fist, then held it over her open hand and told her to say her favorite magic word.

Lisa said, "Shazam."

I laughed and dropped a diamond tennis bracelet in her hand. Why change a good trick, it worked great the first time.

Lisa loved it, she said, "You're my Wizard."

Snake said, "Is he a prestidigitator or a charlatan?"

It was my turn to laugh. Those were two words that I didn't think Snake would even know.

I said, "Oh, I'm a true Wizard. In fact, while we're eating I'm going to make something appear for you."

The people at the table raised their eyes with a look of interest. I merely smiled and dug into my food. When we completed our meals Snake held up his hands and said, "Well, where is it Wizard?"

I smiled and said, "You guys wait here. Snake, follow me to my truck and I'll show you."

Everyone watched us walk to the door with me smiling ear to ear. When we got to my truck I told Snake to step up on my back tire and look under the tarp in the back of my truck.

Snake looked and said, "Hot damn, you are a Wizard."

There were two brown cardboard barrels with blue plastic lids under the tarp. Anyone who knew anything about manufacturing meth knows a 110 pound drum of phenylacitic acid when they see one, or two. Snake had been unable to get any recently so I thought I would oblige him. That left me with eight more drums. Plus, I had two and a quarter thirty-five gallon drums of raw P2p and twelve gallons of distilled P2p. I could spare two drums.

I smiled and said, "That magic trick is going to cost you."

Snake couldn't believe I came through for him and he hadn't even asked. When we walked back in the door, Snake yelled, "He is the Wizard."

I gave Snake my keys so he could have his guy drop off the drums and the party began. When Snake and I went outside, I had retrieved my overnight bag from my truck. I had brought Lisa a soft, sexy little Teddy I wanted her to wear for me.

It was black with little pink and purple bows. While we were talking I told her I'd brought something for her and that it was in my bag. She grabbed my bag and took off to the ladies' room. When she came back out I almost fell out of my chair. She had put it on, then put her jeans back on to cover the bottom part. She had on her black leather jacket, her hair was fluffed up and she's put on red lipstick. I could see the front of the Teddy through the front of her open jacket.

She walked up to me and said, "It's the softest thing I have ever had against my skin."

It would have been impossible for me to love Lisa any more than I did at that moment. She meant more to me than life itself. That night we made passionate intense love then we made slow and tender love. I would have been happy to just hold her and look at her. While I laid there holding Lisa in my arms I said, "When you graduate, I hope you'll consider marrying me."

Lisa said, "For someone that Snake thinks is a genius, you're pretty dumb. Of course, I'll marry you. I love you with all my heart and soul. I would marry you today and live in a shack with a dirt floor if it would make you happy." I pulled her closer and said, "Don't you think I'm a genius?"

Lisa elbowed me in the ribs and said, "Yes. You're my genius, honey. Now shut up and go to sleep."

I wasn't finished, so I said, "You'll never have to live in a shack. By the time you graduate from college I'll be done with all the craziness I have going. I promise and you know I don't make promises lightly. I've already bought sixty acres in the country that has some nice big trees. I'll build you a little house." I fell asleep with my last words.

When Snake got there that morning I was cooking breakfast. I was making my Jeff's omelets extraordinaire. They consisted of anything I could find in a refrigerator that I thought was tasty. One time, I even cooked some ground up hamburger and made hamburger and cheese omelets.

After we ate I kissed Lisa and headed out with Snake. I told Snake that I asked Lisa to marry me after she graduated and that she said yes.

Snake said, "Good, this family needs a Wizard. Welcome aboard."

He was milking everything he could out of the Wizard nickname. I loved it.

The fact that Snake trusted me enough to take me to his lab took our relationship to another level. It made us more than brothers. Snake's lab was almost in downtown Dallas. It was on the top floor of a six story brick industrial building. There were other businesses on the lower floors. The top floor had its own loading dock and freight elevator. Definitely a nice setup. It didn't take me long to figure out what the problem was. The place was huge and far too open. There was no way to control the humidity, barometric pressure, or cooling, to the degree necessary to do the job correctly.

Snake had three, fifty-five gallon drums of used ether. One of which had the ether that hadn't produced any meth. I told Snake that, under these conditions there was a good chance all three drums still had meth in them. I explained what we needed and why. Then I made a list of the supplies I would need. Snake sent two of the guys that were working there to the lumber yard to pick things up. Snake and I went to an appliance store and bought a large chest type freezer and a window unit air conditioner. By the time we got back the other guys were there with the lumber. I then sent them for the final things I would need and got busy building a sixteen by sixteen foot room with an eight foot ceiling. The top floor of the building had twenty foot ceilings and it looked like a huge open warehouse. My new enclosure only took up one small corner. It took most of the day to get everything ready. We built the room, using sealer to bond it to the floor.

We used two by fours and plywood for the walls and roof, then covered the entire structure with heavy plastic and used duct tape to seal the edges.

I bought twenty new plastic five gallon cans. I filled ten of the cans with used either then gassed each one lowering the PH to five and a half. I put three in the freezer. I then made a funnel out of a ten feet long, four inch PVC pipe. I used wire to suspend one end of the pipe two feet off the floor and the other end I wired six feet off the floor. I made a filter out of a roll of paper towels to go in the low end, which I secured with wire, held on by small screws. With the pipe at that steep angle, I could pour most of a five gallon can of ether in the pipe at one time. With the ether coming right out of the freezer most of the moisture would be frozen to the cans. We would recover that ice and get meth out of it, as well. Any additional moisture would be trapped in the filter.

The air conditioner had the room about fifty degrees. Using Snake's ventilation system, that I slightly modified, I sealed the enclosure and pulled a vacuum on the room, lowering the barometric pressure inside our enclosure.

I was ready. I figured that each can of ether needed to sit in the freezer at least two hours and it would take an hour to run each can through the pipe. As I poured the ether in the top of the pipe Snake was waiting at the other end with another five gallon can that had a wire basket that contained a huge filter Like the ones used in industrial size coffee makers. As the ether started coming out of the low end of the pipe it looked like a pink strawberry milk shake, it was moisture free and heavy with pink meth.

It took us three days to complete the task and get everything cleaned up. When we were finished Snake had over fifty pounds of pink meth. I advised him not to dump the used ether in the city sewer system for fear of blowing up half of Dallas. His boys took it out and dumped it in an oil field tank, as I had in the past. Snake offered to give me half the load but I only took ten pounds.

He had also saved his waste water in four fifty-five gallon metal drums. I fixed a way for him to distill the whole drum at once, by sitting the drum on top of three concrete blocks and putting a propane burner under the drum for heat.

I used metal fittings on top of the drum, with a heavy rubber connection to a distilling condenser. The acitic anhydride cooked over at a lower temperature than water. We recovered almost twenty gallons from each drum, for a whopping eighty gallons of acitic anhydride. Snake was very pleased. My position as The Wizard had grown exponentially.

Snake said, "The way I'm looking at it you made me a half a million. What can I do for you?"

"Take care of Lisa for me,"

I added, "I am coming back to marry her."

I told Lisa I would see her for Christmas, apologized for not being able to make it for Thanksgiving and assured her that we would do something special for New Years. Lisa said, "Be careful Wizard. I love you." And I drove away.

CHAPTER TEN:

Tragedy

On the way back to Oklahoma, I had my stereo cranked listening to Flirt'n With Disaster by Molly Hatchet. It was exactly the way I felt. Daniel was tossed into the lion's den. I was walking right in on my own accord with hopes of being as fortunate as Daniel. Bopper was more than mad and he had already threatened to kill me. I had no doubt that if he could figure out a way to kill me, without getting caught, he would. I was going to have to be extra careful.

When I got home, Russell came by on his Harley. He told me that Bopper and Richard were hanging out at a girl's house in Okmulgee.

Russell said the girl was afraid of Bopper and scared to tell him to stay away. That made me mad.

I started watching the house and figuring out Bopper's routine.

Bopper was usually alone. But sometimes he would have Richard with him. Bopper would stay for hours and people would come by, obviously buying dope, throughout the night. I think Bopper was trying to show off for the girl, in hopes that she would have sex with him.

It wasn't working out. I could see through the window that she was watching television while Bopper made his deals. Bopper was parking behind the house in an alley. When he arrived, he would get out of his truck, look around, open the hood and then remove a small bag from the driver's side fender area.

One night it was storming real hard. Rain was pouring. I picked up Russell, got four cement blocks and two four-way lug wrenches and went to work. I parked my truck on the next block then Russell and I each put a four way lug wrench down the back of our pants and grabbed two blocks each. We walked between two houses, at 2:00 in the morning and slid a block behind each wheel, then removed all of the lug nuts from each tire. Then all we had to do was pull the top of the tire and the truck rested on the blocks. We worked the tires off and rolled them to my truck. I felt like they were mine anyway since they came from the tire shop I bought out.

I waited in the rain next to an outbuilding until Bopper came out.

He opened the hood of his truck and hid the bag on the driver's side. Up in the front corner. Then he got in the truck, started the engine and put it in gear. Nothing happened, so he gave it some gas. He then killed the engine and got out, saw his tires and wheels were missing and ran around the truck cussing a blue streak.   As soon as he went back in the house I ran to his truck and popped the hood. Using a small light, I looked in the corner, grabbed the bag he'd stashed, closed the hood and walked away. It was too funny. I'd put him afoot and got his money and dope all in one swoop. It was less than two thousand and a half ounce of my "pink" meth. That meant he was getting my meth from someone I was selling to in Tulsa.

I went to Tulsa and told my guy there part of the story on Bopper.

I described Bopper and what he drove. He knew who Bopper was and it was one of his guys that was selling to Bopper. My guy was obsessed with my Colt Python .357 magnum. The guy said, "If you'll sell me that gun, I'll make sure Bopper never buys another gram of dope in Tulsa, Oklahoma."

Parting with the gun was no problem for me. Revolvers were going out of style.

I sold him the pistol then bought a Mark V, long slide .45 magnum, automatic. It was almost too big to hold with one hand. I bought it mainly for show.

On Thanksgiving Day, I took one of Mom's homemade pumpkin pies and went to Mr.

Connor's house for Thanksgiving dinner. Mom was somewhat put out with me for not being there for Thanksgiving dinner, so I assured her that I would help her eat all the leftovers. Alice was wearing a pretty dress and had her hair fixed nice. The house smelled terrific. I helped in the kitchen, then ate so much I hurt. Alice and I washed the dishes then sat down to relax. I got the bag I'd brought in with me and pulled out a pin, notepad and a Sears catalog. I handed them to Alice and said, "I'm going to be doing most of my Christmas shopping at Sears, because they have gift wrapping. My gift wrapping sucked. I want you to look at the Sears catalog and make the biggest Christmas list ever. "If you want, you can pick a bunch of school clothes, so you can finish school next year. Or anything you want."

I didn't want to seem like I was pushing her, so I let it go at that. When I got ready to leave, I told her I'd be back the next week to pick up the list. I love Christmas, it's my absolute favorite time of year.

When I came back the next week to pick up the list, Alice had only written two things on her list. A work coat and hiking boots. The kind she might use to help her grandpa around the farm. I said, "Well that won't do. Let's all go to Tulsa and do some shopping. I'm in the Christmas spirit. Come on, we'll get grandpa a new pair of boots while we're there."

I took Alice and Mr. Connor to Mervyn's and Dillard's. We had a great time. Things started off a little slow. Then I picked out a little tiny outfit that was for a child and said, "Here, try this on." Then I picked a real big ugly shirt and said, "How about this?"

Alice smiled. She knew I was playing with her. I had the ladies working the clothes area help Alice get going. I had an idea that Alice was scared of going back to school, so I said, "This doesn't mean you have to go back to school. That is entirely up to you. I just want you to have some new nice things. This is fun for me and I want you to have fun. Let's buy some clothes, then go some place nice to eat. What do you think?"

Alice shook her pretty little head, "Yes," and the shopping began. Alice opened up just a little more that day and it made me feel great.

When I took them home we had the back of my truck full of all kinds of girly things. I even bought her the work coat and hiking boots and I later bought her four special Christmas presents and dropped them off before Christmas.

Things happen real fast around the holidays. One day it's Thanksgiving, then Christmas pops up and New Year's slaps you on the rear. Two days before Christmas I made my rounds delivering Christmas cheer. On Christmas Eve my mother and my sisters Susan and Jody and I drove to grandma's. On Christmas, about 3:00 in the morning the telephone rang. My mother answered the phone. It was her next door neighbor back in Henryetta, reporting the news that my mother's house had burned to the ground. We drove back to a smoking pile of ash. All of our childhood memories were gone, along with everything my mother and sisters owned. My mother held back her tears and said, "Oh, well. We needed new things anyway." Bless her heart.

My first thought was, Bopper. But why would he burn my mother's home, rather than mine. The fire investigators later determined that it was probably a faulty hot water heater. That still didn't make it any less of a tragedy.

We were very fortunate that I had a big enough old house to hold all of us.

The house actually belonged to my mother, who had bought it from a friend. I used to say that mom bought the house for me, in order to get me out of her hair. My mom wasn't like that. She did everything out of love. She worked very hard to make sure us kids didn't do without. We may not have had as much as some of the other kids in town, but we had something many of them didn't have, we had an abundance of unconditional love. I look back and wish I'd been a better son.

It wasn't hard for mom and my sisters to move in with me. All they had was their overnight bags they had taken to grandma's house. I moved all my stuff to the back bedroom. My little sister Jody slept with mom in the front bedroom and my sister Susan got the middle room. It was a perfect fit and it brought us all closer together. Mom had her phone transferred to my house and my little sister, Jody became my answering service.

I had already planned to have Christmas with mom, my sisters and grandma. Lisa was having Christmas with her parents. We were going to spend New Year's together. The day after Christmas I drove to Lisa's apartment in Texas.

There wasn't much I could do, at that time. Mom and my sisters needed some time to get settled. Lisa was waiting for me when I got there. She had dinner made, like a cute little housewife. Her best friend, Veronica had been living with her since she got the apartment, which I thought was great. They made a cute little team and were going to college together. That night we had the apartment to ourselves. We opened each other's Christmas presents, had dinner, made love and fell asleep in each other's arms.

The next morning, I told Lisa to pack a bag, because we had to hurry to the airport. All I would tell her was to bring enough warm clothes for four days. We flew from Dallas to Denver, then rented a four wheel drive Blazer and drove to Steamboat Springs. During the day we snow skied and swam in the hot springs. The hot springs had glass walls around it to block the wind and an open roof. The steam hung on the water in a foot thick cloud and huge snowflaks cascaded from the sky and melted as they hit the steam. I will always remember how pretty Lisa looked with steam up to her breasts and snowflakes in her hair. At night, we picked a different place to eat then went dancing. We would then go back to our lodge and make love in front of the fireplace. On New Year's we were at the lodge, halfway up the mountain, kissing at midnight when the fireworks started. Fireworks were going off above and below us, reflecting on the snow. It was a beautiful sight. Magical. When I looked in Lisa's eyes I had no doubt that she loved me. When we flew home we officially joined the mile high club.

At Snake's club Lisa told everyone about the trip and how I taught her to ski. She was as happy as I was.

I hated to leave the next day but I had to get back to mom and my other business. Mom had been having difficulty swallowing for some time. While I was gone it had gotten much worse. It was so bad that she finally had to go to the doctor, because she couldn't swallow. The doctor looked her over and sent her directly to an oncologist. Mom had cancer in her throat and stomach and they had no choice but to operate the following week. I didn't realize the gravity of the situation until I saw her come out of surgery.

At first, I was in shock, then as the days went by I went into denial. The best part was, mom could eat again and at first it looked like she was going to be fine. She never complained, not once. She was up moving around, cooking, cleaning, sewing and eating in no time, singing as she went.

A month went by and all looked well.

I stayed kind of close to home throughout that month, taking care of business, as usual. Some of my friends and I hauled off the remains of mom's burnt down house and cleaned the site, so a construction crew could start framing her new home. I was in the back yard working on a truck when my little sister came outside and told me I had a phone call. I'll always remember how pretty the day was. The leaves were starting to come out on the trees and the grass was turning green. I ran in the house and snatched up the phone.

Snake said, "Man, brother, I'm sorry to have to tell you this on the phone. Lisa was killed in a car accident. You need to come down. The funeral is Saturday. I'm sorry."

Once again, I was in shock and denial, all at once. I wanted to say it couldn't be, to tell him it must be a mistake or it was a sick cruel joke. All I said was, "I'm on the way."

On the way to Texas I was kind of in a trance. I stopped to buy a new suit.

I had told Lisa the story about me buying a new suit before I went to the chemical place and bought a truck load of chemicals.

She said she would like to see me in a suit someday. On the drive South I listened to the Eagles, Hotel California. We had jokingly agreed that when we died, we weren't going to Heaven, we were going to the Hotel California, because it had room service.

The song goes, "You can check in, but you can't ever leave." I hoped to meet Lisa there some day.

When I arrived at Snake's club there were at least fifty people there and no music was playing. Almost everyone in the place hugged me and said how sorry they were about Lisa. I was maintaining my composure fairly well. I just couldn't stop the flow of tears. I got Snake off to the side and asked him what happened. He had just gotten all the details himself. Lisa had left Snake's place, riding with one of her girlfriends. A drunk driver had fallen asleep at the wheel and ran into the side of the girl's car, forcing it off the road where it collided with a cement containment wall. Lisa wasn't wearing her seat belt and her beautiful little face was smashed through the windshield. She was ejected from the car. The doctor said she probably died instantly when she hit the windshield and her neck broke. All I could think about was that she didn't die instantly. I pictured her dying on the cold pavement, in the dark, all alone, as she cried out my name. Then Snake dropped the hammer and told me that Lisa was two months pregnant. The news couldn't have hit any harder if it would have been a real hammer.

I had gotten Lisa pregnant on our trip to Steamboat Springs. She must have been waiting to tell me until I came back to see her. I hadn't only lost Lisa, the love of my life, I had lost a child.

To get my mind on something else, Snake started telling me about all of the funeral arrangements. He and the family had taken care of everything and it was all the best. It was to be a closed casket, because of the facial damage. In a way, it hurt because I wouldn't get to see Lisa one more time, but in a way, it was a relief because I didn't know if I could take seeing her, lying there in a casket. If a broken heart could kill a man I would have surely dropped straight to the ground dead. I was crushed. I felt like it was my fault for not being there.

Snake felt like it was his fault. Lisa's best friend and roommate, Veronica, felt like it was her fault and Lisa's mother was blaming herself for not being a better mother, which wasn't true, she was a wonderful mother, even to me. It wasn't our fault. It was the drunk driver's fault for running them off the road and I was too upset to be mad at him.

Lisa and I were both big ZZ Top fans. Her song for me was Sharp Dressed Man and mine for her was Legs, of course. When I got in my truck and started the engine, Legs came on the radio and I lost it. Snake saw me, just sitting there crying and came over and climbed in the truck with me. When he heard the song, he reached over and turned off the radio.

With the music gone all I could hear was myself sobbing and I was embarrassed.

Snake said, "You want to come back in and have a drink or something?" It was obvious that asking me if I was okay would have been a dumb question.

I said, "No. If I start drinking now I may never quit."

I spent the night in Lisa's apartment. In her bed. As I laid there, I heard Veronica crying herself to sleep in the next room. The next morning, I took Veronica with me to the church for the service. I had Veronica on my left and Lisa's mother on my right. Snake was always close. Lisa was loved by many and there were at least a hundred people there for support and to look at the closed casket with Lisa's smiling picture sitting on top.

I walked by the casket and said, "I wore a suit for you, Lisa."

We had four limos for family. I rode to the burial with Lisa's mother and father.

Seeing Lisa's casket being lowered into the ground brought another flood of tears. It was the last time I saw Lisa's mother. I kissed her goodbye and left with Snake and Veronica. On the way back to the church, Snake told me that he had discussed it with Lisa's mother and if it was alright with me they wanted to give everything of Lisa's to Veronica. I thought it was a wonderful idea and said that's what Lisa would have wanted. I then added that I would pay another year's rent so Veronica would have a nice place to stay while in college. Like Lisa, Veronica was a good girl. Veronica rode with me back to her apartment. I walked down to the office and paid another year's rent and gave Veronica the receipt. Then I changed out of the suit, left it hanging in the bathroom and left. I didn't want to see that suit again, or Texas.

What does a man do when his life is shattered? He can either pick up the fragments and move on, or he can let it eat him up and kill him. I wasn't ready to die, I was too mad. But I wasn't ready to live either. I was stuck in the middle somewhere in my own personal purgatory.

I wasn't ready to go home yet either. My mother had enough problems without having to help me deal with mine. Mom had recently started her chemotherapy.

I stopped at my sixty acres in Pauls Valley and dug into my storage. I stored many things in that hole in the ground, including money, drugs, guns and personal items I didn't want to lose. Snake had given me a bag with pictures of me and Lisa in it and all of the jewelry I bought her. I gave the jewelry to Veronica before I left.

I wanted to look at all the pictures and store them in my secret safe place. I must have looked at the pictures a hundred times before I put them in a box and stored them away. As I sealed the entrance and buried it I felt like I was burying Lisa all over again.

I stayed the night with Mikey. We bought a few more cows the next day and had them delivered to his place. It helped keep my mind busy, as we rode around and smoked pot all day. I bought a lot of cows that summer.

I didn't feel like talking about it so I just kept it bottled up inside.

Without realizing it I started doing more drugs and taking bigger risks. I could mask my pain and hide behind drugs and not have to deal with the reality of things. It is a sorry way to live and it clouded my judgment.

Mom was losing weight and her hair. I was gone most of the time, so I didn't see how she suffered every day, without complaint. I still couldn't get over Lisa and reach some kind of new starting point. I kept remembering that old saying, that someone made a song from, "Only the good die young." Lisa was the good part of me.

Mom's new house started off nice. The contractor got the framing done, the roof on, the siding on and the windows in before he went bankrupt and stiffed mom on finishing the house. Mom had used the insurance money and paid him in advance. She didn't want to tell me, for fear that I might do something rash. The construction slowed down on the house. After the electrician installed the wiring and it was inspected, me and some of my friends put in all the insolation and hung all the sheetrock.

In the interval. I was just acting a fool.

One day Deena called me. I had just gotten out of the shower and she wanted to come by and see me. Someone dropped her off at my house and we went for a ride. We smoked some pot, got something to eat, (which is usually what I do after smoking pot), then did some meth and went to a motel that had whirlpool baths in the rooms. We played in bubbles for a while then we started having sex on the bed. It was the first time I'd been with a woman since Lisa died and I felt a little odd at first. Like I was betraying her memory. That saying that "Man has a brain, and a penis, but only enough blood to run one at a time," is certainly true. Once the penis takes over the brain goes on vacation.

Most generally an earthquake wouldn't stop me, but all of the sudden someone started pounding on the room door and the joy of sex went right out the window. It was Bopper, Carl, Wade and Floyd at the door yelling and banging. The only way they could have known that I was at that Motel, in that room was for Deena to have called them. Deena had set me up and she couldn't even look me in the eyes.

I started for the door with my .45 magnum in one hand and a 9mm thirteen shot automatic in the other and thought, "No, in order to make this seem at least a little legal, I needed to wait until they kick the door open." I had been betrayed by someone I trusted and it hurt, bad.

I put on a fake smile and said, "Methinks some skulduggery is afoot" in my best pirate voice. Then I said, seriously, "I'm sorry you're going to have to watch me shoot these guys. I'll try to just hit them in the legs." Then I calmly added, "You might want to get dressed."

After that there was a commotion outside in the hall and the idiots left.

One of the other guests must have called the front desk and complained about the noise. I finished dressing and took Deena home without another word. It seemed that there was no end to the lessons I kept learning. With knowledge and wisdom often comes sorrow. At first, I was mad at myself for not throwing open the motel door and shooting Bopper and his buddies. That would have been a stupid move and I was later glad that I didn't shoot them because tormenting them was far more fun.

While I was having dinner with mom and my two sisters that evening, Louisiana called. He told me that the Sons of Satan, the biker group I had sold the sixty pounds to, had started their own manufacturing operation and it wasn't going well. They were asking for assistance. I knew that the Sons of Satan were going through a power struggle and I was reluctant to get involved.

I knew that there had been some serious trouble between group members, which could make for a dangerous situation. The problem was, too many Indians wanted to be chief. The gang had basically split into two groups. One group was out of control and had even made the National news. The other group was trying to be more organized and business minded. The business minded group was the one I had already dealt with.

They had set up a lab in Nevada and they wanted me to come fix some problems they were having. I would be dealing with a guy called Bear, who was the guy I had done the previous exchange with. I needed some time to clear my head and get off the dope, so I agreed to call him.

When I called a girl answered the phone and said, "How may I help you?"

I thought that an odd way to answer the phone. I said, "Tell Bear that The Wizard is on the line."

Bear came on the line and said, "Hey, Wizard, I've been hoping you would call. I'm sorry to hear about your girl. Come up here for a few days and I'll help you take your mind off things."

That softened me up and I said, "I hear things aren't going too well for you and that you've been having some problems. Am I coming into a war zone?"

Bear said, "Hell, no. This is a party zone."

I told him I'd be there and he gave me directions to a club which was not too far from Las Vegas. I had sold most of my vehicles and I had wrecked my beloved Challenger. All I had left was the Chevy Laguna, my service truck, the black 1970 Chevy truck I bought from Snake and the black Lincoln I'd fixed up.

I wanted to drive something that wasn't in my name so I headed out in the Lincoln with its great air conditioner. Being in Nevada was a temporary thing for Bear, he was actually doing his thing in Indiana. I was glad to be going to Nevada, because I was hearing that the main trouble was in Indiana.

I drove to Las Vegas and rented a room for the night. I took my time the next morning asking questions about the best places to stay and eat. I was planning an escape route in case of an emergency. I rented a U-Store-It and backed the Lincoln in for safe keeping.

In the Lincoln was extra guns, money, meth and clothes. I called a taxi to take me to a car rental. All I took with me was my overnight bag that contained a new thirteen shot 9mm automatic, a change of clothes, my toiletries and a pound of pink meth.

When I pulled into the parking lot of the bar it was afternoon. The parking lot was full of nice cars and Harleys. I slipped on my shoulder holster and bomber jacket and went in to test the water. It looked like a nice crowd. A lot of pretty women. I went to the bar and ordered a long neck bud.

The bartender said, "It's a little warm for a jacket."

I replied, "It's a little hot everywhere I go. It looks like you have a lot of people in here who don't mind the heat."

I smiled and looked around at the many guys wearing jackets, of the heavy black leather variety.

I told the bartender, "I'm looking for Bear."

He said, "Most people hunt Bear up in the mountains. But you'll find a lot of good looking Beaver in here." He laughed and I smiled.

I said, "It would be helpful if someone would let Bear know that The Wizard is here."

The bartender said, "You don't look like a Wizard."

I said, "I hear that a lot."

Most of the places where I could sit with my back to the wall were already taken. Sitting at the bar with my back to the room was out of the question. Apparently, other people felt the same way. There were only two people sitting at the bar and they were girls. I walked as far away from the loud jukebox as I could and acted like I was watching two girls play pool. I was amazed at the number of pretty women in the place and at the number of big ugly guys. A few minutes passed and Bear came out of a back room with two girls on his heels. It seemed that the girls there came in pairs. Bear and I saw each other at the same time and I held up my beer in that, "Hey, there," fashion.

Bear yelled across the bar, "Hey, man, I'm glad you could make it."

Then he announced to the entire bar, "Hey, everybody this is my friend, The Wizard." So much for keeping things quiet. The sounds in the room increased and some of the girls waved.

Bear walked over and said, "It's alright, they just thought you were a cop, man."

Bear laughed and everyone close to us was laughing, as well. The tension in the bar dropped, some.

Bear said, "You still packing that big gun?"

I said, "I left the big gun at home. I didn't think I would need it. I brought a little one instead."

We went in a back room where Bear introduced me as The Wizard.

Everything was real laid back and I was starting to relax. Bear asked if I wanted another beer and I told him some food and ice tea would be better.

Bear said, "Cindy and Tina here will be taking care of you while you're here. Anything you need or want, just tell them and it will be taken care of immediately. Right girls?"

They both said, "That's right," in unison. They had to have practiced that and they took turns answering questions.

I asked Cindy, "Do all the girls around here travel in pairs?"

Cindy said, "It's safer that way. Some of the guys get a little out of hand when they're drunk. It's best to have an extra pair of hands to crack them on the head with a bottle. And we like to keep each other company, if you know what I mean."

I knew what she meant and it put a smile on my face. I told Bear, "I brought something with me but I didn't want to walk it through the front door."

While Cindy went to order the food, Tina showed me to a side door and walked with me to the car to get my bag. When we got to the car I opened the trunk and got my bag. Tina inched up real close to me and kissed me on the lips and said, "You know, anything you want means anything."

I was happy to hear that we were all on the same page. When we went back in I pulled out the pound of pink meth and laid it on the table.

Cheers went up around the room. While I ate the girls made lines on the table and the party was on.

There was a long line of house trailers behind the bar and several other old buildings. We all went to one of the nicer trailers where Bear showed me some brown meth and told me how much yield they were getting.

They were only getting a fourth of what it should have been. We agreed that I would go out the next day and see the set up and meet the guy who was making a mess of things.

I spent the night with Cindy and Tina and oh what a night it was.

They showed me some things I hadn't seen before. I was definitely impressed and was welcoming the direction things were heading.
Being with two beautiful, very horny women, at the same time, was inspirational. They were bendy, hot, wet and tight and I was loving every minute.

I was sorry to see the night end because I knew it was time to get to work.

CHAPTER ELEVEN:

Dreamer

Work came early. Bear got there at daylight and we headed into the desert, with only one stop for gas, where I also picked up some groceries. I wasn't going to get stuck out some place without my favorite foods.

We drove for an hour, then turned on what was nothing more than a dirt path to nowhere. I couldn't see anything but sand, rock and a few cacti. About a mile down the path we started veering around a small mesa. We traveled around the mesa and into a small valley that contained four house trailers and lots of small barn type buildings. The power lines came in from a different direction than we drove in and there were two windmills pumping water. It was very picturesque. There were many small trees dotted around the place. I was thinking that, although we could see the cops coming for miles, the cops would be able to see us leaving for miles and there was nowhere to run. I was hoping this didn't take long.

We drove to a small structure that was at the back of the little community. There were at least three dozen fifty five gallon drums lined up on the side of the building. They were a little too obvious for my liking.

Anyone that pulled up, or flew over, could see them. We knocked on the old barn door and a small insalubrious man, with a bald head, who hadn't had a shower in a week answered the door. Bear introduced him as

Fester. He was a rude little pus pocket of a man, so the name was fitting. I looked at Bear with a "save me" expression and pointed at the old man. Bear shook his head "No."

"Thank God, I thought. Mr. Fester didn't have enough wit about him to take a shower, care less manufacture methamphetamine. My point was proven when Bear later told me that it was Fester who made the brown meth.

Bear showed me around the barn. He had a lot of good chemicals to work with, but the set up was crude and dirty. I told Bear that "This will not do," meaning the nasty barn and asked to talk to the chemist. We drove back to the first house trailer and walked around to the back where a very pretty woman, about 35 years old, was taking a pot from a pottery kiln. I noticed a pottery wheel and dozens of prettily painted pots sitting on shelves on the back porch. The porch had a roof for shade but the sides were open to allow the breeze through. I later learned that she sold her pots in a store on pier 39 in San Francisco.

"These pots are really nice," I said.

She replied, "Thank you. I hope everyone likes them and buys a million of them. I'm Renee and my friends call me Dreamer. You must be The Wizard. You don't look like a Wizard."

"I get that a lot," I said. Then added, I left my pointy hat at home, looks can be deceiving."

Renee said, "You're not deceiving me, are you, Wizard?" She spoke with very proper English.

I said, "I don't have that nasty trait in me. I only want to be around people who I wouldn't have a reason to deceive. To do otherwise would be contrary to a happy, peaceful existence. I like keeping things simple."

Renee said, "I like you."

"Thank goodness," I said. "Because I'm hoping you will sell me some of your pots before I leave."

"And I hope you stay awhile," said Renee.

Bear said, "Dreamer is our new chemist."

"Oh, hell," I said. "I have strong reservations about getting a woman involved in the meth business. Especially the manufacturing end. It's against my moral code."

Renee said, "Every time you say something, I like you more. You should Know that I have worked around chemicals most of my life. My father owns a crop dusting service and I have a sizable investment in this already.

If I can't put this together, I will lose a considerable amount of money."

She had me there. I couldn't stand to see this nice woman lose her money. She assured me that it was only a temporary, one time deal and that the money she hoped to make would solve a problem she was experiencing. From the looks of things she had already spent fifty thousand on chemicals and equipment. It didn't dawn on me until later that she would not have known what equipment to purchase, or where to get the necessary equipment.

179

I explained everything that had to be done and it was a tall order.

First, the old guy, Fester, had to go and we had to remodel the inside of the barn.

Renee said, "We're all short on money at the moment."

"No problem," I said. "Once I'm in, I'm in all the way." I liked her honesty. Bear had sold a good portion of the pound I'd brought in one night. He gave me six thousand that morning and still owed me four. The barn wasn't large, so it wouldn't take much. Renee told me that the fifty five gallon drums were empty pesticide drums from her father's crop dusting business. She was saving them in case she came up with a use for them someday. I suggested that we move them to the back of the barn, out of sight. Then I suggested that when we were done, she might want to have Mr. Fester cut the tops off the drums, haul them to town and set up a sign, selling them for five dollars each, as trash cans. Anything to help.

We went to the barn and I measured the place and made a list of supplies I would need. Bear then went to town to rent a truck and buy the things I wanted. I also asked him to have someone follow him back with my rental car.

Renee looked in the bag of groceries I'd brought and laughed. She said, "Is this what you eat, hot dogs, cheese and Doritos? The only good thing you brought is the wheat bread."

"That's my favorite emergency food," I said. "I didn't know what I was getting into. It's always good to be prepared."

Renee said, "You're a regular Boy Scout. I like that about you and you're cute."

In my best Huckleberry Finn voice, I said, "Ah, shucks, ma'am, now you got me blush'n."

We shared a laugh and I said, "Come on Sugar Britches, we've got a P2p cook to start."

As we headed back out the door, Renee said, "I can't believe you called me 'Sugar Britches.'"

There was an overhang on the opposite side of the barn from the fifty-five gallon drums. Because I was going to be working on the inside of the barn, I moved the old lawn mowers and junk around so I could set up both of Renee's triple neck flasks under the overhang. I then measured and poured the chemicals in and got the heat turned on, using a heavy duty extension cord. Then I took the pump out of a water cooler and made a temporary cooling system for the condensers, using an ice chest. We added ice and I used water cooler line and some rubber tubing to connect the pump to the condensers to get the show on the road. By the time the chemicals came to a boil the condensers were ice cold.

I had to make boiling stones from a broken china plate, but they worked fine. I played with the heat until I had it perfect, then marked the dials so Renee would know where to put them every time. At that point, Renee could see how the boiling stones were moving up as they got hot at the bottom, then went back down, as they cooled towards the top of the mixture. It created a stirring action. She could see how the gasses went into the reflux condensers, then cooled three quarters of the way up and ran back down into the flask.

Together, we moved everything out of the barn. I didn't want to have to work around it as I remodeled the barn, or move the stuff two or three times as I worked. I hadn't noticed any other people and I was glad. I asked, "Where is everyone?"

"I'm it," she said.

She had a daughter who stayed with her mother, in town, close to her school. Her brothers and sister used to live in the other three trailers.

They all moved away and their trailer houses were used for storage.

She said she enjoyed being out there alone, but I could tell there was something more she didn't want to talk about.

I said, "We can't do anymore until they get back with the supplies. We'll have to add more ice later. Why don't we go cool off and eat some of those hot dogs?"

Renee said, "Yuck, not hot dogs."

I jokingly said, "What do you eat, foie gras?"

"Oh yuck," she said. "That's worse than hot dogs. What I want to eat is you."

I said, "This is getting better by the minute. Come on Sweet Cheeks, let's go to your place."

Renee said, "First you call me Sugar Britches, now Sweet Cheeks, you are quite the romantic."

We laughed together and walked back to her trailer. I couldn't help but like her, she was wonderful. She had an outside shower that only had cold water from the windmills.

I said, "That cold water is going to shock little Elvis, right into hiding."

Renee said, "You call your dick little Elvis?"

"Sure," I said. "But not because he's little."

I told her how little Elvis got his name, by singing "Love Me Tender," at night, when I was alone.

Renee got a kick out of that and wanted to know if I was taking LSD.

We stripped off and got in her outdoor shower. It wasn't as cold as I thought it would be and it was fun.

Renee said, "Don't worry, if Elvis shrinks, I know how to cure that problem."

I was too excited for Elvis to shrink, even if it would have been snowing. But just in case, Renee took me in her mouth and got me hard as a table leg, then led me to her bedroom. She wanted it slow and steady. She came twice before I blasted off and then we came together. Going slow drove me nuts, so I rolled her over and took her from behind. Going slow wasn't an option. I held on to her hips and gave it everything I had. When I came, she went with me and it took both of us to the outer limits. There is a reason why an orgasm is referred to as the "Little Death." We collapsed on the bed together, gasping for air.

As she caught her breath, Renee said, "Wow, shit, damn. Let's see, you are a Boy Scout, a Wizard, a carpenter and a hell of a lover, what else are you?"

"Like that's not enough," I said. " I'm also a mechanic. My hobby is restoring old muscle cars."

Then I told her the story about the girl that was married four times. The last time she was married to a mechanic, who tore it apart the first night and has been working on ever since. She laughed and I felt good about making her laugh. While we were eating she asked me if I wanted to tell her about what happened to my girlfriend. I told how Lisa died and about her being pregnant with my child. I asked her what her story was and she told me about an abusive husband that spent most of her money on that barn full of chemicals, then got himself killed in a drug deal. Bear was actually one of her Brothers. Renee and I were kindred spirits of a sort.

We finished eating then walked back to the barn to add more ice to the condenser water. I was explaining the purpose of each chemical and how they bonded, when we saw Bear coming in a truck, followed by two cars. We unloaded the supplies next to the barn door. Then Renee and I moved the chemicals and glassware out of the barn, I inventoried everything and made a list of the things I would need to get things rolling.

I gave the list to Bear and he took off to town.

We were going to have to make our own hydrogen chloride gas, using rock salt, hydrochloric acid and sulfuric acid. I needed rubber tubing, large coffee filter, more jars, plastic cans and a few other easy to obtain items.

Bear still had to get the rest of the things from my first list, as well. It was nothing hard to find.

Because ether was too difficult to obtain and highly flammable, I would be using trichloroethane as a solvent to powder the meth. It was nonflamable and had very little odor. I asked Bear to pick up four, five gallon cans of trichloroethane, which wasn't a controlled chemical, at that time.

Bear left and I got to work. I covered the floor in black plastic then I decked the floor with half inch plywood. I then stapled insulation on the walls, then stapled black plastic over the insulation and duct taped all the seams. I then covered all the walls with half inch plywood, covering all but one window, where I installed an air conditioner. Using plywood for the walls, rather than sheetrock, allowed me to screw things to the walls anyplace I wanted. I built L shaped work benches along two walls. Ran my power lines and hung four new florescent lights. Two over each side of the L shaped work benches. I cut a small hole through the wall, four by six inches, where I mounted a squirrel cage fan high on the wall. I wired the ventilation fan to a variable control switch, so I could regulate the ventilation speed. I then hauled everything back in the barn and organized it in the order needed, while Renee added more ice to the condenser water.

I was done by 5:00 a.m. Renee and I took another shower, had slow intense sex and fell asleep until Bear got there at 10:00 that morning. We walked to the barn and added more ice to the condenser water then had breakfast. As we unloaded the freezer, Bear asked me, "Are you diddling my little sister?"

I said, "Diddling, is not a very nice word."

Bear said, "You got a lot done in one night."

I smiled and said, "That's why they call me The Wizard."

After lunch, I turned the heat off on the P2p cook. By 1:00 p.m. I had the oil separated with lye water and by 2:00 p.m. I had everything moved inside to start distilling. We had the speed cook going by 7:00 p.m. That meant we had twelve hours to play.

I asked Renee what happened to the sixty pounds I'd sold Bear. It turned out that the sixty pounds was what caused the great divide in the biker group.

The two main leaders split the sixty pounds and only five pounds was actually Bear's.

Then there were several rip offs by lower level bikers, which got her husband killed and caused the loss of much of Bear's cut of the meth.

Renee saw the look on my face and said, "It wasn't your fault."

Renee made me a nice dinner of grilled chicken and rice, with pineapple.

It was delicious. We went to bed early so we could get better acquainted and we did.

The days start beautiful in the desert. Renee's little valley faced the East, so when the sun came up we could see it across miles of open desert sand. It was easy to see why she loved it there.

While we were distilling the speed oil I took the two big triple-neck flasks back outside and started two more P2p cooks, which gave us a six hour head start on the next batch. I had decided to stay a few more days because I didn't want Renee trying to handle things on her own. It just didn't seem right. As we worked I asked her where she got her nickname "Dreamer."

Her daddy had given it to her because she was constantly talking about all the wonderful things she was planning to do when she was grown. She asked me how I became "The Wizard," and I told her the story about Alice and Bopper and about my adventures in lab recoveries. I told her a little more about Lisa and Snake and how I'd turned his dope crystal white and recovered over fifty pounds for him.

Renee said, "You are a Wizard and a good man."

"Just like Lucky Charms," I said. "Magically delicious."

She said, "You don't like taking credit for the good things you do and you hide behind a mask of humor. That's a selfless quality that more men should have. Don't let the past stop you from having a future, Mr. Wizard."

Dreamer, my sweet, talented, mystic, hippy chick and wild desert flower had spoken words of verisimilitude, but in my mind, I didn't feel worthy.

Even though we didn't have a vacuum pump and we had to make our own hydrogen chloride gas, by 3:00 p.m. we had five and a half pounds of perfect meth and had everything cleaned up for the next round.

Renee called Bear to come get the meth. By the time Bear arrived I had another small list of needed supplies made for the lab and Renee and I were cleaned up, ready to go to town. We didn't stay long. We had a nice dinner, went to a movie and were back by midnight. Just like Cinderella.

Early the next morning we heard the unmistakable sound of two loud Harleys coming up the road. I was getting dressed, thinking it was Bear when Renee looked out the window and said, "Oh, shit. It's the bad guys, there's going to be trouble. These guys are crazy."

I said, "Stay in the house and call Bear, I'll take care of them."

The two bikers pulled up in front of Renee's trailer and got off their Harleys. Before they could step away from their Harleys I stepped out on the front porch and said, "You're not welcome here. Get back on your Harleys and leave." I had my gun in my hand, behind my leg.

One of the bikers said. "We've come to talk to the bitch."

That was a mistake. I pulled my gun up and fired three quick shots in front of their feet and said, "The lady doesn't want to talk to you, so leave and don't come back."

One of them said, "You'll regret this." "Not today," I said.

The other one said, "Are you The Wizard?"

"Today, I'm The Bad Man," I said. "You have two choices, die and be buried in this desert, or leave. What's it gonna be?"

One of them said, "You son-of-a-bitch."

Before he could say another word, I shot the ground next to his foot and it knocked the heel off his boot. It must have hurt bad, because he was dancing around, cussing. I'd actually missed. I was aiming for his foot.

I intended to blow a hole right through the top of his foot. I didn't like the implication about my mother.

Foot shot guy said, "I can't ride like this."

"I gave you two choices," I said. "So, you can either suck it up and ride, or die."

They rode away cussing. Renee came out and said, "Damn, you're scary as hell.

One minute we're in bed, the next minute you're shooting up the country side, like Clint Eastwood."

I said, "Was I really as good as Clint Eastwood?"

"Better," she said, laughing and giving me a hug.

By the time Bear got there with reinforcements, we had eaten and were ready for the day. Renee told the story about how her "Bad Man," The Wizard, had run off the two big mean men. It was funny, hearing her tell the story. Bear hung around there while Renee and I separated and distilled the second P2p cook and started the speed cook. I told Bear that I needed to pick up my car because I'd turned in the rental. I explained that I had more firepower in my car in case those two bikers got ignorant and came back with friends. Bear watched the place while Renee and I went to Las Vegas and picked up my Lincoln. Even though my Lincoln was older it was in perfect condition and looked nice.

We did some shopping, ate dinner and went back to her place where all was calm.

When we got to Renee's I opened the trunk and got my gun case and gym bag. In the trailer Bear and Renee were looking at the gun case like, "What the hell you got there?"

I put on my best Al Pacino voice and said, "You wanna meet my little frien'?"

I opened the case to reveal my customized Russian AK-47, with black nylon stock and scope set for one hundred yards. My long slide .45 magnum was in the case too, with extra loaded clips for each gun. I plucked out the AK and a thirty round clip from the case and walked out on the front porch with Bear and Renee hot on my tail. I slammed in the clip, jacked a round into the chamber, flipped the selector to full auto and let go about fifteen rounds at a rock a hundred yards down the road.

I said, "Weee!, now that's what separates the men from the boys.

That's how we do things in Oklahoma. If them fellers come back they will be in for a rude awakening.

They'll think they are in Vietnam. At a minimum, they will be walking home, 'cause I'm going to cut their Hogs in half."

Bear said, "Damn, I've got to get me one of those. You sure came prepared." "It's the Boy Scout in me,' I said.

Renee said, "He's my Boy Scout."

We had a good laugh, as I picked up my spent shell casings. The bikers were lucky that they didn't come back. While I was there I showed Renee how to use my 12 gauge pump riot shotgun and gave it to her for home protection. Renee didn't really like guns, but saw the necessity in them and felt better having one. I didn't want Renee taking meth and she didn't really want to either. I stayed long enough to process all the chemicals she had into meth.

When I finished, I'd made a little over thirty-four pounds of meth and used up all the chemicals. Renee had no reason to pursue things further.

I told her she should have the equipment and trash hauled away and use the barn for her pottery. I couldn't bare the thought of her getting in trouble or hurt. I like to believe that she listened to me. I didn't really want to go. I'd been there three weeks and really liked the peace and quiet of the place. Renee was a wonderful woman, who I cared for deeply and will always hold a special place in my heart. But I felt home calling. Seeing Renee wave goodbye to me from her porch was hard for me. If I could have seen into the future, just a little, I would have spent the rest of my life with Renee.

Bear gave me twenty thousand before I left. Ten for the pound I'd brought and ten for my trouble. Staying there with Renee sure wasn't trouble. At that point, I didn't care about the money, I just hoped Renee would be alright.

As I left, depression took over. I didn't want to leave Renee and thoughts of Lisa were flooding back. On top of that I was worried about my mother. As long as I was under pressure and working under the gun I could block out most of my worries. Alone, with nothing to do but drive, I was a mess. I stopped in Las Vegas to wash the dirt and sand from my old Lincoln. Looking around I saw all the people walking up and down the strip without a care and having fun. I thought, why not, I might as well enjoy myself while I'm here. I set myself a ten thousand limit and got a motel room for four days. I met a lot of people I thought were interesting and enjoyed the flashing lights and ringing bells. When I left, I had won three thousand and it had only taken me eight thousand to win the three thousand. HA! As my friend Larry would say, "That's why they call it gambling. If you won every time, they would call it stealing."

When I pulled into Henryetta things hadn't changed. I'd been gone a month and I expected something to be different. My customers were glad about my return, but for the most part, nobody realized I'd been gone. I'd been talking to mom on the phone regularly and she sounded fine, but when I walked in the door and saw my mother, my heart sank. She had lost her hair and was at least twenty pounds lighter. She was never a big woman. The loss of twenty pounds brought her down to frail.

As usual, mom said, "I'm alright. When life deals you lemons, you make lemonade." My way to deal with it was to not deal with it. I ran from it, hid my head in the clouds, did drugs and even drank some, which was unusual for me. I don't like alcohol. And I have never smoked a cigarette. I learned to run from pain and hide from the truth.

Many nights I went spot lighting deer with my friend Russell.

We would drink tequila, smoke pot and do meth. And ride through fields on little dirt bikes in the middle of the night. One night a deer jumped up in front of me and took off ahead of me. I fast drawed my pistol and shot that deer in the back of the head. That was all it took for Russel to start calling me The Wizard."

Escape from reality was the name of the game. I totaled my service truck one night after leaving Russell's house. I rolled it at least twice on Wilson road, which is the back way between Henryetta and Okmulgee. There was nobody there. I was alone and felt like I didn't matter. I walked five miles home without seeing another car. I called Russell and he and a friend of his, that had a wrecker, picked up my truck and towed it to Russell's house. The whole time Russell and I went deer hunting I only shot one deer. I don't like to kill things. Russell shot twelve that I knew about. I sold my Chevy Laguna to one of Russell's deer hunting buddies. I could have bought something else, but I enjoyed driving the Lincoln and my 1970 Chevy truck.

My pot connection in Stillwater got busted and was out on bond. He was short on cash and came to me with a deal. He and his new partner wanted to purchase a thousand pounds of high quality green bud. He showed me a sample of the pot and I was impressed. The load was three hundred thousand and they needed another one hundred thousand to do the deal. I would be the third partner, but I didn't have the cash.

However, I did have a lot of meth and I was more than ready to give up the meth in exchange for the pot. My pot connection called his guy in Arizona and told him that he had ten pounds of pure meth for one hundred thousand toward the pot deal. The guy in Arizona jumped on the opportunity.

I drove to my underground storage in Pauls Valley, got ten pounds of meth from my stash and took it to my pot connection. My pot guy was driving the money and meth to Arizona to make the deal. Our other partner was a wealthy man who lived in Okmulgee and owned a plane. He was flying to Arizona to pick up the load. My job was to meet him at the Okmulgee airport to unload and transport the marijuana. This would be one step closer to me getting out of the meth business, which I had grown to dislike greatly. I was going to sell the meth I had left and shut down that end of things. I had almost eighty thousand in cash, sixty acres and some cattle. It wasn't much to show for all my trouble, but I could make do with what I had. After all, I still had over forty pounds of meth and enough chemicals to make a small fortune. I wasn't in a hurry.

The night the plane was due to arrive I had a cargo van waiting at the airport.

Jimmy was with me and we were watching the sky for an approaching plane. It was late at night, so there wasn't much happening at the airport.

When the plane hit the runway it didn't even bounce. The struts broke, the wheels flew off in opposite directions and the plane belly flopped onto the runway with a horrendous crash and screech. The plane slid down the runway showering sparks in all directions. People ran out of buildings, jumped into vehicles and headed for the plane. I saw the pilot get out, as the plane ground to a halt, and take off running for the trees in the opposite direction from me. That was my cue to leave. I drove out of the airport and around to a side road, which was in the direction the pilot was heading. I drove slow calling his name out my window and Jimmy called his name out of the other window. I made one slow pass and couldn't risk another, because sirens and flashing lights were showing up on the scene. I had to leave or risk arrest. I was sure the pilot was okay. He was running like a bat out of hell as soon as his feet hit the runway. He had a substantial head start, so I figured he would get away.

One of the advantages of being a prominent citizen and wealthy is, when you tell the cops that you have no idea why your plane crashed on the runway with a load of pot, that it must have been stolen, they take you seriously.

Mother and I were watching the news together when the late breaking report came in about the plane crash and pot bust. The cops and media were having a blast laughing about dumb criminals.

Mom said, "What kind of idiot would load that much marijuana in such a small plane. Why didn't he make two trips?"

I thought, "What kind of idiot, indeed." I sure couldn't tell her that I was one of the idiots. What made it even worse, I had been around small planes most of my life. I should have known better, but it didn't dawn on me until after the crash, that the load limit on that size plane was about half of what he was trying to carry. It was a wonder the plane got off the ground in Arizona. Needless to say, we were all three out of the pot business.

It seems like dumb things come in bunches. This girl I knew, Jan, had a friend in Florida that was in the pot business. I'd known Jan for years, had gotten high with her on many occasions and thought she was a reputable person. Jan heard that I was looking to buy some pounds of marijuana and she gave me a call. She said that if I would pay for her trip, she would go to Florida and bring back as much pot as I wanted. She would fly down, rent a car and come right back. I knew she had done the same thing for other people in the past, so I agreed to give it a try. She called Florida and got a price on twenty pounds. It was a good deal, so I gave her the money, plus a thousand for expenses. I was also going to give her a pound when she got back. Funny thing was, Jan didn't come back. She stayed in Florida and kept my money. The only consolation I had was, I hadn't given her enough money to buy one hundred pounds. I still felt like the biggest dumb ass in the continental United States, but what was that chunk of money, in comparison to what I'd pissed away already.

I had worked my rear off, obviously helping many people along the way, which I will never regret and only had sixty acres, some cows and a hole in the ground full of chemicals and meth to show for it. I was at the point where it was either manufacture and sell meth, or get an honest job.

I should have gotten an honest job.

I was a fool for not going back to Nevada and trying to make a life with Renee. We could have had a great life together.

CHAPTER TWELVE:

Sunshine

Because of the benevolent arrangement of things, we have more light in our lives than darkness. We see the sun coming long before it actually appears on the horizon, bringing warmth and life. Biblically, light represents good and darkness represents evil. I was spending too much time in the dark looking for a ray of sunshine. The darkness in my life was enveloping the sunshine. I'd had too many tragedies and unfortunate events. I felt that God knew I was on the edge, that is why he gave me a ray of sunshine before I had to deal with my next tragedy.

The holiday season, which had been my favorite time of year, was a cruel joke. I hadn't even noticed the leaves on the trees changing colors.

Having Thanksgiving with mom and my sisters was almost more than I could bare. Mom looked worse than ever. With every bite of food, I was choking back tears. Mom acted like all was fine. I didn't see any possible way she could lose any more weight. I left after we ate and put my head back in the clouds.

On Christmas, I went to see Alice and Mr. Connor. My mother had taken a bad turn, but she was holding on. I was visibly depressed and I had lost weight, as well.

Mr. Connor said a prayer that included my mother and I had to stifle my sobs and wipe the tears from my eyes.

Alice said, "I'm sorry your mother is ill."

I was dumb struck. It was the first time I'd heard Alice speak. Her voice sounded as lovely as I'd imagined it would. It had been almost two years since Alice had spoken.

God had given me my ray of sunshine. I said, "Thank you Alice. And I am thankful that you finally decided to talk to me. I was starting to think you didn't like me."

"I like you," Alice said, with a smile. My heart lifted with joy and eating became much easier. We all had smiles and I ate too much, again. We opened presents, then I headed home. I was feeling pretty good. Alice didn't say anything else that night, she didn't need to, her smile said the rest.

I had learned that Bopper's friend Wade went into the chop shop business. I knew that Wade had stolen and stripped a new blue Ford truck and a yellow Camaro. I was still mad at Carl and Wade for siding with Bopper. It showed me their lack of moral character. Wade, on the surface, looked like a nice young man. He was the antithesis of Bopper. Looks can fool you. Even Hitler looked nice when he was young. I didn't have any respect for a thief who steals from honest hard working people.

It made me mad. I had taken things from Bopper, but not for personal gain and he most certainly wasn't an honest hard working man.

Wade was a classic example of how you can sprinkle sugar on shit and make it look pretty, but it still doesn't smell or taste good.

On New Year's Eve, I found out that Wade had stolen a new white Dodge Ram truck and I was told where it was hidden. I was faced with some options. I could have reported it, but it is not in my nature to call the police. I'm the kind of guy who believes in that bumper sticker that says, "If you need help, call a Hippie." I could have simply ignored the matter. But I chose to stick my nose in and rub it in Wade's face. In my defense, I wasn't thinking very clear and I didn't know that Wade's step-dad was a local district attorney.

I had Jimmy drop me off close to the location of the stolen Dodge.

I had my trusty tool bag with me, but it turned out I didn't need any tools. The key to the Dodge was in the ignition. It was like divine providence. Taking it was meant to be, so I drove it away. I was having fun breaking one of the cardinal rules of the drug business, which is, never have anything stolen. Stolen property is easily traced and will get a person busted faster than the dope will. The kind of people who deal in stolen property are likely to sell you something, then come back and steal it from you. There is no honor among thieves. That saying is an old myth. Honor among thieves is a fallacy.

I took the stolen Dodge to Preston, Oklahoma, to an out-of-the-way shop my friend Russell rented. I spent New Year's night, alone, stripping the Dodge. Before daylight, I drove out and dumped the hull of the Dodge in the river. I took the front fenders, hood, grill and bumpers to my place for storage. Then I took the motor and transmission to my friend in Tulsa to put in his Plymouth Cuda. After I dropped the tires and wheels off with a guy who owned a motorcycle salvage, I was back at the shop my 8:00 a.m. to cut the frame up and haul it away.

While I was gone Russell's brother dragged the frame out of the building. The frame was sitting outside for all to see. What I didn't know was, the day before, Russell's brother had walked next door and stolen two cement blocks from under the next door neighbor's trash cans. The man's wife had witnessed the theft and called the police. When the police showed up, while I was gone, the frame was already outside. The police saw the new clean frame and recognized it for what it was. The police took pictures of the frame, wrote down the serial number and questioned Russell's brother. Of course, Russell's brother told the police that the frame belonged to me.

Russell showed up when I was about to cut the frame up and haul it away. He told me the news and said that the sheriff told Russell's brother not to move the frame.

It was too late to be mad. I was going to cut the frame up anyway and move it real fast, but Russell was worried about the warning from the police. Russell's brother had gotten me busted over two stolen cement blocks and by pulling the frame outside.

It's the drugged out idiots that will get you busted every time.

When I heard it was Tim Newsome in charge of the investigation, I thought, "Maybe I can buy my way out of this." While Russell and his brother sat there listening I called deputy Newsome and told him that I'd heard he had a building for lease in Beggs, Oklahoma. He said he did, but it had just been leased. He asked who I was and when I told him he wanted to know where I was.

I said, "I'm fixing to go eat some chicken. Why don't you join me."

He said he would and when I met him he had a lady assistant district attorney with him, which was not a good sign.

The conversation started with a question about the frame. I had my story ready. I told them that I had been traveling the old Beggs highway, between Beggs and Preston, New Year's night when I came around a curve and there was that truck frame in the middle of the road. I had barely missed it myself. Thinking of the safety of others I had used a chain and come-along to load the frame on my truck and haul it to my friend's shop, that wasn't far from the potential accident. It was my civic duty not to let someone else get injured. It was as good a plausible lie as any.

At the time, the frame hadn't come back stolen, so I was in luck, temporarily. When the assistant district attorney lady went to the restroom I explained that I needed the problem to go away and showed Mr. Newsome an envelope full of money. He said it was too late to handle it that way.

I thought we were done but the assistant district attorney lady told me that she had a question about a statement that was made against me.

She showed me a signed statement from Wade that said he personally witnessed me steal and strip a blue Ford truck and a yellow

Camaro. (which wasn't true). Wade added that I was manufacturing and selling him meth, which was partly not true. I wasn't selling Wade anything.

I said, "It sounds like Wade has gotten himself in trouble and he's trying to blame his problems on me."

The DA lady then laid a statement on the table from Bopper that accused me of breaking into his house and stealing his freezer. He accused me of stealing his Charger, boat and the tires and wheel from his truck. Then the clencher, Bopper accused me of manufacturing and selling him meth.

I said, "Me and Bopper's been feuding for a long time, you know that.

I'm surprised he didn't accuse me of dirtying his underwear."

There was a statement from some girl I didn't know and one from Bopper's friend Richard, both accusing me of manufacturing and selling meth. I said, "Those are Bopper's friends. That's just more of Bopper plotting against me."

The fifth and final statement was from Russell's brother. He told them that I had stripped the Dodge Ram in his shop New Year's night and that he had pulled the frame outside, not knowing it was stolen.

I said, "Did you ask him where he was when this supposedly took place? He was not at the shop. I'm thinking that he saw that frame and just thought I stripped something."

My answer was lame and they both knew I was lying.

Because the frame number hadn't come back as stolen, yet, they said they would get back with me and left. I knew I was in deep shit and it just added to my depression.

A few days later my mother was admitted to Saint Frances hospital in Tulsa, Oklahoma, where I will always remember the nurses being so kind. The chemotherapy, that had saved the lives of countless people, was too much for my mother. It had caused her kidneys and liver to stop functioning. My mother was dying and all I could do was watch. I felt useless, hopeless and worthless.

My Junior High School sweetheart, Darlene, lived near the hospital.

I stayed with Darlene, going back and forth to the hospital until mom died.

The last thing my mother said to me was, "I'll be alright."

I broke down and left the hospital. Mom died two hours later, while I wasn't there. I regret not being there when she died. I will always remember my mother saying, "Jeff, there are two kinds of people in this world. Rich and good looking. Aren't you glad you're good looking?"

Mom never got to live in her new home. It still lacked carpet and kitchen cabinets when she died.

I also regret not going back to Darlene that day. She was so sweet and understanding and I feel bad not having the opportunity to tell her thank you and to let her know that I care. Darlene didn't have it easy in life either and I wish I would have at least been a better friend. My mother and I were very close. She raised me with the help of my grandparents. My mother's death was a hard time for me and I was thankful that my three uncles took care of the funeral arrangements. I didn't come home until the day of the funeral. I put on my suit and went to the services alone, driving my mother's little car. My Lincoln was at Russell's and my old truck was at Jimmy's house. The church was packed with people from all over. My mother had a lot of friends. Mom looked pretty and peaceful and not in pain, which was my only consolation. Uncle Ronnie pointed out that the wood grain on the coffin lid was shaped like an owl. Mom would have liked that. She always tried to find the beauty in everything. The girl that sang at the church had such a lovely voice. When she started singing I started crying. I couldn't help it. It tried not to, but it didn't work.

When we walked out of the church, behind my mother's coffin, I saw deputy sheriff Tim Newsome's big silver Cadillac sitting across the road.

I knew why he was there. To avoid a scene, I walked across the road and got in his car, where he put the handcuffs on me.

Newsome said, "Boy, you're just like Coca-Cola, you're everywhere I've been. I would show up some place looking for you and you'd just left." He thought he was funny.

I didn't say anything. I was mad, hurt and embarrassed. My uncle Ronnie walked over to Mr. Newsome's car and asked if he could take me to the burial and said he would bring me back. Mr. Newsome declined and pulled away. I didn't get to go to my mother's burial, which was another bad mark against me in life. It added insult to injury and caused me to be even more depressed.

I was charged with many things, including motor vehicle theft, knowingly concealing stolen property (the truck parts) and manufacturing and selling methamphetamine. The district attorney, based on the multiple charges and on a comment by Mr. Newsome that
I had threatened a witness, set a rather large bond. I only had the money in my pocket. What other money I had, that I hadn't blown, was buried in my underground storage. I was effectively broke.

My three uncles, who had always set good examples for me when I was a child, came to see me in the county jail. They informed me that they were not going to make my bond.

Uncle Dewayne told me to, "Say, yes sir and no sir and show these people some respect."

It was another one of those crucial turning points in my life. I knew my uncle could have easily made my bond and taken me home with him and put me to work in his construction business. But he chose to wash his hands of me, which was the same as saying that I wasn't worthy. That added to my depression and I didn't feel worthy. I was left to deal with my pain and suffering on my own, sitting in a jail cell.

I apologized to my uncles for the inconvenience and for making such a mess of my life. I also reminded them that I hadn't asked anyone to make my bond and I thanked them for coming. My uncles are honest men, who would always tell me what was on their minds. I appreciate that fact and I was glad they took the time to come tell me how they felt, rather than just letting me sit there and wonder.

Some of my friends were going to post my bond, but the district attorney had my bond raised, by arguing that I was a threat to society and a danger to the community.

He also told my sister that he would have my bond raised again if I tried to post bond. My sister Susan and I discussed it and I decided that making bond was hopeless and probably not in my best interest. I would have undoubtedly done something incredibly stupid at that point in my life. I didn't think that I deserved to be out. I had been making an absolute fool of myself ever since Lisa died. When mom died it took everything I had left out of me.

When my sister Susan sent my mother's Bible to me, my mother's marker was in Ezekiel, where it talks about Heaven. I knew then that mom knew she was dying and she had been getting ready for it, without a complaint.

Tim Newsome had convinced the district attorney to file the additional charges on me and to keep me in a maximum security lockdown cell so he could put pressure on me and get me to talk. They were hoping that I would admit everything, telling on myself and others and then plead guilty to all the charges. It didn't work.

I spent my time reading and working out in my tiny cell. When the elevator would "Ding," announcing its arrival, thinking that it might be Tim Newsome on his way to see me and it often was, I would start doing pushups. I was acting like jail wasn't bothering me a bit and it wasn't.

I was lost in thoughts of Lisa and my mother. Jail was just incidental to everything else. I was dreaming about being back in the desert with Renee.

Because the county jail wouldn't let me wear my boots I had been barefoot for a month. I didn't think much of it, because it was nothing compared to what my mother had to endure. A wonderful girl I knew, Kelly, came to visit me and noticed I didn't have any shoes. She bought a new pair of tennis shoes and brought them to the jail for me. Kelly was very sweet. She came to visit and wrote me often. Like a fool I messed that relationship up too. Only I did it on purpose because I didn't feel good enough for her. I gave her a reason to break up with me so it would be my fault when we broke up, but that came later.

When Easter came my sister Susan made enough cupcakes, cookies and colored eggs for the whole jail. The people from the local church brought them in to all of the prisoners. It was quite a treat. On my birthday, my sister sent in more treats for the whole jail.

Because I refused to cooperate or plead guilty, we proceeded to jury trial. Prior to trial, the district attorney dismissed the drug charges. There was no evidence to support them. The powers that be were just hoping that I would be dumb enough to admit them and to plead guilty to them.

By the time the trial arrived I had been in the maximum security lockdown cell for six months.

We selected a jury for the short trial and the State presented its evidence.

The State was not allowed to present any testimony about the meth because those charges had been dismissed. Deputy Newsome testified that he had met with me at the chicken place and that I had admitted that I was responsible for the truck frame, not my friend Russell. Russell's brother, who had stolen the two cement blocks that brought the police to the scene, testified that I came by in the white Dodge Ram and asked to use the shop to install a new stereo. He said that when he came back to the shop the next day, the frame was in the shop floor so he pulled it outside.

The man who owned the motorcycle salvage testified that I'd offered to sell him parts from the Dodge Ram. He neglected to mention that he had actually bought the tires and wheels. Finally, another officer testified that they found the fenders, hood, grill and bumpers from the Dodge Ram under my house in a storage area. In the end, the jury convicted me of knowingly concealing stolen property and I was sentenced to four years imprisonment. Tim Newsome and the district attorney were perturbed because I wouldn't cooperate or plead guilty so they protested any type of probation or parole and I was sent to prison, on my first offense.

After my somewhat unpleasant stay in the Okmulgee County Jail, I did most of my time at a work center in Oklahoma City and one in Lawton, Oklahoma. In both places I worked in the maintenance departments and had a perfect conduct record. It took me eighteen months, with earned good time, to discharge my four year sentence.

Upon my release, I stayed with my grandparents for a short while.

I drove my mother's yellow Mustang II. My Lincoln was gone and my old Chevy truck was in bad shape. Kelly came to see me and I messed up that relationship, on purpose. She was a nice girl. I was pretty down on myself and didn't have a real job. I was back doing odd jobs and service work, only I didn't have a truck or enough tools to do much.

Elmore City, where my grandparents lived, was a real small town with little work available. The people in Elmore City are great and I loved the town and being close to my grandparents.

I met a girl in Ada, Oklahoma, Shawyn, who worked for my uncle Max at one of his video stores. She was shy at first and bashful. Shawyn was pretty and lonely, like me so we started seeing each other. I went to a local mechanic shop in Ada and told the owner that I'd been in some trouble and had come to Ada looking for a job and to get away from my past. He put me to work

That day I moved in with Shawyn. I was bound and determined never to use or be around drugs again. Shawyn didn't do drugs and I didn't know anyone in Ada that did.

Things went well for a year. Shawyn and I were relatively happy. Not as happy as I had been with Lisa or Renee, but I was happy living a simple life. Shawyn wasn't Lisa or Renee, but she was special to me.

One afternoon, my boss took me and my coworkers to eat pizza.

One of my coworkers was bad mouthing people in prison.

I said, "Not all people who go to prison are bad. I spent eighteen months in prison before I moved to Ada."

Everyone got quiet and ate their pizza. I thought that, after working around me for a year, they should know that I wasn't a bad person. But that is not the way it works when you are dealing with simple minded bigots. The day after the pizza party my boss fired me. I hadn't done anything wrong, other than making the mistake of being truthful.

I would have been much better off if I would have just kept my mouth shut. I told him I'd been in trouble before he'd hired me. I didn't understand how someone I'd been around for a year could just shit on me like that.

I wasn't independently wealthy. My livelihood depended on me having a job.

I didn't have anyone to help me, I was on my own. I went job hunting and ended up in the unemployment line. To me, there is nothing more degrading than the unemployment line. It was a matter of pride and it was depressing. My past had come back to haunt me.

I had been working since I was a child. I picked up pecans with my grandmother when I was a child in order to help buy my school clothes.

As I got older I worked with my grandmother in a restaurant, washing dishes and I worked with my grandfather restoring old cars.

When I got bigger I worked with my uncle Dewayne in the construction business. I was certainly no stranger to work and I was ready to work. I could not find a job.

Up until that point, I hadn't even considered digging up my stash.

My friend Mikey and I sold twenty cows and split the proceeds so I wouldn't be completely broke. It felt good to have a little cash in my pocket and I vowed not to be broke again. I started my road service, doing twenty four hour on the spot repairs and things were slowly starting to get better. In order to run a business a man needs equipment and I didn't have much. I decided to dig into my storage and get the money I had stashed there. It had been almost three years since I'd been in either of my storage places.

When I got to Pauls Valley I stopped by my friend Kevin's house to say hello.

After I determined that there was no one around I went to my sixty acres and dug into my secret storage. Long before I was arrested, I had given Kevin enough money to pay the taxes for five years. At that point, I planned to transfer the land into my name. All looked well when I pulled into the trees to hide my truck while I was working. The sun was shining and birds were twittering around in the trees. I was day dreaming about building a small home on the place and starting a garden, that small piece of land and a bunch of cows was pretty much all I had.

As I was uncovering the entrance I detected a chemical smell. There should have been no smell, everything was sealed. When I opened the door a cloud of toxic vapors escaped, burning my eyes and taking my breath away. I quickly got up wind from the fumes, caught my breath then angled myself for a closer look with my light. What I saw broke my heart. At some point the heavy rains had partially flooded my storage. The cardboard boxes had gotten wet then collapsed, causing many of the glass gallon jugs of chemicals to break. The several different types of acids had formed a corrosive mixture. Fortunately, most everything had soaked into the ground, over time. My clever storage was mostly a clay hole in the ground lined with heavy wood. The clay didn't allow the rain water to soak in fast enough to keep it from flooding.

There was no way to touch anything in the mix without running the risk of a chemical burn. I went to Walmart and bought rubber wading boots, rubber gloves, cleaning supplies, water cans, trash bags and two wash tubs. I had a big mess to clean up in order to see if anything could be salvaged. I filled four new five gallon water cans and went back to the storage. I had to start at the front and work my way back. The acids had eaten the cardboard and it was mixed with broken glass. I picked the unbroken glassware and jugs of chemicals from the top of the mess then shoveled the muck into five gallon buckets.

Every time I brought something out I would take the time to wash it, rinse and dry it, then mark it with a grease pencil to identify its content for inventory purposes.

The labels were mostly eaten off but I knew what was in the jugs. Because I had to hold my breath while in the hole I obviously couldn't stay in there long.

The acidic chemical mixture was so stout that it had eaten the bottoms off the ether cans and many of the plastic storage containers that were not designed to hold chemicals. The plastic storage containers I'd used for my personal effects were just melted heaps of muck. I was dragging them out as I came to them and bagging it up as trash.

When I came to the container that held Lisa's pictures and my money my heart sank. What was left of the container held unidentifiable muck.

It broke my heart. Those pictures and my memories were all I had left of Lisa.

The container that held the forty pounds of meth was in no better condition.

The meth was gone. The three plastic thirty five gallon drums that contained the raw
P2p still stood in the corner. Those drums were made to hold chemicals. I had gotten lucky there. However, the glass gallon jugs of distilled P2p hadn't made it and four of the 110 pound drums of phenylacetic acid had perished, as well. I had four and a half more drums in the other storage.

I had built a shelf high on the back wall to hold my guns. Four of the guns I had in zip-up carry pouches were ruined, from the fumes. The guns I had in hard plastic carrying cases made it okay. The cases were ruined, even though they only came in contact with the fumes.

What I cared about most, the pictures and money were gone. I didn't have any meth to sell, but I still had enough chemicals to make a lot more meth. Nature, and the chemicals themselves, had reduced my five million supply of chemicals, to maybe one million. I could live with that and be done with the meth business.

I didn't want to haul the chemicals far, so I decided to use an old ravine I knew about for a temporary makeshift lab. I laid limbs over the top of the ravine, tied them together with rope then covered that with an old Army tarp. I then spread dirt, leaves and a few sticks on top to camouflage my hidden makeshift lab. I took a shovel and squared the walls making a level dirt floor. I used some 1 X 12s and 2X 4s to make some shelves and a floor. I hauled the chemicals, glass ware, propane bottle, ice chests full of ice and other necessities into my hidey-hole and started a meth cook. I had the cook going and everything organized before dark. I was shaping a rubber plug when one side of the dirt wall and roof collapsed.

I was buried alive. My legs were pinned by the fallen limbs. And they hurt bad. My upper body was pinned against the opposite wall. I could not see anything. I could move my arms around in the small area. I heard the gas spewing out of the line going to the propane tank. Luckily, I could feel the propane bottle. I found the knob and shut off the propane. I felt around for anything I could use to dig my way out. I found a roll of duct tape and a broken boiling flask. I used some tape to wrap around part of the broken glass then proceeded to cutting the ropes that bound the limbs together. About the time I thought I would suffocate, I was able to push two of the limbs apart a few inches.

I then cut the tarp. Dirt fell in for a moment then I could feel fresh air. I was not out yet but I had hope. I kept cutting ropes and the tarp until I could move more limbs and get my legs free. A short time later I could tell the sun was coming up. Light was coming through the places I cut free.

When I pushed my way through the opening I was so thankful I was alive I just sat there for a bit. I dug my ice chest out and the propane heater. I then cooked myself two hot dogs with cheese and mustard while thinking about how close I'd come to death. From my own stupid mistakes.

I moved the remainder of the chemicals to the lab I had designed and built years before. Which I should have done in the first place. Everything was in order and all I had to do was dust. The lab was small, but that's what I wanted. In comparison to the amount of chemicals I had, the leftovers were embarrassingly pitiful.

I went back to my storage place and hauled all the trash away. I buried the entrance and later caved in the roof with a backhoe and filled in the hole.

The following weekend I went to my other underground storage, which was in far better condition. I got the supplies I would need to turn some of the P2p I had into crystal white meth. I was going to be powdering without a vacuum pump because mine had been ruined by the chemical spill. That wasn't too big of a setback. The setback came when I was about to turn down the road to my hidden lab. There was an oil well on the property and a crew had brought in equipment and was working on the well. I wasn't going to be able to use the lab I'd built for a while.

I turned around and drove back to Ada where I placed the chemicals and equipment I'd brought in the cellar of the house I'd rented. Later that night I drove back to the lab and brought out enough undistilled P2p and other things I'd need to make ten pounds of meth. I had to time everything so I could work in the cellar while my girlfriend Shawyn was either asleep or at work. It took me six days and I had nine and a half pounds of meth. I then moved the equipment back to the lab I'd built.

At first, I only sold to my friend Kevin, who had been selling meth for a guy named Tommy. But Tommy was on his way to prison in Texas. I'd sold Tommy a truck and he knew who I was, so he asked me to hold on to his lab and chemicals while he was gone. I felt sorry for him so I agreed. I also sent him two hundred a month while he was in prison, because he didn't have anyone else he could trust. Tommy wasn't a real good guy. He wasn't very good at making meth and he had a reputation of doing people wrong. That didn't stop me from feeling sorry for him. Kevin warned me, more than once, that Tommy would screw me over if he got the chance. I wasn't going to give him a chance.

I started selling a little meth to my old friend Russell and a few other people I used to know. One thing I was adamant about was not selling any meth in Ada. It would be too much like shitting in my back door. I didn't want any local police problems.

As the money came in I was slowly buying tools and equipment and fixing up my service truck so I would be set to get away from the meth business. I was also buying a few cars and trucks and fixing them up for resale. I wasn't going to be in the meth business long, I just needed a little nest egg.

One weekend I went to Henryetta to see my sisters. They were living in mom's house. While I was in prison my sister Susan had sold my old house and used the money to finish mom's house. It looked nice and I was happy that my sister Susan, her husband and my little sister Jody had a nice place of their own. It would have made mom happy to see the house finished and them living there. I was planning to build a similar small home on my sixty acres.

We had a nice dinner and I told my sister Susan that I had to go see Russell before it got late. She didn't care for Russell, in general, but most of it was based on what Russell's brother had done to me. Susan warned me that if I was doing things I shouldn't be doing, I had better quit before I ended up in prison again. I don't lie to my sister, rather than say I wasn't doing anything I told her not to worry and kissed her bye.

I dropped some meth off at Russell's but I didn't stay long. He had several doped up idiots hanging around working on motorcycles.

I then drove to Mr. Connor's convenience store. Alice had finished school while I was gone and was working in the nice little convenience store. Mr. Connor had aged a lot, but he was still his energetic self. They both greeted me with open arms and wonderful warm smiles. Alice had grown into a beautiful young woman. She still didn't talk much, but she had a nice young man that was coming by regularly to see her. Mr. Connor got on to me for not calling him when I got in trouble. I told him that I was too proud to ask for help and that I had gotten myself into the mess by acting foolish. I had to get myself out. It would have been different if I would have gotten in trouble over the meth, he would have felt obligated to help me.

But it was all over a stolen truck. I knew better and when a man makes a mistake, he has to suck it up and suffer the consequences. I went to prison and didn't take anyone with me, which is a lot more than I can say for the people who told on me.

When I left Alice and Mr. Connor I was feeling pretty good about life.

CHAPTER THIRTEEN:

Betrayal

Things were going pretty good in Ada. Shawyn and I were doing fine. I liked her a lot and she was starting to come out of her shyness. I kept my meth business secret and on a small scale. I didn't need a lot of money.

I was slowly stocking up on tools and equipment to get a solid footing to work with in the future. I kept buying a few cows to help increase my future income. I also bought a large quantity of lumber and supplies I would need to build a house on my sixty acres and stored it all in one of the barns I'd built on Mikey's place.

The news came one day that Bopper had shot and killed a childhood friend of mine, Robert. Bopper claimed it was an accident, but the story was that Bopper had done Robert wrong on a dope deal. When Robert confronted Bopper about it Bopper shot him. Robert was a good man and his sister Robin was a wonderful person. Robert never bothered anyone.

He did a little dope now and then and pretty much minded his own business.

Anyone who knew Robert liked him, because he was a likable person. When we were young, Robert bought an old rusty car that needed a paint job. We were kids and none of us could afford a real paint job. Robert sanded that old car and painted it dark blue with a real fine paint brush.

From a distance, it looked like a thousand dollar paint job. You couldn't see the brush strokes until you looked real close. Robert had a great sense of humor, as well. Bopper had finally killed someone and it was someone we all knew and loved. Somehow, Bopper beat the case. He got away with cold blooded murder. Bopper was not so lucky with the charges of selling methamphetamine. He got some time for the meth charges and was sent to prison. Bopper's friend Richard was in prison on cocaine and meth convictions.

I was staying in Ada, minding my own business and living little. One weekend I drove to Ardmore to eat at Budroux's. I had missed the place. I then drove to Texas to see Snake. He looked a little older, but was doing well. His meth business had slowed down some because the DEA was really cracking down on chemicals, namely phenylacetic acid. He was happy to see me and it was like old times week. He explained the problem and I told him that I would part with two more drums of phenylacetic acid if he would send someone to come get them.

Snake said, "You're still The Wizard."

I didn't feel much like The Wizard. I couldn't bring Lisa back.

Snake told me that Veronica was still in college and that he had continued to pay the rent on her apartment. I thought that was really cool.

When the evening crowd started rolling in, the place quickly filled up with pretty women looking to party. I was going to head home but Snake talked me into staying. Up until that point I hadn't been using drugs. But after eating dinner and drinking two beers, it was either find a place to lay down and sleep or do some meth and party. I felt like joining the party. So I chose door number two and did a little meth. Then it was dancing, drinking and Kimberly. In that order. It was the first time I cheated on my girlfriend Shawyn, but that's not what I was thinking about when a beautiful redhead named Kimberly had her lips wrapped around little Elvis.

It wasn't long before I was taking a short jumper flight from Oklahoma City to Dallas twice a month to party with Kimberly. She was wild. I would fly out on Friday mornings, rent a new Mustang at the airport in Dallas and fly back Sunday afternoon. Kimberly was worth it and not seeing her every day is what kept the relationship hot and nasty.

That first night at Snake's was a lot of fun. Kimberly and I ended up at a motel where we used a half a bottle of coconut oil in our sexual exploits. Fun can be measured in how much coconut oil or baby oil one goes through in a night.

The next day Snake followed me back to Pauls Valley to pick up the two drums of phenylacetic acid. I had him follow me to my sixty acres where I told him about the bad luck with my storage there. I also pointed out the group of big trees where I was going to build a little house for me and Lisa.

He waited in the trees, out of sight, while I went to my other storage and picked up the two drums. Snake left happy and I had an extra ten thousand. The going rate, at that time, was five thousand a drum. I would have given them to Snake, but he insisted on paying the going rate. That's the way things work between real friends.

Back home I was running my road service and working out of my garage. I needed a little help so I hired a guy named Brad to give me a hand.

Brad worked for me part time as a mechanic. Kevin was coming and going a lot and one day he hired Brad to work on one of his cars. I found out later that Kevin paid Brad with meth. Kevin and Brad struck up a friendship and Brad started selling meth for Kevin. I didn't notice because I was spending a lot of time on the road or in the air. I was doing some business in Ardmore and seeing Loretta. I didn't see what was going on between Kevin and Brad. Brad wasn't stupid and it didn't take him long to figure out that Kevin was getting his meth from me.

My girlfriend Shawyn was happy, as long as the money was coming in, because it fit my story that I was working out of town, my road service was doing okay. I could have made a living with that alone. A lot of people seemed to be locking their keys in their cars and leaving their lights on when they went in bars so I was getting a lot of late night calls. It was starting to get fun and I thought some of the girls were locking their keys in their cars on purpose. That was the reason I started running my free drunk service. It was sort of a promotional gimmick and it gave me an excuse to be out late at night. The girls I gave my business cards to could go out drinking and when the bars were about to close they could call me.

I would come pick them up so they wouldn't run the risk of getting pulled over for drinking and driving. I happened to be seeing Brad more and more at bars at closing time.

One day I got a call from a girl whose car wouldn't start. She was stuck in the parking lot of the college campus. When I showed up it was love at first sight, for me anyway. She told me her name was Misty and asked how much it would cost to fix her car. She was looking at me with that I can't believe a good looking guy came to rescue me look. I determined that the starter was shot and the battery was about gone. I told Misty that I would fix her car for free if she would have lunch with me. That took the worried look off her face and replaced it with a sexy smile. We went to lunch, then I bought the part and fixed her car. After that I asked her if she would go dancing with me that weekend in Shawnee, Oklahoma. That weekend we went dancing and drinking then we went to my step-dad, Bob's all night diner, The Rainbow Inn, for breakfast. There is a motel next door to the Rainbow Inn where we spent the night doing the boogie woogie and the hot rumba. After I met Misty my trips to Dallas and Ardmore were less frequent. Misty and I were delving into verboten territory and I was in love.

I started seeing Misty regularly and the more I had her, the more I wanted her. We were trying everything we could think of, sexually and it was intense. I bought her a better car and a house full of furniture. She knew that Shawyn and I were living together and was alright with that. Misty was focusing on college and didn't want any obligations. I was ready to leave Shawyn, but Misty didn't want a steady relationship until after she finished college. I understood that and certainly didn't want to pressure her. It wasn't until later that I found out the real reason. Misty was seeing an older married man and I was just part of a juggling act. But I was in love and didn't want to see what was happening.

Meanwhile, Brad had asked me to start selling him meth. I told him to keep getting his meth from Kevin. That was the beginning of Brad having hard feelings toward me. One afternoon Brad's wife called Shawyn and told her that Brad was messed up on meth and had beaten her. Shawyn was mad and suggested that I run Brad off, so I did. I don't like men who hit women. Shawyn asked Brad's wife to come stay at our house a few days, until she could work something out. Brad was mad because I'd run him off for beating his wife and he started accusing me of having sex with his wife.

I wasn't, but in his mind, I was. Brad called Shawyn and told her that I was selling meth to Kevin and that I had a girlfriend.

I lied to Shawyn about having a girlfriend and told her the truth about me selling meth to Kevin. Shawyn was pissed. We argued and she told me how petty selling drugs was and I told her that was what kept up with her three hundred dollar a week trips to Walmart. I told her that I would leave and she told me no, that I should stop selling dope. I should have packed up and left that day and I would have if I'd known about the other things that were happening behind the scene.

After the argument with Shawyn I went to Misty's and told her I was leaving Shawyn. That's when Misty hit me with the news that she was pregnant. I told her it was great timing. I was leaving Shawyn and Misty and I could get married and have a child. Misty said that she had thought about it and didn't want to get married or have the baby. The news was a heavy blow and I left unhappy.

As usual, I ran from my heartache and started seeing a sexy sweet blond named Gena, that same day. Gena helped me take my mind off the other things in my life. The sex was great and her girlfriend was often in the picture, so I was spending a lot of time with Gena. Brad saw my truck at Gena's. Then one day Kevin and Brad knocked on Gena's door. Kevin wanted more meth. Brad didn't say anything even though I had run him off and he thought I had sex with his wife. I think Brad really knew better he was just making up an excuse to be pissed, I sent them away and told Kevin I would meet him later.

When I met Kevin he again reminded me that Tommy was about to get out of prison in Texas. Kevin warned me that Tommy was a bad person, that couldn't be trusted and told me I should flood my cellar to get rid of any trace evidence of manufacturing. Kevin was the only one who knew that I had done something in that cellar. He had come by one day when I was cleaning the cellar and he could see and smell the reason why I was cleaning the cellar.

Kevin's mention of the cellar and use of the words "Trace evidence," put me on high alert. I had left Gena's and picked up more meth before meeting Kevin.

The fact that Kevin and Brad showed up at Gena's unannounced and Kevin's comments, hit home. It was a set up. I told Kevin I didn't have anything. He didn't believe me and he was mad. I told him not to come to my house, or Gena's and left. I didn't go far. I took the first side road I came to and drove out of town, then pulled over and buried the meth and went home. I knew that I had been betrayed by my best friend.

I started moving a lot of my tools and equipment to Mikey's house, where I was storing it all in a new box trailer I'd bought. I kept the box trailer behind Mikey's barn, which was actually my barn. I then went to Kevin's and told him that I was ready to transfer the sixty acres into my name. That's when he told me the truth about the property belonging to his father and that he would transfer it over to me once he inherited the land. Kevin was my best friend and I thought of him as a brother. He betrayed me and I wasn't mad, I was crushed. Everything between us had been a lie and I was certain that he had tried to set me up. Before I left Kevin told me again to watch out for Tommy and to flood my cellar.

From Kevin's I drove to Dallas to see Snake and Kimberly. I gave Snake the last two pounds of meth I had to sell for me and told him that if I got busted I was making bond. It certainly wasn't going to be like the last time.

I spent a day with Kimberly and headed home. Snake told me to write everything off and stay and I should have. But my house was clean, I didn't have any more dope and I was going to move soon anyway.

I started staying home more, minding my own business. I hired a guy named Ron to work on things at the house while I did my road service.

Shawyn was so happy that she decided that we should get married. In a moment of weakness, I said, "Yes." Misty had wounded me and I was hurting. I took Shawyn to dinner at Polo's where I got on my knee and asked her to marry me. It was romantic and I was getting into the spirit of things. I suggested that we get married in Lake Tahoe.

I told my dad, who lived in Modesto, California, that I was getting married in Lake Tahoe and asked him to come to the wedding. He did better than that; he picked Shawyn and me up at the airport in San Francisco, drove us to Lake Tahoe and paid for everything. A lot of my family, on my father's side, came to the wedding, which was very nice. The only bad thing was, I looked terrible. My eyes were red from being awake for three days and I had lost weight. I didn't really want to get married, but Misty didn't want me, or my baby. I thought that maybe love wasn't in the cards for me and that I should be happy with companionship. We went to a Jude's concert the night we arrived in Lake Tahoe. Then we were married at the "Touch of Love" wedding chapel the next day. We gambled some, then drove back to San Francisco and flew home.

When we got home an engine I'd built was missing and so was Ron, the guy I'd hired to help out. I didn't know it, but by hiring Ron, I'd opened the door for a visit from the police, who were looking for an excuse to come see me.

Shawyn and I had returned from Lake Tahoe, on that day, because Tommy was out and coming after his lab and chemicals the next day.

Shawyn, of course, didn't know that. When the police arrived, Shawyn had gone to her sisters to talk about the wedding and get the pictures developed. It was raining a little, so I invited the two officers in the back door to talk. They asked me if I knew Ron was involved in a chop-shop.

I said, "No," and that it looked like he had taken an engine from me while I was gone. They asked if they could look in my garage and check my vehicles to see if they were stolen. I said, "Yes," and showed them around. I didn't know my phone was tapped and they already knew Tommy was coming the next day. I had been under investigation ever since Kevin and Brad came by Gena's house. Kevin and Brad had been busted and they told the cops everything they knew. A local attorney, Barney Ward, Jr., found out all the details for me later.

I told the officers that Ron wouldn't be coming back to my place and if he did, I'd run him off. When they left everything seemed okay.

I had put everything of Tommy's in a Rent-a-Storage there in Ada. When Tommy called I told him I would meet him at McDonald's. At McDonald's Tommy and I ate cheeseburgers and fries while we talked. I gave Tommy a little money and the key to the storage and left. I no sooner than walked in the door of my house when a police SWAT team raided my place.

I was thinking, "Boy, am I lucky the house is clean."

What I didn't realize was, the day before, when I invited the police into the house out of the rain they saw two of my pistols hanging from both bed posts in their shoulder holsters. It didn't dawn on me that I was a felon and could get in trouble for having guns in my house. While I was handcuffed, an officer came in and said, "There is enough residue in the cellar to give you one hundred years." That confirmed the fact that Kevin, had indeed, told on me.

I said, "I've only lived here six months and I have never been in that cellar." Then I didn't say another word.

I was thinking, "Damn I'm glad I met Tommy in town." I didn't know that another team had followed Tommy to the storage and busted him while he was loading his lab and chemicals in his vehicle.

When I made bond two hours later it was for felon in possession of a firearm. All they had me for was the guns they found in my home.

When I went to arraignment two days later I was charged with conspiracy to manufacture and sell methamphetamine.

Tommy, although caught red-handed, told the police that everything was mine. Kevin had warned me that Tommy would turn on me and he did, but it was Kevin and Brad that got the ball rolling. I told my attorney that there was nothing in the storage that belonged to me and that Tommy was lying. And that was the truth. The only thing the cops had on me was the guns they found in my house. I was adamant about going to trial. The only witnesses against me would have been Tommy, who was caught with the lab and chemicals and had a criminal record. Kevin, who had been caught with meth and who made an unsuccessful attempt to buy drugs from me. And Brad, who had never bought anything from me and he had a criminal record. Brad had done his business with Kevin, not me, which would make Kevin look worse. After Kevin ratted on me I was out of the dope business the next day. There was no way the cops could have a taped telephone conversation of me making a dope deal. I wasn't using my phone like that, even before Kevin got busted. So I was going to trial.

Things don't always go as planned. My attorney summoned me to his office one day for a pow-wow. He explained that, hands down, they had me on the gun charges. There was no way I could argue with that. With the residue in the cellar and the testimony of Kevin, Brad and Tommy the State had a circumstantial case against me that might stick. With that said, my attorney advised me that he had negotiated a deal for me.

If I would plead guilty to conspiracy to possess methamphetamine, they would drop the gun charge and give me ten years probation. I knew that a probation deal meant that they thought they would get another chance, at a later date, to get me on something bigger. It's called a "Trick bag." But the word probation had a sweet sound. I took the deal that day and went before the judge to receive my ten years probation. I also had to forfeit my service truck, but my attorney got my guns back.

I probably would have been alright if I would have left Shawyn and moved away. I could have transferred my probation to another location and been fine. But I didn't. Instead, I bought a newer four wheel drive Chevy truck, jacked it up, put big tires on it and continued my road service. I was not selling any drugs. That didn't stop the police from sending people to my house asking to buy meth and having them call me at all hours. Because of that I started spending more time away from the house. When I stopped throwing money around, Misty got busy and had other things to do. I couldn't go by Gena's house because Kevin and Brad told the police about her and the police had even questioned Gena. When the weather was nice I spent a lot of time at a park called Turner Falls. I would swim, cook hot dogs on a camp fire and drink margaritas in the shade. I wasn't bothering anyone. That didn't stop the police from trying to set me up.

One evening I received a phone call from Brad's brother. I knew who he was, because I'd recently put a water pump on his girlfriend's Camaro.

Brad's brother told me that he had a friend who was trying to sell some big tires and wheels that would fit a Chevy four wheel drive truck.

He knew that I was building four wheel drive trucks. He said the guy wanted to trade them for meth. I told him I didn't sell dope. He then told me that the guy would trade the tires and wheels for a gun. I had over thirty guns that I'd bought at gun shows. I was bringing one gun home at a time and slowly selling them. I certainly didn't need them and I wasn't supposed to have them because of my felony convictions. I thought selling them was the right thing to do and my best option.

In a moment of ignorance, I told Brad's brother that I had a new .44 magnum, still in the box, that had never been fired that I might trade.

He said he would be by later with the tires and wheels.

It was Valentine's Day. I had just finished putting a timing chain in a Chevy truck. Shawyn had come in the garage in a heart shaped teddy and spike heels and said it was time to come in and play. I was ready. I was cleaning my hands when

I heard a siren chirp in my driveway. I opened the door to another SWAT team. The search warrant said they were looking for "a new .44 magnum, still in the box, that had never been fired." Brad's brother had set me up. At first, they couldn't find the gun. On closer inspection they discovered its hiding place and I was arrested. I was charged with felon in possession of a firearm. I made bond as soon as I got to the jail.

In my eyes, I was trying to do the right thing. I had stopped being involved with drugs. I was selling my guns and working every day. I wasn't bothering a soul. The police hounded me until they could figure out a way to set me up. I didn't get mad. I was hurt and depressed. I hadn't done anything to Kevin or Brad's brother. I hadn't done anything to Brad, other than refuse to sell him meth and run him off after he beat his wife. It was Brad's guilty doped up imagination that made him think I'd had sex with his wife. I was having sex with several women, but not Brad's wife.

The second bust put additional strain on Shawyn and my relationship. I would not argue with Shawyn, other than a few words when I told her I was leaving. That made Shawyn mad, because she didn't want me to leave.

I knew it was only a matter of time before I went to prison. I sold my nice service truck and some tools. I put most of my nicer tools and equipment in storage at Mikey's house. I knew Mikey would never do me wrong. We had been friends since childhood and he was independently wealthy. Shawyn and I moved out of the nice house we lived in and into a rented trailer in a trailer park Northeast of Ada. I was going to great lengths to make it look like I was broke. The truck I bought was a 1965 Chevy with a six cylinder. It was primer gray, with rust showing through in spots, with blue front fenders and a faded green hood. What people couldn't see was that the engine, brakes, shocks and stereo system were all new.

I hired a local attorney, Barney Ward, who was a great man and an interesting person. My goal was to put my trial off as long as possible and Mr. Ward took care of that for me. When I was in Ada I drove the '65 Chevy truck. I stayed home most of the time, listening to the Eagles, Hotel California and wishing I was with Lisa. When I left the house, I was usually leaving town. I would drive West through Stratford and Pauls Valley to Elmore City where I would park my old beat up truck behind Mikey's barn.

Then I would visit Mikey awhile and climb into my black 1988 Chevy half ton four wheel drive truck and head to Ardmore then Texas. I'd bought the truck already fixed up with a lift kit, big tires and double shocks. It had a hopped up 454 engine, tinted windows and a fancy stereo system. I was riding in style once I left Ada.

My trial date was a year away. For the first three months after I moved Shawyn into the trailer house, I didn't do anything but party. I went country dancing at the Arbuckle Ballroom and went dancing to rock-n-roll in Ardmore. Loretta went with me some times while I was in Oklahoma and Kimberly went with me while I was in Texas. A lot of times I just went alone, because I liked to meet new people. I spent a lot of time at Snake's place, just doing nothing. They all knew I was going to prison, so we partied hard and wild, Kimberly asked me how I could be so happy when I knew I was going to prison. I told her that just looking at her made me happy and hell, I needed a vacation anyway.

Those three months went by in a haze. As long as I was in that haze, I didn't think about Lisa, or prison. I would stay away from Ada for two or three days, then go back to Ada in my old beat up truck and sleep for a week. Time was going by fast.

One day I told Snake that I was going to Las Vegas to check on Renee, Snake said, "How the hell can you even think about another woman, when Kim's got her mouth glued to your dick half the day?"

I stated, "Kimberly is quite a distraction and I wouldn't trade her for a new truck. But I'm worried about Renee."

Snake said, "Hang on a minute, I'll go with you. I haven't been to Vegas in a while."

Snake was a true friend. He didn't want me to be alone with so much on my mind. We took a flight out of Dallas and rented a car in Vegas.

Driving to the club where I'd met Bear I told Snake more about the unusual events I'd had while hanging out with Renee. He got a good laugh out of my exploits. When we arrived at the club the place was packed. The same bartender that was there years before was tending bar and he looked the same. Snake and I ordered beers and cheeseburgers. I asked if Bear was around. The bartender informed me that Bear was in jail in Indiana, He'd gotten rounded up with a bunch of his biker buddies on a big meth case. I liked Bear and I was sorry to hear about his misfortune. I told him that Bear's sister's phone had been disconnected and I was worried about her. He was kind enough to explain that my help had gotten Renee out of the financial mess she was experiencing, at that time. He seemed to know a lot about what was going on in her life. Renee had moved to San Francisco where she married the man who owned the store that sold her pottery. I was thankful and relieved. I hoped she was happy. Hearing that Renee was okay was all it took to lighten my mood.

Back at the motel I made some phone calls and found out where Bear was locked up. Then I bought two five hundred dollar money orders and sent Bear two letters. A little money helps while a person is in prison. I had a reason for sending two letters. One was funny, asking about Renee and asking Bear to send her my love. The other was serious. Being a biker was a way of life. I didn't try and talk Bear out of being a biker, but I did tell him about the Christian Motorcycle Association. The CMA is full of great people, all bikers, who share their life experiences, trying to make the world a better place. I suggested it might be time to change his colors and ride with a group with a better objective. I hope he did.

That night, Snake and I went gambling. We had a blast losing money. As we were leaving Harrah's there was a beautiful blond, who looked like she should be in a Vouge magazine, standing in the lobby. I told Snake I was going to ask her to go to dinner with me and he said, "She won't go but go for it."

I walked over to the girl and said, "I saw you standing here, looking gorgeous and I thought I would ask you to go to dinner with me."

The girl with the million dollar smile said, "I'm working."

I thought, "That's not a total brush off," so I said, "What time do you get off work?"

Meanwhile, Snake is trying to hold back his laughter. I looked at him like, "What?" and he laughed harder.

The girl said, "Is this your first time in Vegas?"

"Second," I replied.

She said, "I thought so, you're a little green. I'm a hooker, I don't get off work. If you want me to go to dinner with you, it will cost you five hundred."

I said, "That's pretty expensive."

She said, "I'm not a cheap date. 'Sides, it comes with a lot of French benefits, if you know what I mean."

By then I knew what she meant. Snake said, "He's from Oklahoma" and busted out laughing.

The girl shook her head like she understood and laughed a little.

Snake said, "Come on big spender, stop bothering the lady and let's go eat." I told Snake, "I didn't know she was a hooker. She looked like all the other girls I know."

Snake said, "Bro', you're finally catching on."

Neither one of us lost much money on our two day stay in Vegas and we had a lot of fun. We flew back to Dallas with the knowledge that Renee was doing well and that I was a dumbass from Oklahoma. I have no doubt that if Snake saw me today, he would put on a woman's voice and say, "Is this your first time in Vegas?"

We walked in Snake's club to a bunch of sour faces. Snake's partner in the meth business had been busted while we were gone.

Fortunately, Snake's partner had moved the lab to a new location a year earlier. Snake hadn't had any direct involvement in the lab or meth sales for a year. Snake was providing most of the chemicals, through a third party and was sharing in the profits. Even though Snake wasn't there when the bust went down, the risk of his name popping up was fairly great.

Snake was too old to go to jail. It was time for Snake to take an extended vacation and stay out of Texas for a while. We both made haste and exited stage left.

As I drove back to Oklahoma I was hoping that Snake would come out clean. And I started thinking about my future as I listened to "Janie's Got a Gun." I knew I was going to prison, for at least ten years, because of the probation violation. I decided that, if I was going to take any additional risks, it would be before I went to prison, not after. Snake had mentioned before we both left Texas, that with his lab gone there would be a demand for meth. I thought it best to use the time I had left to make as much money as I could. I would certainly need money when I got out of prison.

I made a mental list of the supplies I would need to get busy making meth as I drove. To get in the mood, I put in "Flirt'n With Disaster," by Molly Hatchet. That song always gets me wound up and ready for anything. I changed back into my old truck at Mikey's and headed back to Ada to rest up for my next big project.

I was going for broke and it was going to be all or nothing.

•

CHAPTER FOURTEEN:
Friends

After resting for a week, I drove to Oklahoma City and bought a fifty five gallon drum of trichloroethane, which is a cleaning solvent. At that time, it was not on the government's controlled chemical watch list, so buying it didn't raise any red flags. Trichloroethane is very heavy. It weighs six pounds a gallon heavier than water. Even after I put it all in five gallon cans it was hard to carry and manage. I had to use a wheelbarrow to take two five gallon cans at a time from my truck to the lab. Just moving the chemicals I needed was a tremendous job. Then I went to my underground storage and got cases of more chemicals that I had to haul into the lab. By the time I packed in all the chemicals, the gas for the generator and four propane bottles, I was tired. The last thing I brought in was enough food to last two days and four ice chests full of ice. Then I parked my truck a mile away and walked back to the lab.

I was lucky to be working with raw P2p. All I had to do was distill the P2p and start a speed cook. Of the over seventy gallons of undistilled P2p I had, I was only going to distill four gallons, which is still a big project. I'd brought ice in four ice chests and was using a twelve volt RV water pump and a car battery for my condenser cooling system. It took me several hours to distill the P2p, then I started two full triple-neck flasks boiling using propane for heat. I wouldn't need the generator until I got ready to powder the speed oil into meth. At that point I would need lights, a magnetic stirring table and a ventilation fan. I didn't have an air conditioner, but that wasn't as important with trichloroethane as it was with ether. Trichloroethane was non-flammable and had a low evaporation rate. My setup was a little crude, but it was late in the year and the nights were cool. To keep from needing an air conditioner and freezer, out in the middle of nowhere, my plan was to manufacture only once a year in the dead of winter, when everything was iced over and frozen.

Because of necessity I was going to make the one exception.

When I finished I had used twenty gallons of trichloroethane, four gallons of P2p and I had thirty two pounds of meth. Not bad for two days of hard work. It took a while to get my mess cleaned up then I left to get my truck. The walk back to my truck gave my head time to clear and gave me a chance to look around. When I was certain all was clear, I drove to the lab and loaded the meth, trash, empty ice chests and empty propane bottles and gas cans. As I drove away I was confident that nobody could tell I'd been there.

I left ten pounds of meth secured in the lab. I took ten pounds to Mikey's, where I kept it stored in the woods. I put ten pounds in my underground storage and with the other two pounds I headed to Ardmore.

I fronted one pound to John, my truck driver friend in Gene Autry, Oklahoma. I then fronted the other pound to Sonny, a friend of mine in Ardmore who did landscaping. I told both guys to call me when they got the money together and I would bring them another load. I then went back to Ada to get some much needed rest and to call Snake.

There can sometimes be more than one version of the truth. I told Shawyn I was working out of town because the cops were bothering me so much. That was the truth. Only I left out the part about me manufacturing mass quantities of meth. I was giving her enough money to pay the bills, but not showing any excess. She wasn't suspicious until I got a phone call from John. He was calling from a motel in Kansas. Shawyn answered the phone, listened for a moment, then said, "Your friend John is stuck in a motel in Kansas. Two girls robbed him, took his money, dope and clothes, and he doesn't know where his truck is." Then she handed me the phone.

Sure enough, John was in trouble. Thankfully, he had gotten some sleep, and he realized his mistakes and understood his predicament.

The people at the motel were pounding on the door, telling him it was check-out time. He gave me the phone number of the motel and I called the clerk. I gave the clerk my credit card number and paid for another night. I also told the clerk that my friend had been robbed and that I was coming to get him. I figured John was probably hungry, so I asked the clerk to order him a supreme pizza and put it on my credit card. The clerk said he would and I promised him a large tip when I got there.

I jumped in my old truck and went to Oklahoma City where I rented a nice car for the trip to Kansas. When I got there, I stopped by the front desk and visited with the clerk I'd talked to on the phone. He was happy with the tip. I got John dressed in a sweat suit and took him to buy new clothes.

With that out of the way we drove to the most likely truck stops and happened upon his truck at the second one. The truck had run out of fuel and his load of cantaloupe had spoiled. I didn't have any tools with me so I called a service truck to come fuel up the truck and bleed the fuel lines. That night John and I stayed in a motel. We were going to share a room, but John snored so loud that I had to get another room.

I was joking with John, and said, "You feel like going drinking?"

John said, "Ha-ha, very funny. I'll never drink another drop as long as I live." I hoped that was true, because alcohol can sure mess a person's life up. The next day we headed home. Like Lucy, my friend had "Some 'splaining to do." His brother owned the trucking company he worked for so I had no doubt his job was okay, but he was going to catch hell from his brother and his mother.

On the way home, I traveled a different highway so I would come into Tulsa. I stopped by a friend's house, the one I'd sold my Colt Python .357 to and his wife told me he was in prison on a dope case. I knew she probably needed some money so I bought my Colt Python back and bought some of his hot rod parts. I paid her way more than they were worth and left. Then I drove South on highway 75 to Mr. Connor's convenience store and visited with Mr. Connor and Alice for a few minutes. Alice was getting prettier and seeing them both was uplifting. I drove a little further South to Preston, Oklahoma and stopped in at Russell's house. Russell's wife, who had put up with a lot of crap from Russell, told me that Russell was on the run. He'd gotten caught in a drug deal, but took off before they could arrest him. I went a little further South to Henryetta to have dinner with my sister Susan, her husband and my little sister Jody. Seeing my sisters always made me happy. Then I headed West on I-40 to Oklahoma City to return the rental car.

When I got back to Ada Shawyn was mad. Sonny, my landscaping friend from Ardmore had called. Shawyn told me that Sonny was freaking out on the phone. He thought the police were watching him. It was late, but I tried to call Sonny anyway. He didn't answer and I thought it would be just my luck if the little dumbass was in jail. Shawyn knew something was going on and I had to beg her to stop yelling at me just so I could get some sleep. Shawyn throwing fits was quickly becoming more prevalent.

I was having a nice dream about a school bell ringing. We were all running outside for recess. Then Shawyn elbowed me and told me to answer the phone. I hate it when that happens. Making an educated guess, I snatched the phone out of its cradle and said, "Sonny, what's wrong?"

Sonny said, "How'd you know it was me?"

"The same way I know you're calling from a payphone at that store down the road from your house," I said. "I'm The Wizard."

I could hear a truck going by in the background and I just figured it was the same phone he always used. Sonny was stammering. I'd freaked him out, so I added, "Or maybe you're just predictable."

Sonny was in a panic and about to cry. He said, "The cops are watching my house and they followed me here. What am I going to do?"

I said, "Give me the number and I'll call you right back. I'll take care of everything, just don't move."

John was only twenty minutes away from him, so I called John and told him the story. He agreed with me that Sonny had just been awake too long and was imagining things. I told John where Sonny was and asked him to go get him, before he got himself in real trouble. I then called Sonny back and kept him on the phone until John got there.

John took Sonny to his place, fed him and got him to lay down. When I got there, Sonny was still asleep, so I left him that way. I talked to John for a while and visited with his mother and father, who were wonderful people and we made plans for the next morning.

I called Loretta and went to Ardmore where I rented a motel room.

There is a good reason why they call Loretta "Little Bit." She is only about five feet tall and very petite. She was a perfect, sexy little doll.

We had missed each other so the sex was hot and frantic. The next morning, we were eating breakfast early when Loretta told me that Sandy had called her trying to find me. Sandy supposedly had some kind of emergency she needed help with. Loretta wasn't real pleased about Sandy looking for me, but she thought she better tell me in case it was important. That and Loretta wanted me to know that Sandy's cocaine connection had been busted. My main priority at that moment was Sonny, as I explained to my sweet little friend Loretta. Loretta kissed me bye and I headed to John's house.

While it was early I called Sandy because I thought I would have a good chance of catching her at home. Sandy told me that she had some mysterious problem that she couldn't trust anyone but me to handle.

I informed her that I was in town taking care of another problem and I would love to meet her for dinner. I asked her to call and make reservations at a classy little steak house South of Ardmore that we enjoyed. The place featured a pianist that reminded me of Sam in the movie "Casablanca." He played the blues like a master. Sandy agreed and we were to meet at 6:00 p.m.

When I got to John's everyone was awake, including Sonny.

Sonny was embarrassed because he'd made an ass of himself. He explained that there really was a police car parked down the road from the house he'd rented. I told him that if that was the case, it was time to move. Sonny didn't want to go back to the house. I had Sonny wait at John's and John and I rented a U-Haul and spent the afternoon loading all of Sonny's belongings into the truck. It was easy, because a lot of things were still packed from the move into the house. While we were working, the undercover police car Sonny had seen pulled into a driveway of a house down the road. The officer got out of his car and went in the house.

He apparently lived there. It looked like nothing more than poor planning on Sonny's part. The meth was where Sonny said it would be and we just packed it with everything else. We had the whole house loaded and were back at John's by 2:00 p.m. I called a friend of mine in Oklahoma City who had some rent houses. He said he had one that still needed a little work, but Sonny could move in that day. John agreed to help Sonny move and I went back to Ardmore. Some people can use a little meth and appear normal and unaffected. But when a person is turned loose with a lot of meth, they often go nuts quickly, which is what happened to John and Sonny. No matter how bad they messed up, they were still my friends and I came to their rescue. It was partly my fault anyway for giving them so much meth.

I rented a nice motel room, as nice as can be had in Ardmore, Oklahoma, then I went clothes shopping. I wanted to look good when I met Sandy. I bought a camel hair jacket, matching light brown Roper boots, new matching belt, pants, shirt and paisley silk boxers. It's fun to dress up now and then. I was at the bar when Sandy walked in looking like a million dollars. She was stunning, in a low cut slinky dress that showed her rather endowed cleavage, with nylons and high heels. If the piano player would have seen her even he would have stopped what he was doing. I was impressed and thankful I'd had the foresight to go shopping.

It was a weeknight and our table was ready. The place was only moderately busy.

Sandy said, "Hello, cowboy. It's been too long."

I just smiled. We had chateaubriand and a light red wine that was somewhat tart for my liking. I liked iced tea better. I didn't drink much because I wanted a clear head for what I hoped was coming. As we ate Sandy told me her problem.

Her cocaine connection had received a tip that he was about to be arrested. Based on that news, he had taken a private plane back to Columbia.

The feds didn't know that when they raided his million dollar home where they found cocaine and money in the master bedroom. The feds arrested everyone that was there at the time of the raid and seized the home and its content. Sandy informed me that there was still a substantial amount of cocaine and money in the house. The feds didn't find it, because it was stashed behind the bookshelves in a secret compartment in the library. The problem was, one of the people arrested might tell where the cocaine was hidden in an attempt to get out of jail. The other problem was, the home was in a gated community. To get in you had to stop at the guard shack and get approval. If a person could get through the front gate, then the chance of the neighbors observing was too great. The front door wasn't an option. Fortunately, the home was at the back of the community with a huge open hay meadow behind the house. Sandy wanted me to walk in and get twenty kilograms of cocaine and fifty thousand in cash. I told her I would give it a try, but it would be the following night. Sandy had the security code and knew where the spare key was located. All I needed was some clothes and tools to work with, in case the key was missing or wouldn't work. I asked Sandy to make me a good drawing of the house, as well. I knew I wasn't the first guy to put his neck on the line for a beautiful woman. I would have jumped off a tall building to please Sandy. And it helped that I just loved any kind of James Bond shit.

We left the restaurant and drove by the gated community. It even had its own golf course. I couldn't see the house in question from the road, but the houses that I could see were enormous. We drove all the way around the place and as close as we could get to the rear of the place was two miles. I was in for a long walk. I took Sandy back to her car and she followed me to the motel.

At the motel I had margaritas mixed and ready to pour over ice. I like mine on the rocks. The combination of tequila and Sandy, mixed with a little meth and cocaine on top made me big, in many ways. Sandy had shaved her little love muffin, which made it all kinds of fun for me to keep my face between her legs. She wanted to trim the hair around little Elvis. Her excitement about it was infectious and it made me want to please, so I agreed. Sandy used a small pair of scissors and trimmed the hair all around and under little Elvis. I'm a hairy guy, so it took ten minutes. The left over pile of hair was huge. Little Elvis felt cool and airy. It was new for me and Sandy loved it. Little Elvis was poking out there as big as day. We took a shower together and rinsed the hair away.

Then Sandy expressed her appreciation by affectionately kissing and loving on little Elvis. Sleep came several hours later with total exhaustion.

We had both done our best to bruise each other's pelvic bones, but by morning we were ready for another round.

We had breakfast and went shopping for the clothes and other items I would need. After buying the clothes I wanted we went to a laundry and washed the clothes and duffle bags so they wouldn't be stiff and noisy.

Throughout the day Sandy told me more about the house and the hidden compartment. We would shop, go to the motel and have sex, then go eat and then have sex. We did that all day.

When nightfall arrived, I kissed Sandy and told her to meet me at Denny's the next morning. I'd bought a new lock to put on the gate going in the property behind the gated community. I cut the lock off with bolt cutters, drove through the gate and put on my lock. I took the dirt path all the way to the edge of the hay meadow and parked in the trees.

Everything went well. I simply walked across the hay field, climbed over the back wall and walked around the pool to the back door. The spare key was where Sandy told me to look. I retrieved the key, opened the back door and walked right in. The alarm wasn't activated. The house was in shambles. The police had dragged everything out of its proper places and dumped it in the floor. In the library, all the books had been raked off the shelves and thrown about the floor. The hidden compartment opened at the waist, so the clutter on the floor was no hindrance. It took me a few moments to figure out how to get the small panel open so I could get to the latch. Once I pulled the latch the top half of the book shelf swung open easily. Using a small light, I looked inside at a large stack of cocaine. There was money stacked on top of the cocaine and two nice 9 mm pistols lying next to the money. Seeing all that cocaine and money got me excited and the adrenaline kicked in. I packed the cocaine, money and guns in two duffle bags I'd brought for the job. There was twenty four kilograms of cocaine. That made each bag about forty eight pounds. That didn't sound like much, until I had to carry it out of the house, over the wall and across the hay meadow to my truck. It gave me a whole new respect for people in the military who carry packs for miles. I was happy when I finally got to my truck. It was just after midnight when I left the way I'd came and locked the gate behind me. I went four miles to another location that didn't have a gate and drove into some trees and parked for the night.

I removed the duffle bags from my truck and carried them into the woods. Then I took out four kilos of cocaine, both guns and the money. There were eighty seven thousand in one hundred dollar bills. I put fifty thousand in one of the duffle bags and kept four kilograms, both guns and thirty seven thousand for myself. Leaving the dope stashed in the trees I went back to my truck to sleep until morning. With all the sex and hard work, sleep came easy.

When I woke up I changed my clothes, loaded everything in my truck and went to Denny's. Sandy was there when I arrived and so were four police cars. I drove up like I owned the place and went in for breakfast.

I figured that, if the cops were waiting for me, they sure wouldn't be that obvious. Sandy was happy to see me. I told her that I got everything and we didn't say much after that. She couldn't believe I'd brought it all to Denny's with the police sitting there. I told her that, as long as I can see them, then I knew where they were.

When I told her, I had two duffle bags in the truck with twenty kilos and fifty thousand in them for her, she was more than happy. She didn't complain when I told her what I kept for my trouble. After we ate, I followed Sandy out of town where I loaded the bags in her trunk. I saw Sandy a couple of times after that, but we never mentioned that we'd both made out like bandits on that cocaine deal.

I left Sandy and drove back to my underground storage, where I stored two kilos, the guns and money. Then I went to Mikey's and stashed the other two kilos in the woods with the ten pounds of meth I'd hidden there.

Then I switched back into my old truck and headed back to Ada.

Shawyn wasn't pleased with me being gone so much and with the hair around little Elvis trimmed she was starting to wonder. I lied and told her that working out in the heat with all that hair was just too hot. I explained that by trimming the hair it prevented me from getting a rash. She didn't argue with me because she liked the way it looked. It was a new and exciting thing for her too. Shawyn was actually happy to hear that I'd gotten my friend Sonny squared away.

I stayed home almost two weeks waiting on Snake to call. He would have another person call and simply say, "Call Texas," and I would go to a payphone and call him back. While I was home I spent a little time going around to payphones calling people. I was going through a lot of prepaid phone cards. When I called the rodeo clown in McAlester, he told me that he was doing fine and was out of the meth world. I was glad to hear that he had good sense. The rodeo clown had married Elizabeth and they had a two year old daughter named Crystal, of all things. He jokingly said that it was crystal meth that brought him and Elizabeth together and it was their daughter Crystal that would keep them together. It was good to hear that they were doing well.

When Snake finally called I was ready for a break from home and for some real excitement. Things were going well for Snake. His partner had kept his mouth shut, but was still in jail with no bond. Snake still had his bar and shop, but had relocated for a while. He had other people taking care of his day-to-day business. Snake said he had a couple of problems that he wanted to talk with me about. I suggested lunch at the first place we'd met. I didn't say where in case the phone I was using or his phone was being monitored and he agreed. The cops have been known to monitor payphones, so I was being very careful not to say anything on the phone.

I had seen a telephone truck sitting down the road from my place a few days in a row. After I thought about it, a telephone truck had showed up a day after I came home the last time. I wasn't taking any chances.

When I left Ada, I headed East, the opposite direction of the way I'd been going. Sure enough, I was being followed. I circled around and headed North towards Shawnee, Oklahoma. Four unmarked police cars stopped me before I got to Shawnee. The officers searched me and my truck and didn't find anything. They asked me why I circled around and I politely told them that I started towards my sister's house, then decided to swing by Shawnee to see my step-dad. They let me go, but I knew they were still following me. It was only 8:00a.m., so I went to Shawnee and stopped in to see my step-dad, Bob at his restaurant for a minute. When I left, I drove to I-40 and headed West to Oklahoma City. In Oklahoma City, I drove to the airport and rented a car, then went South on highway 35, toward Texas. I got off of highway 35 in Duncan, Oklahoma and drove the back way to Mikey's. At Mikey's, I loaded the ten pounds of meth and two kilos of cocaine in the black 4 X 4 I kept at Mikey's and headed for Ardmore. The only way the police could have followed me would have been with an airplane or helicopter and I didn't see or hear either. Just in case, I stayed off the main highway and took back roads to Budroux's. With all that drama, I still beat Snake to Budroux's. When Snake got there he was looking fit, well fed and rested.

Snake had two problems. He needed meth and his chemicals were being held hostage. I told him I had already fixed his first problem and that what he needed was in my truck. He thought I was kidding, and I said, "The Wizard don't kid."

Snake said, "Hot, damn."

The second problem was somewhat more complex. Snake's partner had stored a lot a chemical in a guy's barn. The guy didn't know Snake and Snake wanted to keep it that way. When one of Snake's guys went to get the chemicals the owner of the barn told him that he wanted a hundred thousand or he was keeping the chemicals. I suggested that he let the man keep them. That wasn't an option, because it was a lot of chemicals and if the man got caught with them, he might tell on Snake's partner. I also agreed that a hundred grand was too much to pay for his own chemicals.

The man had already threatened to shoot anyone who tried to take the chemicals. For obvious reasons, we needed to avoid a gun battle over chemicals. This had to be a covert operation.

I had Snake explain the layout and draw me a picture of the property.

It was isolated, with the closest house a half mile away. The barn was in the back, with the only doors facing the back of the house. From the back door of the house, a rock could be thrown to the front of the barn. The man had two big dogs that he kept in a pen that ran along one side of the barn. The chemicals were in the back corner of the barn in a tack room, on the side closest to the dogs. The area was pretty open behind the barn, but there was some farm equipment lined up behind the barn. The closest we could get to the back of the barn, without being seen, was a quarter mile. Snake told me the barn was old and made out of wood. I told Snake that if he would give me two guys to carry the chemicals I would take care of the rest.

Snake made a phone call and got two of his guys on the way with a truck. Snake and I went shopping and I told him my plan. We got the supplies and tools I would need then drove to Ringling, Oklahoma to meet our other two partners in the recovery mission. It was more James Bond shit and I was loving it. This time Snake would be with me. By the time the other two guys got there it was 4:00 p.m. I wanted to be behind the place before dark to get a good look at things. Coming in behind something is just a matter of getting the angle right, so the person on the other side can't see you coming. If the man spotted us we would be open targets.

I went as far as the equipment behind the barn and started throwing golf ball size wads of hamburger, with two valiums in each one, into the dog pin. The dogs ran back and forth snatching up the hamburger surprise. Thirty minutes later it was getting dark and both dogs were napping.

I waved for the guys to come. Then I used a hand drill to drill one inch holes next to each other in a horizontal line at eye level.

I had oiled the hand drill and put in a new bit before we came. It chewed the holes smoothly, quickly and quietly. When I had a line of holes all the way across three of the boards, I used a knife to cut the wood between the holes. All I had to do was put the tip of the big knife in each hole and work it back and forth. When I pulled the three boards loose, I had a small doorway in the back of the barn. It was a little tricky at first.

The boxes were stacked against the back wall. I had to push them forward without knocking them over. Then I just stepped into the barn and started passing cases of chemicals out the hole to one of Snake's guys.

Snake and the other guy started moving everything and stacking it behind the farm equipment. It didn't take long to get all the boxes and other containers moved out of the barn. I leaned the section of board back over the hole in the wall and we left. It took nine trips, with two new wheelbarrows and one two wheel dolly to move all the chemicals to the trucks. The trucks were stacked high with boxes, all tied in, when we drove away. I was later told that the man didn't notice the chemicals missing for a month.

After we dropped off the chemicals at another barn in Texas, I spent the night at Snake's new house. The next day I took my time driving back to my storage, where I put up the money I'd brought back with me. Then I went to Mikey's to drop off my truck and then to Oklahoma City to return the rental car.

After getting pulled over leaving Ada I wasn't hauling anything back with me. Not that I would have anyway. And it was a good thing.

When I drove into Ada a police car started following me. As I neared the trailer park two more police cars joined the parade. They pulled me over before I could get to the house. As they searched me and my truck, one of the officers told me that he could arrest me for not having a driver's license, no insurance and a broken tail light. He had my license and insurance verification in his hand and my tail lights were fine. The officer then asked me where my lab was. I told him that he knew that I had been arrested and that all of that was behind me and I didn't have a lab.

He said, "That's what I thought you'd say."

Then he proceeded to tell me that he knew I had a lab on a friend of mine's property just North of Ada. I told him, "No," I didn't have a lab anywhere.

Once again, the officer said, "That's what I thought you'd say."

By that time, I could clearly see that the officer was a stone cold nut and I thought I was being arrested, so I just stood there with my hands in my pockets waiting. When the other officers finished searching my truck, the officer, who I later discovered was from Pauls Valley told me I could go.

He advised me that he was keeping my driver's license and insurance verification and that I had to come to the courthouse in Pauls Valley to get them back. Then they got in their cars and drove away. A few days later the police searched my friend's property and there was nothing there. There never had been.

Shawyn took me to the tag office to get a new driver's license and by the insurance office to get a new insurance verification. I was ready for another go around.

With all the craziness happening, I thought it best to go to a payphone and call Snake. If they were watching me, they might be watching him. I gave him a number of a friend of mine in Ada where he could leave a message for me, rather than have someone call my house. Then I sat at home for two weeks, only going as far as my barbecue grill. While Shawyn was at work, I would listen to the Eagles, "Hotel California," and think about Lisa. One day I took Shawyn out to eat and shopping and took that time away from home to call Mr. Connor. The holidays were coming and I just wanted to say hello. When I asked to talk to Alice he told me that she had gone to a movie with her boyfriend. That made me happy.

The two weeks went by fast. I was bored and ready for some action.

I needed to get the ten pounds of meth I'd left in the lab and I wanted to get ready for my big winter cook. My departure from Ada was uneventful. I drove North to I-40, then West to Oklahoma City. I figured that, if the cops were following me, they were spending a lot of time and money. I went to several places in Oklahoma City picking up some supplies

I would need. By the time I got to Mikey's I was sure no one was following me. I later found out that the police were following me. They had even followed me into the stores and knew what I'd bought at each place. They had lost me when I got on the country roads near Pauls Valley. They questioned me about some of my actions the next year, before I plead guilty to the firearm charge and went to prison.

After I changed trucks at Mikey's I went to my underground storage and loaded up some things I would need to process more meth that winter. Then I drove to the lab as it was getting dark. I moved my things into the lab, did some organizing, made a list of the things I would need, then hauled out the trash and the meth. By the time I got the entrance to the lab buried and camouflaged, it was 2:00 a.m. I knew better than to haul anything at night, so I just sat there in my nice truck and waited until daylight. I was able to sleep for about three hours that night. I went back to Mikey's, burned the trash and had breakfast with Mikey. He liked it when I came by in the mornings. Then he didn't have to do the cooking.

I called Snake at noon and asked him how the weather was in Texas. He told me that the weather was great and that he'd just had a new hot tub installed.

That sounded like a party to me. Snake told me that Kimberly had asked about me. That was good news. My concern was, did Kimberly get along with Snake's wife. He assured me that they got along fine. I suggested that he ask his wife to call Kimberly and invite her over and we could all go to dinner when I got there.

When I came around the corner on the road leading to Snake's house, I could see Kimberly's beat up Camaro parked in front. My spirits lifted.

It's nice to show up to hugs and kisses and a warm welcome from friends. I felt like Kimberly had sincerely missed me. She even had a tear in her eye after she hugged me. I told Snake what I had in the truck and he called one of his guys to come get the meth.

Snake showed me his new hot tub while the girls got us a beer. After Snake's guy picked up the load, we all went to dinner. Then we went back to Snake's and sat in the hot tub for an hour, joking and laughing.

Kimberly was extremely sexy in her little bikini. It felt good just being close to friends I really cared about and that I knew cared about me.

We played Yahtzee and had a normal evening.

I had stopped by a motel and rented a room on my way to Snake's house. I handed the key card to Kimberly under the table and raised my eyebrows. She smiled and we told Snake and his wife that we would see them in the morning.

CHAPTER FIFTEEN:
Risky Business

When we got to the motel the first thing that Kimberly wanted to do was get her lips on little Elvis. Of course, that made me happy to no end.

We helped each other off with our clothes and when Kimberly went down she noticed that little Elvis had a haircut.

Kimberly said, "Oh, this is too cool. You trimmed your hair back for me. Little Elvis looks so big."

"I was hoping you'd like it," I replied.

Kimberly said, "I do, I do."

I thought she was going to suck little Elvis right off my body and I would have died a happy man. Kimberly was wonderful and we had a great night together. She knew that the reason I didn't stay with her was the fact that I was going to prison. I was careful not to give her any false hopes about us living happily ever after, when I was about to go to jail. We agreed that it was best to live for the moment and work with what we had. She was doing a great job of taking my mind off the prospect of prison. I wanted to do something nice for her too.

We went to Snake's the next morning and Snake gave me a bag of cash. I told Kimberly that we were going on a shopping spree. She looked a little perplexed when I suggested we take her car. I asked her to take me to the

Chevrolet dealer so we could check out the used cars. They had three late model Camaros that I liked. I asked Kimberly which one she liked best and she picked the black one.

I said, "Are you sure? Because that's the one I'm buying for you." She went a little nuts. I loved to make her happy.

This was a time when a used car salesman was a "used car salesman," rather than a pre-owned vehicle dealer. The salesman was more than happy to take cash. I paid for a year's insurance then went to the tag office and put the car in Kimberly's name and tagged it for her. I drove her old Camaro to her mother's house for her then we went to the mall. Kimberly had made a comment the night before about needing a new bikini, so I thought it was the perfect time to get her one. I liked seeing her smile.

She tried on two bikinis and she looked hot in both of them, so we got them both. It just made sense to get one for afternoons and one for evenings. At a little jewelry store in the mall I bought her a heart shaped diamond necklace. Of course, she needed new clothes to go with the new necklace. When we left the mall Kimberly's car was full of clothes, literally. It was so much fun watching her eyes light up.

We had a late lunch at a restaurant near the mall, then went back to the motel where we slid into bed and I slid little Elvis into Kimberly. She had a way of looking me directly in the eyes while we had sex, or when she had little Elvis in her mouth, that made me feel like I was the only man she ever wanted. It was a sexy, seductive look that kept me wanting more and more.

We could be in a crowd of people and Kimberly would look at me like I was the only person that mattered in this world. I was afraid to open up and tell her that I loved her. I'm sure she knew. I just couldn't say, "I love you." The L word is dangerous. It brings with it a lot of responsibility.

Once you say it, a person has a duty and obligation to be there and to protect the other person's heart and feelings. The prison thing was hanging over my head like a razor sharp pendulum that cut me to the bone every time it swung past. When the topic of prison came up I avoided it when I could. It was like a cloud hanging over a picnic. When someone brought it up I laughed it off and ran for cover. I became good at changing the subject. I didn't want it to rain on my sunshiny day. It was bad enough knowing that I was going to prison. I didn't want to be around anyone that wanted to remind me of the prison stigma.

When someone would say, "I'm sorry to hear that you're going to prison." I would smile and say something like, "Me too. It kind of sucks."

I always tried to joke it away, but in the back of my mind I was hearing that song "Hotel California, you can check in, but you can't ever leave."

It seemed that my new job was trying to make other people feel better about me going to prison. I would be some place with Snake and Kimberly where people knew I was going to prison and they would look at me with sad expressions. A few times I announced to the crowd, "Okay everyone, cheer up. Yes, I'm going to prison, but it's not the end of the world. Let's lighten up and have some fun." That got most of them smiling. For some of the people it was like I had a contagious disease called "prison" and they felt uncomfortable around me and my situation.

I stayed with Kimberly in a nice motel for four days. We went to the movies, ate ice cream and took some pleasant walks around the mall where it was cool and we could do some window shopping. I love to watch people that are enjoying themselves. We spent some time with Snake and his wife and just had a great time.

Snake was debating on whether to start his lab up again. Chemicals were getting harder to obtain which increased the risk of getting caught. When his partner got busted it was an eye opener for Snake. That, mixed with the fact that I was on my way to prison, had Snake at a crossroad.

I told him that I had another ten pounds of meth and two more drums of phenylacetic acid I could part with. That made him happy and put off his decision on whether to start cooking again. I let him know that, as soon as it got cold, I was planning to whip up a big batch. There was no need for him to start manufacturing until after I was gone to prison, which was still a few months away. Snake had other people taking care of all his sales. At that time, his risk was low and I advised him to keep it that way for a while. I didn't even want him hauling the meth and chemicals back from Oklahoma.

Kimberly wanted to ride to Oklahoma and back with me, but I told her it was too risky. I had been going back and forth so much in my truck that I decided to fly back. I parked my truck at Kimberly's house and she took me to the airport. Back then I could board a plane with only a moments notice.

The flight from Dallas to Oklahoma City just takes a few minutes. We no sooner than got in the air and then we were going back down again. When I got to Oklahoma City I rented an emerald green SUV and drove to my grandparents and spent the night. My grandmother loved to feed me and I loved to let her. The next morning, I ate breakfast with grandma and grandpa then left to take care of my task. Thankfully I was being observant. As I was filling up with gas in Elmore City I noticed two new cars with tinted windows and little antennas. They were parked so the drivers could talk to each other through their open windows and still keep an eye on me. My gut told me that I was in trouble.

I left Elmore City going East, then turned North on the old airport road. The airport road is curvy. I drove slow at first and sure enough I could see one of the cars trying to keep me in sight. When I got to the halfway point, between Elmore City and Pauls Valley, I took off as fast as I could drive, then turned into my old friend Kevin's driveway and quickly pulled around back behind the house out of sight. I jumped out of the SUV and looked around the corner of the house just in time to see both unmarked cop cars roar past on the old airport road.

I got back in the SUV and went back the way I'd come. On the dirt road close to my underground storage there is an oil field location sitting on top of a hill. From the top of that hill I could see the dirt road below me and another paved road to the South. I drove to the top and parked out of view. I then walked to the best vantage point and watched the two roads. It wasn't long before a sheriff's car went by, then one of the other cop cars

I'd seen went by on the other road. I watched the police looking for me for about two hours. When I felt it was clear, I took back roads to the highway and went back to the airport in Oklahoma City. I returned the green SUV at the rental agency then I walked over to another rental agency and rented a burgundy colored SUV. Then I called Mikey and he told me that the cops were watching all the roads coming into Elmore City. Mikey liked to listen to a police scanner while he watched television at the same time.

I knew every back road in the area, but I decided that using extreme caution might work against me. If the cops were watching the back roads then I needed to stay away from them. I got on highway 35 and headed South to Pauls Valley as fast as I dared. I wanted to make it by dinner.

People are creatures of habit. They like to eat their meals three times a day. The odds are pretty high that the cops will be eating breakfast, lunch and dinner at the same time every day and usually at the same places. I got off the highway at the Pauls Valley exit and drove through the truck stop parking lot. Sure enough, there was at least ten marked and unmarked police cars sitting there, including the two I'd seen earlier. Blessed with the good news I eased out of the parking lot and took off for my underground storage. I kept a shovel hidden in the trees so I quickly dug in the storage, got what I came for, covered the entrance and was out of there in thirty minutes.

Then I drove another back road to highway 35 and motivated my way back to Texas. Usually I won't haul stuff at night, but most people I knew, including Kevin, knew that. It was time for a change. I was back in Snake's neck of the woods by 11:00 p.m. It was starting to look like someone close to me was talking to the cops, or the cops were very smart and anticipating my moves. I'm not the paranoid type, but I could feel something was wrong. A few people knew that I had a hidden storage, including Kevin, but nobody knew where it was. They could have guessed the general area, but that was not good enough. My lab was close to twenty miles away from the storage and I was the only person who knew where it was. If the cops caught me it would be coming or going and I was not going to let that happen. I called Snake and he met me at a prearranged spot. I felt better once his guy left with the load. I let Snake know that the cops were homing in on me so I wouldn't be back for a while. It had been a stressful day and I was happy that Kimberly was waiting at the motel room to help me relax.

I wouldn't have even considered going back to Oklahoma, but it was that time of the month. I had to see my probation officer. I slept in with Kimberly, then gave her ten thousand dollars and told her to conserve because I wouldn't be back for a while. By noon I was on the road back to Ada.

My first destination was Budroux's in Ardmore for a late lunch. On the way I had an idea, so I went truck shopping after I ate. I found a sharp 1970 Chevy half ton truck in a faded forest green. It was in excellent condition. I bought the truck and told the man I would be back the next day to take delivery. That night I stayed at Mikey's and he took me to Ardmore the next day to get the truck.

On the way to Ardmore I dropped off my 1965 Chevy truck in Wynnewood, Oklahoma at a friend's house. After I picked up my '70 Chevy truck and went to an insurance company and the tag office, I drove straight to Ada like I owned the road. When I got to Ada I parked my truck behind Polo's Mexican restaurant, then walked two blocks to the probation office.

My probation officer looked a little surprised to see me, but all went well. She asked me if I could pass a urine test and I said "Yes," so she didn't bother testing me. I'm sure she could tell by looking at me that I wasn't using drugs. I was glad to get my probation visit out of the way and knowing that I had another month before I had to worry about it again felt pretty good. I figured that, if the cops were going to harass me, they could find me at the probation office once a month. I was being careful to make sure that didn't happen.

Shawyn was home when I called from Polo's and asked her to come join me for dinner. She wasn't happy with me because I had been gone so much, but we managed to have a nice meal together. I had Shawyn follow me to my cousin's house in Ada, where I parked my truck. My cousin had a nice work shop behind his house where I'd stored a 350 Chevy engine I'd built and some parts I was intending to use to build a hot rod truck. I didn't go around my cousin much. He worked every day and didn't do drugs and I didn't want to cause trouble for him, with the police following me around. I left the truck at his house then I came back the next day to change the engine. I took the seat out and the dash pad and door panels off and took them to an upholstery shop to have them redone in black.

It took me a week working every day to get the truck fixed up to my liking.

When I was finished, the truck had a new engine, transmission, radiator, brakes, electrical system, shocks, tires and wheels, and interior. I then drove it to Oklahoma City and had the windows tinted and a new stereo system installed while I went Christmas shopping at the mall. I called my friend in Wynnewood and had him drive my '65 Chevy truck to Ada and park it in Shawyn's driveway. He had his girlfriend follow him and then take him back home. Then it looked like I was home, parked in the driveway. It took a while for the police to figure out that I wasn't there and that I had another truck. As long as I parked the new truck some place else and had Shawyn pick me up I was good to go. I used my old truck to drive back and forth to the store.

I was sure the police activity "Wasn't coming from Shawyn or anyone in Ada, because I wasn't doing anything in Ada. It wasn't Mikey and it certainly was not coming from Snake's end. I figured it was probably a residual effect from Kevin, Brad and Tommy telling on me. That theory was supported by the fact that the police presence was concentrated in the Pauls Valley, Elmore City area. I decided not to do anything in that area for a while.

If I sat too long in one place I would start thinking of sweet Lisa, or the very sexy Kimberly and the prison thing would start weighing on my mind. The depression was ever present, but I dealt with it okay. I called Kimberly every week from a payphone to flirt. That was fun. Kimberly kept asking me when I was coming to see her, so I thought up a plan and asked her to come see me. I went to Oklahoma City and made flight arrangements.

When Kimberly got off the plane she was so pretty I almost cried.

I kissed her and said, "Hurry, we have another plane to catch."

We picked up her luggage and checked it right back in for another flight. We flew to Denver and stayed the night. While we were there I took her to a rock and roll premier club called Bangles. I had been there before with my friend Pat and it was a pretty cool place. The people there were wearing more leather than you would see at a rodeo in Oklahoma. We danced until the place closed. Our flight out of Denver the next morning was to Reno, Nevada where we boarded a smaller plane for Lake Tahoe. To me, Lake Tahoe is a magic place that made me forget all my worries. One evening Kimberly and I had dinner on a paddle wheel boat. Standing on the observation deck, as the boat slowly made its way around the lake, we held hands and watched the moon and stars reflecting off the water.

The sky is so clear in Lake Tahoe, when you look up it feels like you are up there with the moon and stars. Kimberly asked me what was on my mind. We hadn't talked of love or prison, we were just enjoying the moments we had together. I told her that I wished we could freeze time and just keep riding around that beautiful lake. I told her how lucky I was to have her standing beside me, sharing that wonderful moment. I didn't want it to end, but reality was vastly approaching.

The next day we went shopping for something for Kimberly's mother.

We came to a shop that had these Navajo Indian blanket coats that were soft and pretty. We bought one for Kimberly's mother and we both had to have one, as well. It was a little cool that time of year in Lake Tahoe.

Then we decided to buy Snake and his wife both coats. Before it was over, I bought Alice and Mr. Connor coats too. It was a lot of fun. On the way to mailbox etcetera we saw an Indian jewelry store.

We bought a few nice pieces for Kimberly's mother and I got Alice a squash blossom necklace, matching hair barrette and a matching ring.

I put them in Alice's coat pocket then we mailed everything back to Oklahoma to keep from having to carry it all on the plane.

Leaving Lake Tahoe was hard for me and Kimberly. We didn't want to go because we knew our time together would be over for a while. We flew back to Oklahoma City and spent the night in a motel then Kimberly flew home the next day. Not much could have upset me at that point.

I was happy and just dreading going back to Ada a little bit. The sex was always great with Shawyn when I got back from a trip, so I didn't mind going home.

Halloween came and went without much notice. On Thanksgiving, I went with Shawyn to her grandmother's house at noon for Thanksgiving dinner. Her grandma was a wonderful person who always welcomed me with open arms. I loved seeing her, but Shawyn's mother and father were understandably bothered by the fact that I had been arrested "twice." I didn't stay long. My family was having a Thanksgiving get together in

Elmore City so I drove there after lunch. A lot of my family, on my mother's side, were there. My sister Susan and I visited a little and I tried to give her some money, but she wouldn't take it. She must have had a good idea of where it came from and didn't want any part of it. It hurt my feelings, but I understood. My sister has never done anything wrong in her life. She doesn't smoke, drink or even cuss and she has been a great example of the right way to live. I wish I would have followed her example. I read a study that said the oldest sibling is the smartest. In my family I would have to agree.

Christmas rolled around and I was nowhere to be found. Shawyn's and my relationship was strained. Her mom and dad were giving her a hard time about me and that added pressure caused us problems. I was big on running from arguments and problems, so I left for a while. Kimberly was busy with family matters, so I went to Steamboat Springs, by myself, snow skiing for four days. I met a girl there and we had some serious fun together. She asked me what I did for a living and I told her I was in manufacturing and sales. I just didn't elaborate on what I was manufacturing and selling. She was there with her parents for Christmas and she had to sneak away to meet me. It was more covert, James Bond stuff and it made it that much more fun. She was twenty years old, but still didn't want her parents to know that she was screwing a guy she didn't know while on vacation with them. We had sex all over the mountain, in the hot springs and in front of the fireplace in my room. It was a holly jolly Christmas, that year.

When I got back to Oklahoma it was plenty cold. We don't get a lot of snow in Oklahoma, but we do get some mean ice storms. I was waiting for the first ice storm before I went to my lab. The first night I woke to ice hitting the side of the trailer at two in the morning I got dressed and left before the roads got too bad. I like driving when I am the only person on the road. I didn't think anyone was watching in that weather, but I wasn't taking any chances. I drove my '65 Chevy truck to pick up my '70 Chevy truck. Then I drove to Mikey's and got my '88 Chevy four wheel drive truck.

I planned to return home in the reverse order. I had all the supplies I needed either with me, or they were already in the lab just waiting on me.

The old maxim that anything that can go wrong, will go wrong, is true. The first problem I had was digging into the frozen ground to clear the entrance to the lab. When I finally got in the lab all of my water was frozen, which caused me another problem. I had to thaw enough water to run the cooling system for the condensers. My next task was to start four P2p cooks. I still had the two triple neck flasks with the unfinished P2p cooks in them that I'd recovered years before at the house in Ardmore before the police raided the place. I also had half a drum of phenylacetic acid that I wanted to turn into P2p. That would reduce the amount of chemicals I had stored by a significant amount and leave me with a huge supply of raw P2p.

While the P2p cooks were in progress I took the twenty gallons of used trichloroethane outside into the freezing ice storm. To help set the mood, I kept Pink Floyd, "The Wall." "Machine" and "Comfortably Numb," playing softly. The next problem I had was when I was using a razor knife to trim down some small rubber stoppers. I needed the stoppers to fit perfectly in the necks of the jugs I was going to use to make my hydrogen chloride gas. I accidently cut a deep gash in the meat below my left thumb. I couldn't very well go get stitches at that point so I used duct tape to hold the cut together and stop the bleeding. I then hung a tarp in an L shape, using three trees, so I would have a wind break.

I had twenty gallons of used trichloroethane in four five gallon plastic cans. I re-gased all four cans, lowering the PH to five and a half and poured all twenty gallons through filters. A little over four pounds of pink meth was my prize for all the cold, hard work.

I encountered my next problem when the P2p cooks were finished.

I was using lye water to separate the P2p from the acetic anhydride.

Trying to separate all four cooks at the same time proved to be too much for me. The lye water separation is a very hot and violent reaction.

The trick is to add the lye water slowly so the reaction is controlled. I added too much lye water to one of the flasks and it instantly vaporized the acetic anhydride and lye water, shooting hot gasses into the lab, with a loud whooosh. The hot gasses immediately took my breath away and caused my eyes to slam shut in pain. I had to crawl   blind out of the lab and onto the frozen ground. For a moment, I didn't think my lungs would ever work again.

Right when I started to panic my natural survival instincts took over and I started gasping, choking and coughing, trying to get air. I was never so happy in my life, when I was finally able to breathe. My eyes burned, my lungs hurt and even though I was laying on ice, I was in a dead sweat. When I was able to get up I started my generator and watched as the fumes were sucked out of the lab by my ventilation system. That lesson almost cost me my life. From that point forward I did not work with poor lighting or without ventilation.

The accident and struggle for my life had left me in a weakened condition. I wanted to lay down and sleep but I had too much work to do. With the lights on and the ventilation system going I finished the lye water reactions and separations of all four P2p cooks. I was putting the waste water in five gallon cans. I made the mistake of moving one of the full cans without the cap on and when I sat the can down, kind of hard, the waste water splashed up and hit me in the left eye. I was once again, blind and in great pain. Fortunately, I was next to the ice chest that was full of cold, clean condenser water. I splashed water on my face and into my left eye until I had it flushed. I then washed my face with Joy dish soap and allowed a little to get in my eye to make sure it was cleaned out well. It burned like crazy, but it was either wash out the eye, or take a chance that my eye would be damaged. I was lucky that I didn't lose my eye and I probably would have if that ice chest of water hadn't been at my feet.

By the next day I could see out of the eye okay and I was thankful. I thought I had prepared for everything, but the unexpected still got me.

Even though I had cut myself, gased myself and almost lost an eye, I was thankful to be alive. I started using a lot more caution.

It took me four days to cook all of the phenylacetic acid into P2p and it was time for a break. I shut everything down and went to Ardmore and rented a motel room. After eating a nice dinner, I showered, washed my clothes and climbed into bed. My vision had cleared in my left eye and the redness was gone around the eye. I slept hard. The next day I filled my gas cans and propane bottles, went by good old Walmart for supplies and headed back to the lab.

I had thirty gallons of fresh trichloroethane and I planned to distill only enough P2p to use up all the trichloroethane. When I finished distilling I had over eight gallons of P2p. The speed cooks went well and were uneventful. I'd powdered about twenty pounds of meth when my next problem occurred. I was using thick, clear one gallon glass jugs to make my hydrogen chloride gas in. The size was easy to manage and I could see inside the jug and watch the foam level inside. If the foam level got too high I could simply slap the side of the jug and the Foam would fall back down.

I had powdered about one third of the speed oil and was on my ninth jug of rock salt mixed with hydrochloric acid and sulfuric acid, (which makes hydrogen chloride gas), when I slapped the side of the glass jug to knock the foam down and the bottom blew out of the jug. Luckily, the acidic mixture blew downward on the right leg of my coveralls and the floor. I held my breath and backed away as I peeled off my coveralls. Then I poured water on my boots and the floor to help neutralize the acids.

The ventilation system did its job.

I quickly scraped up the rock salt, broken glass and watery acids with a dustpan and put it all in a five gallon can. Then I placed my smoking coveralls on top of the mess and snapped the lid on the can. I was ready for that accident. If the ventilation system would have been off the hydrogen chloride gas would have likely killed me before I could get out of the lab. It was one of those times when I did not know whether to feel smart for being prepared, or feel dumb for being out in the middle of nowhere, by myself, making dope. If I'd died, it would have been a long time before I'd been found. Even if I would have been badly injured I could have frozen to death before I got back to my truck. Being a one man top secret operation can have some serious drawbacks.

When I was finished I'd used up all of my phenylacetic acid, all of my acetic anhydride and all of the trichloroethane. To finish my project, I had to distill some of the waste water to recover part of the used acetic anhydride and had to reuse some of the trichloroethane twice. The result was that I had turned eight gallons of P2p into sixty-four pounds of meth, with the additional four pounds I had recovered from the previous cook, was sixty eight pounds of meth. Eighteen pounds were pretty pink and the rest was crystal white. I spent a whole day cleaning out the lab and burning trash. It took two trips with my truck to haul all the waste water and used trichloroethane to an oil field location in the country and pour it all in a tank. I burned all of the plastic cans, buckets and other containers, then moved all the remaining chemicals to my underground storage. It was difficult lowering the two full thirty-five gallon drums of undistilled P2p into the storage, but I persevered.

I loaded forty-five pounds of white meth and five pounds of pink meth into three Army duffle bags and added one kilo of cocaine. Then I called Snake from Ardmore and told him that "Santa Claus was coming to town."

It was a little late for Christmas but I had a feeling that Snake wouldn't mind. I'd spent my Christmas in Steamboat Springs with a girl I didn't know, having sex all over the mountain. And I'd spent New Year's in my lab, all alone, almost accidentally killing myself half a dozen times.

I was ready for a party.

Snake must have thought I would show up with ten pounds again.

When I told him, I'd brought fifty pounds of meth and a kilo of cocaine he was a little shocked. It put a big smile on Snake's face and he said, "Damn, you are a Wizard."

I knew he wouldn't have all the money, but that wasn't my concern at the time. My concern was to provide Snake with enough meth to last him a while and allow me to put some money away for when I got out of prison.

I told Snake that I wanted him to hold half the money, two hundred and sixty thousand, until I got out of prison. I wanted money in three locations. With Snake, Mikey and in my storage. I figured it would give me a better chance of having something when I got out. I still had all the building materials stored at Mikey's and I planned to buy some land and build a house when I got out. Snake was reluctant at first. He didn't want to be responsible for my money. I didn't blame him, it was a lot of money. But he understood my position.

I was going to start a salvage yard and a bar and grill in Ada, but then I got busted and had to take things slow because too many eyes were on me. Then I got busted the second time and certainly couldn't open a business with me on the way to prison. Obviously, opening a bank account was out of the question. I couldn't account for where the money came from, so if I put the money in the bank, it would likely get seized and be further proof that I was doing something wrong. Putting that kind of money in the bank would be like handing it to the authorities as a de facto confession. My thoughts were if I could store the cash some place safe and reliable I could slowly put some in the bank when I got out of prison, from the sales of cattle that I had at Mikey's, then I could open a bar and grill and a salvage yard. I could live off the money I already had and show a moderate profit.

Having a lot of illegal cash wouldn't be too much of a problem for a person who had a legitimate business that generated a lot of cash, such as a restaurant. Sliding a little additional money into the till to show a better income wouldn't be noticed. That's why some of the old mobsters had clubs and restaurants. Same thing with the casinos. Who's to say how many people lost money, or how much, on a given day. My problem was; I got busted before I could open a real business. I was running some money through my road service, but I could only show a reasonable income. Most people who do anything illegal, such as sell drugs, only make a little bit of money and it goes unnoticed. Then there are the real big crooks that have so much money that a few million here and there just mixes in with the legitimate funds. I was in the middle some place. The law is like a fish net, or spiderweb. Small things go right through. Big things break through. It's the medium size people, like me, who get hung up in the system and can't get free. I was stuck in the net, or web, depending on which metaphor one likes best.

Because the probation thing had me doing drug tests, I wasn't doing drugs. That fact, mixed with the fact that I ate when I was depressed, had me looking pretty healthy when I got to Snake's place. I was feeling good and I didn't have any immediate problems. The lack of sunshine left me a little pale, but I was fine. Red hair runs in my family. I'm blond, but I have fair skin and I don't tan well. If I stay in the sun too long, I just turn red and burn. I do better at night, or in the shade.

Kimberly was happy to see me. She and Snake's wife were planning a going away party for me. I still had about four months before I would be going to prison. I told them that I would be coming back in a few weeks and I would let them know when so they could plan a date for a party.

I had to come back to pick up some more money from Snake, but the girls didn't need to know that. Kimberly and I went dancing that night at a club in downtown Dallas. At first, I didn't notice the other people around us, but after a while I noticed that I was getting some funny looks. When I looked around the club I saw only women. There wasn't another man in the place. I brought the point up to Kimberly and she said, "Silly, it's a lesbian club. I want you to pick any girl in here and I'll get her to go back to the motel with us."

I said, "That's very thoughtful of you, but I only want you."

Kimberly hugged me tight, kissed me hard and said, "I love you Jeffrey Dan." We left and went back to the motel where I showed Kimberly just how much I wanted her. I stayed for two days taking Kimberly to nice places to eat, doing some shopping, site seeing and living on love and room service. I really didn't want to go back to Oklahoma, but I had obligations there too.

When I got back to Oklahoma I changed trucks at Mikey's and took my circular route back to Ada, where I changed trucks again. Shawyn was her usual pissed off self and I couldn't blame her. I once again told her that we should get a divorce before I went to prison so she could move on with her life. I was going to leave her with everything and take my clothes and move out, but Shawyn said "No." I agreed to stay, but only if she would stop yelling at me. I had enough on my mind without her screaming. I stayed there, watched a few good movies and listened to "Hotel California."

CHAPTER SIXTEEN:

Birthday Bash

The weekend before my 30th birthday my good friend, Pat, called me and asked me to go with him to the Flea Market in Oklahoma City. It was Pat's place that the police had searched looking for a lab. Pat was never involved with drugs and I felt bad, because just knowing me caused him to be harassed by the cops. There was never a lab, or anything illegal on Pat's property. Pat and I went to the Flea Market and walked around buying a few things and visiting with people. My birthday is in April, so it hadn't gotten hot yet. It was a pleasant day, with a mild breeze blowing. People were milling around enjoying themselves.

I didn't realize it, but Pat knew that my birthday was coming up. He also knew that I was going to prison and I'm sure he felt sorry for me.

Pat has a good heart and he was a great friend. When we left the Flea Market Pat suggested that we stop at a club.

I usually didn't go to clubs, but I was enjoying spending time with my friend and being away from Ada. When we arrived at the club it was a strip club, commonly known in Oklahoma as a "Titty Bar," but pronounced "Tiddy Bar," in Okie speak. I was about to turn thirty and I had seen and done more in my short life than many people do in a lifetime, but I'd never been in a "Tiddy Bar."

When we went in it took a moment for my eyes to adjust to the darkness. I followed Pat to the chairs that ran around the stage and sat down. Pat later told me that the seats in front of the stage are referred to as pervert row. Thanks Pat. As soon as our asses hit the chairs a pair of perfectly formed breasts appeared on my left shoulder. The face above the "tiddies" asked if I wanted a pitcher of beer. I tried to look the girl in the eyes and said, "Yes." No sooner than the first boobs walked away another pair of perfect boobs appeared at my right shoulder and the pretty girl asked me if I wanted a pitcher of beer. I was so stunned and feeling so uncomfortable and out of place, I told her "Yes," also. Before I knew it, I had two pitchers of beer and I was shaking so bad I spilled beer on my hand trying to pour it into a mug. Pat was laughing. He thought my reaction was pretty funny. A few minutes later, both girls came back, kissed me on each cheek and wished me "Happy Birthday."

Pat leaned over and told me, "Happy birthday, buddy."

I was nervous, so I drank three mugs of beer in about ten minutes. Not being a drinker I was feeling the beer, quick. Another pair of "tiddies" showed up with a jar and asked for a five dollar donation for the jukebox. At that point, I would have bought her a new juke box if she would have asked. I gladly donated the money. In less than an hour I was shit faced. Pat asked me which girl I would pick if I wanted a lap dance. I wasn't exactly sure what a "lap dance" was, but the word "dance" sounded promising. I wasn't sure I could dance in my inebriated condition, but I was willing to try. I chose a perfectly gorgeous girl with long, wavy, dark hair. She had a little playboy bunny just above her g-string. It was where she placed a bunny sticker while she tanned, then took the sticker off and it left a little white bunny. The girl was so pretty that I fell in love with her from across the room. After Pat went to the restroom the girl with the bunny came over and whispered "Happy birthday" in my ear. Bunny girl also told me to find a table against the back wall because she was going to give me a lap dance.

Pat and I moved to a back table and a few minutes later the beautiful girl came over to me and started dancing in front of me. I was sitting there with money in both hands, plenty drunk, with this hot girl bent over in front of me with her finger going in and out of her sweet spot. My brain was on hold, my animal side took over and I was stuck on stupid.

In my slightly slurred speech, I asked the girl, "Can I lick it?"

She said, "No."

"Why not?" I asked.

"Rules," she replied.

I said, "Whose rules?"

This amazingly beautiful girl turned around to face me, put both hands on her hips and said, "Do you see anyone licking anybody's pussy in here?"

Feeling like a chastised school boy, I said, "No."

I can honestly say that I wasn't very bright in that intoxicated, sexually overwhelmed condition. I looked at the girl, standing there with her hands on hips and an expression on her face that could have only meant she was thinking, "Dumbass," and I said, "It's my burfday, will you do to dinner wif me?"

She shook her head, smiled, and said, "No. I don't date the customers."

A light came on inside my drunk little head and I realized that I wasn't just a guy asking a pretty girl out. I had graduated to a "customer." That realization repulsed me. I handed the girl the money I had in both hands and apologized for being a bother, then I left. Pat took me home and put me to bed. The next time I saw Pat, the first thing he said to me was, "Can I lick it?" Then he cracked up laughing. Pat is the best and he will never let me live that one down. I can count the times I have been in a "Tiddy Bar" on one hand.

Shawyn didn't show any sign that she knew it was my birthday, so the day before my birthday I took off for Texas where Kimberly had planned a party for me. Once again, I changed into my '70 Chevy truck and left Ada heading East. I went through Allen, Oklahoma and drove to McAlester where I got on highway 75 and headed South. I then drove through Paris, Texas and cut across on back roads to Dallas. I was feeling a little lonely, because the cops weren't following me.

I usually love to drive, but thoughts of prison were weighing on my mind pretty heavy. I had come to terms with the fact that I was on my way to prison, but that didn't stop the depression. As I drove I tried to focus on how nice it would be to see Kimberly and my friend Snake. I thought of Snake as a brother, even though we hadn't been friends long. I knew that Snake had been testing me when he asked me to do the recovery jobs for him. By taking me to his old lab to help him recover the meth he lost, Snake had shown me that I'd earned his trust. It was my turn to do the testing by trusting Snake with a large chunk of my money. We had already established a bond and a level of trust that many people have never experienced.

Since things went okay after Snake's partner got busted, Snake was hanging out at his bar and grill again. I was supposed to be there by 7:00 p.m. for my combination birthday and going away party. I had asked Kimberly to keep it small, but when I pulled into the parking area it was obvious that small was out of the question. As I was locking my truck my friend Muscle came walking out to greet me.

Muscle held up a large hand and said, "Hey bro, you're a little early. We got to take a ride."

He informed me that Kimberly and her helpers were putting on the finishing touches. We drove to a motorcycle shop to see if it was open late.

It wasn't, so I turned around and headed back to Snake's place.

Muscle was impressed with my truck. He was keeping me talking because he knew I was nervous about the party.

All my reservations disappeared when I walked through the door.

The back half of the club was made up with stars and moons. There was a live band cuing up happy birthday in a traditional manner as I walked in and the whole place started singing "Happy birthday." Smiling ear to ear, I took a bow and told the crowd "Thank you," as I went to Kimberly who had her arms open waiting for me. The cake was cool. It was three layers high, shaped like a pyramid with the top cut off. On top was a five inch tall medieval pewter wizard holding up a crystal ball and a five inch tall pewter fairy with her wings spread and a single white candle burning between them. When I blew out the candle everyone yelled and clapped their hands. Tables were lined with food. I was hungry. I'd been on the road most of the day. While we were eating, Snake made a short speech. He went up on the little stage and the band stopped playing.

Snake said, "The fact that I'm standing up here talking on this microphone should be enough to let you know that I value our friendship. But if that's not enough then knowing that I'm not going to throw any of these other guys a party like this should seal the deal."

Everybody laughed and clapped. Then it was my turn.

I took the microphone and said, "I could have searched the world over and never found as good of friends as all of you. Everyone has a purpose in this life. It may not be something big, like being a movie star or President, but we have a purpose. Even a candle maker has a noble purpose. He brings light into people's lives. Tonight, my purpose in life was to get Snake to spend his hard earned money on this party. I'm going to be gone for a little bit, but when I get back, the next party is on me."

That got a nice round of applause and some great laughs, but it was Kimberly who stole the show. Kimberly stepped up on the dais, grabbed the microphone and said, "When I get him in bed tonight, I'll show him what my purpose in life is."

She bent over, slapped herself on the ass, then took my hand and we walked off the dais to another round applause and cheers.

It was a wonderful party and a great night. About midnight Snake said he had a gift for me. One of the things I'd insisted on was no gifts at the party. But I wasn't the boss of Snake. We went to a back table where Kimberly and Snake's wife were putting away food. Snake handed me a small present. Kimberly and Snake's wife were looking with interest as I opened the package. I pulled out a soap on a rope. Snake and I just busted out laughing. Snake's wife saw what it was, she hit him and said, "You insensitive asshole."

We all started laughing again at the unintentional pun that made us think of a sensitive asshole.

After we could breathe again without laughing, Snake said, "Buddy, if you drop the soap in the shower, just leave it."

We didn't say our good-byes that night because I was planning on staying with Kimberly for two days and we were meeting Snake and his wife for lunch the next day. Knowing that it would be our last time together, for a long time or maybe forever, the lovin' reached a full spectrum of hot, passionate and tender. The next morning Kimberly woke to find little Elvis standing at attention with a tiny smile on his face, just begging for more attention. I came fully awake when Kimberly straddled me and lowered herself down on little Elvis. I took hold of Kimberly's hips and helped her grind forward and backward until she orgasmed. It was then my turn, so I rolled on top, pulled her legs up over my shoulders and slammed little Elvis home until I exploded inside her with enough force to scoot us off the bed, on to the floor. We held each other's sweaty bodies until little Elvis relaxed. What a great way to wake up in the morning. It was a true breakfast of champions and I was ready for lunch.

We showered and went to Snake's for lunch. The hot tub looked so inviting that we decided to sit in it a bit before we ate.

Snake said, "Bro, I know how you got fingernail scratches down both sides of your back, but how did Kimberly get those bruises on her hips?"

My thumbs had left bruises on each of Kimberly's hip bones where I had hold of her, sliding her back and forth that morning until she gushed like a water faucet being turned on when she came. It was a flood and I loved it.

I said, "Oh, but the real question is, 'Why doesn't your wife have bruises like that on her hips?'"

His wife said, "Yeah, where are my bruises, mister?"

We all had a good laugh, relaxed awhile, then got out of the hot tub and fired up the grill. That's what men do, make fire, cook meat. The meal was better than great, because I was having it with friends that truly cared.

After lunch, Snake and I discussed some business while the girls cleaned up our mess. (It's another man thing). Snake was pretty much set.

He still had thirty pounds of the last batch of meth left. He had the chemicals we'd recovered from the barn in Ringling and the four drums of phenylacetic acid I'd sold him. But he had lost all of his glassware when his old partner had been busted. The DEA was not only watching precursor chemicals, they were monitoring the sales of certain glassware that could be used for manufacturing. Buying more glassware could be a huge problem.

I told Snake that I would give him all of the glassware I'd obtained from the two recovery jobs I'd done for him. I also said that I had ten more pounds of meth that I could leave with him. I asked him to give Kimberly ten thousand for me and that would mean he would be holding three hundred and fifty thousand for me when I got out. He agreed, we shook hands and that was that. Snake had my other money already counted out in ten thousand dollar bundles, waiting for me in a brown paper grocery bag. Snake always took care of his end of things. I quietly gave Kimberly ten grand of that money, as well and she put it away.

Snake and I went for a drive, because he said he had something to show me. We went to a secured storage facility. He handed me the entry code on a piece of paper with the unit number on it and a key. We drove around to the correct unit, then we got out of my truck and I opened the door with the key Snake had given me. When the door rolled up, I saw the sun shining off the chrome of two new Harleys. One was electric blue and the other was candy apple red.

Snake said, "I remembered that you like blue, so the blue one is yours."

"Blue is perfect," I answered.

Snake went to a stand-up tool box in the back of the storage and opened one of the drawers. He showed me the title. It had been signed over to me and notarized. All I had to do was tag my Harley and transfer the title. They both had temporary paper tags, so we rolled them out, fired them up and went to pick up the girls. I left my truck parked at the storage and we took the girls for a ride. There is nothing like the freedom you feel while traveling down an open highway on a Harley with the wind in your hair and a beautiful woman holding you tight. It's exhilarating. We rode to San Antonio, Texas for dinner and stayed in a motel that night. The next morning, we rode back to Dallas and dropped the girls off at Snake's house. We then rode the Harleys back to the storage place. Snake had paid the storage for five years. I didn't know how long I'd be gone, but based on what my attorney told me, I figured five years was about right. Snake said that he would stop by now and then and start the Harleys, so they would be ready for a long road trip when I got out. He kept a key to the storage and I had one and the slip of paper with the entry code and unit number. We each kept a key to our Harley and locked the spare key and titles in the big tool box. Then we each kept a key to the tool box in our Harley tool pouch. Snake said that if anything happened to him, my money would be locked in the tool box. It was a good plan.

We went back to Snake's, loaded up the girls and headed to Oklahoma in a caravan. I was leading with Kimberly beside me, Snake and his wife were behind us and two of Snake's guys were following in a van. Kimberly had a thing about entertaining little Elvis while we drove down the highway, any highway, which drove me wild. About the time we crossed the State line into Oklahoma, I was coming in Kimberly's mouth.

We got two motel rooms in Pauls Valley, Oklahoma next to the highway. Everyone waited at the motel while I drove the van out to my hidden storage. It didn't take me long to dig in, get everything out that I wanted and loaded it all in the van. It was a lot of glassware and other equipment. The van was half full. I put a large part of my money, with the other money I had stored and buried the entrance. When I got back to the motel Snake's guys took off in the van with the laboratory equipment and ten more pounds of meth. Snake and I then took the girls out to eat, then back to the motel for some fun lovin'.

The next morning, we had a quiet breakfast at the truck stop across the road from the motel. Kimberly was set for a while and I felt pretty good about that. Money is no substitute for companionship, but it does take the edge off. I knew she would miss me. I would miss her too, but she would get over it pretty fast. She worked at her father's business and lived at home. I knew she would be fine. It was tough for all of us, saying our good-byes. It was hard watching them drive away.

After they were out of sight I got in my truck and drove to Mikey's. I gave Mikey fifty thousand to take care of the cattle for five years. I figured ten thousand a year would do it and none of us thought I'd be gone more than five years.

Even though the district attorney was recommending thirty years, Mr. Ward, my attorney, had assured me that I would get ten years and be out in less than five. I put some more money in the tool box I kept locked in the trailer behind Mikey's barn. I had taken the tires and wheels off the trailer so it couldn't be stolen easily. I put twenty thousand, the keys to the trailer and tool box at Mikey's and the key to my new Harley and the storage key and code in Texas, in a Crown Royal bag and hid it under the dash of my '70 Chevy truck. Mikey gave me a hug and waved bye to me as I drove away.

On the way back to Ada I was thinking that this really sucked. The thought of going to prison had me a little down, but on the other hand, I felt good about having most of my affairs in order before I left. I had given Shawyn enough money to pay off a little bank note we had, but I found out later that, rather than pay the note off, she transferred it into her name.

When I got back to Ada I went by my cousin's house and asked him to take care of my truck while I was gone. We had already talked about it and he didn't mind. He dropped me off at Shawyn's trailer and told me good luck. I felt like I would need some luck.

I hadn't been gone long, so Shawyn was in a fair mood. After dinner a friend of mine from Wynnewood, Oklahoma rode up on his Harley with his girlfriend. He didn't stay long. He just wanted to let me know that if I needed anything to call him. He and his girlfriend hugged me and rode away. I told Shawyn, again, that we should go ahead and get a divorce, but she insisted that she loved me and would wait on me. I knew better.

She was just lying to herself.

I got up early the next morning and took a shower and shaved. I woke Shawyn up and asked her to take me to the courthouse, but she didn't want to get out of bed. She told me to take her car, because I had sold my '65 Chevy truck to her brother.

I didn't feel like arguing, so I got in her car and drove to the courthouse by myself. I hadn't told my sisters about me going to prison. There was no reason for them to worry about it any longer than necessary. I had gotten myself into the mess and there wasn't anything anyone could do to help.

On my way to the courthouse I stopped by my uncle Max's video store to tell him goodbye. He fixed my tie and hugged me with tears in his eyes.

I was in a good mood when I got to the courthouse. I went to the second floor and was sitting in a chair in the hallway waiting on my attorney and the appointed time when the deputy sheriff walked up the stairs and took a seat beside me. He asked me if I was alright and I said, "Yes, sir." I'm sure he was just making sure I showed up for court, but it was nice of him to ask. The sitting was a little awkward and I was thankful that my attorney and his secretary showed up about two minutes later.

We went into the judge's chambers where the district attorney recommended that I get thirty years. The judge asked me where the gun was and I told him it was in my closet. He asked me how the police found the gun and I told him the truth about the phone call setting me up and my agreeing to trade the gun for some tires and wheels for a four wheel drive truck I was building. To my surprise, the judge said that he could see that I would not be in his courtroom if it wasn't for an informant. He shook his head and sentenced me to ten years for the gun to run concurrently with the ten years probation that he revoked.

I apologized to the judge for being a burden on the Court, then I asked if I could have a few minutes with my attorney. The judge told me to turn myself in at the county jail when I finished talking with my attorney. I went to Mr. Ward's office and called Shawyn to let her know to pick up her car keys at my attorney's office. She freaked out and started crying. I didn't know why she was crying. I was the one going to jail and I knew that she didn't really care about me. I gave Mr. Ward my nice silk tie and asked his secretary Linda to give Shawyn her keys and my wedding ring. Then Linda walked with me to the county jail door and gave me a hug. I had been through so much in such a short time, I was ready to get it all over with.

The county jail in Ada sits on a corner of the courthouse lawn. It is a small concrete bunker, with no windows that holds about thirty prisoners.

It was nicer than the Okmulgee county jail, but jails in general are not nice places. In his book, "Pretty Boy Floyd," Larry McMurtry wrote that Pretty Boy Floyd once said, "I have a powerful lack of affection for jails."

That is my sentiment, exactly. My wife Shawyn never did come see me. She sent me a letter about four weeks into my county jail stay that said, "I think I want a divorce." I called Mr. Ward and he took care of it for me. All I wanted was my clothes and wedding ring. My sister Susan, who had been trying to pick up after me and watch out for me most of her life, went to Shawyn's to get my clothes and Shawyn kept most of them and flatly refused to give my sister my wedding ring. That hurt my feelings, but I expected as much from Shawyn. Shawyn and I had grown apart and the longer I knew her, the more I disliked her. I was just thankful to get her behind me, as well.

With prison overcrowding problems, I had to sit in the county jail for several months waiting to be transported to prison. I will always remember just how good it felt on Thanksgiving when the ladies from the local church brought us all a Thanksgiving meal that was fit for kings. We had turkey, dressing, fresh baked bread, cranberry sauce, corn, green beans and pumpkin pie. It was the first time I cried. I was so touched that I must have told them "Thank you" twenty times. After Thanksgiving I was transferred to the Assessment and Reception Center (A & R), in Lexington, Oklahoma where I spent my Christmas. A & R is a processing center that all State prisoners go through to be evaluated before going to prison.

After a short stay in the A & R Center I was sent to the trustee building for the maximum security prison in McAlester, Oklahoma. The new underground death row unit was under construction and they needed a welder for the finishing touches, so I was delegated the job. I wasn't there long. The final projects were small and didn't take me long to complete.

While I was there I started lifting weights for the first time and it felt great. From McAlester I was sent to Lawton Community Correctional Center (LCCC), where I went to work in the maintenance department. I can fix just about anything, so the maintenance department was the perfect place for me.

One afternoon I received a letter from Misty letting me know that she wanted to come see me. Looking back on it, she must have thought that there was still some money stashed some place and she didn't want to burn any bridges until she found out for sure. My problem was, I'm a "dumbass." I was still in love with her so I sent her a visiting form.

About two weeks later I was called into the Administrator's office. He had Misty's visiting form in his hand. In the box on the form that said, "Reason for wanting to visit this inmate?" Misty had put, "To further a better sexual relationship." I thought it was a perfectly fitting answer, but the Administrator disagreed. I told him that she was just having fun and he stressed that it was a serious matter. In the end, he approved her visiting form.

Things went well at Lawton (CCC) for a few months. My boss would sign me out some weekends and drop me off at a motel where I would spend the afternoon doing Misty or Suzanne. Then he would pick me up and take me back to the center before shift change. All good things seem to come to an end. The Administrator figured out what was going on and transferred me to the work center at Ardmore Airpark. I liked it there.

They took us to Walmart on Saturdays and we got to go to church in town on Sundays. I met a nice girl at church, Tammy, who I enjoyed getting to see and visit with.

One fall evening I was walking the track and the facility did an unscheduled (special)count. I wasn't in the building, but when I heard my name called I reported to the office. When I got to the office I was given a write up and sent to a low security prison called Jess Dunn.

Being sent to Jess Dunn was one of the best things that happened to me while I was in prison. In the early '90s Pell Grants were still available to qualifying prisoners. I took advantage of the Pell Grants and went to college full time. The courses were offered through Bacone College in Muskogee, Oklahoma. The teachers came to the prison to teach the classes. What amazed me was how few prisoners utilized the college program. Out of about nine hundred men, only about 30 took courses.

I carried a 4.0 GPA while in prison. I love college and lifting weights. I also worked as a GED math tutor and spent most of my off time working out. The feel of the weights and watching my body grow was an exhilarating experience for me. When I started lifting weights I was small compared to the other guys. When I got to Jess Dunn I worked out with my friend Big Jeff. I was still so small that our other friends referred to me as Little Jeff. That changed over two and a half years.

I had been at Jess Dunn for a year when I received a letter from Alice.

The letter wasn't from the little girl Alice I had known, it was from a grown up Alice who was the mother of a two year old beautiful daughter.

The picture she sent me showed Alice and her daughter playing in a pile of fall oak leaves. They looked so happy. It had taken several years and some amazing will for Alice to overcome the bad things that happened to her. I was proud of Alice and still mad at the bastards that hurt her. If you want to know how devastating drugs are and how evil drug dealers can be, Go Ask Alice and the countless girls just like her. People like Snake and I were part of the few exceptions. We weren't mean or cruel. We were just trying to have fun and make some money. Go Ask Alice, she could tell you the difference between good and evil. Evil has a common face and it may look like your next door neighbor.

Evil doesn't come with horns, it's in the heart. You can't always see evil on the surface, because it lurks within. Alice had looked evil in the face and she knew what evil lurks in the hearts of men and I was thankful that she was able to put it behind her and move on with her life.

Time at Jess Dunn went by fast for me. Tammy and one of her girlfriends came to see me once. Loretta came a few times and I often went to visit with a good friend of mine, Jack, who was like family to me.

I had a serious crush on Jack's niece, Elizabeth, who was absolutely beautiful. My sisters came from time to time and my dad would fly in from California once a year to see me.

One of the hardest things about being in prison is not knowing what is going on out in what we called "the real world." Unless someone wrote me and told me what was happening, I had no idea. I just had to hope things were going well and that everything was in order. I made it a point not to worry about anything. Things have a way of taking care of themselves over time.

Some nights I would listen to the radio and think about the things I wanted to do when I got out. I heard an advertisement about a new sports bar in Tulsa called Hooters. I told myself that when I got out I was going to see this Hooters. One night I heard a song by Alice and Chains, on their Dirt CD, called "Rooster" and it struck me as funny. It was just how I felt. I was about to get out of prison and the song was perfect. The song goes, "Here comes the Rooster." I had been lifting weights and going to college and I was feeling pretty cocky. I had made a lot of mistakes in my life and I was determined not to make any more. I was in great shape and I was hoping that my educational background would help me overcome the prison stigma. I knew it wouldn't be easy when I got out, but I was ready for the task.

CHAPTER SEVENTEEN:

Rooster

In October of 1994, I'd been in prison for three and a half years and I was about to walk out the front door. I was scheduled to get out at 3:30p.m. and it was the longest day of my life. It seemed like the clocks were running at half speed. At 3:30, the prison staff told me good luck and opened the door to let me out. I walked outside into sunshine that looked brighter and air that smelled sweeter. To help get past my nervousness, I kept thinking, "Here comes the Rooster." There is a part of the song that goes, "Can't kill the Rooster," and oddly as it sounds, that's the way I felt. I had been shit on by most of my friends and locked in a cage, but they couldn't kill the Rooster. I was a new and improved Jeffrey Dan.

My brother-in-law, who had taken off work to come get me, was waiting in front to pick me up. On the ride home, I sat with my hands clasped in my lap because I had ridden so many times handcuffed it was a force of habit. We stopped in Muskogee at a Pizza Hut to eat. It smelled wonderful. I was used to eating small portions of bland food. The pizza was like little bites of heaven, only I couldn't eat much.

We left the Pizza Hut and drove through Tulsa to Sperry, Oklahoma and stopped at my sister's place of work. She hugged me, cried and introduced me to everyone there. That was the first time I met Cathy, who worked with my sister. I was one of the lucky people that was fortunate enough to have a loving sister who was willing to give me a place to live when I got out of prison.

It was the first time I'd seen my sister's new home. She and her family had moved from Henryetta, Oklahoma to Sperry while I was in prison.

The house was a large two story that had plenty of room for me.

I was used to living out of a small locker and sleeping on a single bunk. Everything I owned fit in one closet.

My sister cried when she saw how I had everything organized in the one little closet.

Even though my sister and brother-in-law did everything they could to make me feel comfortable, it was several weeks before I adjusted to freedom. I spent a lot of time working in the yard and the garage. One of my sister's friends took me to get my driver's license and my brother-in-law took me to Ada to pick up my '70 Chevy truck. My cousin had been using my truck to haul things in, so it was pretty run down. It needed new brakes, shocks, tires and the engine rebuilt, again. When I got the truck home I looked under the dash and got out my Crown Royal bag that had twenty thousand and my keys stashed in it. I was thankful it was still there.

My dad had sent me some money too, so I was, once again, a lot more fortunate than most people getting out of prison. I was set for a while.

Loretta came to see me twice after I got out. She was living in Arkansas and the second time she came she informed me that she was pregnant by her boyfriend in Arkansas. She went back to Arkansas and I never saw her again. I wanted to have a relationship with my friend Jack's niece, Elizabeth. I put out the effort, but it didn't work out. I took her to dinner at Red Lobster, we went bowling once and she invited me to her company Christmas party. We danced and I had a great time with her.

However, she was in love with a guy who was at the party. She only invited me to make him jealous. That was a kick to my already wounded ego.

My sister had innocently mentioned to her friend Cathy that I was hurt over Elizabeth. Low and behold, Cathy called me at home one afternoon.

Cathy was very pretty and married. She told me she was coming by on her lunch break. When she got there, she kissed me and said she didn't have a lot of time. I knew what that meant. We went inside and Cathy pulled out little Elvis and wrapped her lips around him. After that I did her standing up, laying down and from the behind. I loved it, because she was great and it was more secret James Bond stuff, but it was eventually my downfall. My big plan was to go to college to help get "prison" behind me and to start my road service using my old truck. I knew a job application would look better if I could honestly say that I had just completed college, rather than just completed a prison sentence. That and I really wanted to get my associates degree in psychology.

I got a membership to a gym in Skiatook, Oklahoma, less than five miles from the house, where I worked out at least three times a week. One of the first places I went by myself was Hooters. I wanted to see what the fuss was about.

My Hooters girl happened to be named Lisa. When she told me her name it brought back a flood of memories. Hooters Lisa was extremely sweet. She peeled my boiled shrimp for me, then fed it to me. We dated and I met her family. I even put an alternator on her car, but it also needed a water pump. Before I could put the water pump on, something came up with Cathy, she was separating from her husband and moving in with a friend. That and every time I heard her name it brought back too many memories of my Lisa from Texas. I felt like I was disrespecting my first Lisa.

I guess there are some things in life we just can't get over and I am very thankful that I don't forget. I just wish the memories were not so painful.

I started college in the spring semester taking a full load of honor classes. I really enjoyed getting up every day with a purpose. Going to college, coming home and doing my homework, then going to the gym was great. I wish I would have stayed in that mode and I did for a year.

During that year I found out that my old friend Mikey had a heart attack. He sold out everything. His land, home, my cattle, building supplies, tools, truck, equipment and cash were gone. Mikey had moved away and none of his family would tell me where he went. I lost close to four hundred thousand and one of the best friends I ever had. I wasn't mad. I was heartbroken and hurt. It wasn't the money and things like my tools and truck being gone that hurt, or the cows, I would have given him all of it anyway. Selling it all behind my back and sneaking away showed me that Mikey didn't value our friendship like I'd valued our friendship and that hurt.

There is an old Arabic saying, "What leaves the eyes, also leaves the heart."

It's kind of like our saying, "Out of sight, out of mind." That must be the way it is for some people. For me it is, "Absence makes the heart grow fonder." I guess I'm just a sap or a sucker. I should probably change my name to Lollipop. I miss the people I care about and would never do them wrong. I could not understand how Mikey could do me that way.

Life is a series of tests. How we handle each test is what defines us as a person. If we cheat on a test we are known as a cheater, but if we pass the test with hard work, we are known as an achiever. Mikey had cheated and flunked the test and all that money couldn't buy him a place in heaven.

I dusted off all the disappointment and moved on.

I was thankful that I'd had the foresight to put some money in my hidden underground storage. The new problem I was faced with was a big one. I had buried the old hundred dollar bills and needed to change them all to the new hundred dollar bills. Walking into a bank with four hundred thousand in cash was out of the question. I went to my storage and got out one hundred thousand and started driving all over Oklahoma changing old hundreds for new ones two or three thousand at a time. It took weeks in my spare time to exchange all the old bills.

The problem with Mikey had left me concerned about Snake. His home phone had been disconnected and the guy who answered his shop phone said he hadn't seen Snake in two years. The first chance I had, I drove to Ardmore and had lunch at Budroux's. I then drove to the outskirts of Dallas to Snake's bar and grill. The place looked the same but the people were different. I asked about Snake and was told "He ain't here no more." I didn't press the issue, I just drove by his house then to Kimberly's mother's house. Kimberly's mother informed me that Snake was gone and she didn't know where. She also told me that Kimberly had married and moved away. I didn't ask where she moved. The last place I went was by the storage. My entry code worked on the gate so I was hopeful. My key worked in the lock, but when I opened the door my heart sank. Both of the Harleys were gone, but in the shadow at the back of the storage stood the big tool box.

The tool box was full of nice tools, all made by Snap-On, just like the tool box. I opened the drawer where my title was and found a letter with one word on the envelope, "Wizard." The envelope contained a letter from Snake and ten thousand in old hundreds. The letter informed me that he had some tax issues and felt it was best to relocate. The letter further stated that my Harley and money were safe and that I needed to go see the attorney listed on the attached card for further instructions. The only problem was that the attorney was in Belize. It was a year before I went to Belize to meet the attorney, but I called him that day and left a message for Mr. Snake, from Mr. Wizard.

During this time, Cathy and I were in a heated sexual relationship.

She liked to do methamphetamine and suck on little Elvis and have wild sex. The harder I gave it to her, the better she liked it. I could keep up with her pretty good and I wasn't using meth, at that time. But I knew Cathy was also doing her husband and probably the guy she got her meth from. I could tell by looking at the meth she was getting that it was very poor quality. She was also doing a lot of it, which supported my conclusion that it was surely nothing more than crap.

A year went by before I finally caved in and broke my rule not to be involved in drugs. I'd told Cathy many times that she should stop using the cut-up meth, because she didn't know what it was cut with. Her response was to taunt me by saying that if I didn't want her to do the cut dope, then I should get her some that was not cut. Cathy was so sexy and seductive with her bright green eyes, I wanted to make her happy. I'm a sucker for a pretty face. I think part of it was that I wanted to show off a little.

The day I put the shovel in the back of my truck and headed for my storage, my mind, heart and my stomach were telling me to leave it alone.

I went as far as going back in the house and turning on the television. Then the phone rang and it was Cathy asking me when I was leaving and how long it would take me to get back.

At that point I had a choice. I could have dumped Cathy and the great sex, or I could take the road trip to get the meth. I made the wrong choice.

When I got back with a pound of meth from my storage, Cathy could not believe the extreme difference in the quality. She had never seen good, high quality, meth. After having wild sex every way we could think of, all night long, I forgot all about making the wrong choice. It felt like the right choice at that point. Cathy was wild and I loved every minute we spent together. But she kept going back and forth between me and her husband. I felt guilty for being in the middle and it hurt my feelings.

I wasn't selling any meth because I didn't need to, or want to. But it wasn't long before that changed and everything went to hell in a hand basket. I had easily managed to stay clean and on the straight and narrow for a year, while maintaining an outstanding GPA. That too changed in a blink of an eye. All it took was a little meth and the hot, wild sex and I was a goner.

When I first got out of prison, as a courtesy, I called the people I knew to let them know I was out. I had been out a year and a half before Louisiana gave me a return call. He caught me early one morning after my sister left for work. It just so happened that I was between semesters and had some free time. He wanted me to drive down that night and meet him for lunch the next day. Cathy had been spending a lot of time back with her husband. I figured she was sharing my meth with him, so I decided to take the trip. I needed some time to think.

I spent the day driving and checked into a motel in Lafayette, Louisiana by 6:00 p.m. I had a nice dinner and hit the sack early, because that long drive was tiresome. The next day at the appointed time, 11:00 a.m., I pulled into the parking lot of a nice little out-of-the-way steak house to meet my friend. The place had just opened and the lunch crowd was yet to arrive.

There were only three cars in the customer parking area. The place was surrounded on three sides with huge pine trees. Only the front was open to the road. It was the kind of secluded restaurant that I wished I owned.

When I walked in the front door, the first waitress I noticed didn't look up to see who I was. I thought that was odd. When I spotted the second waitress, she was looking at me, but her eyes darted quickly to the left and right of the room. I took it as a silent warning and looked left, then right.

There were five tables occupied, each with two men wearing either a suit coat or jacket. I did the math. With five tables occupied with what looked to be cops and only three cars in the lot besides my truck, I figured two or three cop cars were parked around back. It was a setup and I cursed under my breath at the knowledge of it. I should have drove around the place before I parked. Louisiana was supposed to be my friend. I was quickly learning that my so called friends were few and far between.

Louisiana was waving me over to his table as I looked his way. I walked over with a fake smile and shook the hand of the dog that was trying to bite me. He told me that he was glad to see me and introduced the fellow he was with as Todd Granger. I shook his hand, knowing he was a cop there to bust me.

As soon as I sat down, Louisiana said, "Todd here has a business deal for you."

"I thought we met at a steak house to eat a steak? I was wondering why we didn't meet at your house for lunch. I would have liked to see little Lucey. I bet she's grown a foot." I said, quickly.

Todd said, "We thought this kind of business would be best discussed away from the house."

"Is that right," I said. "Look, if it is some kind of shady business I don't want any part of it. I told you when I called a few months ago that I am going to college and staying clean. I've had all of prison I want. I've done my time and

I don't want to do any more. My road service is doing okay and I'm not going to do anything to risk my freedom."

Todd started dominating the conversation by explaining that he had a large quantity of chemicals. Enough to make five hundred pounds of meth.

He went on to tell me that he had all the lab equipment and a secure place to do the cooks.

He said that his father was a prominent local politician and nobody would suspect that I was making dope on his land. He asked me to come out and take a look at the lab. I just looked at him with raised eyebrows, like he was crazy. Then he told me that he would give me one hundred thousand dollars to cook the meth for him. It was a cornucopia of information that was clearly well rehearsed to get me life in prison.

When I could finally get a word in, I said, "You really shouldn't be telling people that you don't know all that. It could get you in a lot of trouble.

I wish you hadn't told me. I don't want any part of your business opportunity. Besides, I noted that you didn't bring the money. This looks more like some kind of setup to me."

Before anyone could say anything, I continued, by looking at Louisiana and saying, "I thought you were my friend. I guess I should have known better when you didn't come make my bond when I was arrested at my mother's funeral. I would have made your bond, even if I had to borrow the money. It hurt knowing that you could have gotten me out but chose to let me sit there. That is not exactly how I picture friends acting. Now you hit me with this. You called me up and asked me to a steak dinner and I drove all this way, as a friend, then you introduce me to this guy with an outlandish deal. I'm thinking that you are either in a lot of trouble, or you have lost your mind. I'm not getting involved with anybody or anything."

Even though I was plenty mad, I said all that in a low friendly voice, with a half smile on my face, as I shook my head in that "I can't believe you did this," manner.

I had a lot more to say, but before I could get a breath to proceed, Todd chimed in with, "Calm down. We just wanted to talk a little business.

If one hundred thousand isn't enough, then name your price. I'm flexible. I've got a lot tied up in all these chemicals and I got to get it turned into meth so I can recoup my money."

"I guess you aren't listening," I said. "I'm not interested. No amount of money is worth going to prison over. I've done my time and my life is on the right track. My past is just that, my past. The only reason I sat here this long was out of respect for my old friend here."

Louisiana wouldn't even look at me. Todd said, "let's have some lunch so you can think about my offer. We can talk about something else. I have a nice gun collection. I hear you do too. You like guns? (I shook my head yes). So do I. What kind of gun do you carry?"

"I like guns," I said. "I used to have some nice ones. I collected guns since I was young. I grew up in the country where everyone had guns.

That is common for a country kid who likes to go deer hunting.

But I'm a felon now. I can't have guns. I don't want to be anywhere around them."

Todd was pretty slick. He changed the subject to cars. It was a fairly good attempt to try and be friendly and to find out what kind of cars I might have.

"I love old cars. I just can't afford to have one. All I have is my old truck out there and I can barely keep it running."

I wasn't about to show him the three-thousand-dollar engine I had under the hood of my truck. I'd heard enough and it was time for me and little Elvis to exit the building.

I said, "Guys, I've lost my appetite. It was nice meeting you. I'm going to head back to Oklahoma while it's still early. My advice to you is to abandon this plan of yours before you end up in jail."

Todd quickly said, "If you won't help us, I guess we'll have to call your friend, Mr. Connor."

I looked at him, knowing he was baiting me, trying to get me to admit that I knew a Mr. Connor. It was obvious to me that my old friend wasn't just whistling Dixie. He was singing a serious tune of betrayal, in an attempt to save his own ass from something.

I got up and said, "Don't bother calling me again." Then I walked away. I didn't shake their hands and I didn't bother looking back.

I was surprised that I made it out the door into the bright sunshine. I was even more surprised that I made it to my truck and out of the parking lot. Since they didn't arrest me there, I figured the next thing would be to pull me over and search my truck before I got the one mile to the highway.

I took the first side road I came to and started zigzagging my way through an industrial park. I pulled into a parking lot where I saw an alley running behind the big buildings and dropped my 9mm in a dumpster. I then continued in the direction I was heading until I came out on the next major road. I turned in the direction of the highway and stopped at the first fast food place I came to. I went in and went straight to the pay phone and called Mr. Connor. I kept it short, and told him not to take any calls from Louisiana. For all I knew his phone was already tapped.

I took my time eating while I watched the road. Too many police cars were driving back and forth. When one of them drove through the parking lot and back out again, I knew they had me. I thought I was going to jail so I walked up to the order counter and bought an apple pie with a hundred dollar bill and told the pretty girl to keep the change. She was shocked. I considered it to be my last act of chivalry. Then I went to the rest room and put most of my cash down my pants. I didn't have much on me anyway, but I didn't want to lose what I had.

When I left the restaurant, I drove out of the parking lot from the rear and went down a block before I pulled on to the main road going to the highway. I hadn't gone a block when a police car pulled out in front of me and another one pulled in behind me. The police car behind me hit his lights and as I stopped. The police car in front of me stopped too. It was the full court press, with other police cars showing up around us. Officers got out of their cars with their guns drawn, pointed at me.

One of the officers behind me got on his loud speaker and told me to turn off my engine and put both hands out the window. Then he told me to open the door and get out with my hands on my head, which I did.

I was then instructed to lay down on the ground. At that point they came up to me yelling things like, "Don't move or I'll blow your head off."

It was very dramatic and certainly uncalled for. I hadn't done anything. Not even a traffic violation. They jerked me up from the ground, searched me, then placed me in the back of a police car. They must have searched my truck for an hour before another cop showed up with a drug dog. The dog didn't find anything. The officers checked under the hood and did a lot of pointing and talking and searched under my truck.

A new officer showed up and got in the front seat of the car I was in, after he talked with the other officers. He asked me, "Why are you in Louisiana?"

I said, "My question is, why was I pulled over and treated like this? I sure haven't done anything."

"Just answer my question," he said.

I said, "Sir, with all due respect, you know who I am and that I have been arrested before. My attorney told me never to answer any questions. I wasn't asked for permission to search my truck and nobody has read me my rights. I don't understand why I have been arrested."

The officer said, "So you want to play tough guy, do you?"

I said, "No, sir. I'm not tough. I'm just being sensible. You didn't pull me over like this because you're my friend and want to visit. I would like to know why I'm under arrest?"

"You're not under arrest," he shouted.

"Then why am I handcuffed in the back of a police car? I'm certainly not free to leave. What About Terri v. Ohio?" I said.

The officer then got out of the police car, acting all mad and conferred with the other officers. There were over a dozen of them by that time.

I was thinking that there sure as hell wasn't anything like constitutional rights in the heart of Dixieland. They held me there for another hour. I figured they were going over the tapes of our conversation at the restaurant to see if they could find something to charge me with.

Finally, some of the officers started leaving, then one of them let me out of the police car, took off the cuffs and told me to "Stay out of Louisiana." After being treated like that only a dumbass would come back.

On the long drive back to Oklahoma, I was thinking about how lucky I was that they didn't--nail me while I was in the steak house. It was the last time I ever carried a gun into a public place and the last time I ever went to Louisiana. The only reason I ever carried a gun in a public place was that I had some romantic notion that someone might try and rob the place and I could be a hero and save the day.

When I got back to Oklahoma I came to the realization that I could no longer stay with my sister. I never kept dope or guns in her house. I kept them stashed in woods out by Skiatook lake. But I figured that the cops were out to get me, thanks to Louisiana and I didn't want them coming to my sister's house looking for me. The very next week I put a down payment on a small place down the road from my sister. It had big trees and I really liked it. It was nothing fancy on the outside and I kept it that way.

The thing about having a lot of cash is, a person can ease around and pay cash for all nice new furniture and household items and nobody will notice. The inside of my house was nice. I installed an oversize whirlpool tub with eight jets and put in all new carpet. I still had a lot of cash from the old days. I didn't need to sell dope. Of course, because I had so much money, people thought I was selling a lot of dope.

I was hurt by the way Cathy was acting. I also felt like a jerk for getting between her and her husband. One day I went out to a truck stop West of Tulsa to have a chicken fried steak. I wanted to be alone and it wasn't likely that I would run into anyone I knew there. As I was eating, this extremely sexy, beautiful, petite young woman came in and started talking to the lady at the counter about a job application. I got up and gave the girl my business card and told her that I had some friends in the restaurant business and if she needed a job to give me a call and I would see what I could do. A few days later she called me and asked me to meet her for coffee. I got there early, which was my habit in those days. When she walked in the door she was even prettier than I'd remembered. I introduced myself and she told me her name was Eileen. She was small, sexy, and I had the hots for her in a big way. I asked her on a real date and she said, "Yes." Life was good.

When I came to pick Eileen up at her sister's apartment, for our first date, Eileen was putting on the finishing touches. Her sister was chopping up a couple of lines of meth on the kitchen table when I walked in the room. She asked me if I wanted a line and I said, "No." They both did a line, as I looked on. If I would have had any sense I would have walked out then.

But all I was thinking about was having wild sex with the sexiest little gal I'd seen in a long time. I fell in love with Eileen and it was the second stage of my downfall. It was too soon for me to know what kind of a person she was, but I soon found out. Some girls have a way of covering up their real selves until they get their hooks into you and then it's too late.

Two nights later, I was driving to Tulsa to Eileen's apartment, late at night, after working all day and I fell asleep at the wheel. I rolled my slick old '70 Chevy truck two times. The truck was totaled, but fortunately, I didn't get a scratch. I had a mobile phone in my truck, so I called a man I knew that had a wrecker service, then I called Eileen to come get me from the side of the road. She probably thought I was crazy. I was tired, mad at myself and just generally pissed off.

The wrecker showed up first and I had the man tow the truck to my house. Then Eileen came and took me to her apartment. I was a little sore, but in good enough shape for sex. I think I would be able to have sex even if I was dying.

The next morning, I had Eileen drive me by a few used car lots until I spotted a red four wheel drive Toyota pickup. It was used so I knew it wouldn't cost too much. Eileen asked me if I wanted her to wait, I said, "No," and told her I would see her later that night. I kissed her and got out with my overnight bag.

I walked into the used car office and said, "Who do I talk to about the red Toyota pickup?"

One of the salesmen spoke up and we went outside to look it over. It had plain tires and wheels, with no extras. I knew how to fix that. I asked the clerk how much it cost. He informed me that it was sixty-eight hundred. I asked him to call and see if his boss was willing to take a six-thousand-dollar cash offer. In less than thirty minutes I was the proud owner of a nice little red truck. I then headed for a tire shop where I bought new wheels and big tires. By the time I had the new stereo system installed I was riding in style. I later put a roll bar, sidebars and a crash grill on my little truck.

My new truck made me bold, so I took the next step and asked Eileen to move in with me. The next day we were hauling her things to my house.

CHAPTER EIGHTEEN:
Outlaw

At first, I thought Eileen was the answer to all my problems in life. The sex was better than great and she looked like a little playboy centerfold. My girlfriend Cathy was back with her husband, most of the time and I was in the process of cutting her loose. But when Cathy called I would come running. I just couldn't let her go. What I didn't realize was, Eileen was following me whenever I left the house. She saw me meet Cathy one day and after I left, she approached Cathy. I hadn't been home but long enough to take a shower when Eileen walked in the door with Cathy. Of course, Cathy knew about Eileen but Eileen didn't know about Cathy. That didn't matter. I was busted and they both ganged up on me. I could tell that Cathy thought it was all very funny. Eileen said that I had to make a choice. I said I wanted them both, which was the wrong answer. Cathy liked the idea, but Eileen wouldn't go for it. When Eileen told me that she had followed me I should have let her go and ran for the hills. What more of a sign did I need? Did the sky need to fall on me?

Cathy said that she was worried about her two children, so she was going back to her husband. The choice was made for me. After that incident things started happening pretty fast.

The next day I was called by one of my friend Jack's nieces. Jack was my friend that was still in prison. Jack, my friend Russell, who was in prison with us back then and I had told Jack's three sisters about what I was in prison for. Russell had made me out to be a big time meth man. Jack's sister must have told her daughter about me and that was who called me. She told me who she was and said that her boyfriend wanted to meet me. I was at a friend's house swimming in the pool when I got the call. I was alone and a little sad about what happened between me, Cathy and Eileen.

It was early, just after lunch, so I gave them the address and invited them over. I knew why he wanted to meet me, even though she hadn't said. It certainly wasn't because he was in need of a tennis partner.

Before I loaded my shovel in the back of my truck, I did a lot of reasoning. Based on past experiences and my limited knowledge of the law, I figured that if I didn't make or sell meth, if I happened to get caught with a little meth, it would only be simple possession. In State court, simple possession of meth, by my reasoning, would be either probation or maybe three to five years in prison. I figured that, if I got three to five, or even ten years - like I did the previous time - with good time I would be out in one to four. I didn't really like that thought, but I weighed the risks based on that reasoning. As long as I wasn't making or selling meth, I knew my chances of getting caught were slim to none. At that time, I had no idea that the federal government has drug conspiracy laws that enabled them to charge and convict a person on nothing more than the statements and testimony of other people who have been arrested and charged with a crime.

The federal government can simply use those unreliable people, with no corroborating evidence, to charge a person with conspiracy and then give that person up to life in prison. Had I known that, the risk would have been far too great, in my mind, to get back into drugs. I wouldn't have even considered it. I would have said "No," to Cathy, even over the great sex. But I didn't know how the federal government worked and I didn't know anything about federal drug laws.

When they arrived I was a little shocked. Jack's niece was a white girl, and her boyfriend "Outlaw" was half black. The thing is, I liked him from the moment I met him. He had a firm handshake and a no nonsense way about him. I invited them both in and fixed us all a glass of tea. Outlaw got right to the point. He told me that he had just gotten out of prison and didn't have a thing. I knew how that felt and I respected his straight forward honesty and was ready to help. He was a down to earth country boy and I could tell by his manner that he was intelligent. Outlaw told me that if I would front him an eight ball of meth, he would be right back with the money. He said that he would never let me down.

I was impressed by his boldness. He had enough nerve to come in and lay his cards on the table and I liked him. I decided right then not to bullshit him and to give him a hand. I hadn't been selling anything, but I felt I could trust him. I asked the girl to wait in the kitchen and had Outlaw follow me into my friend's garage. I told Outlaw that he couldn't make much money on an eight ball, which is an eighth of an ounce. Plus, he would be making too many trips back and forth to see me, so I fronted him an ounce. To me, it was worth an ounce just to test his integrity. I gave him the ounce for twelve hundred and told him, "As long as you do me right, you'll be able to count on me."

From that point forward, Outlaw and I were the best of friends. He never lied to me and I trusted him with anything I had. It was the beginning of a short lived relationship. I'm certain that if Outlaw and I had been wealthy men, we would not have sold dope. We just wanted what everyone else had, but didn't have the opportunities that many people have. If we could have gotten jobs, at something other than digging ditches or washing dishes, we would have been working like normal people. Once a person has been labeled as a criminal, or convict, good jobs just aren't available. Reputable companies don't want to take a chance on tarnishing the company name. That is understandable, with so many young people just getting out of college trying to establish themselves in the work place. Why take a risk with a convicted felon?

Things started happening rather fast after I got home that day. While I was gone, I got a call from a guy named Bobby who lived in Texas.

When I returned his call, he informed me that a lawyer from Belize called him with a message from a mutual friend of ours. Bobby wanted to know that if he came to see me, could we go to dinner and visit a little.

Hell, he sounded like me. I told him that if he came up I would fire up the grill.

It took Bobby about four hours to get to my house. He brought a nice looking young lady with him. She and Eileen got busy in the kitchen while Bobby and I went out back to start the grill. My friend Russell, right after he got out of prison, had started a small (two man) construction company. Their first project was to build me a real nice back deck. The deck was impressive and I liked to show it off.

Bobby told me that he and Snake had become good friends about a year before Snake had to leave the country. That would have been about the time I went to prison. Snake and Bobby were complete opposites.

Snake was big, wild, tattooed, long haired and hard looking.

Bobby was tall, clean cut, business like and a general all around good guy, with a very friendly smile. It is not often that I meet two people in one day that I like. I felt that I'd made two friends that day and I did.

The first thing I told Bobby was that I didn't want to talk or do business in front of the girls. I knew they would figure it out, but I didn't mix business with women. Bobby told me that he had been selling for Snake and doing pretty good. He missed the good meth and the extra income. From the way it sounded, it seemed that after I left for prison and Snake left for points unknown, the quality and quantity of meth dropped considerably.

I informed Bobby that quality I could handle, but I wasn't ever going to have quantity again. He said that he was only interested in making a couple hundred thousand and he was getting out too. I like people who have goals and set limits. A person needs to know when to quit. That didn't apply to me, because I already knew that I was blowing it by getting back into it, even a little. I told Bobby that I had a few pounds we could work through, but I wasn't planning on making any more. I figured that I could manage selling what I had to two people, as long as they never met and didn't know each other. I could sell them what meth I had in less than a year, and then I would be out for good. That would give Outlaw and Bobby a leg up and me a little money to retire with. It sounded like a good plan and I wasn't planning on making any more.

Bobby's next question was, "Could you show me how to do the new short phosphorus cook, using ephedrine?"

I said that I would look into it. We both knew that getting the chemicals for the old P2p cook was close to impossible. I didn't tell him that I had P2p and a bunch of the required chemicals to process it, because I was never going to cook meth again. However, I was curious about the ephedrine reduction method, so I decided to see if the chemicals were easy to obtain. I soon learned they were.

My new friend Bobby had brought enough money with him to buy an ounce of meth.

After we ate, I drove out to Skiatook lake and brought back a quarter pound of meth. I had made a real nifty stash spot out in the woods. I didn't see any point in Bobby making too many trips. When he left, I was certain that he was happy and that I had made a new friend. I was right.

The next morning, feeling pretty good about the previous day's events, I went to a small salvage yard in Turley, Oklahoma. Turley is between Tulsa and Sperry, where I lived. I had noticed that it was also a car crusher and scrap metal place. I wanted to see what kind of cars and parts they had.

I met a guy named Pete who worked there part time. They let me look around some and I found a few things I wanted and decided to try and deal him out of them. I could tell Pete was already wired. He had a Chevy four speed transmission I wanted, but he didn't want to part with it. So, I pulled out a small bag of meth, (about two grams), and said, "Let's do a line and talk it over." I then handed him the bag. When he made up two rather large lines, I knew he hadn't seen real good meth before. I told him it was as pure as it comes, but he didn't seem to care. He did his long line and I did about a fourth of mine. He looked at what was left of my line and I said, "I'm not doing that much," and laughed. Then I said, "In about thirty minutes you'll wish you hadn't." I knew what was about to happen.

We walked around the salvage yard with Pete showing me around and me telling him what kind of parts I was interested in buying. It didn't take long and Pete was breathing harder and sweat was popping out on his face.

He wiped his face and said, "Damn." A couple of minutes later he wiped his face again and said, "Damn."

I said, "Brother, you're going to need a lot of water."

"That shit is good," he said.

"It don't come any better," I answered.

Before I left, I traded the meth I had left in the little bag for the parts I wanted, including the four speed transmission. We swapped numbers and I told him that if I had something he might want, or if he came up with some parts I might be interested in to give me a call.

I went from the salvage/crushing yard to Home Depot. As I was walking through the store filling my basket with the things I needed and many things I didn't need, I heard a voice I recognized from prison. I turned the corner and looked down the next aisle. Low and behold, the tall lanky form of my old prison buddy Brian was standing there visiting with a clerk. When I walked up to him, I noticed that Brian was in the process of buying some plastic tubing. I was gathering up the equipment and chemicals I was going to need to experiment with the ephedrine reduction meth cook. I needed some plastic tubing too. Imagine that.

I said, "That's some pretty small tubing for such a big guy."

Brian spun around, wide eyed, like he was busted. I thought to myself, "Is everybody in Tulsa wired?" His expression went from shock, to relief, as a smile emerged on his face.

He said, "Jeff!"

I said, "Brian!"

After we bought our tubing, I told Brian to meet me at my truck. When he came out, I gave him the other two grams of meth I had with me and told him that I was in the market for small block and big block Chevy hot rod parts. New and used. I gave him my number and told him where I lived.

I made it clear that he should never come over without talking to me first. I also advised him to never talk any business around my girlfriend.

When I got back to the house I had a call from Outlaw. I called him back and he said that he was ready to come see me. I told him to give me an hour and gave him directions to my house. I jumped in my little red truck and drove to my stash spot, where I picked up a quarter pound of meth.

I didn't want much traffic at my house, so I was giving him more that trip.

While I was waiting on Outlaw I decided to call my old friend Sonny to have some landscaping done. I also called my old friend Plumber Joe, to ask him to come out and take care of some plumbing projects for me.

I wanted everything fixed up and out of the way by the time I ran out of meth.

When Outlaw got there we walked out back to my little shop, while the girls stayed in the house. Outlaw not only brought the twelve hundred he owed me, but also brought an additional eight hundred to pay towards the next ounce. I told him that there was no need to rush things and advised him not to take any risks, because I was not in a hurry for the money. Then I handed him a quarter pound.

I could tell by his look and the way he said, "Thank you," that he knew that, (in one day), we were at another level of trust and he appreciated that trust. The money it saved him. I just smiled.

Sonny called me before he came and wanted to know if our old buddy "Shitty Leg" could come with him. I said, "Yes," and when they arrived we had a little party. I was glad to see my old friends. Shitty Leg brought some good pot with him and I made my famous margaritas. We had a great time.

I broke out some meth and all three of us and our girlfriends, did a little. From that point forward, Eileen started acting like a complete nut case. She had followed me in the past, but that was nothing compared to the way she started behaving. She became very, very paranoid and was accusing me of all kinds of things I wasn't doing. I begged her to stop using meth because it was making her crazy. I didn't realize that she had watched me hide some outside, then after I went to sleep, she went outside and got into my stash. For a month I didn't know she was getting into my meth.

I wasn't giving her any, but it was obvious that she was wired out of her head.

One night, Eileen - as small as she was - attacked me and started accusing me of having sex with her sister. Then she claimed that I had a secret, hidden door in the back of my shop where girls came in to have sex with me. I told her there was no secret door and even offered to show her.

She said, "Then why do you keep the door closed and locked?"

"Because of the air conditioner," I replied. "If you would have bothered knocking I would have opened the door and let you come in."

I was in the shop, where it was cool, building engines and transmissions. I had no way of knowing that she was outside the shop pulling on the door trying to get in, looking through the cracks and hunting for a secret door that didn't exist. The more she acted crazy, the more time I spent in the shop.

On afternoon Eileen's sister came by to see her. I heard Eileen yelling so I went inside. Eileen was accusing her sister of having sex with me.

I managed to get between them and said, "Hey, calm down. I'm not having sex with your sister and you need to get a grip."

Then Eileen went crazy on me. She swung at me and said I was taking up for her sister and screwing her. She then stormed off into the bedroom and slammed the door. Eileen's sister, Lanette, told me that Eileen was strung out.

I said, "Yes, I see that, but I'm not the one giving it to her."

Lanette looked at me like I was plain stupid and informed me that Eileen had been getting into my stash, without me knowing it and selling meth to her for a month. I hadn't noticed any missing and I never thought she would do that. But it sure explained a lot.

All my friends quickly learned that Eileen was strung out and nuts. They stayed out of her way.

I had two friends, Delbert and Kevin. Kevin lived near Pauls Valley, Oklahoma. Kevin was the guy who screwed me out of the sixty acres and ratted on me when I was in Ada. My other friend Delbert was from Henryetta, Oklahoma. I'd known them both for many years. Delbert was the person who provided me with the recipe and detailed instructions for the ephedrine reduction cook. I had already heard several stories about mistakes that had been made by other people that had disastrous results. I didn't want to share the same misfortunes so I asked Delbert to introduce me to his friend in Tulsa who was doing the ephedrine cook. Delbert talked to his friend and we agreed on an exchange of information.

I knew the P2p cook and had P2p meth. The guy wanted to know about the method I used to cook the P2p dope and he wanted to compare P2p meth to his ephedrine meth. It was a classic, "You show me yours, and I'll show you mine deal." I also took the time to buy a new Merck Manual. A chemical cross reference. I then studied the relationship of the chemicals involved in the ephedrine reduction process. I wanted to know more about it than the person I was about to meet.

Before I went to meet the guy, I made him a copy of the recipe and detailed instructions for the P2p method, complete with a chemical and equipment list. When I met Delbert I brought an ounce of the P2p meth with me, then we went to meet his friend. When we got to the guy's house, it looked like any other house on the street. Delbert introduced me to his friend Marty and we struck up an immediate friendship. To break the ice, I handed Marty an ounce of P2p meth and the copies of the recipe and instructions for the old P2p cook. Marty informed me that he had seen my dope many times in the past, because Delbert had brought him some way back when I first started out in Henryetta, and again when I was in Ada, before I went to prison.

Marty showed me some of his ephedrine meth and I showed him the recipe and instructions I had for the ephedrine cook. He knew the information well, because he was the person who wrote it. I had found some things in the instructions that weren't clear and didn't make sense.

I explained my misgivings to Marty and asked if it would not be better if a few things were slightly changed. It didn't take me long to explain why I thought the changes would help and Marty said, "Let's try them and see."

Marty showed me to a back room in his house where he commenced to opening boxes and cabinets, pulling out his lab equipment and chemicals. The ephedrine reduction cook, using red phosphorus, is simple and quick, but it can be very dangerous. If not done properly, it can blow up in one's face. I called it the "New 1-2-3 cook." It takes one part red phosphorus, two parts ephedrine and three parts iodine crystals. The combination of the three chemicals causes an intense heat reaction. The result is, the ephedrine molecules bond together making methamphetamine. However, many things can go wrong, which means that the majority of the people trying the ephedrine cook get a poor quality product because all of the ephedrine doesn't make the transformation into meth.

It didn't take long for Marty to set up his little lab and produce about fifty grams of meth. As Marty was going through the process, I noticed several things that needed to be changed, just a bit, in order to perfect the process. When I discussed them with Marty, he agreed and we made the changes on the next go around. One thing was very obvious, because the heat reaction produced a lot of foam that had to be watched and controlled, large cooks would be difficult and dangerous. In contrast, small cooks would be relatively simple, safe and easy to manage. I was not planning on doing much anyway. I was mainly trying to satisfy my curiosity, and be able to show Bobby the cook. That is, if he really wanted to learn how it was done. Bobby already had a pretty good idea how to do it anyway and so did my friend Outlaw, who had also asked about the ephedrine cook. I wasn't the first person they had talked to about it. Over time, the main problem I saw with most people was, they were all in a hurry and tried to rush things. Taking things slow, starting cold and finishing hot, was the only way to get the ephedrine cook to come out with quality meth.

By the time Bobby called the following week, I had been through the ephedrine reduction process several times and had all the bugs worked out. In order to keep things safe and easy to store, I designed a small setup using a two thousand milliliter flat bottom boiling flask and a reflux condenser, that was fast, clean and efficient. It would turn out one hundred and fifty grams an hour. To keep the odor and fumes down to nothing and to be environmentally friendly, I used a one inch clear plastic tube connected to the top of the condenser, looped around and down into a large jug of hydrogen peroxide. This additional attachment, not only filtered the exhaust, it also reclaimed a significant portion of the iodine crystals.

With my method, a person could turn out over a pound of meth in about five hours, if they started with the ephedrine ready. Of course, it took several hours to properly prepare the ephedrine. Again, the key was to not get in a hurry, keep the smell down and not make a mess. It is best to use water to extract the ephedrine, because water doesn't smell. That and the process of boiling the water from the ephedrine changes its chemical structure to chloro-ephedrine which produces a higher quality methamphetamine.

The other methods of doing the ephedrine reduction cook are very smelly and toxic, so I wouldn't even consider using them. To use things like anhydrous ammonia would be like hanging a sign around your neck that says, "Come bust me." The smell of ammonia is very pungent and easy to identify. It would be almost as bad as using ether back in the old days.

When Bobby got there, I took the risk of setting up the small lab in my workshop, after we had a nice dinner with our girlfriends. Eileen was already mad because I had cut her out of the loop by moving my stash.

She had been accusing me of things and asking me questions, the answers to which she had no business knowing. She wanted to know everything and was asking people behind my back what was going on. Some of the guys thought it was more fun to tell Eileen unbelievable stories, rather than just say nothing. Or course, Eileen believed the wild unbelievable stories. She became more agitated and aggressive towards me.

This, in turn, made me want to run for the hills and it ultimately led me to enlisting the help of Eileen's sister Lanette.

As I was setting up the little lab in the shop, Eileen banged on the shop door. I opened the door to her standing there acting all happy with Bobby's girlfriend. I let them both come in so Eileen could see that no girls had come through a secret trap door to have sex with me and Bobby. While I took Eileen aside to explain what I was doing and the importance of not being disturbed, Bobby's girlfriend took him aside and told him how crazy Eileen was acting. Bobby and I told the girls to just please give us a few hours and we would be done and back in the house. I found out later that the only thing that kept Eileen busy in the house with Bobby's girlfriend was some interesting sexual activities.

Bobby and I went through the process twice and he had a pretty good idea, I thought, about the chemical relationships. It didn't dawn on me that some people could just never understand. It was like speaking Chinese to a third grader in Oklahoma. Bobby had an expression on his face that said, "What?" But he kept shaking his head "Yes," like he understood everything I was telling him and showing him.

By morning we had everything, the lab I put together and the left over chemicals, boxed up for Bobby to take with him and he had a quarter pound of meth. The sun was starting to peak over the trees when we loaded everything in his truck. We went in the house to find the girls curled up naked together, asleep. It was a nice picture. Bobby and I made breakfast, then woke our girlfriends up to eat and start the day.

Eileen was okay until Bobby and his girlfriend left, then she went nuts on me again. I told her that I couldn't deal with her anymore and that she had to go. I said that I was going to rent her an apartment for a year and she said she wasn't going anywhere.

Because of Eileen's refusal to leave, I decided to employ a new tactic.

I was going to leave my own house. Rather than sleep that day, I spent the day making sure that the few people I'd been dealing with, Pete, Brian, Outlaw, Delbert, Marty, Bobby, Sonny, Plumber Joe and Eileen's sister Lanette, knew not to call or come by the house. I got a new mobile phone, rented a Post Office Box, because Eileen was going through my mail (including my bank statements) and made new schedules for people to call and meet me. I wanted to be in my work shop or away from the house when I got a call. I was basically pushing everyone away and shutting down. Which is easier said than done.

People get angry when they can't get what they want.

Things don't always work as planned. When I started telling people that I couldn't help them when they called, they started coming to the house. Outlaw and Bobby were the only two that I would meet anytime they called. Bobby wasn't calling as often and when he did it was because he had a problem with a cook. I would go to him and show him how to fix it. One time Bobby called me from my old friend Shitty Leg's house in Oklahoma City and asked me to come fix a problem he had. When I got there, I found out that Bobby had been showing Shitty Leg and Scott, from Tulsa, how to do the cook. That put me in a bad position, but I showed them all how to fix the problem they were having.

I didn't want to leave Outlaw hanging, so I decided to show him the ephedrine cook. That way he could branch out on his own and I could get out of it all together. I gathered everything up for another small lab, then once again, took the risk of setting it up in my workshop.

As I was finishing the second cook and showing Outlaw how to turn the speed oil into powder, Eileen started banging on the shop door. I had to open up, or she would have woke the neighbors. Eileen had convinced Outlaw's girlfriend that we had girls in the shop. To shut them up, I had to sit them both down in the shop until we finished. I was beyond mad.

I couldn't believe that I had gotten myself into such a sorry position.

When Outlaw left that morning, I packed up my things to leave too.

Before I could get away from the house, Brian showed up with his friend Scott, who had been with Shitty Leg and Bobby when I went to Oklahoma City to help Bobby and a guy named Gary. They had some hot rod part they wanted to trade for meth. I traded for the parts then left the house. I went to check on my friend Outlaw, then drove to Ardmore to meet Bobby at Budroux's for dinner. I told them both what the problem was. They already knew, because Eileen had been calling them too.

For a while I kept my phone off. That was an even bigger mistake. People started calling Eileen at the house and she invited them over.

Then she would grill them, asking them questions about me. She would lie to them and tell them that I should be back any time. They would wait for me and use my home phone to call my mobile phone. Then when they left, Eileen could use redial to call me. It was a nightmare. I thought Eileen would just go away. I was wrong.

It was my good friend Outlaw that finally told me that I needed to go back home and deal with the problem. He was right, I should have never tried to run from it.

CHAPTER NINETEEN:

Dumbass

When I went home Eileen was acting like I never left. She hugged me, kissed me and said she missed me. But the look in her eyes said it was all a front for my friend Delbert, who was waiting on me when I got there. Delbert had brought glassware and chemicals to trade for meth. I told him that I didn't want them, but I gave him a little meth and told him not to come back. I didn't want him to be seen leaving my house in the middle of the night, so I had him and his friend wait until daylight to leave.

Delbert asked me outside where he told me that Eileen had knives hidden all over the house and she was planning on killing me in my sleep. I thought that was a little much. I didn't believe him. I went into the house and started looking around the bedroom where I found a knife under her pillow, one under the mattress and one on the night stand behind the clock. When I started looking hard, I found eight knives just in the bedroom. There was no way I could sleep in my own home, as long as Eileen was there.

I stayed up most of the night talking with Delbert, and trying to figure out a solution to my problem. I had tried to talk Eileen into drug rehab several times, but she would not go. When Delbert left that morning, I called Eileen's sister and told her what the problem was. She told me that people had been coming by my place looking for me and giving Eileen dope. That fit, based on Eileen's condition. I asked Lanette for help getting her sister out of my life and she agreed to help if I gave her some meth. I knew I was getting played, but I reluctantly agreed. Lanette came over that morning and tried to get Eileen to move in with her. Eileen went crazy again and accused me of having sex with her sister. It went on for most of the morning with me begging Eileen to eat and get some sleep so she would be rational. That made it even worse.

Sometime after lunch I got a call from an old friend of mine from Henryetta, who informed me that Delbert was in jail calling him to come make his bond. The guy wanted to know why Delbert wasn't calling me to make his bond. When the guy told me that Delbert was in Osage County Jail, I knew that Delbert must have been busted leaving my house. Based on the fact that Delbert, my old childhood friend, wasn't calling me, it was obvious that he ratted on me.

No sooner than I hung up the phone, it rang again. It was another friend of mine that told me that the cops were suiting up behind the church across the road from my house and it looked like they were going to raid me. I told Lanette to leave and had Eileen get in the car with me, I was driving a rented Mustang and we all left just before the cops ran in on the place. Fortunately, there wasn't anything there. While the police searched my home, I drove to Pawhuska and bonded Delbert out of jail. I wasn't mad, I was broken hearted and hurt. When the bondsman brought Delbert back to his office where I was waiting, Delbert just about freaked out. It didn't dawn on me why he was acting that way until we got down the road a ways and Delbert asked, "Are you going to kill me?"

I replied, "Hell, no. We have been friends for most of our lives. I would never hurt or betray you. I'm taking you back home to Henryetta. I hope you realize what you've done and have to live with from now on."

I stopped and checked into a motel, then asked Delbert's friend Marty to take him home. Marty was disgusted with him too, but he took him home for me. To this day, I don't understand why Delbert and so many others betrayed me. It must have been the dope talking, because surely people aren't normally that evil. Even in the motel with Eileen that night, people tracked me down wanting dope.

I woke up to find Shitty Leg in the room talking to Eileen. I had Eileen's sister come get her at the motel and Eileen still beat me home, when I decided to return four days later. It was like a reoccurring nightmare.

Eileen's sister called me and told me that Eileen was back at the house acting all normal like nothing had ever happened.

I had bought Eileen a little red car that she liked and I told her that when she left the house to make sure she didn't have anything illegal in her car. The police were clearly watching the house from down the road and had already pulled a few people over that left the house. One afternoon I get a call from Pete and he tells me that it looks like the cops may be going to raid my place again. They were a couple blocks away suiting up again. So I called Eileen and told her what was going on and asked her to leave the house and come meet me, but not to carry anything illegal in her car. She left the house and was pulled over and searched.

The police found meth and arrested her. I had to get the bail bondsman to meet me there to bond her out and she lost her car. I felt bad about it, so I bought her a little white truck and she came back to the house.

One afternoon I came home and Eileen was there with four other girls. One was her sister Lanette and one was a six foot tall gorgeous blond named Katherine. It was like Katherine made the room glow and I just couldn't keep my eyes off her. Lanette had been sharing the meth I'd been giving her with these other girls. It was at that point when my little head took over all of my bodily functions for my big head. I wanted to impress Katherine. I had a total of five good looking women in my bedroom waiting for me to break out the meth.

When Eileen had previously accused me of having sex with her sister, I was not. But once I started bribing Lanette with meth to get her help with her sister, I was doing her every chance I got. I wasn't sure why Lanette brought three good looking girls to my house with her, but I certainly didn't mind.

The thing was, I was then interested in only Katherine. I wanted her from the moment I laid eyes on her. I broke out some meth and we all did a little. Then I went outside to talk to my friend Pete, who had just arrived.

After the girls left, I gave Lanette time to get home, then went to see her. We had quick, hot sex, as usual. She liked me to do her from behind, then pull out right before I came and she would spin around and suck the come out of little Elvis. That drove me wild and made me last a lot longer the second time around. When we finished, all hot, sweaty and out of breath, I told Lanette I was having a party at a motel and asked her to come.

She looked at me, smiled and said, "Do you want me to bring Katherine? I could tell by the way you were looking at her that you want her."

I must be transparent. I said, "Does that make me a bad guy?"

Lanette laughed and said, "That makes you a horny Devil. That's why I like you. Hell, I want to fucker her too"

I'm sure it also had something to do with the fact that I was giving her money and meth any time she asked. The only reason I was still giving her meth was the fact that she was handling it well and not acting stupid. That and the great sex and the help with her sister. Lanette was level headed. I would have been happy to give her a lot more, money or meth, if she would have asked. I made it a policy not to volunteer.

That night at my small party at the motel, my mind was distracted by thoughts of whether Katherine would show up with Lanette. It was more of a social event than a full blown party. I had beer on ice and pretzels in bowls around the three room suite. It was nice, quiet and real friendly. Girls were playing in the hot tub together and the guys were watching.

When people would show up they would drink a beer or two, do some meth, then get their own rooms. About thirty people came and went that night. Things went pretty well until one of the girls flopped down on the glass coffee table and it shattered. I was thankful that she wasn't cut.

I didn't care about the table, it only cost money, but I couldn't replace the girl's ass.

When Lanette and Katherine showed up I was a little looped and feeling happy. They walked in the door looking hot, dressed to the nines, all sexy. I had picked up six point beer in Texas, so the people that were used to the three point two Oklahoma beer were feeling pretty good. Even the other girls in the room were looking and flirting with Lanette and Katherine. I got them both a beer, showed them where the meth was and started paying exclusive attention to Katherine. It was obvious to everyone in the place and to Katherine, just what my intentions were.

When people started leaving I asked Katherine to stay and play in the hot tub with me. Katherine took me to the side and said, "I want to get it straight from the beginning that I won't mess around on my husband unless I get paid."

I was somewhat taken aback, but I didn't let it show. I had just found out two new developments. One, she was married. And two, she needed money. Me being a dumbass, I simply said, "How much?"

Katherine said, "Three hundred. I need to make my car payment."

I would have given her whatever she asked for and not for the sex, but because she was asking. I pulled three hundred from a rather large wad and asked her to stick around. When everyone was gone I changed the water in the hot tub while we talked. A lot of people had been in and out of the hot tub and I'm a clean freak. At first Katherine left on her bra and panties. I'm more bold than that. I just got naked and jumped in with a smile. Little Elvis was all excited and wide awake thinking about the prospect of formally meeting Katherine. When I told her the story about how little Elvis got his name she got a big kick out of that and wanted to hear him sing Love Me Tender. I told her that he might sing to her once he got to know her better.

It didn't take long to migrate to the bed. Katherine was nervous, so I pulled her on top to give her control. She said, "Don't hurt me. Be easy." That confused me again. All the other girls I knew liked it and wanted it hard. She was a six foot tall blond wanting it easy. I said, "You're on top, so it will be as easy as you want it. You set the pace and I'll do my best to follow your lead."

That made her smile. We had an easy version of wild sex, for about two hours, in every position we could think of. It was the beginning of an interesting and enlightening relationship. Even though her motivation was money, I soon fell in love with her. I'm a dumbass when it comes to women.

After Katherine left, Eileen found out where I was and started calling the motel. I begged her to stop calling and to please let me sleep. She called about six times in a row and threatened to kill herself if I didn't come home right then. I started to believe her, so I said I was on my way. I had just bought a 1988 Chevy short and wide bed truck, black on black from my little sister's husband. I only had it one day. I almost made it home. I fell asleep at the wheel just down the road from my house and hit a tree.

I hit the tree so hard that it totaled the truck. It knocked the motor and transmission out from under the truck. When the wrecker moved the truck away from the tree, the engine and transmission was left there stuck down in the dirt. I woke up just before I hit the tree. My head hit the windshield and blew it out. The camper shell windows exploded and the tinted glass went flying up into the air.

It was amazing and beautiful, because the light was reflecting on the flying glass as it shot into the air. I thought I was going to heaven.

My knees caved in the dash and tore out the tendons, so when I crawled out the window of my truck, the doors were buckled and stuck, and tried to stand the pain in my knees was excruciating. I had hit a tree that was close to the road in one of my next door neighbors front yards. I noticed their porch light came on after I hit the tree, but it went back off before I could manage to get to their door. By the time I knocked on their door I was hurting all over. The man and his wife opened the door together as they turned on the porch light. I remember both of them looking at me with their mouths open. I didn't know why until later. I had blood and dirt all over me.

All I could manage was a weak, "Can I use your phone? I wrecked my truck."

They handed me a phone and brought me a chair. The lady wanted to know if she should call an ambulance. I put on a fake smile and said, "No," and called my friend with the wrecker, who only lived down the road. Then I had to call Eileen to drive about a block to pick me up. Eileen wanted to take me to the hospital and I said "No." I wanted to lie down.

I called my sister and asked her to call Katherine for me. Katherine worked for a veterinary clinic. I thought, "Who better to come pick the glass out of my head." Katherine came and dug the glass out of the top of my head and then looked me over. She checked my eyes and said I had a concussion. I smiled. That was nothing new, I'd had one before and a similar head injury, only the time before it was gravel being picked out of my head, not glass. Katherine said that I needed to go to a hospital, but I wouldn't go. The pain in my knees was so bad that I was sure something was broken. The knee pain masked the pain in my head, shoulders and chest.

Rather than go to the hospital I had my little sister drive me to Skiatook to see our family doctor. He x-rayed my knees and said nothing was broken. They hurt so bad I had tears running out of both my eyes. I could barely walk. I was bent over at the waist because I couldn't straighten my legs. When I came back into the reception area, I remember seeing a girl I knew named "Rebel." I could tell by the shocked expression on her face that any chance I might have had of getting a date with her was gone.

I later found out that my ACls were torn out in my knees. The right one was the worst. Not only were my knees messed up, I had a concussion, torn tendons in both my shoulders and my sternum was cracked. It was the second wreck I'd had because of Eileen and I was pissed. It was a miracle that I was alive. I finally put my foot down and told Eileen she had to go and I wasn't taking "No" for an answer.

I called Lanette to come get her and both of my sisters stayed there with me until Eileen left.

It took me a week to get pretty much back to normal, except for my knees. It was a month before I could straighten my legs all the way out.

Then I had to learn how to walk with my ACLs torn out, which took several months.

During my recovery Eileen rented a U-Haul and showed up at my house while I was gone. My new friend Scott called me and told me that Eileen was at my house stealing everything with a U-Haul.

I called my sister who only lived two houses away and asked her to go to my house and told her I was on my way. When I got home, Eileen had her brother and boyfriend loading up all of my living room furniture.

I made them put it all back in the house. Then Eileen called the police. When the police arrived, Eileen had the nerve to ask the officer to make me leave so she could empty the house. The officer politely told her that it was my house.

It was the only time that the police ever took up for me and I was thankful.

On the other hand, I was mad at Eileen, but my brother-in-law pulled me to the side and told me to give her whatever she wanted to get rid of her. He was right. I let her load up about half the house then told her if she came back I would get a restraining order against her. It was just another bit of drama and part of the ongoing nightmare.

Shortly thereafter Katherine told me that she was leaving her husband. We had been seeing a lot of each other and I thought she was leaving him for me. I was making her car payment and I had given her the money to pay fourteen hundred in fines she had from some kind of mess she'd gotten into with her previous fling.

I ended up paying the fines twice, because she lied to me the first time and used the money for something else.

I was pretty gullible when it came to women. When they said, "I love you," I thought they really meant it. So, I asked Katherine to move in with me, which she did. I loved the attention and it was great having a woman around that wasn't crazy. Katherine didn't try to get in my business all the time. I felt that she truly just wanted to be with me. That was short lived.

Katherine had only been staying with me a short time when Thanksgiving rolled around. She told me that she was going to spend the morning with her mom but would be home by 2:00 p.m. I went to great lengths preparing a huge Thanksgiving dinner. It was to be our first Thanksgiving together and I wanted it to be real special. Katherine didn't show. I called her mother that night and asked what happened and she said she didn't know. I was crushed. The next day Katherine showed up with bruises on her arms, legs and neck. She looked like she had been in a fight, or an accident.

I told her that she missed a nice Thanksgiving dinner and asked her if she wanted to help me eat the leftovers. I wasn't going to ask how she got all the bruises, but I guess she thought I needed to know. She volunteered the information. She told me that she had promised one of her ex-husband's friends that if she ever left her husband she would go out with him. My only question was, "Where did you go?" On a date, a person usually goes to some place like a movie or dinner, but I didn't know of anything that would have been open on Thanksgiving Day. She told me that she went to his place. I knew what that meant. That was not a date. Then

she told me that she got the bruises because she wouldn't have sex with him and he tried to force her, which apparently took some time, based on the amount of bruises. I was born at night, but not last night. It was obvious that she'd had some rough sex with someone. It was no wonder that she asked me to be easy with her all the time. She was probably bruised in places I couldn't see, as well.

That's when it dawned on me that I was a dumbass. She hadn't left her husband for me. She was shopping for the best deal and I was the best deal of the moment. Rather than get mad, I was hurt and actually embarrassed. I was wondering how many people were laughing at me behind my back. So, I rented a room at the Double Tree and called Cathy.

Wild sex is good for a broken heart. A week later, Katherine went to lunch with another old friend of her ex-husband's. By then I knew that I was only a fling for her so it didn't hurt, as bad. I went and had sex with my friend Cathy again and it was great.

It was at that point that I came to terms with the fact that, when Katherine, Cathy, Lanette and some of the other women I knew, said, "I love you," what they really meant was, "Give me some more dope." I also realized that when they said, "Oh, honey, you're the best I ever had," that really meant, "Give me some more money so I can go shopping." Once I discovered these revelations it no longer hurt so bad, because I knew they were lying every time they said, "I love you."

In one way it was comforting, in another it was depressing. Then Katherine acted like she couldn't understand why I was "cheating" on her.

Life can be odd sometimes.

Up until my house was raided I'd had a guy called Harley living in a trailer house on my property. He was working as a mechanic for me.

After the raid I asked Harley to move. I wasn't going to let anyone live in the trailer. But I met Scott's friend Gary, who had a family and needed a place to live and who was a pretty good mechanic. I let Gary move in and gave him a job. It wasn't working out real well, but I didn't want to run him off because it was the holiday season and he had a wife and daughter. Gray brought several vehicles onto my property telling me that they were his or family members that he was working on. I didn't mind and I hoped he was making some extra money.

Katherine told me that if I ever messed around on her again, the girl better be better looking than her and a rocket scientist. One night I rented a room on the top floor of the Double Tree downtown and asked Katherine to meet me there. I had champagne on ice, for its romantic value because I don't even like it, a food platter and some fun sex toys waiting on her. She didn't show up. She'd pulled another disappearing act. I called her mom and got that same, I don't know where she might have gone, just like I'd gotten from her the time before. I was pissed.

I'd met a girl named Stephine a few days before when I was buying some parts from a friend of Gary's. It took me a few calls to locate her, but then I called Stephine and told her where I was and asked if she would like to join me. She said, "Yes," so I went and picked her up.

First time sex, with the right girl, can be super hot. It's fast, intense and you want to try everything. Then you want to slow down and do it all again. It is a good sign when you use half a bottle of baby oil and have to take three showers. By the time morning arrived, Stephine and I were ready to go home and get some sleep. Stephine was another six foot tall blond who used to play basketball in high school. She was in great shape and enjoyed showing me just how great of shape she was in. We did everything we could think of that night and I am sure that she slept as good as I did that day. Only my sleep was delayed.

After I dropped Stephine off, with promises of coming back for more, I got a call from Katherine. She had the maid let her in the motel room after I left and she had just ordered room service for two and wondered if I would like to join her, since I was paying for it anyway. I could tell she was mad. When I got there, there wasn't any denying what went on in the room and I didn't even try. She had done the old rub a pencil on the motel note pad trick and retrieved Stephine's full name, address and phone numbers. The bedding looked and smelled of sex. The bathroom was a wreck and the discarded items in the trash painted a vivid picture of the night's events. That and I was give out. Stephine and I had a hell of a romp.

Needless to say, Katherine was not pleased. She had met Stephine before and knew that Stephine was gorgeous. Katherine told me before that if I messed around on her the girl better be better looking than her and a rocket scientist. To me they were both equally stunning and beautiful.

When I came into the room, Katherine asked me, "Is Stephine a goddamn rocket scientist?" I knew where she was going with it and that wasn't really a question that was meant to be answered.

I said, "Since you pulled another vanishing act on me, I figure you blew me off and went out with another one of your ex-husband's friends." "So, you just screwed another girl?" she asked.

"Well, yes," I said. "What did you expect me to do, sit her all night and cry?"

I wasn't going to argue. We ate our breakfast, then Katherine went to her mother's house. A few days later she rented an apartment in Tulsa, that I was paying for, of course. It gave her more freedom and made her feel like she was in control. I had already figured out that she wasn't serious about me. Even a dumbass could see that, but we were still seeing each other.

I was spending a lot of time at Katherine's apartment and Katherine was still coming out to my place a lot. I was helping her financially with anything she asked for. One day I came home, intending to fix some fried shrimp and a steak. When I opened my freezer, it was completely empty.

Katherine was the only one who had a key, so I knew she must have taken everything. I went out to eat, then drove to Katherine's mom's house to ask her why she emptied my freezer. Katherine said that her mother needed it and I didn't eat much of it anyway.

"No problem," I said. Then I told her that the next time her mother needed something to tell me and I would get it for her. Her mother, who is very sweet, spoke up and told me that she needed a new washer and dryer and that she wanted me to pay Katherine's fines. Even though I'd given Katherine the money to pay the fines once already, I just smiled and said, "No problem," again. I took Katherine to the courthouse and paid her fines, then went and bought her mother a new washer and dryer. I would have gladly done anything, all they had to do was ask. They just didn't ask for much, or I would have done more.

Meanwhile, back at my house, I'd had some problems with Gary stealing from me. The Holidays were over and his wife had left him and moved out of State.

I had no choice but to run him off. I told him to pack up and get his cars off my property. After I went to bed, rather than move his own vehicles, Gary stole one of my trucks that I had for sale and was towing one of my cars away, when he was pulled over by the police because the truck wasn't tagged. The cops arrested him for back traffic tickets and impounded my vehicles and car dolly. Gary made up a story about me having a lab at my house, machine guns, a room wired to blowup and more. The police got another warrant and raided my house, again.

They came in at 4:00 a.m., while Katherine was on the back porch eating ice cream. It just so happened that Eileen had shown up and I felt sorry for her, so she was asleep on the couch.

When the police searched they found a 9mm pistol under the file cabinet in my bedroom and a very small amount of pot rolled up in a sock.

They also found meth in Eileen's pocket. I was arrested and charged for the gun, pot, and the meth in Eileen's pocket. I was also charged with possession of the stolen vehicles that Gary brought onto my property.

I didn't know they were stolen. Gary told me that they were his and his families. One truck they said was stolen, I'd bought from Gary and I had the title for it.

Because I was the owner of the property, I was charged with everything. The police also seized all of my tools and equipment and accused me of running a chop-shop. Fortunately, Katherine was not arrested. I made my and Eileen's bond and was back at my house before Gary showed up with a truck and trailer with the intent to rob me while I was still in jail. I found out later that Gary had done the same thing to another guy in the past.

I told Eileen not to ever come back and started spending more time with Katherine at her apartment in Tulsa. Bobby and Outlaw were doing fine on their own, so I was shutting down the meth business. I was sick of it and the crazy people that went with it I just wanted to be left alone.

The more I avoided people, the harder they tried to find me.

A guy named Ricky Dale had been coming around trying to buy meth from me. I wouldn't sell him any, so the story was that he was going to try and rip me off. I got a phone call one afternoon from a girl I hardly knew and she told me that Ricky Dale and one of his friends were on the way to my house to rob me.

Sure enough, Ricky Dale showed up with his buddy knocking on my door. I had a long slide .45 caliber magnum in my right hand when I answered the door. I asked them what they wanted and Ricky Dale said they wanted to buy some meth. I told them to show me their money. They didn't have any money, but said they each had a pistol that they wanted to trade for meth. I had them step in the door and show me the guns while I kept my gun in my right hand. They handed me their guns so I could look them over, at my request, and I asked them how much they wanted for them. They informed me that they wanted to trade for an eight-ball of meth each. I told them that I didn't have any meth. Then I placed both the guns on the counter behind me and paid them each two hundred and fifty dollars for their guns, which was the going rate for an eight ball.

They wanted dope, not money. I told them to take the money and go by some dope some place else and not to ever make the mistake of showing up at my house with guns or I was going to assume that their intentions were to rob me and I would just shoot them on the spot. Even though I never sold him anything, Rick Dale later ratted on me anyway. He just made stuff up that sounded like what the cops wanted to hear.

I built a jacked up hot rod Chevy Blazer and sold my red Toyota to Scott. I also bought a white short and narrow '72 Chevy truck that was customized. It had Raisin Hell on the door panels and the tail gate, with a cool California Raisin painted on the tail gate, as well. It was nice, but I later sold it to Scott too. My pride and joy was my black short and wide Chevy truck. I put a big block in it with a four speed. I was changing vehicles around in hopes of not being noticed or followed.

Somehow, Eileen found out that I was spending some nights at Katherine's apartment. She was probably following me again. She stopped by the apartment one evening and asked me for money. Me being a dumbass, I gave her some money just to get rid of her without an argument.   Little did I know she was scoping things out. During the night Eileen and one of her boyfriends broke into my '70 Chevy truck and stole everything I had in it, including the tools. Saying I was mad would have been an understatement. I wasn't just disgusted with my old crazy girlfriend Eileen, I was disgusted with the whole dope crowd.

I parked my old truck and started driving the white Blazer to throw people off. Before I had time to think about things much, I got a call from a bail bond agent in Beggs, Oklahoma. The lady told me that Outlaw was in jail and asked her to call me.

I just asked, "How much do you need?"

She told me and I asked her to go get him. She bonded him out and met me at a fast food place in Tulsa where I paid her and thanked her for her help. Outlaw left with the bail bonds lady, then called me back an hour later. His girlfriend, my old friend Jack's niece was in jail too. I met Outlaw and gave him a thousand to bond her out. It was just a few days later that Bobby was arrested and I had to go make his bond too.

I went to Katherine's one morning and visited with her until my little sister got there. I was going to take her to lunch. As we were leaving the apartment my Blazer blew a line of the transmission cooler. I pulled into a church parking lot and called a friend to bring me some transmission fluid. After I fixed the line the police came running into the parking lot - with guns drawn – yelling for me to get on the ground. One of the officers searched me and acted like he found a small amount of meh in my pocket. It was the cop, J.J. Gray's meth, not mine. They arrested me and placed me in the police car.

Two officers jumped in the car and said, "Where's your apartment?"

"I don't have an apartment," I said.

One officer asked, "Where's your girlfriend's apartment?"

I said, "If you don't know, I'm not telling you."

They knew because they drove me straight back to her apartment where a search was already under way. They had a warrant, but only found a very small amount of meth and they found a gun. I don't know why Katherine had a gun. They took us in and we were back out on bond within the hour. That was it, I knew I would be going back to jail. didn't know it at the time, but Pete had been arrested a week before and so had Marty. They had neglected to mention that to me. The only reason that I found out was that Marty called me to borrow money for an attorney.

I met Marty at the attorney's office and paid him five thousand for Marty's representation. The attorney informed me that Pete had been busted too. It was time for me to get ready for prison. I sure felt like a dumbass.

CHAPTER TWENTY:

Belize

My main concerns were to put things off for a while and to get the charges from the arrest at my house and the second arrest ran concurrent so I could serve them at the same time. At that point, there was no doubt that I was going to be in prison for a while. Being set up didn't matter, I could not prove it. The only question was, for how long? My attorney was still shooting for five to ten.

I ran just about everyone off and was laying low. To keep my mind off things I worked all the time. I had money because I was working, not dealing drugs. I had given my old friend Russell some guns that he liked and we shot them at some cans one day at his house by the lake. Someone must have reported the shooting because Russell was later raided by the police and arrested for the guns. And as luck would have it, he ratted on me too.

Eileen didn't show up for a hearing and they issued a warrant for her arrest. For some reason she went to my house while I was gone and broke in. Her sister called me and told me that Eileen was at my house and that the bail bondsman was on his way to pick her up. I drove home and got there at the same time as the bondsman. It was a mess. The bondsman acted like it was all my fault and Eileen had the nerve to blame me.

Eileen made statements against me too and so did her sister Lanette, at a later date.

I could deal with five to ten years in State prison, even though I was far from happy about the situation. I started getting everything in order for my departure.

I rented an apartment in Tulsa and moved out of my house. My little sister moved into my house and her boyfriend started stealing everything that wasn't nailed down. He was trading my things to Scott for dope.

None of the people around me were smart enough to realize that I was leaving things out just so I could see who the people were that were sorry enough to steal from me.

I had already moved anything that I really wanted to keep to storage. I didn't care about any of the stuff, not even the things in storage, I knew it would all be stolen as soon as I went to jail. If not sooner, as the day of me going to prison got closer. I didn't tell anyone where my apartment was and to this day I don't believe anyone ever figured it out. I was finally getting some rest and having some time to relax, with a girl who didn't do drugs and who I won't name. She knew I was about to go to prison, she treated me great and she was the one I loved the most.

Katherine checked herself into a drug rehab. She pretty much had to in order to get probation. I was still proud of her for making the effort.

She told her mother that the place didn't have any fruit. I went to Walmart and bought a small plastic kiddy pool. Then Bobby and I went to a store and bought twenty watermelons, twenty bags of ice and ten large bags of apples. The rehab place would not let me bring them in the building, so I put the kiddy pool next to the front door, put the watermelons and apples in it, then covered them with ice. I would have done more but the place said no. I asked about having pizzas delivered for everyone there but they wouldn't let me.

One morning I got up early and drove to Mr. Connor's in time to ride with him to check on his cows. I told him I was on my way back to prison.

It depressed him and he chewed me out pretty good. I had it coming. I was trying to make him feel better about me going to prison, so I started telling him about the funny and dumb things that had been happening to me. We were laughing so hard that Mr. Connor had to stop the truck several times before we got back to the house. Mr. Connor was getting up there in age and I was worried that he would laugh himself into heart failure. The stories about Eileen had him rolling with laughter. When we got back to the house, Alice and her sweet little daughter were there making grandpa Connor's breakfast. They saw me and Mr. Connor laughing, so they started laughing at the sight of us.

Alice and her daughter hugged me and gave me a kiss on the cheek.

Alice had seen my truck and was making breakfast for all of us. I didn't talk about jail or prison around Alice and her daughter. I was just so happy being there close to them in a normal family situation. When I left that morning, I didn't know it would be the last time I would see Mr. Connor. I am thankful that our last moments together were happy ones.

I started spending some time with an old friend of mine, Tony, who lived in Oklahoma City. It was a place I could spend an afternoon with no dope heads around. I was also seeing a girl in Tulsa named Kara. One afternoon she called me and asked if I would come bond a guy called Skip out of jail. According to Kara, Skip was a really nice guy. I drove to Tulsa and made Skip's bond and then spent the night in a motel with Kara. I was driving back and forth from Oklahoma City to Tulsa a lot, but I didn't mind.

On the day Katherine got out of rehab I went to pick her up. I had started a wrecker service with a guy called Harpo, who also ratted on me later. I had to stop by the shop on the way to Katherine's mother's house.

While we were at the shop Skip showed up with a car problem and asked me to fix his car. I said yes and I agreed to give him a ride home. Before I could leave the shop, Kara called and said that she was stranded at a motel and needed me to come get her because it was check out time. I felt that something was wrong, but I didn't listen to my heart. I just acted. Katherine and Skip got in the truck with me and we headed for the motel. We didn't get far. It was a setup. The police pulled me over and said a truck like mine had been reported stolen. I had just bought the new Z71 4X4 and I had all the paperwork with me. The truck and all the papers checked out. The officer asked to search the truck and I said "No."

The officer then told me to get out of the truck. I got out of the truck. Then the officer told me that the guy in my truck (Skip) was known to carry guns and drugs so he had to search my truck. The officer wanted my consent to search and I said, "No." I further told the officer that I hadn't done anything wrong and asked to leave.

The officer then had Skip get out of the truck and searched him and he didn't find anything. Then he told Katherine to get out of the truck and made her wait in the police car. By that time several other marked and unmarked police cars showed up and officers were standing around talking with each other. Sometime later they brought in a drug dog. Drug dogs are the biggest scam the cops have. All the cops have to do is say the dog alerted to something and they can search the car. If they don't find anything, the cops say, "Sorry for the inconvenience."

If the cops do find something they say, "Good dog." When the dog walked around my truck three times it never alerted to my truck. Then the officer handling the dog pulled a small black object from his pocket and tapped it on the passenger door of my truck. The dog started barking at the black object and the officer started yelling, "The dope is in the door." It is nothing more than a game the cops play because they know the courts will let them get away with it.

The other officers laughed and started searching my truck. There was nothing in the passenger door. The cops found a small amount of meth, some pot and a few valium in a little black bag that was in my briefcase, not mine but put there by Skip while I was out of the truck. All of it would have fit in the palm of your hand. They also found a 9mm Glock that Skip had dropped into my briefcase while I was out of the truck. I was arrested, again and charged with possession of the gun and drugs. Kara and Skip set me up.

I felt bad because Katherine hadn't even made it home from rehab and she was arrested too, simply because she was with me. Her charges were later dismissed, thankfully. Katherine was let go without bond and I made my and Skip's bond, because, at that time, I thought the cops had planted everything. I hadn't been selling any dope and I wasn't bothering anyone, yet it seemed like everyone was out to get me.

I talked to my attorney, who was actually a bum and just milking me for money and he believed that because I hadn't been caught selling anything, he was still hopeful that he could get me the five to ten year deal with everything running concurrent. It was at that point that the attorney started including a disclaimer of, "If the case doesn't go federal." It was obvious that there was something he wasn't telling me. I was going to tough it out, because I knew that the conduct I'd actually been arrested for was relatively minor. Simple possession of small amounts of drugs and firearms. I could not prove I was set up. How bad could it be? There were no sells or manufacturing charges. I was thinking that even if my case went federal I was still looking at no more than ten years.

It was time for me to take a trip. I called the attorney in Belize and asked when would be a good time to come see him. We agreed on a date and I drove to Mexico, then hopped a plane and flew to Belize. The attorney was very friendly and professional, as I expected. His firm represented Snake in his legal and financial needs. The attorney and I met for lunch at a very nice restaurant where we enjoyed a fine meal. I told him that I had been arrested three times in Oklahoma and was going to prison for a while. I explained that I came to Belize to see my old friend and have a little vacation before I had to go away.

I was fairly certain that the attorney was already aware of my situation and was simply feeling me out to see if I'd tell the truth.

The attorney said, "You don't seem very concerned about your predicament."

I laughed and said, "No, I'm not. I have been to prison before. I don't particularly like it, but I am not going to cry about it."

According to legend, Pretty Boy Floyd once told a police officer in Oklahoma that he had "A powerful lack of affection for jails." That summed up how I felt.

He told me that he would relay my message and that I should check into a hotel where a room was already waiting on me. When I arrived at the hotel I asked the concierge where best to do some shopping and about the best places to eat. Working with the very distinguished concierge's recommendations, I set out to do some shopping. Once I had the things I needed I went back to the hotel and took a hot bath. I always feel better after I get cleaned up and put on new clothes. I'd had the hotel laundry service wash and iron my new clothes and they were ready by the time I was ready to go out and eat dinner. I ate my dinner on a patio overlooking the ocean. The sky was a deep red and bluish purple as the sun went down. By the time I finished dinner there were many people dancing under the lanterns that were strung around and over the outside dance floor. It looked like a scene out of a movie. The live band and singer weren't loud like they are in America. It was peaceful and romantic. I wished Lisa was there.

While I was watching the people dance an exotic, sexy, dark-completed young woman with big eyes and wavy long black hair, came and sat down at my table. Her hair was so black it had a blue shine to it. Her mouth was large and her teeth perfect. When she smiled, all I could do was smile back.

She said, "You look sad. No one should be sad after such a fine meal and a beautiful sunset."

The patio faced the Northeast so I thought she must have been on the roof to see the sunset. Her English was perfect, with a slight sexy Spanish lilt. I told her that I was thinking of an old friend that I missed very much.

The girl said, "She must have been very special for you to look so sad."

I told her that it was a long time ago and I was just wishing she could be there to enjoy the spectacular view.

As soon as she sat down I perked up. I would have been happy to just sit and look at her. I ordered myself a margarita and white wine for her.

After our drinks came she asked me if I would like to dance. I said that I would love to, then warned her that I was not a good dancer. We danced to several songs with her showing me the steps. It was a lot of fun.

We walked down the beach talking about nothing in particular and listening to the waves rolling in. There was a bright half moon that provided plenty of light for us to see each other well. We took off our shoes and walked in the sand with the warm water lapping at our feet. It was very romantic and picturesque. I walked her back to her room and kissed her good night. I gave her my room number and told her that if she wanted me for anything I'd be there. She told me that I was a nice man and that most men would be trying to get in her bed.

I said, "I'm not that nice and if you want me in your bed, you let me know."

I then kissed her lightly and walked away. As I was returning to my room, I was thinking "nice guys finish last." But I'd been told most of my life that finishing last isn't always a bad thing.

Since then, I read a book by Nelson DeMille, where the main character, John Corey, was thinking about a woman and said, "My hearts on fire, and she's sitting on my hose." That summed up how I felt back then. But I was tired and a little drunk so sleep came quick and easy.

I woke the next morning to the sound of the telephone ringing. The phones don't ring the same in Belize. It's more like a zing-zing. At first, I thought it was a fire alarm, so I jumped up looking around. Then I grabbed the phone from its cradle and said, "Yeah?"

Snake said, "Wizard, come have breakfast with me."

I said, "You old dog, where are ya?"

He told me that he was down stairs in the restaurant. I asked him to order me whatever he was having and I'd be right down. I had been in prison for three and a half years. Then it was almost a year after I got out when I went to the storage and I'd waited close to ten months after that to go to Belize. It had been over five years since I'd seen Snake, but he hadn't changed much. I was so glad to see him that I had tears in my eyes. On the other hand, I looked a lot different. I had been working out for those five years and I was looking pretty good.

Snake said, "Damn, boy, what'cha been eatin'?"

We spent the morning walking around talking about what was going on in our lives and doing some shopping. I told him that Bobby was doing fine and all about the big mess I was in. He asked me what I wanted to do about it. I said, "Nothing." I told him that I was going to do my time, then I wanted out for good. I had the option of staying with Snake, but I didn't want the pending charges hanging over my head. I knew that with the charges not taken care of I would never be able to completely relax and enjoy myself. Plus, the cops would mess with my family if I went on the run. I had to go do my time.

Snake was living in Brazil. He had flown to Belize just to see me. He showed me beautiful pictures of his home and the surrounding mountains.

His wife looked the same and she sent her love. Snake showed me a picture of his and my Harleys sitting in his garage, with his wife waving at me. After lunch we met the attorney for drinks. The attorney showed me my portfolio, that I didn't even know I had. Snake had put one hundred thousand in an investment account for me. The money had been in the account four years and had grown to one hundred and sixty two thousand and change. That was a fairly good return with minimum risk, according to the attorney. Snake said he had my other two hundred thousand for me and we agreed that he should put another hundred thousand in the investment account and hold on to the other hundred thousand for me. I didn't need any money, so it sounded great to me. I also arranged with the attorney to

send him another hundred thousand in cash to put in my investment account, which I sent him after I got back home.

Snake also informed me that he could have a beautiful cabin built for me with two bedrooms, two full baths, two fireplaces and a two car garage, right next to his place on five acres for forty thousand. I knew I would need it when I got out of prison so I said, "Yes." I wanted to make sure I had a hundred thousand there with Snake in cash, so I later sent him the forty thousand to take care of the cabin.

We took care of everything that day because Snake had to catch a plane home at 5:00 p.m. that day. I hated to see him leave, but I knew he had to. He had taken a risk just coming to see me and I appreciated it more than words could say. I knew Snake was sitting on at least a couple of million, so keeping his word to me didn't put him in a bind. He showed me what a true friend is and anything less is just a bum.

After I'd had lunch with Snake that day and found out when he was leaving, I'd taken the time to call my new friend's room and was transferred to poolside. I asked her if she would meet me at 7:00 p.m. for dinner. Then Snake and I did some more shopping before we met the attorney for drinks. While we were shopping I bought myself a nugget ring with four small diamonds and I bought a tear drop necklace with a tear shaped emerald in the center surrounded by little diamonds on a platinum chain·. I told Snake who it was for and he jokingly called me a "Dog" and said I hadn't changed a bit. We had several good laughs that day.

After I saw Snake off at the airport I went back to my room, got cleaned up and put on another freshly pressed outfit. I'd only had one drink when we met the attorney and I wasn't planning on drinking anymore.

I wanted to be sober for dinner and dancing. It didn't seem wise to be drinking in another country.

When I met the young woman in the hotel lobby at 7:00 p.m., she turned everyone's head in the place. It was hard to believe that she was even more beautiful than she was the night before. The odd thing was, I still didn't know her name. It hadn't come up the night before.

When Snake asked me her name I couldn't tell him and when I called her at the hotel I asked to be connected to the lady in room 416. The man at the desk told me that the lady in 416 was at the pool and he took her the phone. I couldn't very well ask him what her name was without sounding like an idiot. Plus, the clerk probably wouldn't have given me her name anyway. I wondered if she thought I was mysterious, because I was in a hotel room by myself in another country. I certainly thought she was mysterious for being there alone.

When she walked up to me I handed her the single red rose I'd bought from a lady in the lobby and said, "You're so pretty I could stand here and look at you all evening."

She said, "Then people would think you touched and we would go hungry, no?"

We laughed and she recommended a restaurant down the beach.

We hailed a taxi and rode the short distance to the restaurant where I thought we were going to have to wait in line. I was wrong. The maître d came right over and said, "Good evening miss. It is a pleasure to see you.

I have a table waiting for you and your companion. Right this way."

I was a little jealous of the guy. I followed them to a table where the man handed us menus and informed us that our waiter would be right with us.

"He seems like a really nice man," I said.

"I've known him since I was a child," she replied.

That explained a lot. When the waiter came and asked what we would like to drink, I ordered hot tea. My date looked at me a second and then said she would have the same. I explained to her that hot tea seemed to bring the flavor out in the food and alcohol covered up the flavor. I like to taste my food. I also explained that when I went to a nice place, most people are drinking and they expect you to drink.

"I'm just not much of a drinker," I said.

She ordered some kind of avocado salad with fish. I ordered a steak. My dad told me a long time ago that, "Son, when you go to a steakhouse, you order steak." I made the mistake of ordering a cheeseburger at a steak house once and I thought dad was going to throw his plate at me.

While we were waiting on our food, I said, "We don't even know each other's names. It would be helpful if I knew what to call you."

"Names aren't important," she said. "I know more about you than you think, Mr. Wizard."

That shut me up for a second. "Well, then you have me at a disadvantage," I said.

She thought the shocked expression on my face was rather amusing.

Before I could ask her how she knew, she told me.

"Your friend left me a message," she said. "He said that you are a very good person and that your friends call you The Wizard, because you are magical. Do you always have your friend call pretty girls for you?"

"No," I said. "My friend is always trying to protect me and he worries about my feelings. He knew that hearing you call me The Wizard would shock me and make me smile. It was his way of saying that he will always be looking out for me. He is a very good friend."

I didn't go into an explanation of why I was sometimes called The Wizard. I simply said, "You can call me Jeff, or Jeffrey."

"Jeffrey, I think," she replied. "My friends call me Mia."

"Mia sounds sexy. I like it," I stated.

We enjoyed a wonderful meal, with our hot tea. The waiter took our plates and we ordered dessert. Then Mia excused herself and went to the restroom. Our dessert came while she was gone and I put the necklace on the table and had the waiter place her dessert dish over it.   There was a ridge running around the bottom of the dish that held the center of the little plate off the table. The necklace fit perfectly under the plate. I didn't start my dessert until Mia returned to the table. Then we talked about how beautiful Belize is that time of year. When the waiter took the dessert dishes away, Mia simply looked down at the necklace with raised eyebrows. She then looked up at me with a questioning expression.

I said, "That is one of the reasons they call me The Wizard."

She smiled, then looked at me with a serious expression and said, "Does this mean that you expect me to have sex with you?"

I would have laughed but she looked so serious. "No," I said. "It means that I consider you a special friend."

"Do you have a lot of special friends," she asked.

I looked at her as the tears welled up in my eyes and said, "Not any more. I had one once." I thought I was doing something nice but Mia looked offended. All thoughts of sex left me and I started thinking about Lisa and my next trip to prison. I was in no position to have a relationship and I didn't want to hurt Mia's feelings.

It wasn't really late, but I said, "let's call it a night."

I needed some space. We rode back to the hotel together and I walked Mia to her room. Things had changed between us. I was then more concerned about Mia's virtue than I was about sex, which was odd for me.

At her door, Mia said, "I would invite you in, but my grandfather would think I'm a very naughty girl."

Based on my questioning look, Mia said, "My grandfather owns this hotel. He knows everything that goes on."

I laughed, because it explained a lot. I kissed her on the cheek and said, "Goodbye."

"Not goodnight, but goodbye. Will I not see you again?"

"Maybe someday," I said. "It has been delightful knowing you."

I would like to think that she wanted me to talk my way into her bed, I sure wanted to, but I couldn't bring myself to do it. I went to my room and packed. I then checked out and moved to another hotel. I spent two days there crying in my beer, so to speak, then I flew back to Mexico and picked up my truck. The drive home seemed like it took forever. I stopped in my underground storage and picked up some money and the little pewter fairy that had been on top of my combination birthday and going away cake so many years before. I just wanted to look at the little fairy and carry it around.

I then went to a big mall that sits just off I-40 and I-35 in Oklahoma City, Cross Roads Mall, where I bought four expensive dress shirts and asked for boxes to mail them in. Two were for the attorney in Belize and two were for Snake. I went to my truck and wrote a note for the attorney and put one hundred thousand between the two shirts and taped the box closed. I put forty thousand between two shirts with a note for Snake and taped the box shut. I went back in the mall to a mailing place and had the two boxes wrapped in brown paper and mailed to where they needed to go.

When I got back to Tulsa nothing had changed. Katherine and I both had court dates coming up. I was taking care of all my loose ends and getting ready for prison.

The day I was scheduled for court in Osage County, I got word that my case was going federal and that I would be arrested at the hearing and held without bond. I took Katherine to court that morning, then I sold my '70 Chevy truck to Scott and let Scott's cousin drive my new Z-71 truck. I knew the cops would be looking for me and my truck. I needed another two weeks to get things situated before I went to jail. I wasn't trying to get away or run. I just wanted to say goodbye to a few friends, or I should say, people I thought were friends. People can't run away from their troubles or the law. It all catches up with you eventually. It is far better to keep your mouth shut, stand up and be a man and face the music. After all, I was the one that turned on the stereo and got the music playing.

Prison is only a place to fear if you have done something to be afraid of. I hadn't crossed anyone, so I had nothing to fear or worry about. I wasn't thrilled about being locked away and forgotten about, but I had to deal with it. One thing prison does well is, it shows you who your friends really are.

I was staying in a motel in Bristow, Oklahoma next to a discount mall, just off I-40. From there I could jump on the highway and go to either Oklahoma City or Tulsa with little trouble. Aubrey was staying with me and we were spending a lot of time in the hot tub and in bed. Aubrey was a dancer with an attitude. She was cocky and would tell a person where they could go, right quick. I liked that about her. She was sexy and a lot of fun.

Her birthday was in the first part of September, so I bought her new tires for her car and took her on a shopping spree at the mall. That was before a tornado blew the mall away. We had a great time visiting each one of the little shops buying whatever she wanted. When I kissed her goodbye in the mall parking lot I knew I probably wouldn't ever see her again. It broke my heart.

By the time I saw Aubrey off at the mall, several people had figured out that I was staying in the motel next to the mall. It was time for me to move on. I went to Oklahoma City and stayed at a friend's house for a few days while I got ready to go back to prison. I wasn't doing much those final days and when people started showing up in Oklahoma City, I knew it was time to turn myself in and get it over with.

The night before I was going to turn myself in I had a friend drive me to Tulsa. I got a taxi when I got to Tulsa and had the taxi run me around to the places I needed to visit. I bought Katherine some birthday presents then met her and my little sister at a chicken place to say goodbye. Saying goodbye is not easy for me. I mainly wanted to tell them I loved them before I left. I had also picked up a few things for Bobby and I had to leave them someplace for him before I left.

After I left the chicken place and Katherine and my little sister went their way, I got a call informing me that the police had surrounded the chicken place after I left. They were looking for me. I had the taxi driver take me to pick up Michelle, a sweet girl I'd been seeing off and on for some time. Michelleis wonderful. When she has an orgasm, she goes ridged and her legs shake real hard. It is great. There is no question that she came. I loved that. We were on our way to a motel when I got a call from a girl who said her son was in jail and she needed some money to make his bond. I told her that I would meet her and give her the money.

I was always helping people. Helping people was my way of justifying the things I was doing wrong. Before I· could get to the arranged place to meet her the taxi was pulled over by a dozen or more police cars.

I don't know if the girl who called me set me up, maybe the cops were listening to and tracking my phone, or maybe they followed us from Michelle's house. I don't know. But I was surely caught before I could turn myself in. I felt bad because Michelle had to experience my arrest. After I got out of the taxi as instructed by the police I laid face down on the ground with my hands behind my head. The officers put the handcuffs on me then started asking me who I was as they beat me in the legs, knees and ribs with their big black Mag lights. I don't know why they did it. I did exactly as I was told and didn't say one word to provoke them. Then they placed me in the front passenger side of the police car and drove me away. The woman officer in the back seat wrapped the safety belt around my neck and pulled me back against the seat, while the male officer who was driving put on a black leather glove and started back handing me in the face as he yelled questions. When I wouldn't answer he hit me more. I never said a word, but got a dandy beating anyway. I will never understand why or how a police officer can be that violent, for no reason and get away with it. Why would a police officer, who is sworn to uphold the law, act in that manner? It was all completely unnecessary. I didn't have a gun and I complied with them in every respect.

What I have learned from personal experience, and from observation, is that law enforcement is no longer a noble and honorable profession. The few very bad apples have spoiled the reputations of the whole profession of cops. All you have to do is watch the show Cops, or the movie Training Day and you can see how violent, aggressive and corrupt some cops are. What people don't see, unless they are a victim of it, is how some cops use their badges and guns to hide behind while they literally rob people.

We are living in sad times and there is no one to police the police, or check the oppressive government that is running over the constitutional rights of American citizens with the "Patriot Act."

CHAPTER TWENTY-ONE:
Prosecution

My arrest and beating was based on a failure to appear warrant from Osage county. It made me wonder how they would have treated me for an unpaid traffic ticket. I was held in the Tulsa county jail for a few days, then transported to the Osage county jail in Pawhuska, Oklahoma where I'd failed to appear for court.

The first thing I did was hire another attorney to represent me on a bond hearing. The State called one witness at the bond hearing, the officer who had backhanded me in the face a dozen times while I was handcuffed and his female partner choked me with a safety belt. He testified that I was a known drug manufacturer and should not be allowed bond. I had two bail bond agents there ready to make a new bond, if it was reasonable. It wasn't. Even though the pending charges were nonviolent and only involved the conduct from the raid of my home, the court set my bond at over six hundred thousand. I didn't have the collateral for that kind of bond, so I was done.

I hired two local attorneys to represent me on the Osage county case and got ready for the long ride. I had a pending motion for return of property already in the works and the new attorneys filed a motion to dismiss all the charges stemming from the raid of my home. Hiring those two local attorneys was one of the best things I could have done. They were honest and did a great job of representing me. At all times, I felt that they had my best interest in mind and they did, as time proved.

While I was in Osage County Jail, during a visit I advised Katherine to go visit her sister in England. She got permission from her State probation officer and left the country. It was the best move she could have made and it prevented her arrest when the case went federal a short time later.

I hadn't been in Osage county long when a deputy told me to pack my things, I was leaving. Two Marshals were there to pick me up. They transported me to the Tulsa county jail where I was booked again and held without bond on a federal warrant. Then I was taken to the federal courthouse where I was formally arraigned on federal drug and firearm charges that included conspiracy to manufacture and distribute methamphetamine.

I had been charged by "The State of Oklahoma" before and that wasn't a very good feeling. That didn't compare to the feeling I had when I received my first federal indictment and it said, "United States of America versus Jeffrey Dan Williams." Knowing that you are going up against the United States of America kind of takes all the wind out of your sail and leaves you dead in the water.

One of the things I don't understand is the amount of violence the prisoners exhibited in the Tulsa county jail. I realize the circumstances were stressful, but rather than try to help each other, in an already oppressive situation, the prisoners wasted time fighting amongst themselves and trying to kill each other. It was a sad situation that severely hindered the prisoners that should have been spending their time learning more about the laws that held them captive. Instead, they were fighting like gladiators, or were too afraid to speak to anyone. I was the proverbial peace maker that tried to help the other prisoners get along and learn something. Some of the prisoners even resented that. But I was just big enough that people left me alone and when I spoke they listened. I wouldn't tolerate bullies, so the people around me were mostly okay guys.

The first attorney I hired to represent me on the Osage county charges and the two Tulsa arrests, pulled out on me when the case went federal. I was actually glad to get rid of him. It was the reason I hired the two good attorneys in Osage county. It was also part of the reason I went through three other attorneys on my federal case. I have learned the hard way that an honest attorney can be your biggest asset and a crooked attorney can be your greatest liability.

Before the first attorney quit me, he came to the Tulsa county jail to see me. He told me that one of the investigating officers, J.J. Gray, had contacted him about a large amount of money that I supposedly had buried. According to the attorney, the officer wanted me to turn over six hundred thousand I supposedly had buried. In return, the officer would assure me a sentence reduction. I didn't have six hundred thousand buried. But I am pretty quick on my feet, so I said, "Tell the officer that it's only five hundred and eighty thousand and if he doesn't turn me loose and try to catch me with it he doesn't have a hair on his ass." I thought it was a fine answer, but the attorney didn't. I think the attorney was just trying to rob me. By the time I was arrested most of my money was gone. I had sent some to Belize, some to Snake and a lot of it was spent making peoples bonds and paying for their attorneys. Some went on failed business deals. It was just gone.

I found out later why they thought I had six hundred thousand buried. Eileen had seen a bank statement, from my secured credit card account, from a bank in New York City. That was one of the reasons I'd gotten a Post Office Box. Eileen wouldn't stay out of my mail. The statement showed six thousand in the account. Somehow, in Eileen's disturbed, drugged out mind, it grew to sixty thousand. It was Eileen's sister Lanette who told me that. By the time Eileen told the story to the police it had grown to six hundred thousand, not in a bank in New York City, but buried in my back yard. After I went to jail, people actually went to my house in the middle of the night and dug up parts of my backyard looking for money that didn't exist. Thank you, Eileen. It's funny now, but it sure wasn't funny then. It caused my little sister a lot of grief. She was living in the house while people sneaked into the back yard digging holes.

My first attorney didn't even make an appearance in federal Court.

He ran for cover as soon as the case went federal. The Court appointed an attorney to represent me, but I didn't know about it until he showed up at the Tulsa county jail one day demanding that I sign a drug quantity stipulation. He told me it was a great deal and that it would get me twenty-one years.

I refused to sign anything and my only question was, "Who are you?"

When he told me who he was I told him that I was going to trial, then I told him to leave and not come back. I would have signed a plea deal for a guaranteed ten years, but that isn't how the federal government works. The federal system is purposely designed to mislead and trick people into pleading guilty to one thing, then they add enhancements and sentence you to another. In many cases a person enters a plea to a crime that carries an indeterminate sentence. Then he finds out at sentencing, when the Court imposes a thirty or forty year term of imprisonment, that he got screwed. That happens a lot more often than one would think.

After I ran off the second attorney, who was just a bum like the first one, I retained one of the top three attorneys in Tulsa. We had the same last name, but no relation. That was about the time the government filed its "first" superseding indictment against me. Filing a new indictment is a tactic the government uses to prolong the speedy trial date and pressure the defendant into pleading guilty. In federal Court, normally, the defendant has a right to trial within seventy days, but the government, being the trickster that it is, has developed many ways to get around a defendant's right to a fast and speedy trial.

I told my new attorney, Mr. Williams, that I would plead guilty to ten years, but no more. If I couldn't get ten years, I was going to trial. Mr. Williams was honest with me. He explained how the federal guilty plea process worked. I was disheartened, to say the least and I refused to plead guilty and insisted on proceeding to trial. I was not going to plead guilty to a life sentence. That would be stupid.

After my attorney informed the prosecution that I was going to trial, the prosecution, once again, put off my trial date by filing a "second" superseding indictment. It was nothing more than a strategic ploy to put more pressure on me to plead guilty. It also gave the government more time to build its case against me.

When my new attorney came to see me after the "second" superseding indictment, he brought a long list of witnesses and a synopsis of their statements. He explained that the government needed no supporting evidence. That is when he informed me that I could be found guilty on the informant testimony alone. To me that didn't make sense.

I had studied Oklahoma State law and knew that the State required real factual evidence, not just unsupported statements from a bunch of people who were caught breaking the law and doing nothing more than trying to get themselves out of trouble. From the first day my case went federal I had been studying federal law and I didn't like what I was reading. It was looking bad for the home team.

Hearing what some of the people said in their statements broke my heart. I was very upset, to say the least. There were statements from people I didn't even know. There were statements from people like Ricky Dale, who I'd refused to do business with. Some of the statements were partly true, but they were mostly lies.

After seeing the names on the witness list and reading what they had said, I was mad. When I went back to my cell I made three or four phone calls and told some of the informants exactly what I thought about them.

I was beyond hurt and I said some nasty, mean things, but I never threatened anyone. Soon after I made those calls, I was taken back before the judge and arraigned on a "third" superseding indictment. The new indictment included additional charges for tampering with witnesses and encouraging perjury. That was not good news and it made me look even worse.

My attorney's visit after that "third" superseding indictment was not very pleasant. Mr. Williams was pretty disgusted with me and I deserved it. I'd made some shitty comments on the phone that were all recorded.

Those calls caused me to lose my attorney's respect. I had blown it with my attorney by letting the informant statements get to me.

Mr. Williams informed me of another new development that was far more disturbing than the new charges. I was advised that if I didn't plead guilty, the prosecution intended to file a "fourth" superseding indictment that would include the new charge of Career Criminal Enterprise (CCE) and my little sister would be added to the indictment as a defendant. The government doesn't play fair. I had seen them do the same thing to some of Outlaw's family and I knew they would do it to mine without any compunction. I couldn't take the risk. My little sister was pregnant and had two small children, at that time. She hadn't done anything wrong, but I knew that wouldn't stop the government from charging her, arresting her and prosecuting her for no other reason than to hold her over my head to pressure me into pleading guilty. I couldn't stand the thought of them arresting my little sister, so I agreed to plead guilty. I was tired and just wanted to get it over with.

It didn't take the prosecution long to come up with a plea agreement, which is a ready made confession, based on what all the informants told them. When I read the plea agreement I refused to sign it because it went to great lengths to implicate my girlfriend Katherine. I told my attorney that, if the government would take Katherine's name out of the plea agreement and agree to dismiss all the charges against her, I would sign the plea. Katherine was still in England, but I still didn't want the charges hanging over her head. For all her faults, Katherine was a good person and she did not deserve to be charged in a federal indictment.

The very next day my attorney brought me a new plea agreement with Katherine's name removed. I signed the ready made confession, feeling like an idiot. I was agreeing to plead guilty to the four counts that were in the original indictment. My attorney managed to get all the new charges dismissed, including the tampering with a witness and encouraging perjury charges. However, getting some of the charges dismissed wasn't the primary reason I agreed to plead guilty. It was obvious that my acquiescence was more to assuage the wishes of my attorney and sister and to protect the people I love. Katherine meant more to me than I was willing to admit, even though she had proved that she thought our sordid relationship was little more than a joke and a joke on me, at that.

Most people, like myself at that time, have never seen a federal plea agreement and would be shocked by its one sidedness. A plea agreement is considered a contract that is generally tailored in favor of the drafter, in this case the federal government. While the government retains all of its rights and options in a plea agreement, the defendant must agree to waive many of his basic rights, leaving the sentence determination to the sole discretion of the judge.

Signing a plea agreement is not enough. The government then takes the defendant before a judge to enter a formal plea. I told my attorney that I wasn't going to stand up there in front of the judge and admit to everything in the plea agreement. I told him that I was only going to say I was pleading guilty to the charges. My attorney informed me that was not how the federal government worked. They wanted me to confess everything on the record. I wasn't going to do it.

The Court started by asking me the basics, like my name and education level. I didn't have a problem answering those questions, but when the Court asked me to tell the Court about my crime, in my own words, I refused. I simply said, "It's all in the indictment." That didn't seem to be good enough for the Court, so the judge started reading me parts of the indictment, then asking me if it was true. That didn't work very well either.

I said, "For the purpose of this hearing, it's true."

When the Court came to the part about me being arrested that day in my truck after Skip planted the drugs and 9mm Glock, things got more interesting. The Court said that I had drugs, scales, and a gun in my briefcase. I said, "No, sir. There were no scales in my briefcase and the drugs and gun were not mine."

The prosecutor spoke up and said, "We would be prepared to prove that there were scales in the briefcase."

I said, "No, there wasn't, but for the purpose of this hearing, I'll agree there was."

The scales were not in my briefcase. The officers searching my truck had found them in one of the four boxes of Aubrey's clothes that were in the back of my truck.

The police put her scales in my briefcase, then said that was where they found them. Logic and reason tells us that I would not have had a tiny, plastic, "pink," cheap, scale in my briefcase. Simply not going to happen.

It took some time to get past the scale issue.

Then the Court wanted me to agree that the gun was there to protect the drugs. Well, it wasn't, so I said, "No, sir."

The judge asked me why I had the gun and I couldn't/wouldn't tell him that Skip had just planted the gun. So I told the Court that it was just for my protection.

The judge wasn't going to give up that easy. He asked me why I needed protection and I said, "It's the 90s, everyone has a gun." Then I told the Court that, "No amount of drugs or money would be worth hurting someone over." I hadn't been carrying a gun for a long time and it was just chance that I had one planted that day. That and bad luck.

The judge, seeing that he was going to get some resistance, changed his tactic and asked me if there was anything else in the plea agreement that I didn't agree with. I didn't agree with most of it, but the only specific point I could think of at that moment was a comment stating that I had given a girl named Debbie some of my checks, so she could write hot checks on my account. That wasn't true. I told the Court that I didn't give her my checks, that would have been stupid and I added that if she had my checks I didn't know how she got them.

Finally, the Court seemed satisfied and accepted my guilty plea to each of the four counts. Pleading guilty left me feeling like a cow being led to the slaughter house. I'd went along with it peacefully, without putting up a fight. I was mad at myself for giving up so easy. Shortly after my guilty plea, the Tenth Circuit issued its initial decision in the Singelton case.

The Court ruled that offers of leniency in exchange for testimony violated the federal bribery statute, Title 18 U.S.C. § 201(c). That ruling would have rendered all of the informants statements in my case tainted because they were obtained with offers of leniency.

I also discovered that my attorney, Mr. Williams, one week prior to my guilty plea, filed a Motion to Withdraw from my case, stating that circumstances had arisen and exist where he could no longer render me effective assistance of counsel. That motion was pending at the time Mr. Williams represented me when I entered my guilty plea.

Based on the above two points, I asked my attorney to file a Motion to Withdraw my guilty plea. I also sent two letters to the judge asking to be allowed to withdraw my guilty plea. That prompted my attorney to file a "second" Motion to Withdraw as Attorney of Record. The Court granted Mr. Williams' Motion to Withdraw and appointed me new counsel.

My new attorney filed my requested Motion to Withdraw Plea of Guilty and Nullify Plea Agreement. The Court subsequently held a hearing on my Motion to Withdraw Plea and denied the Motion.

After a person pleads guilty in federal Court, the prospective sentence calculation is determined by a Probation Officer in a Presentence Investigation Report (PSI).

The Probation Officer takes all the statements from the informants, the information in the indictment, the stipulations by the defendant in the plea agreement and any recommendation of the prosecution to use for sentence enhancement and calculation purposes. It is not necessarily based on the truth. It is the government's version of the truth. The PSI assigns points for the crime committed, which is called the Base Offense Level. Then it assigns points for each of the proposed enhancements, or reductions, which formulates the Total Offense Level. Once those factors are determined, the Criminal History Score comes into play.

Using a Sentencing Chart, the Criminal History is shown in a horizontal manner across the top of the Chart. The Total Offense Level is represented vertically down the left side of the Chart, then vectored to the correlating sentencing range. It is not a complicated calculation. The thing is, the enhancements are largely based on the whims of the Probation Officer and prosecution, which makes the enhancements arbitrary and capricious. The application of uncharged enhancements has been a hot topic of debate since the Federal United States Sentencing Guidelines (U.S.S.G.) were enacted.

After the PSI Report is prepared, the defendant gets an opportunity to file objections to the report. In my case, I objected to most everything.

The drug quantity was based on lies and in some instances, from people I didn't even know. I was enhanced for being an organizer or leader and enhanced for obstruction of justice. The obstruction of justice enhancements was based on the dismissed tampering with a witness and encouraging perjury charges. I certainly didn't see anything fair about that.

The government filed an answer to my objections to the PSI Report, explaining how the enhancements were justifiable. It was like trying to argue with God.

You are not sure if he can hear you and don't always get the answer you want. God works in mysterious ways and so does the federal government.

On the day of sentencing, the Court overruled my objections, adopted the findings of the Probation Officer in the PSI Report and started explaining its reasoning for imposing the sentence. Because I disputed the drug quantity, the government called the Probation Officer to testify at sentencing. The Probation Officer stated that he based his drug quantity calculation on the statements of the informants. He then named the particular informant and the drug quantity that each informant said I was responsible for. The quantities were huge and completely unrealistic.

At least one of the informants, Greg, I didn't even know. This Greg person said he saw me manufacture 385 ounces of methamphetamine.

That was a lie. I didn't even know a Greg. The Probation Officer swore that his calculation was reliable and my attorney told the Court that there was no way that the Probation Officer could be certain it was reliable.

The whole thing was staged to give the "appearance" of fairness, when there was absolutely no fairness to the process, at all.

I knew the moment I walked into the courtroom for sentencing that it was all staged. There were a bunch of juvenile offenders seated in the jury box that were brought there to observe my sentencing. I was being used as an example of what could happen to you if you broke the law.

Before the judge actually imposed the sentence, he gave me an opportunity to speak. It's called allocution and it is another process that is merely there to give the "appearance" of fairness. I told the judge that the drug quantity calculation was wrong and that I didn't even know a Greg, as the Probation Officer had alleged. I might as well have been talking to a wall. The judge, hang'em high Cook, imposed a sentence of 360-months on the drug counts, then imposed an additional 60-months for the firearm count, to run consecutively to the drug counts. That resulted in a whopping 420-month sentence, or 35-years.

I figured something like that was coming, so I just shook my head and walked away with the Marshals in tow. I felt much better after I got out of that damn courtroom. I was even happy to get back to my jail cell.

My newly appointed attorney, who did a great job at the sentencing hearing, especially when considering that the deck was stacked against me, filed a timely Notice of Appeal to start my appellate process.

Most people I met after they were sentenced were depressed. It was the opposite for me. I was relieved and thankful it was over. The heavy weight of uncertainty and anticipation had been lifted from my shoulders.

I had been lied to, stolen from and just generally shit on by people I thought were my friends, people I had helped and trusted. I was thankful to be away from them. I was also more than ready to get out of that nasty Tulsa county jail. I knew that federal prison had to be better than the sorry county jail conditions.

The feeling of being prosecuted and the turmoil that comes with it, is one of the worst feelings there is. The loss of property and liberty, the feeling of helplessness, hopelessness, being isolated and lonely, are just a small part of what a person goes through while being prosecuted. I needed some relief and the only place I could get it was in my mind and it started with closure. I had part of the nightmare behind me and I was thankful for it. I spent a lot of time reading books in order to help escape reality. Books helped a lot and I was also studying federal law. That kept my mind occupied. But what helped most, I'm sad to say, was getting the prosecution part behind me and moving on to federal prison.

Early one morning, not long after my sentence was imposed, a deputy came and told me to pack out. I thought I was on my way to federal prison. Little did I know. I was surprised to find out that I was on my way back to the Osage county jail. I had been gone from the Osage county jail so long that they had time to build a new jail. The jail looked clean, but looks can be deceiving. The kitchen must not have been too clean, because the first day I was there I got sick from an egg salad sandwich. Just my luck.

One of my Osage county attorneys showed up the next day and informed me that I was there for a hearing on my Motion for Return of Property. That was an interesting development. The day of the hearing I was brought before the judge. Both my sisters and my brother-in-law were there. Initially, the district attorney told me that if I didn't agree to forfeit the seized property he would refile the State criminal charges. I laughed and told him that I'd just been sentenced to 35 years in federal prison.

I didn't care if he refiled the State charges. My attorney advised me that it would be far less costly to go ahead and let the State have the property than it would be to proceed to trial. I agreed, but even then, my attorney managed to negotiate the return of a large portion of the tools and equipment that was seized. I was thankful that my family was getting a little bit of something back. The seizure was not legal or justifiable, but that has never stopped law enforcement officials from just taking anything they want. After the search of my home, I discovered that the cops had stolen blue jeans out of my closet, a new car stereo system that was still in the box, many of my CDs, a coin collection, my new chainsaw and some of my Coca-Cola collectables. They simply took what they wanted and then they have the nerve to call other people crooks.

After my small victory at the property hearing, I was soon transferred back to the Tulsa county jail to await my transfer to federal prison.

CHAPTER TWENTY-TWO:
Federal Prison

Waiting on almost anything can be stressful. Especially when considering that you don't have a choice and you are completely at the mercy of others. You have absolutely no control of the situation when you are in jail. Your fate is in the hands of others. My thoughts were not about the length of my sentence, or how long I would be away from my family.

I knew that when I came home it would be in a pine box.

Imposing a 35-year sentence was the Court's way of saying "life" in a less shocking manner. I knew it was not likely that I would outlive my sentence.

My immediate concerns were, how long would I be forced to endure the Tulsa county jail before transferring to federal prison and to which prison would I be sent. The wait and not knowing where you are going is stressful.

The day an officer told me that I'd been designated I was relieved because I knew I would be leaving soon, but that relief was short lived.

The officer then informed me that I was going to the United States Penitentiary (USP) in Beaumont, Texas. I wondered what I'd done and who I'd pissed off, to be sent to the worst maximum security prison in the federal system. The prison's nickname was "Bloody Beaumont." I was being pushed out of the frying pan, right into the fire.

When a guard finally came, early one morning and told me to grab my bunk, I was thankful to be leaving, but apprehensive about where I was headed. I was put in a van, all chained up with no place to go and taken to the Oklahoma City transfer center. It was clean and compared to what I'd been forced to eat for a year in county jails, the food was great. People were telling me that I would be there two to four weeks, but to my surprise, I was shipped out in only four days.

The trip to USP Beaumont was uncomfortable, long and tiresome.

Riding on a bus for twelve hours in chains is not a pleasant experience. Even though I was sitting still for the entire ride, I was worn out by the time we arrived.

My arrival at USP Beaumont was very dramatic. The bus pulled up to the back entrance gate that is next to a gun tower. As the officers in the bus get out to put up their guns, two trucks pull up and the drivers got out wearing bulletproof vests and sporting shotguns. Before driving in the first gate the officers are required to disarm and place their weapons in a compartment at the base of the gun tower. Then the bus is allowed to proceed through the first gate. Once through the first gate the bus must stop while the first gate closes, then the second gate opens. At that point the bus clears what is called the outer perimeter fence. Both fences are topped with razor wire and there is razor wire stacked between the fences.

When the second gate closed, the bus then drove a short distance to a set of steel doors that are thirty feet tall. The doors slowly open and you get the impression that you are about to enter the gates of Hell. As the bus goes through the gates you get the feeling that it is the point of no return and for many people it certainly is. The bus then turns and stops. at an odd angle that I realized was to force a prisoner to run around the bus to get back to the gate. That act would be futile anyway, because no one gets off the bus until the steel doors slowly grind their way closed and seal with a loud boom. Only then, after the buzzer and flashing lights announce that the door is secure, do the officers unlock the bus door and have all the prisoners line up beside the bus. The officers take their time matching each of his new prisoners with the pictures and papers he has in his hands and he has each prisoner state his name and date of birth.

Once satisfied that they have the correct prisoners the officers march them through a back door to a holding cell in the Reception and Discharge (R & D) wing where the chains are finally removed. Once again, all prisoners must be dressed out. which is a humiliating process that a person sadly grows accustomed to because it happens so often.

From the holding cell a prisoner must see a psychologist, doctor, case manager and counselor. It is a screening process to help evaluate whether a prisoner can be in general population.

The very first question they asked was, "Have you ever been sexually assaulted?"

I answered, "No," but in my mind I was thinking, "What the hell kind of place were they sending me into?"

The next question was, "Are you an informant?" I said, "No."

I soon learned, from observation, that the life expectancy of informants in a maximum security prison is short. At a minimum, they run the risk of being severely injured. In most cases, background checks are easily done, even from prison. Informants, if not killed, are often beaten and spend most of their time in the Special Housing Unit (SHU), which is commonly called the corner pocket. Even in most medium security prisons, informants don't fare well. Because the problem is so large scale, the federal government now has prisons where most of the population are informants. We are living in sad times.

Because I didn't have any skeletons in my closet, I was sent into general population my first day. It was the first week in January of 1999 and it was obvious from day one that I was a sheep amongst the wolves.

Believe me when I say that there is definitely a need for maximum security prisons. There are people in them that you would not want to meet on the street. I didn't want to meet them in prison.

The prisoner custody classification system is supposed to be designed to separate the nonviolent prisoners from the dangerous nuts and killers.

It works most of the time, but then you get some people, like me, that get sent there simply because their sentences are so long. I wasn't there because I was bad or mean, I was just unfortunate enough to have a long sentence. I'm the kind of guy who can get along with most anyone.

But I quickly saw that it was best to stay to myself. I could see in many of the prisoners eyes that the lights might have been on, but they were far from home.

The orientation process took place on my third day at USP Beaumont.

All of the new arrivals are required to meet in the chapel to undergo a series of speeches from various staff members. The first person that spoke was in charge of security. His primary point was to advise us to make no mistake about the men in the gun towers. Their job was to kill us and they were good at their jobs. He let us know, in no uncertain terms, that if we attempted to climb over the wall, we would be shot. As tall as the wall was, I was thinking that a person would have a real hard time flying out if he had wings.

The next person to speak told us that we had to learn one thing, "Tolerance of others." He explained that we would see a lot of things that we didn't like, but if we wanted to survive, we better learn to mind our own business and stay out of everyone else's. He said there were five things to stay away from because they would get you hurt or killed quickly: (1) drugs; (2) alcohol; (3) gambling; (4) homosexual activity; and (5) getting in debt. He pointed out that if we avoided those areas we would all probably make it okay. He also added that if anyone was a rat, they had better check in right then, because the other prisoners would find out.

One guy actually raised his hand and walked up front and checked in right there on the spot. The other staff that spoke mainly filled us all in on day to day prison life. The next day I got a job in the prison law library, where I spent most of my time researching and learning more about federal law.

The first three weeks I was there were uneventful. That soon changed. The prison had two men cells and I was fortunate enough to get a cell mate named Tom who was an older gentleman, in for bank robbery. He was a great guy. He had a serious side, but was mostly funny and pleasant to be around. I was thankful to have his friendship, guidance and insight, even though when he farted it would almost peel the paint off the walls. I like old Tom so much, that a few farts were no bother. It reminded me of that one word, "Tolerance." I gladly endured a few farts for the knowledge he shared with me and the everlasting friendship.

I learned that prison life can be endured if you have one good friend. Tom helped me find my laughter again. No matter how tough life gets, a person will be better off if he can find something to laugh about.

Mixed with the bad, there is usually some good if you look hard enough.

The fourth week was a different story. I was walking back to my unit after the evening meal, just at dusk, when the guard in the gun tower next to me (the gun tower was in the center of the compound) slid his window open, thirty feet above my head and started yelling, "On the ground. On the ground," as he fired two warning shots. I was shocked. The other prisoners laid down, so I followed suit. At first, I didn't see anything wrong, then a lot of guards started running towards the far unit where I lived. There were three units with four dorms on each unit. Then the guards turned and started running towards the center unit, then they broke up and started running to all three units. Medical staff and more guards were arriving and going to dorms on all three units. Almost immediately, the officers started bringing out prisoners in handcuffs that were covered in blood. There were at least thirty bloody prisoners in all. It was like a war zone. There was blood all up and down the sidewalks. I couldn't figure out what happened.

I was later told that eleven white gang members had previously witnessed another prisoner get stabbed. The eleven men made statements and agreed to testify about the stabbing. A copy of the witness list had been sent to one of the white gang leaders and a massive hit was orchestrated against all eleven rats, at the same time.

The entire prison was locked down for eight days, while staff searched every cell for weapons. I learned then that it was best to keep a two weeks supply of food and a large stock of reading material in my locker, at all times. During the lock down, the staff conducts interviews. Every prisoner is handcuffed and escorted to an office and asked if they saw "The incident," and if they knew anything about "The incident."

After being told at orientation that any rat better check in to SHU or risk being killed and seeing eleven rats get beaten and stabbed at the same time, the prisoners in their right mind said that they didn't know anything. What better example did a person need than eleven rats getting beaten and stabbed for ratting. If there was ever a better example for prisoners to learn to mind their own business, I never saw it. One time I was taken into an interview on another "Incident," and I said, as I always did, that I hadn't seen anything. The counselor popped in a video and pushed play and low and behold, it showed me wide eyed, looking at a guy being stabbed then turning and walking away. He said, "You were standing right there. How come you didn't see anything?" I told him again that I didn't see anything. I didn't want any part of that situation.

Criminals have never really been classified as smart. They certainly don't seem to get more intelligent after incarceration. Several months went by without another large "Incident." There were many small ones where prisoners tried to kill and maim each other. That usually resulted in a short lock down. I spent my time working every day in the law library doing research to help with my appeal and compiling case law I would later need for a post conviction motion. A post conviction motion comes after a direct appeal. It's called a Motion to Vacate, Set Aside, or Correct Sentence, pursuant to Title 28 U.S.C. § 2255. It kept me busy. When I wasn't working I was walking the track, or reading and writing. I was also helping a few other prisoners with their § 2255 Motions and other legal matters.

One morning I heard there was going to be a work strike. My question was the obvious one, "Why?" What were they trying to accomplish? What was the ultimate goal? What were the demands? I asked my cell mate Tom these obvious questions and he promptly informed me that "These idiots don't even know why they are striking."

I thought, "Surely not. There has to be a reason."

I decided to discreetly ask a few prisoners I knew what the strike was about. I asked several prisoners and got the same answer from all of them.

"I don't know," they told me. I asked what the goal was and what would be the demands and I got the same answer. "I don't know." What it all boiled down to was, when I asked them, "Since you don't have any goals or demands, what's the point of striking?" The general answer was, "Everybody else is." It was crazy and stupid. The day the strike started, I walked outside at work call, then looked to see if other people were going to work. There were about a hundred of us just standing there waiting to see what would happen. I wanted to go to work. I had things to do, but I couldn't risk getting killed over it, so I went back inside.

There I was, stuck in a strike I didn't want any part of. One that had no meaning or purpose. One that other inmate would kill you if you did not comply with. It was stupid and I was pissed off because it reflected poorly on me.

The federal government has been running prisons for a long time.

They know how to handle problems. We were locked down for fourteen days. For breakfast we got one boiled egg. For lunch we got a cheese or bologna sandwich and the same thing for dinner. The prisoners were thankful that lock down was over and we could get back to the dining hall. In fourteen days, we got two showers.

Our cells were searched and we were generally treated like crap. All for no real reason. Nobody knew why they were striking, they were just following the lead dog. I was just trying to stay out of the way and not make waives.

In the later part of 1999 the prisoner custody classification system changed. Under the old system, a prisoner with more than twenty-five years had to start in a maximum security prison. That was raised to thirty years. With my projected good time, I had to serve thirty years and I had been in two years at that time, so that placed me under the thirty year requirement. The change in custody scoring lowered me to medium status.

My transfer packet said, "Texas to El Reno, by 11/30/99."

I never made it to El Reno. Just before my transfer, the medium security prison in Beaumont, Texas experienced a large riot. Over four hundred prisoners were shipped to other institutions. I was transferred across the street to the medium to fill bed space. Just my luck. Arriving at FCI Beaumont (Medium) after a riot was interesting. To say the least.

The prison was on high alert. The staff and prisoners were all watching each other carefully, wondering what was going to happen next.

The tension was high. I was trying to act like nothing was wrong and it wasn't for me. I had learned by being at the USP that all a person had to do was be respectful and mind their own business and you can avoid trouble. A maximum security prison teaches a person to maintain a high level of respectability. I got a job in the law library the first day I was there. That was my center. It gave me purpose and allowed me to conduct my personal research while helping others with their legal woes. Because I was honest with people about their possible chances of attacking certain issues in Court, I earned a good reputation. I only submitted cases I felt had a fairly good chance of winning, so I had a higher success rate than many of the other, so called, "Jailhouse Lawyers."

The other prisoners knew that if I told them they didn't have an issue that was worthy of challenge, or that they did, I was right. I would take the time to show them in a law book why and how I came about my position. Trust is a difficult thing to build in prison, but over time, my fellow prisoners knew they could trust my opinion. They knew that if I didn't have the answer to their question, I would say so, then take the time to help them find the answer. They knew that I was not a hustler like many of the other "Jailhouse Lawyers," that would tell them whatever they wanted to hear, just to get their money. I was, and am, brutally honest, even if the reality version sucks. People don't like it sometimes, but I would rather them be upset with me now for telling them the truth, than being upset later for being told a lie. Sadly, very few of the prisoners in the federal system have a valid issue they can raise in a collateral petition. I told far more people that I couldn't help them, than people I told that I could. Even those few people that I decide to help are told from the beginning how difficult it is to win even a valid claim. The Courts just aren't very receptive of a prisoner's plight.

There was a lot of gang violence at the medium in Beaumont, Texas. It was mostly between the Mexicans and on a rather large scale. It was common to see two to four hundred prisoners rioting. Then we would be locked down for a week or two.

Four Christmases in a row we were locked down. I think part of the problem was that right before the holidays, the BOP would let a lot of the prisoners out of the hole for Christmas. That and Beaumont Medium was where the BOP was sending a lot of prisoners with a history of disciplinary problems. Mostly it was rival Mexican gangs trying to kill each other.

I didn't understand the Mexican politics behind the riots, but I could see that it was serious. The first riot or two I was somewhat nervous seeing two to four hundred men stabbing and beating each other with anything they could find. But then it became such a common occurrence that I became indifferent. I would shake my head in disgust and walk back to my cell and get my little water jug and fill it with ice before the lock down.

While I was in Beaumont Medium I had several friends, but two good friends, both named Larry. Big Larry worked at UNICOR and I ate lunch with him every day. The other Larry was my cell mate. I used to say, "This is my brother Larry, and my other brother Larry." They were both great guys and I miss their company. We all three had commissary on different days. So, for almost five years we would each buy three ice creams from the commissary every week. That way we all three ate ice cream three days a week. Yes, we were spoiled. Prison is not a real bad place, if you have some good friends to share it with. It has its good points.

I was at FCI Beaumont for five years. Then hurricane Rita hit the coast of Texas and caused the medium to temporarily close. The prison was locked down the day before the hurricane. During the hurricane, the prison lost power and water. The damage to the prison, from what I could see, was extensive. We all spent nine days locked down in our cells with no lights, no running water and no air conditioning. It was hot. The guards stuck it out with us, bringing us drinking water and food. I felt sorry for the guards I'd come to like and respect, because they were also dealing with similar problems at home, then coming to work and suffering the same miserable conditions the prisoners were.

On the eighth day we were all advised that we were being transferred. On the ninth day we were all shipped out. One of the hardest things about being in prison is getting separated from your friends.

It had been so hot in my cell for that nine days that I'd hardly slept. The humidity was so high during those nine days that water was running down the cell walls and puddling in the floor. When they chained me up and put me on the air conditioned bus I fell asleep for the short ride to the airport. As soon as they loaded me on the Con-Air plane, I fell asleep again.

I didn't wake up until the plane touched ground at a military base in South Carolina. That was when we all found out we were going to a new medium security prison in sunny Bennettsville, South Carolina. I was never so happy to eat shitty prison food

in my life. I will always remember that they fed us meatloaf and I thought it was the best meal ever. It had taken from 7:00 a.m. that morning to 5:00 p.m. that evening, chained up on a plane and buses to get to the new prison and we were all so thankful to be out of that post hurricane heat and to get a hot meal, that nobody was fussing. You could have heard a pin drop while we ate.

The fussing came weeks later when we didn't get our property, or when we did get it and it was damaged. We were also fussing because we wanted to be moved closer to home. But on the other hand, the food was far better in Bennettsville and it had a better commissary.

What I didn't realize until later was, the medium in Bennettsville was full of informants and sex offenders. I never saw so many perverts in all my life. It was like a protective custody (PC) yard for rats and child molesters. Where I came from, those two types of people were beaten and checked in the hole. All of the sudden I was dumped at a prison where most of the population were on somebody's hit list. We Beaumont boys did not fit in.

I wanted away from there. I submitted a transfer request that was denied, because prisoners are required to stay at an institution for eighteen months with clear conduct before they can apply for a transfer. I was stuck, even though I had clear conduct.

Fortunately, I got a great cell mate the first week I was there. His name was Clyde and he was only in prison for some income tax problems. I have learned over the years that there are a few good people in prison, many of whom shouldn't be there.

Clyde was one of those people that should never have been sent to a prison. Things like income tax law violations can, and should, be handled with restitution and a small fine. Prison is completely unnecessary for those types of victimless crimes. I don't even like calling them crimes, when they should be called infractions.

I have been blessed with a few good friends at every prison I've been to. I think true friends are a gift from God. Just when a person starts losing hope for mankind, or at least prisoner kind, God gives us a friend to restore that hope. Over the many years that I've been incarcerated, I have developed a mere handful of true friendships and we will be friends for life.

Prison is not the best soil to cultivate friendship, but I have been lucky in that respect. There is a quote by Oscar Wilde that says it well: "The vilest deeds like poison weeds bloom well in prison air: It is only what is good in man that wastes and withers there." That quote is all too true.

It's sad to see good men in prison.

Another quote I like is by Richard Lovelace and it makes a valid point, as well. "Stone walls do not a prison make, nor iron bars a cage." Prison isn't just fences and razor wire, it is a frame of mind. Some people are imprisoned in wheelchairs, some in bad relationships, or by debt. Even drug addiction is a prison, or alcoholism. A man can be free to roam, but still imprisoned in his heart and mind. Lack of liberty isn't the worst prison.

Think of the prison of ignorance or bigotry. Although it sounds like a cliché, a person can be a prisoner of love. There are many people who love someone they know they can never be with. I was in prison, but I prefer to look at it as an adventure and an opportunity to learn. I don't let a little thing like prison rob me of my joy, but to say that I'm not suffering would be a lie and unrealistic. Not even a dog wants to be in a cage. J.K. Rowling, in Harry Potter and the Deathly Hallows, said that "There are far,

far worse things in the living world than dying." I know that is true and so does Alice.

For twenty-one months I worked in the prison law library at FCI Bennettsville. I helped a lot of prisoners with their legal problems. While I was there I read a book by Steve Martine, called Double Tap, that made an interesting point that I will not soon forget. It said, "Unfortunately, the criminal law was never equipped to prove innocence. It was crafted to establish one thing only: guilt. In the eyes of the public, which holds the collateral to all our reputations, the absence of guilt is seldom seen as the equivalent of innocence." It really does not matter if you happen to win in court, or if you get a sentence reduction at some point. In the public's eyes you are still tainted if you have ever been as much as arrested. And for a man who has actually been to prison, the public will never let him live it down.

Finally, I was able to procure a transfer to Forrest City, Arkansas.

It took me three weeks to get from Bennettsville, South Carolina to Forrest City, Arkansas. I was at the USP Atlanta holdover for that three weeks and the conditions were sorry at best. I was certainly thankful to get to Forrest City, which is closer to home. I call Oklahoma home, it's where I was raised, even though I was born in California. My sister Susan came to see me the first weekend after my transfer. Bennettsville, South Carolina was too far for her to travel, so I hadn't seen her in over two years. My sisters and I are close and it was good to actually see her.

Many years ago, federal prisons were mainly full of white collar criminals and bank robbers. In the mid 1980s, after the Federal Sentencing Guidelines were enacted, there began a huge increase in the federal incarceration of drug offenders.

When crack cocaine and methamphetamine became the scourge of America and the drugs of choice, federal prisons started filling up with crack and meth heads. Just in my seventeen years in federal prison, I have seen a serious increase in gang members in federal prison, which resulted in a sharp decline in the quality of life in federal prisons. I can only imagine what the next twenty years will be like for me and others in federal prison. With the large amount of informants and sex offenders I see coming into federal prison, it is obvious that there has been a drastic moral decline in today's society, as well.

I don't see how the government can continue at its present rate of incarceration. The cost alone is staggering, not to mention the implications on World opinion. I don't understand why the government insists on keeping something like marijuana illegal when it has so many benefits and far less negative aspects than alcohol. Marijuana grows seasonally and can be used for paper, cloth, rope, oil, medical reasons and other things, of course. It could be taxed and sold in liquor stores, just like alcohol, which would generate huge revenues. It would help with prison overcrowding if marijuana offenders were not locked away like murderers. With a stroke of a pen, Congress could decriminalize marijuana and create thousands of new jobs, virtually over night. But as we can see, the federal government isn't famous for doing the right thing. Rather than change with the times, they will keep enforcing draconian drug laws, even at the cost of billions each year to the tax payers and even if it ruins the lives of millions of Americans.

It is bad enough that some people have drug problems, but why does it have to be criminal, as well? Drug problems would be easier to manage if they were only a social issue and not a criminal issue. Decriminalizing drugs in general would cause the collapse of drug cartels. Drug dealers could not sell their drugs at inflated prices if they were available at the local drug store at a fraction of their street value. Our current system isn't working. It's time to try something new. Ultimately, it would be far better if people would just stop using drugs, but that approach has proven to be unrealistic, so let's try something else. Let's try taking the profit out of the drug market, which will reduce the crime rate because people would no longer need to steal to afford drugs. That way your children can go to rehab if they have a drug problem and not prison.

I also don't like the idea that drug laws are helping to create a society of informants. In a time when people need more God in their lives, I don't like it that prayer is being removed from our schools. Even if a person doesn't believe in God, that person would still have to agree that the teachings in the Bile are good. The Bible provides us with guidelines for a wholesome way of life. You can watch the news and see that something is missing in our lives. Could it be God and the discipline it takes to get out of bed and take your children to Church on Sunday?

I'll always remember when Alice started talking again. One day while we were sitting on the porch waiting on grandpa Connor to get home, she said, "I wish I never would have stopped going to Church with grandpa."

I held her there on the porch while she cried. She didn't have to explain. I knew what she meant. If she would have been at Church with grandpa Connor, she would have never met the Devil. If she would have been spending her time around good people, she sure wouldn't have been doing drugs and would not have had to suffer the consequences. Life is hard enough as it is, we certainly shouldn't do things that will make it harder. The choices we make can either make us and be a good example for others, or they can be our downfall. We should not intentionally expose ourselves to unsavory people or situations. If you want to have some fun, try dancing without drugs or alcohol, it is actually more fun. But if you want to see the face of evil you won't have to look far or long, because he'll find you. There is a drug dealer or a sick pervert on almost every corner. The problem is, they look just like you and me. Most people aren't evil by nature, thank God, but drugs can bring it out in them. Go Ask Alice!

My position on drugs may seem somewhat contradictory, but it is the allure of the criminality of drugs that entices our youth to experiment with them. It is the money involved that causes people to deal drugs.

Remove the carrot and the horse won't follow the stick. Take away the risk and the glamour and the excitement goes with it. Look at the historical effects of alcohol. When a child sees a drunk on the street the child never says, "When I grow up I want to be a drunk." The visual aspect says it all. The same thing would eventually happen with drugs if our televisions didn't portray the money and excitement side of the drug world. In a perfect world, our children wouldn't use drugs, but we don't live in a perfect world. There will always be a small part of civilization that do things that are not good for them, but they shouldn't be put in prison for it. People smoke, drink and eat too much, but do we lock them up for that? No.

That same principle should apply to drugs. Think of how bad it would have been if Alice would have been sent to prison for drugs, after she had been raped, beaten and burned. It would have added insult to injury.

The only reason there are sick, crazy drug dealers is the high profits which are brought on by the fact that the drugs are illegal. Take away the profit and you reduce crime.

Alice and I both know about the negative aspects of drug use. If a person doesn't end up dead, raped or beaten, they will likely end up in prison if they make the wrong choice and use drugs. What you won't do if you use drugs is live happily ever after, because drugs bring misery. Life doesn't always have a happy ending. I know.

AFTERWARDS

Alice and her daughter are doing fine. They live in grandpa Connor's farm house and Alice still has the little country store. I have never met Alice's husband. I don't think anyone could be good enough for her. But he must be a great person. He works for an oil company and still takes care of the cows as he has sense he became part of the family. He is a good father and Alice is certainly a wonderful mother.

Mr. Connor passed away in 2005. He was like a father to me and was more than a father to Alice. He was her guiding light. He will always be remembered and missed.

My friend Bobby passed away alone in a motel. He died of an asthma problem that brought on respiratory failure that was more than likely caused or at least aggravated by using meth.

Jimmy, my good friend, died of cancer.

Outlaw is out of prison and I hope doing well.

The charges were finally dismissed against my girlfriend Katherine. I'm thankful for that. It took a lot of work and me filing several pleadings.

She has moved on with her life and I hope she is happy.

Snake is still living in Brazil with his wife. I'm sure he is doing fine. I hope so anyway. He is ten years older than me, so he is over seventy-two now.

The attorney in Belize got in some kind of trouble over laundering drug money. Imagine that. So, all the money that Snake and I had invested with him was lost. Another example of my luck and that crime doesn't pay.

Me, I always advise people to stay away from drugs. While in prison I spent most of my time working in the law library and helping others with their legal concerns and wishing I would have made better choices in life.

Cathy went back to her husband. She knows now what happens when you make the mistake of opening Pandora's box. She was a lonely housewife looking for some excitement and I turned out to be more excitement than she could handle. To use a vehicle metaphor, she got my motor running, then I got in a wreck. I hope she is happy and doing well.

The worst part for me is the broken heart.

Eileen was another wreck that I didn't see coming. After causing me to wreck two trucks, literally and tormenting me for a year, she told on me and herself and got six months for misprision of a felony. Wherever she is, I hope she is not using drugs and I hope she is okay.

You are probably wondering what happened to Bopper. I heard recently that he passed away. But I am certain that if he was still alive he would be up to no good. There are a lot of Bopper's in the world. All wanting to be big shots. The Bopper I knew, or one just like him, could be your next door neighbor.

ABOUT THE AUTHOR

The author was born in 1960, which, for many people was an exceptional year. John F. Kennedy was elected President. Theodore Maiman invented the laser. The price of gold was $35.00 an ounce.

Gasoline was only .26 cents a gallon. And I was brought into this world screaming and kicking I'm sure, on a beautiful April night in Tracy, California. I'm sure my parents thought I was destined for greatness. I'm sorry, they were mistaken. But it was my fault, not theirs. I was given all the necessary love and perfect examples of how to live my life, I just didn't follow them. Growing up in the 60s and 70s was a great time for me.

Life was much simpler then. The World seemed like a lot bigger place back then. I wish that I would have been a better son, father and person. I love the part in the movie, "As Good As It Gets," where Jack Nicholson says, "You make me want to be a better man." As we get older, we can all look back and find something that we regret, I just have far more regrets than most. I now live each day trying to be a better man.

I wrote this book many years ago while still in federal prison. Today, December 1, 2022. I just completed editing this book as a free man. In 2010, the same police officer that were involved in my case were arrested and charged with corruption. The same thing I accused them of in 1997. My case was reopened and I was exonerated on April 18, 2014, and released from prison. I wrote all of my own legal pleadings that resulted in my release. After I filed my motions in federal court I was appointed a federal public defender and an investigator. They are both wonderful people and were instrumental in helping me with my case.

Sadly, fifty-nine days after my exoneration and release, the government appealed arguing only one point, that the judge lacked jurisdiction to release me. The government did not attempt to argue the innocence finding. I knew when I read the government's appeal that I was in trouble. I was exonerated based on fraud on the Court under the principles set forth in the Supreme Court's decision in Hazel Atlas Glass Co. v. Hartford Empire Co. from 1944. Very well established law, but seldom used. The government did not argue the validity of Hazel Atlas. They argued that the motion I filed to reopen my case (Motion to Withdraw Plea of Guilty) that the judge construed as a fraud on the court argument, was not authorized by the Tenth Circuit Court of Appeals as required by Title 28 section 2255 for a second or successive petition.

Reading Hazel Atlas, and its progeny, it is clear that a judge has the authority to grant relief for fraud on the court. It is also clear that a federal prisoner who has exhausted his appeal and first Motion to Vacate under 28 section 2255, must file for permission to appeal.

However, I did not file an appeal or fraud on the court motion, I filed a request to withdraw my plea, which was authorized by Tenth Circuit case law. It was the judge who utilized Hazel Atlas and made a valid fraud on the court determination.

The Tenth Circuit ruled that it was my motion that triggered the judge's fraud on the court decision and since it was not authorized they overturned my case and ordered me back into prison.

However, the Tenth Circuit did agree that, based on the testimony of witnesses at my 2012 hearing, I met the actual innocence standard on the firearm charge and gave me authorization to appeal the firearm charge.

I filed my new "authorized" appeal shortly before I checked myself back into federal prison at Texarkana. Walking into that prison, after being free for a year and a half, was one of the hardest things I ever did.

Four months after turning myself in, the District Court judge granted my appeal, dismissed the firearm charge and ordered me back to the Tulsa County Jail to await resentencing.

I was transported back to Tulsa county, once again. At my resentencing, the judge dismissed the firearm count and gave me time served on the drug counts.

That ruling left me guilty on the drug counts and stopped me from getting any compensation for wrongful conviction.

I am currently a pumper checking oil wells seven days a week. I also buy and sell a few cars and do a lot of mechanic work. I am thankful that I am a free man. My discharge date was March 18, 2028.

If not for the corrupt police officers who created my case being arrested and convicted I'd still be in prison.

Made in the USA
Middletown, DE
30 May 2023

31624532R00239